WORLD WAR 2
OPENING GAMBITS

The Manstein Alternative: Part 3

OPENING GAMBITS

WORLD WAR 2

The Manstein Alternative: Part 3

JOE AVINGER

Copyright © 2023 by Joe Avinger

All rights reserved. No part of this publication may be reproduced, distributed, or transmitted in any form or by any means, including photocopying, recording, or other electronic or mechanical methods, without the prior written permission of the copyright owner and the publisher, except in the case of brief quotations embodied in critical reviews and certain other noncommercial uses permitted by copyright law. For permission requests, write to the publisher, addressed "Attention: Permissions Coordinator," at the address below.

ARPress
45 Dan Road Suite 5
Canton, MA 02021

Hotline: 1(888) 821-0229
Fax: 1(508) 545-7580

Ordering Information:
Quantity sales. Special discounts are available on quantity purchases by corporations, associations, and others. For details, contact the publisher at the address above.

Printed in the United States of America.

ISBN-13:   Softcover   979-8-89330-541-8
                eBook   979-8-89330-543-2
                Hardback   979-8-89330-542-5

Library of Congress Control Number: 2023904133

TABLE OF CONTENTS

TIMELINE

January 1917

Germany adopts the Manstein Alternative.

Unrestricted Submarine warfare is not resumed.

April 1917

The League of Nations is formed by the United States.

March 1918

The Treaty of Washington ends the Great War.

Many colonial territories change hands.

Ukraine becomes an independent country.

The Kingdom of Lithuania and Poland becomes an
independent country.

July 1920

The United States of Greater Austria (USGA) is
formed.

It joins the League of Nations in September.

October 1922

Mussolini stages a coup and takes over in Italy.

February 1923

The First Serbian Insurrection begins and quickly
spreads to Albania and Macedonia.

October 1929

A financial crisis rocks the world.

Controls enacted during the Great War ease effects
in the United States.

Charles de Gaulle becomes the French President.

German Kaiser Wilhelm II abdicates in favor of
Wilhelm III.

Germany becomes a constitutional monarchy.

Erich von Manstein becomes Chief of Staff of the
German Army.

November 1929

The Second Serbian Insurrection begins.

Economic disparities are cited as reason.

March 1930

Charles de Gaulle pushes for the modernization of the
French military.

French nationalism surges.

Religious rhetoric also rises as Protestants are blamed
for the failures in the Great War and for the financial crisis.

June 1932

The New Entente is formed between France and Italy.

Pope Pius XI denounces Fascism.

October 1932

Japan and Britain formalize their alliance.

Spheres of influence are laid out.

Pope Pius XI dies under questionable circumstances.

November 1932

A hardline French cardinal is elected as the new Pope.

He takes the name Pius XII.

December 1932

Pope Pius XII declares de Gaulle and Mussolini to be
defenders of the faith.

April 1933

Erich von Manstein becomes Chancellor of Germany.

Catholicism is made the official religion of France and
Italy.

The New Entente is renamed the Catholic Entente.

June 1933

Unrest in French and Italian colonies is quelled when
Pope Pius XII announces tolerance of other religions.

Protestantism is named as heresy, not a separate
religion.

Papal primacy is renounced and tensions between the
Eastern Orthodox and Roman Catholic Churches ease.

July 1933

The Central Coalition is formed by Germany, Ukraine,
and Turkey.

Lithuania-Poland joins the Central Coalition as a
conditional member. Defensive pact only applies to
the USSR.

April 1934

Bulgaria and Romania join the Central Coalition.

July 1936

The Spanish Civil War begins.

Republicans are supported by USSR and Mexico.

Nationalists are supported by Portugal, Italy and
France.

August 1936

Non-intervention Agreement is signed to prevent
foreign involvement in the Spanish Civil War.

Most signatories almost immediately start violating the
agreement.

September 1936

The Third Serbian Insurrection begins and quickly
spreads to Albania and Macedonia.

Lack of state participation in federal government is
cited as the primary issue.

October 1936

France and Italy intervene in the Spanish Civil War.

The League of Nations vacillates on what action to take.

Tensions mount between the Catholic Entente and the
United Kingdom.

November 1936

The Spanish Civil War ends with a Nationalist victory.

Pope Pius XII helps heal Spain.

Franklin Delano Roosevelt wins US election.

January 1937

Spain and Portugal join the Catholic Entente.

France helps Italy begin modernizing its forces.

Older military equipment is used as payment for
resources from South America.

Roosevelt takes office, works on restoring League
prestige and influence.

March 1937

Pius XII begins a tour of South and Central America.

French and Iberian agents seek trade agreements.

The Third Serbian insurrection ends, USGA Senate
formed.

June 1937

Brazil, Uruguay, Paraguay, and Bolivia leave the
League of Nations and create a new alliance – the
Organization of American States (OAS).

Trade agreements are signed with the Catholic
Entente.

The OAS receives older Entente tanks and airplanes.

Brazil receives the Italian battleships *Conte di Cavour*,
and *Giulio Cesare*.

July 1937

Japan invades China.

The League of Nations imposes sanctions on most
exports to Japan.

The United Kingdom increases its exports to Japan.

The USSR moves troops into Xinjiang at the request of
Sheng Shicai.

The Soviet Great Purge begins in earnest.

August 1937

The Sino-Soviet Non-Aggression Pact is signed.

More Soviet troops move into Xinjiang province of
China to help repress Uighur rebellion.

September 1937

Chile leaves the League of Nations and joins the OAS.

Chile receives two French heavy cruisers as payment
for trade agreements with the Catholic Entente.

The United States begins expansion of military.

US Congress approves military aid for Argentina to
keep them in the League of Nations.

November 1937

The USSR attacks Turkey in the Caucasus.

Finnish troops lead the way.

Ukraine and Lithuania-Poland mobilize.

To deescalate the situation, Germany does not
mobilize.

Large French maneuvers take place on the German
border.

December 1937

The Rape of Nanjing begins.

Belgium joins the Catholic Entente.

January 1938

Venezuela, Peru, and Ecuador leave the League of
Nations to join the OAS.

All three receive older Entente tanks and airplanes.

Venezuela receives two French battleships, the
Dunkerque and the *Strasbourg*.

The League of Nations votes down intervention in
Turkey.

February 1938

The Central Coalition and the Catholic Entente sign a
five-year non-aggression pact.

France renounces its claim to Alsace and Lorraine.

Benelux is split into spheres of influence.

All major French naval units are moved to ports on the
Bay of Biscay.

Britain responds by reinforcing their Home Fleet.

German troops head east.

US Congress approves military aid for Colombia to
keep them in the League of Nations.

March 1938

Bulgaria begins genocide in Macedonia.

The USSR advance in the Caucasus stalls as troops are
moved to reinforce the borders with Ukraine and
Lithuania-Poland.

April 1938

The USGA intervenes in Macedonia with approval
from the League of Nations.

Bulgaria invokes the Central Coalition defense clause.

Germany uses diplomacy to defuse the situation.

Tensions remain high between the Central Coalition
and the USGA.

May 1938

South America erupts in war.

Venezuela, Peru, and Ecuador invade Colombia.

Much of the Colombia is quickly overrun.

Brazil, Chile, Paraguay, Uruguay, and Bolivia invade
Argentina.

Buenos Aires falls in the first week.

Argentina establishes a temporary capital at Bahía
Blanca.

The League of Nations imposes sanctions despite
protests in the United States.

Neville Chamberlain looks for a diplomatic solution and
fails to find one.

Naval units are sent to Argentina to protect British

economic interests.
The League of Nations protests intervention and
imposes sanctions on the United Kingdom.

MAPS

GENERAL MAP
EUROPE 1938
SCALE OF MILES
USSR
UKRAINE
TURKEY
RUMANIA
BULGARIA
GREECE
LITHUANIA
POLAND
USGA
GERMANY
SWEDEN
NORWAY
DEN.
ITALY
NETH.
BELGIUM
LUX.
SWITZ.
FRANCE
ALGERIA
UNITED KINGDOM
IRELAND
SPAIN
PORTUGAL
MOROCCO
BRITISH EMPIRE
CATHOLIC ENTENTE
CENTRAL COALITION
LEAGUE OF NATIONS

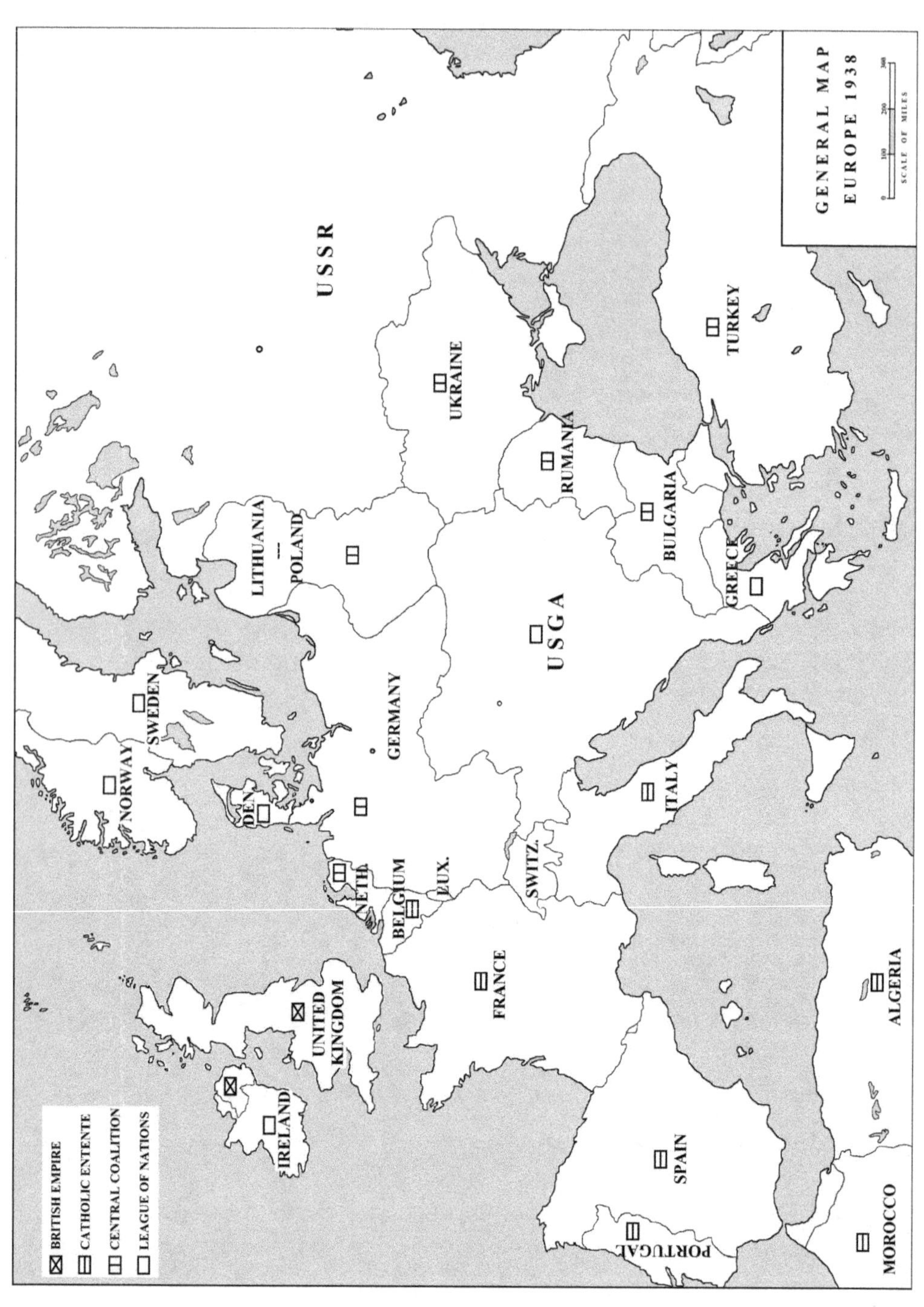

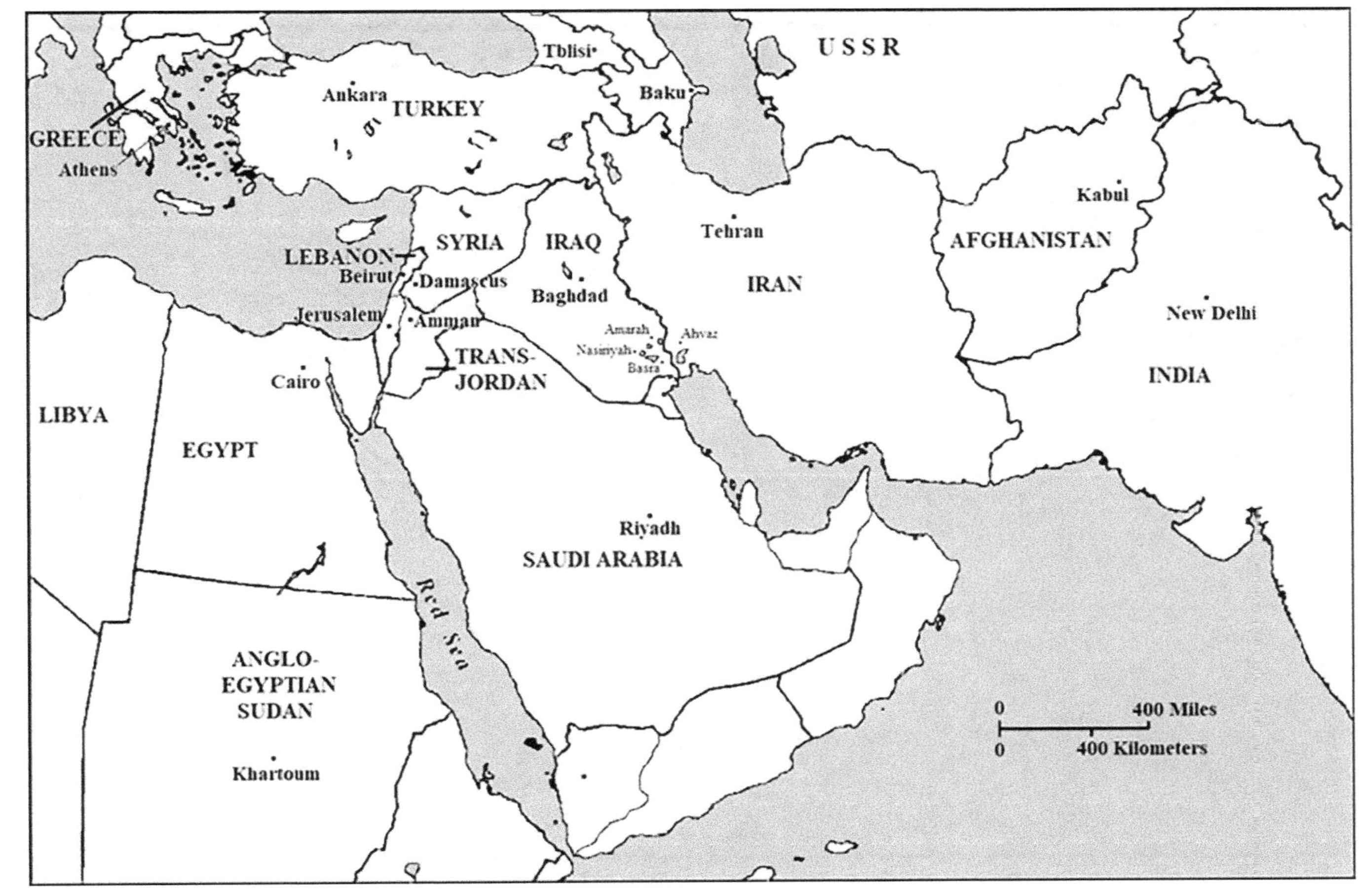

The Middle East – 1938

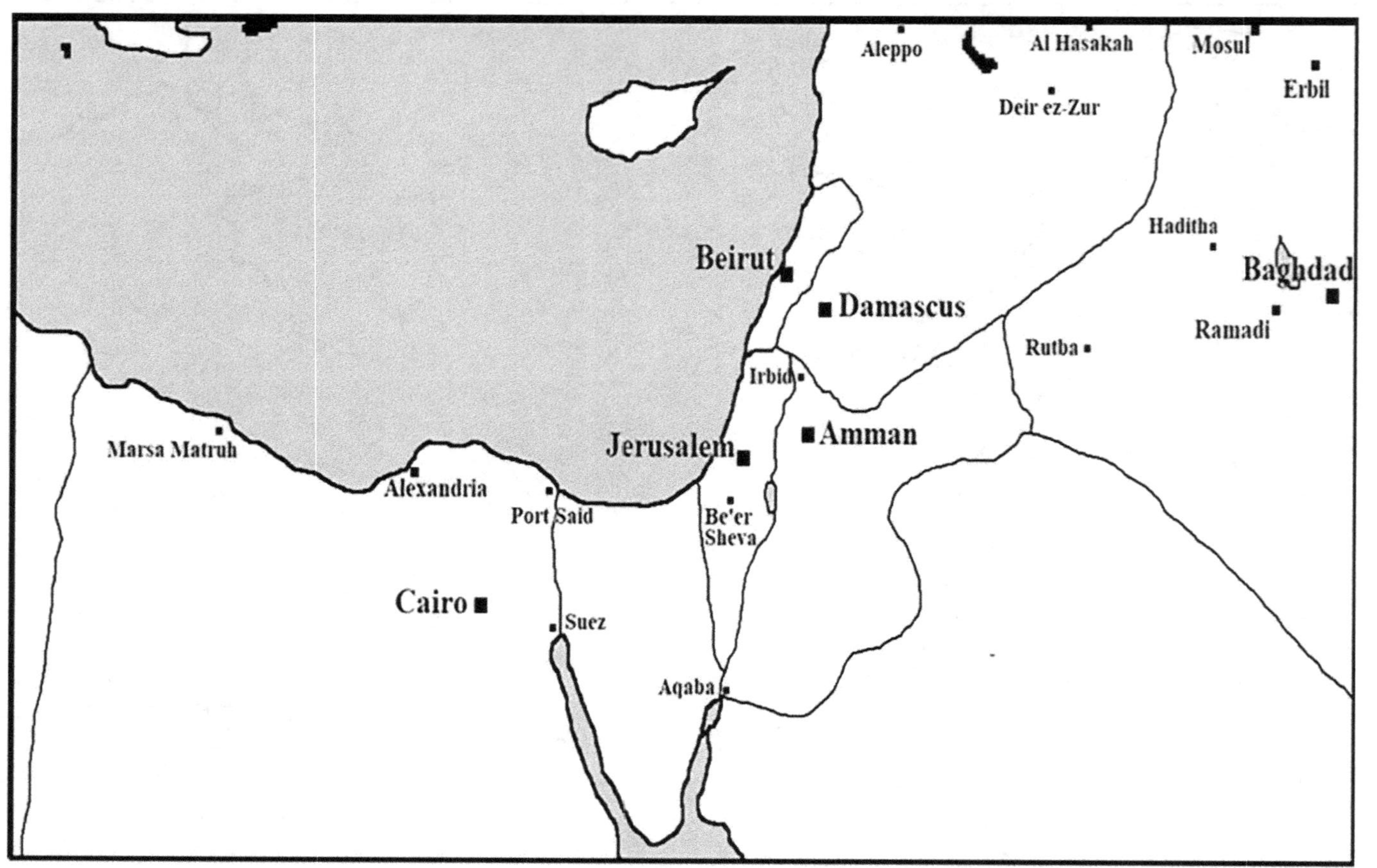

Closeup of the Middle East - 1938

Eastern Europe - 1938

South America - 1938

SPANISH MOROCCO
SPANISH GUINEA
FRENCH WEST AFRICA
LIBYA
EGYPT
GAMBIA COLONY
SUDAN
BRITISH SOMALILAND
SIERRA LEONE
NIGERIA
FRENCH EQUITORIAL AFRICA
ITALIAN EAST AFRICA
UGANDA
LIBERIA
GOLD COAST
CAMEROON
BELGIAN CONGO
KENYA
British Empire
Catholic Entente
RUANDA-URUNDI
TANGANYIKA
NORTHERN RHODESIA
NYASALAND
ANGOLA
SOUTH WEST AFRICA
SOUTHERN RHODESIA
BECHUANALAND PROTECTORATE
MOZAMBIQUE
MADAGASCAR
SOUTH AFRICA

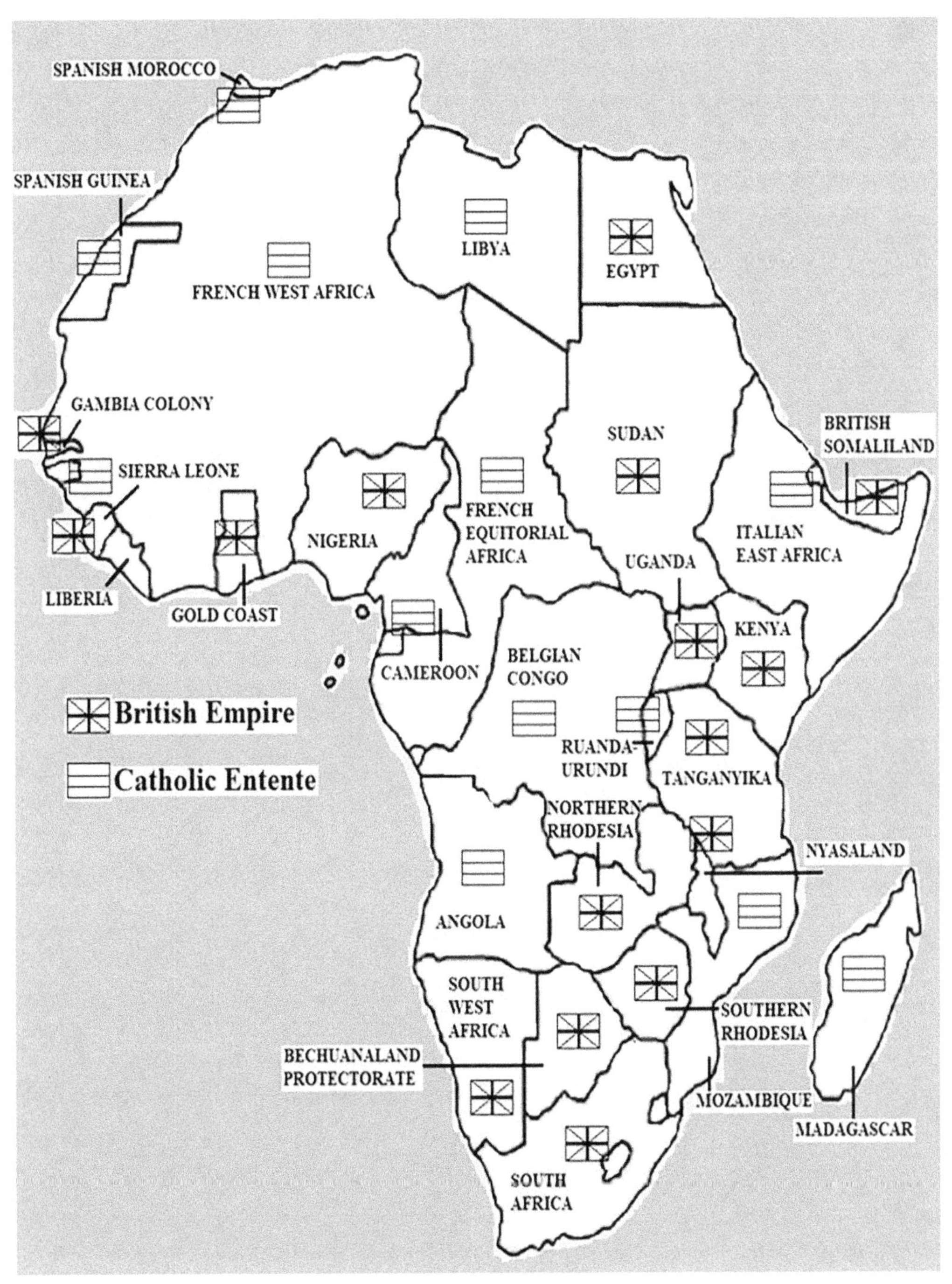

Africa – 1938

Part III
World War 2 – Opening Gambits

The Chancellery, Berlin, Germany

I sit down at my desk and place my arms in the clear space at its center, ready to start another day as Chancellor of Germany. It's my sixth year in the position and I still have the confidence of Wilhelm III and the Reichstag. I must be doing something right. Or maybe it's just inertia on their part. I do happen to be one of the few people who's not too closely associated with a specific faction in the Reichstag. Regardless, my office chair now fits me like a glove and its rich leather smell seems to settle my mind.

I think back on how I got here and wonder what my life would be like if I hadn't met General Ludendorff during the Great War. He and my uncle, Paul von Hindenburg, basically ran Germany for Kaiser Wilhelm II. They liked my idea of working with the United States to end the illegal blockade of non-war material that the British had enacted. The Great War had finally ended in a negotiated peace that left the German Empire intact, but it seems to have generated an even deeper hatred between us, the British, and the French. Maybe things would have been better if I'd kept my mouth shut. Then again, I would never have known the joy of meeting Brenda in Washington, or the birth of our son, Brent. Or the pain of Brenda's death from the Spanish Flu within the next year. Or the joy of finding love again.

A light rap on the door signals Edna's arrival with my morning coffee. This has also become a part of my morning routine, though the kiss she plants on the top of my head when she puts the mug on my desk is still rather new. She's been my secretary for four years and my wife for almost one. I wasn't sure how Brent would react considering Edna is only ten years older than him, but my son seems to be happy that I finally have another woman in my life. Brent is wrapping up his first year at the Military Academy in Lichterfelde and it won't be too long before he's ready to join our men in harm's way. I'm both proud and terrified at the thought.

Edna taps the top folder on the right side of my desk and I look up with a bemused smile on my face. She just shakes her head in exasperation.

"Stop the woolgathering, Erich. Ambassador Henderson will be here soon and you haven't looked over the latest reports from South America."

My "Yes, dear" is accompanied by the meekest look I can muster which makes Edna laugh. She kisses me before she flounces out of my office. She peeks around the door as she's closing it to offer a final word of advice.

"Don't forget to wipe my lipstick off your mouth if you don't want Ambassador Henderson wondering about you."

She giggles at my sour look and closes the door, leaving me to prepare for my meeting with the British diplomat. I use my handkerchief to wipe her lipstick off my mouth then take a quick swipe at the top of my head. Nothing seems to have stuck in my hair. I read the summary and check the details on a few items, placing the folder back on its pile just as Edna knocks on my door before opening it to usher in my guest. I stand to receive the prickly Sir Nevile Henderson and miss the more convivial relationship I shared with his predecessor, Sir Eric Phipps.

"Good morning, Ambassador Henderson. Please have a seat. Is there anything Edna can get for you?" Greeting, seat, and the offer of refreshment, or his nose and his attitude both rise.

"Good morning to you, too, Chancellor Manstein. A spot of tea would be greatly appreciated. I believe your delightful secretary knows how I like it." He takes his seat as Edna leaves my office for a few moments. Edna returns and presents Sir Nevile with a cup and saucer by the time I've settled back into my seat. No magic here. Sir Nevile has been the British Ambassador for almost a year, and he always wants a cup of tea.

"What can I do for you, Ambassador?"

Sir Nevile savors a sip of his tea before placing the cup and saucer on the end table next to him. A little bit of tea coats the bottom of his mustache, giving it a two-toned appearance. If things go as they usually do, that's the one and only time he'll touch the cup. I mentally sigh as I prepare for one of Sir Nevile's monologues. He stands and begins pacing around the room as if trying to decide how to phrase what I am sure is a well-rehearsed speech. His thin build and pasty complexion match the bland speech I expect to hear. He finally stops and clasps his hands behind his back. My mental sigh doesn't reach my lips. I have learned a few things over the years.

"Chancellor Manstein, the French and Italians are working to start a general war and our countries are squarely in their crosshairs. Ever since de Gaulle came to power in France, he's done little other than plot ways to exact revenge on your country for attacking France and on mine for 'abandoning' France when we were on the brink of victory. Both reasons are pure rubbish. We both know that France was looking for revenge for the Franco-Prussian War when they joined the Great War and that their men were exhausted and mutinying at its end. It would have been a question of which of you broke first if the Yanks hadn't bailed you out.

"The Entente is using religion to whip its people into a frenzy that will drag us all down into a war with no quarter and no prospect of peace without absolute victory or absolute defeat. Whether or not we like it, we are both targets of that religious fanaticism, and we will be hard pressed to survive if we don't work together. The Yanks are too insulated to mobilize for the coming war, and it will be down to us to defeat the Fascists.

"The Yanks could at least help supply our men, but their League of Nations is proving to be easily manipulated by the Entente. The Organization of American States is nothing but a surrogate of the Entente and they are using it to drive wedges between the other alliances of the world. They're the new flag to waive in the League's face to keep them distracted.

"The same goes for the Communists. The Entente has been working with them to keep your alliance preoccupied while they work on consolidating their grip in South America and the Mediterranean. Do you really believe that it's coincidence that the French have given up their claim to Alsace and Lorraine and offered a non-aggression pact just when the Soviets were pushing on your eastern front?"

"No, I don't." Sir Nevile may have intended it as a rhetorical question, but I can use it to interrupt his diatribe without being too rude. He stammers for a moment and seems to be searching for his place in his planned lecture. Let's see if I can get past another one of his effusive explanations of the British world view and shock him with bluntness.

"We know the Entente is trying to manipulate the world to its own ends. So are you British. So are we. This is what world powers have always done. So? Is there some reason for today's meeting?"

Sir Nevile looks indignant for a moment before responding, his puff of exasperation sends the ends of his mustache dancing. I simply smile while he regroups. He's never liked my approach to diplomacy and I'm fine with that. He looks at me like I'm a child who doesn't understand how the game is played. I understand the game perfectly well, I just don't like how much of my time is wasted when we play by his rules. Sir Nevile sits back down and gives me his best exasperated sigh before continuing.

"There are several, Chancellor Manstein. I'd like to discuss dealing with the Soviet Union, trade issues, dealing with the League of Nations, and the possibility of an anti-Entente pact. And, as you know, they're all interrelated. Where would you like to start?"

It's about what I figured, though he has spread the OAS into his other categories. "Let's start with the Soviet Union."

"Very well. As we've offered in the past, the United Kingdom and the Empire of Japan can assist you in dealing with the Soviet Union. We already have a large number of their troops occupied in east Asia. We could maneuver our forces to pin down more of them. We could attack to keep them busy and strain their ability to supply their armies. Or we could negotiate with them to free up more of their troops to deal with your alliance's armies. Which would you prefer?"

His proposals are the same ones he's been pushing for months. Carrot, carrot, stick. I put on my best innocent smile as I wonder if there will be anything new today or if it will be the same discussion we've been having for months. "Why, we'd be happy if you attacked them, of course. Isn't that what the Japanese want to do?"

Sir Nevile goes back to his usual bland and patient demeanor. "That is one possible strategic direction for us in east Asia. The question is, why should we choose to benefit the Central Coalition?"

I lean back in my chair and cock my head to the left. "Are you sure you'd be helping us and we wouldn't be helping you? We're already at war with them and pushing them back everywhere except for Georgia, Stalin does seem to be determined to retake his homeland. We expect to push further east as the mud dries. Would an attack by you or Japan help? Sure, but not enough to make a major difference to us. Would an agreement between you and the Soviet Union hurt us? A little, but once again, not enough to make a major difference. Stalin might pull a few troops to our front, but he trusts the Japanese about as far as he can throw one of their battleships."

Sir Nevile's expression devolves from sour to annoyed while I talk. I lean forward and clasp my hands on my desk returning his annoyed look. "I think our current war with the Soviet Union helps your cause a lot more than anything you could do for us. We also keep the Dutch supplying you and Japan with oil and resources. We know you could take the Dutch East Indies, but they just might have things rigged to disrupt production for months or years. Also, invading the East Indies would annoy us a great deal, and do you really want us being more cooperative with the Catholic Entente?"

I stop and try to look innocent, "My apologies, Ambassador Henderson. I seem to have bled over into trade and the Entente."

I'd spit out his carrots and broken his stick. The British had been throwing their weight around since before Napoleon and had managed to alienate most of the rest of the world in the process. Their intervention in Argentina caused the League to impose sanctions and their Home Islands are looking more and more isolated. I am in no mood for bluster and baseless threats. We sit in silence for most of a minute while Sir Nevile appears to contemplate how he'd like to torture me and I serenely smile back at him.

"Please don't insult our intelligence, Chancellor Manstein. We both know that the Entente has no interest in a long-term peace with either of us. They're working to undermine your alliance with the Ukraine and Lithuania-Poland and the USGA's position in the League of Nations. Or do you really think the Pope has been trying to heal the schism with the Eastern Orthodox church because it's 'God's will'?"

"I didn't say that we wanted to work with the Entente, only that we will if you force us to do so. And attacking the Dutch East Indies would throw both us and the League squarely against you. You spoke of trade issues, well here's one. We're providing you the Dutch resources while at the same time, you're cutting off the resources we had been getting from China. That doesn't seem very fair to us. What can we do about it?"

Sir Nevile's mood seems to improve a bit. I guess I'm nibbling at the right bait.

"China is a mess and has been for decades. Their civil war may be at a pause because of the Japanese invasion but it would pick right back up if the Japanese withdrew. It was the Juye Incident where German missionaries were killed that kicked off the Boxer Rebellion and they've been fighting each other and everyone else since then. That fighting has constantly disrupted their trade and made any agreements with them unstable at best. What can we do about your loss of resources from China? We can replace their warlords and communists with a far more stable government that can be counted on to uphold its agreements. All of us would be able to benefit from China's potential."

There's the mark of the true Imperialist I was expecting. Britain and Japan will fix China by putting a puppet government in charge. That way they can exploit it without having to worry about those pesky desires of the Chinese people. But it's all for their own good ... honest. Time to see what role he wants Germany to play.

"And you and Japan would happily provide us with those Chinese resources rather than using them for yourselves, right?"

"The Chinese government would be free to negotiate trade agreements with everyone. Considering their past dealings with you, I wouldn't be surprised if they were happy to work with you in the future. Germany would simply need to negotiate with the new, stable, government of China and ship their resources."

"I see. Our ships would move the cargo through Entente controlled waters so they wouldn't interfere with it while you and Japan split the profits. Add in that any deals between Germany and your new government for China would mean that we recognize it as the legitimate government of China and that's a triple advantage for you."

"And an advantage for you. Germany will get a larger and more reliable supply of those needed resources."

I look at his bland smile and it reinforces my earlier impression. He thinks that just because I don't like his game, I don't understand how it works. I sit back and nod my head as if I see the proposal's merits but not its implications. In many ways it's a variation of my original proposal to the Americans during the Great War. The neutral power ships the goods through contested waters with the hope that any incidents shift the neutral into your camp. Your country benefits either way. It's a proposal that will have to go to the Reichstag regardless of my personal feelings. That doesn't mean I won't tell them what I think of it, or put warning labels all over it.

"True, but if the expense is too great, we could simply get those resources from the Americas like we currently do. We're still on good terms with both the League of Nations and the Organization of American States."

"I'm sure there are people in the United Kingdom who would be happy to purchase any excess you might accidentally import at a price that would profit both of our peoples."

This is also known as using us to get around the League and potentially Entente embargoes. Wouldn't that make them oh so happy with us. Those warning labels are going to have to be huge. I nod thoughtfully.

"I'll make sure that information is presented to the Reichstag. How about we discuss the League next, Ambassador?"

He contemplates me for a moment, trying to determine if he's won his point or I'm patronizing him. "Very well, Chancellor. The League of Nations is coming apart at the seams. The Catholic Church in the United States of America is fighting tooth and nail to keep them from acting against either the OAS or the Entente. The OAS is de Gaulle's brainchild to keep the Americans focused on the western hemisphere and it seems to be doing a terrific job. They're so worried about the Panama Canal that they don't care what's going on in the rest of the world.

"Meanwhile, both the Catholic and Eastern Orthodox Churches are doing the same in the United States of Greater Austria. The Austrians have been obsessed with the Balkans for hundreds of years and the churches are trying to keep their attention focused there. The only thing keeping them from absorbing Romania, Bulgaria, and Greece are the ties our countries have with them. Add in that Mussolini has been stirring things up in the USGA for over a decade and the chances of the Austrians doing anything approach zero. When we showed them our evidence that the Štip Incident that kicked off Bulgaria's ethnic cleansing was an Italian operation, they ignored it."

Our intelligence services had come to similar conclusions two months ago, although there were a few differences. Everything had been relatively tranquil there until late last year. The Bulgarians were surprised by the massacre of the Bulgars in Štip in January. The Macedonians were uncooperative in tracking down the perpetrators. Then the local troops, who had lost family members, started reprisals. From there, things devolved into retaliatory revenge killings. Italian agents were known to be in the area at the time and the animosity the killings caused between the USGA and the Central Coalition only benefited the Entente.

"We think the Štip Incident was a setup, too. That's why we did our best to reduce the tensions in the area."

I stop for a moment, both to see Sir Nevile's reaction and to decide whether to say the rest. Sir Nevile looks thoughtful and nods his head, so I decide to push onward. Just as I begin speaking again, a little voice in the back of my head points out that I had nodded and tried to look thoughtful only a few minutes ago. And I thought he was full of shit. Oh, well.

"We think the OAS was set up for a similar reason, driving a wedge between you and the USA. You may not have a defense agreement with Argentina, but you do have a lot of business dealings with them. I think that you made Charles de Gaulle a happy man when you answered Argentina's request for aid."

Sir Nevile sits back in his chair and sighs heavily before he gives a slight shrug. "That's our opinion, too. The problem is that de Gaulle was going to be happy regardless of what we did. If we had done nothing, Argentina would have fallen by now. True, the USA and the League wouldn't be mad at us, but we know the OAS had plans to go after the Falklands if we didn't react. We were going to be on the wrong side of the League one way or the other.

"The Spanish Civil War showed that half measures aren't going to work against the Entente. My counterpart in Washington is trying to get that point across to the Yanks. That's why we believe our countries need to work together to keep resources flowing from the League. Those resources will be vital once the real shooting starts."

I shake my head sadly, "I know it would have wounded British pride, but I still think you would have been better off if you hadn't taken an active role with Argentina."

"Possibly, but our efforts at a negotiated peace came to naught. One must stand up to aggression at some point. And sooner is usually better. That's one of the reasons we want to discuss coordinating our efforts against the Entente. Your non-aggression pact with them just lets them concentrate on us separately. You must drop your blinders and see the urgency of the threat."

Sir Nevile had gotten more animated during that last part. It was probably part of his rehearsed speech that I muddled up. It doesn't happen often, but I sit back and get to look smug for once.

"Blinders? I don't think so. With the Russians on the march, we would be hard pressed if fighting broke out between us and either the League or the Entente. We gained time to deal with the Russians while our western border and that of the Netherlands are secure. Also, the USGA is likely to be more reasonable if we aren't stretched by other conflicts. The agreement also removes most of the pretexts the Entente might use to justify attacking us or the Netherlands. That means your Far East supply lines should remain intact.

"It also means that we should have unfettered access to global resources. And while the League would frown on us if we seemed to be bypassing their embargo against you, there are some Scandinavian members of the League that don't have grudges against you the way Norway does. We do a lot of business with them, and they aren't overly interested in seeing the Catholic Entente on their Protestant doorsteps."

Maybe that's a big enough hammer. Sir Nevile sits back and stares at me for a moment. "So, Sweden and Denmark are willing to risk censure by the League to transship resources to us?"

I smile as innocently as I know how. I've been working on those two countries since the OAS formed almost a year ago. That was also when we hired my son's old art teacher as an intelligence analyst. Hitler had accurately predicted the extension of the Entente into South America and the resultant economic distress of the United Kingdom. He'd also made a prediction of where the Entente would strike first when the fighting started. A prediction I thought had a lot of merit.

"That's something you'd have to take up with them. They aren't members of the Central Coalition. We can no more influence their trade deals than we can do anything about the security of British colonies in Africa."

That gets a long stare from Sir Nevile. He might not have thought about where the Entente would strike, but hopefully one of his superiors had. The British Isles would be pretty isolated if the Entente controlled Africa in addition to South America. They already ran more of Africa's land area, though the British ruled more of its people.

Sir Nevile purses his lips and stands up. I rise too. In a gesture unusual for him, he extends his hand. I shake it.

He pauses for a moment as if mentally weighing something. "I think that covers things for now. Thank you for your time, Erich. I'll inform the home office of your responses and concerns."

He knows I was on a first name basis with his predecessor but has never used mine before. My reports said he considered it too familiar and unprofessional. Either his attitude has changed, or he thinks he can get more information out of me by playing my version of diplomacy. Time will tell.

"And I'll relay your proposals to the Reichstag, Sir Nevile. I look forward to our next meeting."

"As do I, Erich. As do I."

Damascus Air Base, Damascus, Syria

Général de Brigade Roger Noiret sat at the conference table with the other division commanders of the Levant Corps. They were waiting for their commander, Général de Division Alphonse Pierre Juin, to arrive and begin the weekly status meeting. Their executive officers and aides stood unobtrusively behind them while most of the assembled generals made small talk and waited. Most of those generals were at least ten years older than Roger and didn't have much in common with him, so Roger simply sat and thought.

A letter from his wife, Catherine, had arrived last night. Junior, their youngest son, wanted to know if Roger would be able to make it home for his birthday on June 3rd like he had for the birthday of Guy, their eldest. That had only been a couple of weeks ago and there was no way that Roger would be able to make it back so soon, especially with the probability of war on the horizon. That same probability meant he couldn't really explain why he wouldn't be able to make it. Roger was a little worried about how his namesake would react. It didn't help that one of Junior's school friends, Pierre Moreau, and his family had been arrested for heresy. Roger wished he could be there to celebrate with and help guide his youngest son. He wished he could be there to hold Catherine in his arms. He wished Lucifer hadn't deceived so many by twisting God's Word, but that was his role. Roger's role was to fight those forces of darkness and return them to the light if he could. And fight them, he would.

There was no mistaking the look that came to Roger's face as anything but predatory. It appeared he would finally get to deal with some of the heretical Protestants. His 1st Armored Division had been sent to Syria just after it had been formed in mid-January. It would have led the strike into Turkey if the Catholic Entente had gone to war with the Central Coalition. In retrospect, it seemed that possibility had primarily been a diversion to encourage the Central Coalition to sign the Non-Aggression Pact in February. His men and the rest of the Levant Corps had remained in Syria to acclimate and practice desert maneuvers. Their sights were now set on a different target.

President Charles de Gaulle intended to get some use out of the hundred thousand men he had sent to the Middle East. They had been accumulating supplies and planning attack routes for an offensive against the British for the last three months. Now, it looked like the offensive might start sometime soon.

Roger wasn't sure what was causing the delay. They could be waiting for the Italians in Libya to get ready. They could be waiting for the fighting in South America to provide a reason for war that would keep the League of Nations from jumping in on the side of the Brits. It could be both, or something entirely different. Regardless, Roger hoped things would kick off soon. The Brits were building up their defenses in the area which would make things more difficult. Even the Syrian government was beginning to wonder if the French were there to fight someone else or violate the Viénot Accords which unified Syria and promised them self-governing independence.

Général Noiret's train of thought was interrupted when Général Juin arrived, and he and his fellow division commanders rose from their seats. Général Juin didn't demand that they come to attention, but they all did anyway. Anything less would have been an affront to the older generals present.

"At ease. We're here to discuss our plans, not look pretty on a parade ground."

Roger had accepted Général Juin's left-handed salute far more easily than some of the older generals in the Levant Corps. Général Juin had lost the use of his right arm during the Great War. Juin was also a Warrior for Christ like Roger. They both had two sons, though Roger's were eight years older, and they often shared tales of the exploits of their boys.

Roger had liked Général Juin since they'd first met in January. He was the second youngest general in the room, only seven years older than Roger, and he was far more interested in results than ceremony. His experience with rough terrain and colonial troops should prove to be useful.

Général Juin moved to the center of one side of the conference table and the division commanders remained standing. One of Juin's aides unrolled a large map of the Middle East on the table before withdrawing. Général Juin gave his subordinates a chance to look over the new plan before addressing them.

"As you can see, things have changed. We've been tasked with invading Iraq in addition to our drive on Egypt. The British are moving an Indian division to their Habbaniya air base just east of Ramadi. This poses a threat to our flank as we advance, but it also provides an opportunity.

"The Iraqi government hasn't been happy with the Anglo-Iraq Treaty they were forced into eight years ago. Now, the Brits are deploying troops and requisitioning the Iraqi infrastructure without regard to how it will impact the Iraqis. King Ghazi was less than pleased that they didn't bother consulting his government. So, he asked President de Gaulle if we could help get the Brits out of his country. de Gaulle happily added it to our plate.

"We'll need to modify the original plan to send a force into Iraq. My initial thought is to take the 8th Motorized and send it from Deir ez-Zur, down the Euphrates to Haditha, then on to Ramadi and Baghdad. Any thoughts, gentlemen?"

Général Juin looked around the table at each of the other generals, but his gaze lingered on both Roger and Général de Brigade Marie Joseph Edmond Welvert, the commander of the 8th Motorized Division. Roger simply raised his left index finger indicating he had an idea before turning to look at Général Welvert for his thoughts. They all studied the map for a few more moments as his fellow generals waited for Général Welvert's reaction to the change in his role.

"It's doable, Sir. The Euphrates should help with our supply situation as we push forward. My major concerns are air cover, how well they're dug in when we get there, and how the Iraqis react to our presence."

Roger turned back to Général Juin for his reaction and nodded his head slightly, indicating he had the same concerns.

"Général de Niort?

Général de Brigade Marie Alexandre Martin Henri Fondi de Niort was the commander for the Levant Corps' air assets. He had seventeen squadrons to support us. He was another of the younger generals present. Roger thought he was a bit verbose at times, but generally liked him.

"Our intelligence says that the Brits have around a hundred land-based planes in the area. About half of them are their new Spitfires, which are a match for our D.520s. The rest of them are bombers, about evenly split between Battles and Blenheims. They also have the combined air wings of the *Courageous* and the *Glorious*. That's almost another hundred planes. We don't know of any combat craft currently stationed in Iraq."

de Niort pointed at various places on the map, "We have about two hundred planes, roughly evenly split between fighters and bombers. The Italians will be advancing from Libya with about a hundred and fifty planes, also split almost evenly between fighters and bombers. There's also an Italian group down in East Africa that's about the same size that's supposed to keep the Brits from bringing reinforcements up the Red Sea. The Brits will be able to attain air parity with one of our groups if they throw all their assets in one direction."

de Niort looked around the room. "Our top priority will be to hit their airfields and try to gain air superiority. Their Spitfires have a significantly shorter range than our fighters so we'll have an extra advantage if we can make their fighters base further back from the front. Any planes we catch on the ground will be a bonus.

"Our next priority is to hammer their fleet so it doesn't interfere with our operations. Our current plan is a joint strike with the Italians. Which planes take the lead will depend on the location of the British ships and the condition of our planes after our initial strikes on their airfields. The *Joffre* has been assigned to the Italian Fleet to provide it some intrinsic air cover. They're supposed to attack whatever is left after our combined strike. The *Joffre* is only carrying MS.406Ns, so it can provide some extra fighter support if we can chase off the Royal Navy.

"Ground support will come after that. Hopefully, the Italian fleet will be able to bombard anything along the coast. Since the British can concentrate their aircraft on either front, I don't feel comfortable detaching more than a squadron of fighters to Iraq until we've got a handle on the main fronts."

"Any chance we can get some more planes assigned to our theater?" Général Welvert asked.

Général de Niort shook his head no.

"The airbases are about as packed as they can be right now. Any more planes would just get in the way of flight operations. I have been assured that we'll get replacements for our losses as fast as they can fly here, but there's just no room for more operational aircraft."

Général Juin nodded to his Air Commander and looked back around the table before his eyes settled on Général Noiret. The other division commanders had looked concerned and thoughtful. Only Roger was looking back expectantly.

"Général Noiret?"

"I've been tinkering with an Iraq scenario for a couple of weeks, and I think a modification of your attack plan might have a better chance of success, Sir. I propose that we attach a battalion each of light and heavy tanks to the 8th Motorized. The light tanks could lead one of the 8th's regiments through Mosul and Erbil to advance on Baghdad from the north. The B1s would advance with another regiment down the Euphrates. The original attack plan for my division had me sending a battalion of G1s to Rutba to protect our flank. Now they can continue advancing towards Baghdad. If the 8th's third regiment is attached to my division, my attack towards Amman won't lose much firepower. The extra regiment could then act as a reserve to aid the push from Rutba or our drive on Egypt depending on our progress.

"Each column should be able to handle itself if the Brits concentrate against it. The Brits shouldn't have any anti-tank guns better than their forty-millimeter guns, which need to be very close to disable a B1 or G1. The northern column would be the most vulnerable, but a concentration against it would leave Baghdad and the Brits' supply line unprotected. Don't forget, the light tanks are the new AMX38s with their five shot magazines. That added firepower should keep the northern column safe."

Général Welvert stared at the map on the table for another moment before looking up to find Général Juin waiting for his reaction.

"I think supplies will be tenuous for the flanking columns, but it should keep us from having to assault prepared positions. The additional mobile firepower should help make up for a lack of air support. Things will go smoother if the Iraqis help us. All things considered; it looks a lot better than a simple frontal assault along the Euphrates."

Général Juin saw confidence replacing the doubt on Général Welvert's face and looked around at the rest of his commanders. Each gave a nod of acceptance to the modified plan and Juin moved on to the next item on his agenda.

"Are there any issues with your units?"

Général Juin had established a reporting order early in his tenure as the corps commander. The colonial units reported first, followed by the French infantry, with the mobile units reporting last.

Général de Brigade Godefroy Louis Pfister, commander of the 1st Colonial Division, was the first to report. He had been in the Levant for five years and his division was based at Aleppo. He would coordinate our response if the Turks came across the border or the Syrians got out of hand.

"Nothing out of the norms on readiness, Sir. Things are running smoothly, Sir."

Général Juin simply nodded in acknowledgment and looked at Général de Brigade Paul Émile Britsch, commander of the 2nd Colonial Division and the oldest member of our group.

"2nd Colonial is doing fine, Sir. Since we're based at Al Hasakah, I'll get my quartermaster to work with the 8th Motorized on its supplies.

We should be able to keep them going, though it means we'll be a bit slower to respond if you need us to move."

Général Juin considered for a moment before responding. "I think that's a fare trade-off and we'll keep it in mind if Général Pfister or I need your men." Général Juin's glance at Général Pfister was met with a nod of agreement.

He then turned his attention to the last of his colonial troop commanders, Général de Brigade Jean Ris. Général Ris had been using his alpine experience to get the 3rd Colonial Division ready for its part in the assault on the British in Transjordan.

"We're set, Sir. One regiment will be going over the hills to hit Irbid while the other two support the drive on Amman. It would help if the artillery from that regiment of the 8th Motorized provided fire support since we're losing some of the tanks that were going to help."

"That can be arranged, Général Ris." Juin continued his circuit around the table. "Général Alaurent?"

Général de Brigade Auguste Alaurent was the commander of the 14th Infantry Division. His division would attack southwest into Palestine from the Golan Heights while Général de Brigade Charles Marcel Louis Lucien Trinquand would lead the 26th Infantry Division south from Lebanon.

"Our stockpile of artillery shells is on the low end of what we need, Sir. We've got enough for what's expected but not a whole lot in reserve."

Général Juin looked back at Général Pfister. "Move your reserve shells down to Damascus. We'll work on getting them replaced but that will make them more readily available if Général Alaurent needs them."

Both Pfister and Alaurent nodded agreement and Général Juin turned to Général Trinquand.

"The 26th is ready, Sir, though I will say that sooner is probably better. It looks like the British have moved a second regiment to the border and are digging in for all they're worth. I know we're primarily a holding attack, but the longer we wait, the more men we're going to lose to keep the Brits pinned."

"Understood, Général Trinquand. Unfortunately, I'm not in charge of the timetable. I'll do my best to keep from needlessly losing any of our men."

Général Juin's gaze came to rest on Roger once again.

"I need to cut the orders to transfer the two battalions to the 8th Motorized and figure out where we should station the extra motorized regiment. Beyond that, 1st Armored is ready to go, Sir."

"I think that wraps it up for today. Noiret, Welvert, and Britsch, stay for a few so we can work out the updated plans. Everyone else, dismissed."

20 Miles South of Montevideo, Uruguay

Vice Admiral Sir Geoffrey Blake sat at his desk reviewing the latest report from the temporary Argentinian capital at Bahía Blanca. There were at least fifty dead British merchantmen among the casualties. While the Brazilian battleships were shelling the city, Uruguayan destroyers had specifically targeted the ships in the harbor. There was little doubt in his mind that this was the beginning of open conflict with the Organization of American States and probably with the Catholic Entente. He wanted to teach the pissant countries of the OAS a lesson. The politicians and Admiralty had finally decided on what they wanted to do in response to the murder of His Majesty's people. Now, the question was how the League of Nations would react.

Sir Geoffrey shook his head in disgust. The League was a skirt that lesser countries hid behind after they'd poked a major power. And these days the major power being poked was usually the United Kingdom. Ever since the Great War, the League had been trying to prevent the Commonwealth from dealing with the problems caused by other countries.

That ended today. It had to end. The Catholic Entente was working on isolating the home islands and starving their factories of resources. At least Parliament had seen the writing on the wall after the Spanish Civil War and begun expanding the production capacity of the colonies. But with the Entente in control of western Africa and South America, the only lines of supply left were the north Atlantic and through the less than friendly Central Coalition.

A knock on his door was quickly followed by the entry of his new aide, Lieutenant Gregory Everett. The dark-haired, broad-shouldered young man wore a look of concern as he came to attention in front of Sir Geoffrey.

"Report from the *Indefatigable*, Sir. It looks like most of the OAS navy has sortied from Buenos Aires. They make it four battleships, four cruisers and six destroyers making about ten knots, Sir."

"Have Commodore Moore send the orders for Plan One. I'll be on the bridge shortly."

Lieutenant Everett bobbed his head with a "Sir!" and closed the door as he left to relay the order.

Plan One dealt with the arrival of the OAS navy by dividing his ships, Task Force South Atlantic. Task Group SA.1 consisted of four destroyers of the 6th flotilla and the five light cruisers of the 7th Cruiser squadron. They would carry out the punitive shelling of Montevideo, the Uruguayan capital. Task Group SA.2 consisted of four more destroyers of the 6th and his battlecruiser squadron. Their mission was to engage the OAS navy. His last destroyer, the *Firedrake,* was assigned to escort the *Indefatigable* as Task Group SA.3. The carrier would stay behind both groups and provide air cover. That would keep the *Firedrake's* new captain, Lieutenant Commander Travis Caldwell, out of harm's way. Sir Geoffrey's previous aide had only taken over the new responsibilities a week ago and the Vice Admiral was concerned about him trying to prove his worthiness.

Plan Two was the optimistic possibility that the OAS navy would display some common sense and stay away from the Royal Navy's retaliatory strike. Plan Three dealt with the remote possibility that the Venezuelans could get their battleships to the scene. The two ex-French battleships would even the odds some if shooting started, but Sir Geoffrey was confidant they would have ended just up as more victims for his guns.

Sir Geoffrey felt the *Marlborough* turn to port and accelerate as he finished dressing. He headed to the bridge with equal feelings of anxiety and anticipation.

Thirty minutes later found the 1st Battlecruiser Squadron in line across the wide stretch of the Rio de La Plata. The cruisers and battleships of the OAS squadron were ten miles to his west, trying to form their own battle line. Sir Geoffrey didn't like giving his enemy the first shot, but his orders were to hold fire unless fired upon or the OAS navy tried to approach the punitive mission at Montevideo.

Vice Admiral Blake lifted his binoculars and scanned the OAS line. The battleships, all Brazilian, drew his scrutiny. The *Minas Geraes* was the most dangerous of the OAS ships. She'd just finished a refit in April so her guns would probably be the most accurate.

The *Deodoro,* and *Floriano* were next. The ex-Italian battleships had been partially modernized before being traded to the Brazilians for their loyalty last year. Just how much they had been upgraded was the big question. They looked like they still carried the original twelve-inch main guns that they had when they were built, the same guns that were used on the home-grown Brazilian battleships.

The final battleship, the *São Paulo,* was barely more dangerous than one of the cruisers. Her condition was so poor that her refit had been canceled. She was probably the reason the OAS squadron was only doing ten knots. He left the railing and headed back into the bridge. It was almost ten and the bracing ten-degree morning was making him antsy.

Commodore John Moore greeted him when he entered, "Any changes, Sir?"

"None yet, though I expect them to make a decision soon."

"They did come out to greet us. Maybe they're hoping a show of force will convince us to leave. It did *seem* to work for the Italians off Spain."

That action, or lack of it, still rankled Sir Geoffrey and Commodore Moore. The Admiralty had wanted a show of force but had refused them the option of initiating any action. The Italians had simply ignored their ships and sailed around them.

"I don't think they would have gone into a line-of-battle if they were going to try that. I think they're trying to coordinate something. Anything new from our scouts or the *Indefatigable*?"

"No, Sir. No submarine sightings or ships trying to run past us."

"They're up to something. The easiest way for them to coordinate action would be based on the clock. Warn the *Indefatigable* and *Firedrake* that …"

"Airplanes due west, Sir!"

The radioman's call interrupted Sir Geoffrey and he knew he'd been right. The clock showed ten on the dot. The other ships in his task force would have heard the message, too. Sir Geoffrey simply waited for more information, there was nothing else for him to do yet. Everyone was already at battle stations and knew their assignments. Fifteen seconds crawled by before an update.

"Scout Two reports twenty planes approximately fifteen miles out circling... the *Indefatigable* is sending her combat air patrol our way and she's turning into the wind to launch the rest of her fighters... Scout Four reports torpedo boats leaving Montevideo Bay and heading south... OAS battle squadron is turning east."

"Prepare for battle" was all Commodore Moore said; a call that echoed through the ship.

Sir Geoffrey watched as controlled chaos broke out on the bridge. His battle plan was in place and there was little for him to do until the situation unfolded. Captain Jonathon Lucas of the *Leander* had his orders for the cruiser squadron. The *Indefatigable* was new but Captain

Cedric Holland had commanded the *Ark Royal* before he got his new ship. He would scramble the rest of his Gladiators but keep his Skua dive bombers and Swordfish torpedo bombers on deck. The new carrier had twice as many planes as the older *Ark Royal*, something useful for his isolated task force and something the OAS apparently didn't realize. Meanwhile, the *Marlborough* and *Benbow* were training their guns on the *Minas Geraes* while *Hood, Tiger,* and *Renown* trained theirs on the *Deodoro*. Where the OAS would shoot remained to be seen.

"OAS squadron continuing due north and picking up speed. The *São Paulo* is continuing east. OAS planes are heading southeast."

Sir Geoffrey's calm command voice broke through the buzz of low conversations on the bridge.

"Port turn to bring us about. Match speed with the main OAS force. Maintain separation."

Meanwhile, his brain tried to figure out what the enemy aircraft and the *São Paulo* were doing. The aircraft were probably either going after the *Indefatigable* or lining up for a run at his ships from the southwest. The *São Paulo* might be trying to force the engagement or simply trying to close enough with his ships where she might actually hit something. Either would split the fire of the *Marlborough* when the shooting started, unless...

"Send the distance warning to the OAS again. Have our destroyers prepare for a possible long-range launch on the *São Paulo*."

That might dissuade the Brazilian battleship and at ten knots, she would be an easy target. The destroyers' Mark IX torpedoes could run for around eight miles if they were set for long range. A salvo of sixteen of them had a decent chance of hitting the *São Paulo* if she stayed on her course.

It was 10:10 when the OAS fleet changed course again. Sir Geoffrey had expected the course change to lead them back to the *São Paulo* to come a bit later.

"OAS squadron turning west. *Indefatigable* reports the OAS planes now circling fifteen miles south of her position. Scout Four reports torpedo boats idling just outside Montevideo Bay."

He'd thought that was their game. Draw his ships west and closer to the *São Paulo* as they headed south. It also meant a closer shot for his destroyers though the angle wouldn't be as good. He expected the OAS to start things while the *São Paulo* was still south of his force.

"Starboard turn to bring us about. Inform the other Task Groups that action is expected in five minutes."

The turn away from the OAS ships would open the range, which was fine with Sir Geoffrey. The fifteen- and sixteen-inch shells from his ships would still penetrate the OAS battleships' armor while the extra range would reduce their accuracy and ability to damage his ships. When the opposing groups had finished their turns, he wasn't surprised when the OAS squadron started sidling east to close the range.

At 10:14, Vice Admiral Blake turned to Commodore Moore.

"Inform the task force to load for the current range and that England expects every man to do his duty. Destroyers will begin their run on the *São Paulo* and launch at first shot."

The captain of the *Marlborough* passed the orders while Sir Geoffrey turned back to watch the opposing ships. He might be jumping the gun, but he was confident of his assessment of the OAS intentions.

The clock on the *São Paulo* was apparently a little slow. She was a good five seconds behind the rest of the OAS fleet with her opening salvo. His ships had already returned fire by then. Now came the waiting. The flight time for the shells was around thirty seconds at this range. That was also about how long it took to reload the guns, though his crews would delay their second salvos until they saw the results of their first.

"Scout Four reports enemy torpedo boats accelerating towards Task Group 1. Enemy aircraft approaching Task Group 3."

The news confirmed Sir Geoffrey's expectations as did the reports of the second salvo from the enemy ships he faced. They hadn't waited for the results of their first salvo before firing. Based on their splashes, the OAS had decided to target his older battlecruisers. The deck armor on the *Hood, Tiger* and *Renown* was barely half that of the *Marlborough* and *Benbow* and their belt armor was thinner too. Even the guns from the cruisers could be dangerous to them. Luckily, the first shots from the OAS were short so the second ones should be too. His crews knew to stagger the range on their shots and wait for the results so they could zero in on their targets faster. They also staggered the timing of their shots so they could tell the splashes apart when shooting at a common target.

It was another ten seconds before the guns of his flag ship roared for a second time. The *Marlborough* might be big, but the combined power of her nine sixteen-inch guns could make even a hundred million pounds of ship stagger.

"Destroyers launching torpedoes against the *São Paulo*. Task Group 1 engaging enemy torpedo boats. Aircraft engaged south of Task Group 3."

Sir Geoffrey clasped his hands behind his back. The engagement was being run according to his plan, but the ships were run by their captains, their crews. Until the tactical situation changed, Sir Geoffrey was little more than a spectator. All he could do was project calm and confidence and stick his fingers in his ears when the main battery was ordered to fire.

The third salvo from the main OAS group was ragged. Their guns should've finally started correcting for the results from their first salvo, but an unsynchronized firing of the main guns would throw off all the shots after the first one. He hoped they would keep it up. Meanwhile, the *São Paulo* had finally gotten her second salvo off. Her maintenance might not be good, but her fire discipline was.

Sir Geoffrey and the bridge crew got to experience a solid two seconds of jubilation as the second salvo from X turret bracketed the

Minas Geraes. Its center shot slammed into the front of the forward turret of the Brazilian battleship. The shell sliced through the turret's armor and the resulting explosion blew sheets of flame out of the gunports. Even if the guns were still serviceable, every seaman working on them was dead and the *Marlborough* had her range.

Commodore Moore had just started to commend X turret when the scream of incoming shells announced the arrival of the *São Paulo's* second salvo. Nine of those twelve-inch shells threw plumes of water high into the sky. The tenth shell found its mark. The eleven-hundred-pound shell hit the forward superfiring six-inch secondary battery. Armor from the two-gun turret was blown thirty feet into the air. Some of it found the bridge.

Sir Geoffrey found himself trying to focus on the ceiling while his ears rang and his body decried its indignity at being blown off its feet. A surge of adrenaline and anger brought him to his senses as he regained his feet. There was glass everywhere and the bridge was a mess, but only three crewmen were down. Lieutenant Everett was desperately trying to stop the blood flowing from the leg of a Petty Officer where a large piece of metal had lodged. Commodore Moore was busy getting damage reports and fighting his ship, so Sir Geoffrey made his way over to the radio operator who was back at his post. The seaman held up a restraining finger on his right hand while one from his left was firmly lodged in its ear. After a moment, he dropped the finger and looked up.

"Report."

"*Leander* reports no damage but fish in the water. Three of twelve torpedo boats sunk. Fire from shore batteries at Fortress General Artigas. *Indefatigable* reports aircraft engaged. *Firedrake* moving to interpose. *Deodoro* bracketed but no hits yet. Torpedoes on their way towards *São Paulo.*"

"Fire!"

The order from the gunnery officer made both the Vice Admiral and the radioman plug their ears as the big guns roared for a third time. Those guns would be spewing death faster now that they had the range to the *Minas Geraes*. The slight rolls from the easterly breeze would complicate things, but that was always true for combat at sea. The fourth salvo from the OAS battleships was hurled his way almost simultaneously.

The staccato pop of the six-inch guns firing at the enemy cruisers and the low conversations of medics tending to the wounded were all that disturbed the next thirty seconds. Sir Geoffrey shifted his location and raised his binoculars to get a view of the *Minas Geraes*.

A small smile came to his lips as the shells from his flagship landed. The salvo from A Turret was a little long and had led the Brazilian battleship too much, a fountain of water splashed across the battleship's starboard bow. B Turret was a little short and fountains of water blanketed her centerline gun turret. The salvo from X Turret found its mark. Two of its three shells hit the *Minas Geraes* aft of her stern turrets and the battleship that was barely half the size of the *Marlborough*, staggered as the sixteen-inch shells tore through her armor.

Sir Geoffrey had just enough time for his smile to turn into a snarl of satisfaction when the shells from the *Benbow* arrived at the stricken battleship. Her salvo was staggered differently and it was her A Turret that found its mark. All three shells impacted on the port bow of the *Minas Geraes*. The resulting explosions blew a ragged hole almost fifty feet long in her side that was low enough that she was taking on water with every wave. Whether or not it was fatal remained to be seen, but her speed and stability would definitely suffer.

Sir Geoffrey shifted his gaze to the *Deodoro* though he had to wait for a moment as smoke billowed past. The ex-Italian battleship was bigger than the *Minas Geraes* but still much smaller than his battlecruisers. It had smoke billowing from a hole amidships and its triple-turret there seemed to be out of action, but its other ten guns still belched defiance. He lowered his binoculars and tapped the radioman on the shoulder just as another call to fire the main guns forced a delay.

"*Renown* reports a hit amidships. Three boilers down but no major damage. *Leander* reports four more torpedo boats sunk, torpedoes still inbound, shore batteries still active. *Indefatigable* reports six enemy planes down, one Gladiator down. Six torpedo planes making launch runs."

Sir Geoffrey's expression turned grim. Six torpedoes headed towards the *Indefatigable* could ruin his day. Her planes didn't have anywhere else to land so he would lose them all if his carrier couldn't continue flight operations. Only time would tell. He turned back to survey his enemy and project the calm confidence his men relied on.

Two more salvos were exchanged between the opposing battle lines before Sir Geoffrey gave new orders. The *Minas Geraes* had been hit by eight more shells from the *Benbow* and *Marlborough*. Both of her forward turrets were out of action, as was her turret amidships. Her aft superfiring turret was still firing but its lower partner seemed to have jammed. She was also definitely settling in the water and her speed was dropping as she turned out of the battle line. The *Deodoro* had fared better but had still taken a pounding. Smoke spewed from multiple holes but three of her turrets still engaged the *Tiger* and had managed to knock out its A Turret. The shell that hit it hadn't penetrated but the concussion had killed most of the gun crew and damaged the guns. Several other hits had done minimal damage.

The *Renown* was getting the worst of it. The *Floriano* didn't have anyone shooting at it and its gun crews had finally found the *Renown's* range. *Renown* had taken at least a dozen hits now and her X Turret was a total loss. She was taking on water but her damage control crews had it under control. Amazingly, her speed was unaffected.

Sir Geoffrey placed his hand on the shoulder of the radioman who looked up for orders.

"*Renown* to accelerate and take station one thousand yards east of *Benbow*. *Benbow* and *Marlborough* will engage the *Floriano*."

The "Aye, Sir." from the radio operator was echoed by Commodore Moore. Task Group 2 would start crossing the T of the *São Paulo* soon, but Sir Geoffrey didn't want to give her any reason to change course. The long-range torpedoes were still on their way and the *São*

Paulo had proven unable to deal with the range adjustments needed for shooting at an enemy who wasn't running parallel to it. She'd only hit the *Marlborough* one more time and that shot had done little damage. Once his orders had been relayed, the radioman looked back up and began the latest battle report at Sir Geoffrey's nod.

"Task Group 1 reports all enemy boats destroyed. Enemy shore batteries silenced. Proceeding with punitive mission. Task Group 3 reports enemy aircraft have disengaged. Two Gladiators and ten enemy aircraft down. *Indefatigable* undamaged. *Firedrake* listing heavily to starboard from a torpedo strike. Heavy casualties but Lieutenant Commander Caldwell reports she's not in danger of sinking. Captain Holland says one of the torpedoes was headed for *Indefatigable* and *Firedrake* interposed when it looked like it would hit the *Indefatigable*."

Sir Geoffrey used his acknowledgement to cover a brief look of concern. So much for keeping Caldwell out of harm's way until he was used to his ship. Time to get back to the rest of his command.

The minutes crept by as his ships sped past the *São Paulo*. She continued her charge as the British ships crossed her bow. The change of course for the *Renown* had thrown the shots from the *Floriano* off and she'd escaped further damage. *Floriano* had shifted her fire to the *Tiger* in an attempt to take out at least one of Sir Geoffrey's battlecruisers. The *São Paulo* had shifted her fire to the *Hood* and had a single hit that caused little damage.

The captain of the *São Paulo* must have thought she'd been lucky to be ignored. Maybe he took it as the insult it was intended to be. Either way, he kept steaming east and was finally getting his rear turrets into the action when the torpedoes from Sir Geoffrey's destroyers finally arrived. Sir Geoffrey couldn't see them hit, but Scout Two reported the results. Their aim had been true, and four out of the sixteen-shot spread found their mark. He would never know if one of the torpedoes found a magazine or if bulkhead doors had been left open. Either way, there was a secondary explosion moments after the torpedoes arrived. It blew the forward turret at least thirty feet in the air and it was headed back down when a third, larger explosion, broke the battleship's back amid a spectacular fireball.

Sir Geoffrey had no idea how the explosion affected the OAS sailors, but everything on the *Marlborough* seemed to stop as everyone stared at the carnage. Commodore Moore was the first to recover.

"Prepare to fire on the *Floriano*."

His simple order was a reminder that they had jobs to do, and the bridge crew shivered as they went back to work. If that didn't take the fight out of them, then the Royal Navy would pound them to scrap. Sir Geoffrey tapped the radioman.

"My compliments to our destroyers. Good shooting."

The OAS ships took a few more hits as they turned west to try to break contact. Smoke from their destroyers quickly obscured them and Sir Geoffrey had to check his instincts to pursue them and finish them off. His orders were explicit in that regard. He could defend his ships and the punitive mission. He was not allowed to chase them once they'd broken off.

"Have Scout Two keep an eye on the OAS squadron and report any changes in their heading. Bring us about to cover search and rescue operations for the *São Paulo*. I'll want damage and readiness reports for the task force as soon as possible. Send my compliments and a 'Well done' to the task force."

It was late that afternoon when Lieutenant Gregory Everett brought Sir Geoffrey the full battle reports. It would take the OAS a while to fix the damage to their three remaining battleships. They'd also lost fourteen torpedo boats, ten aircraft, and at least a thousand men on the *São Paulo* alone. The Uruguayans had been given thirty minutes to clear the ships and docks in and around Montevideo Bay before the punitive shelling had begun. Seventeen cargo ships and most of the dock facilities had been destroyed. It would take them months to repair the damage.

The Royal Navy had ruled the day but there was always a cost. One hundred and forty-three of his men were dead and another two hundred and six were wounded. The *Firedrake* should be able to be fixed at the

Falklands, but the X Turret of the *Renown* would have to go back to England for repairs. Whether or not the A Turret of *Tiger* would need the same treatment was still up in the air.

Sir Geoffrey made notes as he went through the reports. He would recommend Lieutenant Commander Caldwell for the Distinguished Service Order for his actions to safeguard the *Indefatigable*. Battle honors would be up to the review board, but he would recommend them for the *Firedrake* specifically. His men had performed their task well. Now the question was what would come of the action.

Dire Dawa, Italian East Africa

Colonnello Guido Nobili enjoyed the feeling as he put the new G.51 Freccia through its paces. He might be the Air Commander for Dire Dawa, but he'd been out of the cockpit for too long. His stint as liaison with the French had lasted almost a year and a half. In that time, he'd worked hard to get the Italian Air Force fighters to a level near those of the French. The G.51 was the first fighter to show the fruits of his labor, and the three squadrons he had here were the first ones in the Regia Aeronautica. The G.51 wasn't as heavily armed and didn't have the same range as the French D.520, but it was ten kilometers per hour faster than the French fighter. It was so much better than Italy's old, front-line fighter, the CR.32. Guido was proud of the airplane his countrymen had created.

He blew past a pair of Italian Z.1007s and slowly overtook the French MB.175 ahead of him. The CR.32 he'd flown in Spain had a top speed of three hundred and sixty KPH and wouldn't even have been able to chase down the Italian bombers. They were almost a hundred KPH faster than his old biplane. The French bomber had a top speed of five hundred and fifty KPH and the G.51 was only twenty KPH faster, but that was a hell of a lot better than almost two hundred slower. Guido slowly closed on the French bomber as it desperately tried to lose him. Moments later he cried "Gotcha!" over the radio and headed back to the airbase for the next part of the exercise. Time to see how the Italian fighter would fare against its French counterpart.

"Your turn, Commandant Lefebvre."

"Yes. Sir."

Guido had met Commandant Claude Lefebvre during the Spanish Civil War. They'd shared an airbase and supported the Catholic Entente's offensive that broke the back of the opposing Republican forces. The campaign had only lasted a month, but a major Republican offensive had killed a third of the men under his command and taught him painful lessons. It had also made him the only ace to come out of the conflict and given him the opportunity to apply those lessons to the Regia Aeronautica. Guido had spent time as an instructor at the Fighter School earlier in his career and his desire to understand the abilities and limitations of the G.51 were behind today's exercise. It had nothing to do with his love of flying. Honest.

The next ten minutes were filled with rolls, slips, wingovers, and Immelmann's as Guido and Commandant Lefebvre put their fighters through their paces while the rest of the fighter pilots at Dire Dawa watched from below. Sweat beaded on Guido's one hundred and seventy-five-centimeter frame by the time he decided to break off the demonstration.

"I think that's enough, Commandant Lefebvre. Let's land and see what our men think of our efforts."

"Sounds good to me, Sir."

As they landed, Guido saw his pilots streaming towards the control tower and its briefing room. Maybe they would come up with some good questions when he and Lefebvre ran the debrief. He hoped so. Their lives might depend on it.

Guido and Commandant Lefebvre headed straight to the briefing room from the flight line, only pausing to each get a glass of cool water. They entered and the waiting pilots snapped to attention. They took their place at the front of the room and finished their drinks before

Guido ordered his men to ease. Guido smoothed his rumpled and sweaty black hair and smiled as he saw Claude doing the same.

"As you may have noticed, the G.51 and the D.520 are well matched. The G.51 turns a bit better than the D.520 while the D.520 is better at rolling. The most advanced enemy fighter we may face in the coming campaign will be the Spitfire that the English recently introduced. It's about the same speed as our fighters but we don't know how it handles in the air, so I hoped you paid attention to how Commandant Lefebvre and I moved to negate the advantages the other enjoyed.

"A major part of our mission is to interdict any attempts to reinforce Egypt via the Red Sea. Given that, we will probably tangle with the 1st and 2nd Battle Divisions of the Royal Navy. Both are supported by two aircraft carriers though the 2nd Battle Division is the more dangerous of the two. It has all five of their *Queen Elizabeth*-class battleships as well as the *Courageous* and *Glorious*. Those carriers each operate forty-eight aircraft. The 1st Battle Division is based around the five, older, *Revenge*-class battleships and has the *Indomitable* and *Formidable* as air support. They only carry thirty-six planes each. All the British carriers operate Gladiators for their fighter components. Think of them as slightly faster CR.32s with more guns.

"Intelligence reports that the British have Spitfires in Egypt but it's unlikely we'll face them initially. The British also have a small number of Hurricanes based around the area, but most of our opposition will be carrier based."

Guido paused for a moment as his pilots murmured excitedly amongst themselves at the prospect of facing the slow biplanes in their new fighters. Guido let them babble for a few moments before loudly clearing his throat to call them back to the briefing.

"The expectation of facing mostly Gladiators is the major reason we were equipped with CR.32s for our Italian component until the G.51 became available. Fighter pilots, remember the tactics the Italian pilots used when practicing against the French during dogfights. We should expect similar maneuvers to be used against us by the British pilots though they may have a few extra tricks up their sleeves. We'll get to see how well the tactics we developed for the D.520 work against real opponents. And in case anyone has forgotten, the D.520s racked up a good kill ratio in our training but several of them were still deemed to have been shot down. I'm pretty sure both groups held back some of their information to try to keep an edge for their group during training. So, both groups of pilots need to share all of their secrets about fighting the opposing planes. If you learn from each other, we can minimize the number of pilots who don't make it home."

That quieted them down a bit. Confidence was good. Over-confidence could get you killed for stupid reasons.

"Bomber pilots, you are faster than the British Gladiators once you've dropped your ordinance. Push your speed when leaving the battlefield. Escorts should prioritize any newer model fighters they encounter so that our bombers won't need an escort as they return to base.

"You may have noticed that we have retained twenty CR.32s. Each day, one Italian squadron will fly them against one of the squadrons flying newer planes. The other squadrons will face off against each other to get experience facing foes on an equal footing. Hopefully, everyone will feel comfortable against either type of opponent by the time we get into real combat."

Guido fell back into his old teaching habits from Fighter School and another half hour was spent discussing tactics with his pilots before the session finally ended. He felt both physically and mentally exhausted when the group broke up and headed back to their barracks. Guido slogged back to his quarters to clean up a bit and change his uniform. His flight suit had been soaked but had quickly dried out in the arid conditions of East Africa. Still, Guido had gotten used to being as presentable as possible during his assignment in Paris. It was a change in his attire habits that Aurora had enthusiastically supported. He stood in front of his bathroom mirror, lost in thought.

Aurora...

Saying Guido missed his wife would be like saying an amputee missed their lost limb. He'd met her when he was called to Rome to receive the Medaglia d'oro al valor militare from Mussolini himself. She was a Colonnello in Intelligence assigned to show him the capital and keep an eye on him. It had been a whirlwind romance that continued with them getting married last June. They had spent their honeymoon in Paris, finally getting to see the sights rather than pass by them on their way to factories and conference rooms. The view of the City of Light from the top of the Eiffel Tower had been almost as beautiful as Aurora. The just-past full moon had made her long black hair shine and created a halo around her athletic figure. She was his angel, his heart, his soul, and his best friend. Guido came back to reality with a sigh. She was also five-and-a-half months pregnant with their first child and back in Rome.

Even if things went well, Guido wouldn't see his wife before their first anniversary on June 26th. He might find a way to get back to her for the birth of their child in September, but even that wasn't assured. If the British were pushed out of Egypt quickly, there were plans to push south through Africa, liberating its people and cutting off British access to its resources.

The hope was that those resources could be redirected to the Entente, but supplying the advancing troops and returning with raw materials would have to be a primarily seaborne operation. And security for those lumbering transports would rest on the shoulders of the Italian Air Force as much as its navy. That's why he and his men were in East Africa. And that's why both Guido and the High Command hoped the British would commit their Eastern Fleet to the defense of Egypt. Every ship they could sink or airplane they could shoot down from the British carriers was one less that could raid the Entente supply lines as they advanced down the African peninsula.

Generale di Corpo d'Armata Guglielmo Ciro Nasi, and he preferred you use all of that rather than just Generale Nasi, had eleven infantry divisions and two tank battalions to provide security and start the initial push to drive the British from Africa. Eight of those divisions were Ethiopians, whose quality was dubious at best, but the same was true of most of the enemy forces in the surrounding countries. Taking the Horn of Africa should be easy as long as Guido and his pilots could keep the British Navy from interfering. Holding it and advancing further south would be the hard part. They depended on capturing the Suez Canal so that supplies could be sent down the Red Sea.

And that brought everything back to his pilots and the British Navy. Virtually all of their supplies came through the port of Djibouti in French Somaliland. Generale Nasi's first objective was to take over British Somaliland. Guido and the East Africa Air Fleet were supposed to handle the rest.

Guido shook himself out of his introspection and finished getting dressed. It was almost six o'clock and time for the evening meal and discussions with Generale Nasi and Generale di Brigata Attilio Matricardi, his immediate boss and commander of the air base.

The food would be good and too plentiful, just like the wine. The discussion would center around their readiness and how they were going to kick those haughty British asses across the border. Neither of the Generales would worry about the cost of doing so, or how much of that cost would be borne by the five-hundred pilots under Guido's command. At least his men weren't being used as bait like they had been in Spain.

Cross Anchor, South Carolina, USA

Manly Lee Wilburn put down the Spartanburg Herald-Journal and shook his head. News spread slowly in rural South Carolina, so M.L., as he was known to his friends, made a point of reading the local paper from front to back to try to find out what was going on in the world. Most of it was local gossip but their Saturday edition tended to carry more national and international stories from the Associated Press and United Press Associations. Those stories were not painting a pretty picture. It looked like another big war was coming and it was only a matter of time before it landed in America's lap. He felt a lot older than his fifty-one years now that the shooting had started.

Wilma Leila came in from the kitchen and set a cup of coffee and a slice of her birthday cake on the end-table next to him before sitting in her chair on the other side of it. Her forty-ninth birthday had been this past Monday and she'd saved a slice of her cake for his Saturday morning reading time. It had been a near thing a couple of times as the kids tried to sneak away with it twice. That second attempt had earned Junior a whooping with her broom that finally got the point across to the kids. How his five-foot two-inch wife managed to keep control of their six kids still at home was a testament to her force of will. That was part of what made making those kids so much fun. It was probably also why they'd had ten of them.

"Thanks, m'Love."

"You're welcome, Honey. Anything interesting in the paper?"

M.L. knew she'd already glanced through it. She always did while she was directing the making of breakfast for the family. Saturdays and Sundays were her days off, too, as she made Jewel, Sybil, Betty, and Rita do the actual work. It usually involved breaking up at least one fight as the sixteen-year-old Jewel tried to make the twelve-year-old Sybil and nine-year-old Betty do as much of the work as possible. Seven-year-old Rita mostly just got in the way. But that question about anything interesting was her normal way of announcing she wanted to discuss things that worried her.

"Not much locally. The Piggly Wiggly in Spartanburg is having some kind of sale for Decoration Day, so it might be worth going up to look around. We could pile the kids in the truck and make a day of it if you want to."

"That's probably a good idea. The kids would enjoy it and we could stock up on things before they start going up in price."

"They do tend to do that when a war is abrewing."

Leila's nod was her only response, so M.L. knew she had more on her mind.

"Maybe I oughtta talk to Jim about a raise. Get things moving before it's too late."

Another nod, accompanied this time by a quizzical look.

"And I'll check with him to see if he knows what's likely to happen to my schedule and hours." As the head mechanic at the Spartanburg depot of the Seaboard Air Line Railroad, M.L. would likely end up with extra work if traffic picked up for a war effort. If that happened, the kids would have to do more of the work in their five-acre crop field. Leila would also have to shuffle their chores around to balance their workload.

Leila gave another nod and stood. Apparently, M.L. had found what she wanted him to do so it was time for her to return to the kingdom she openly ruled, the kitchen. She bent down and gave him a quick kiss before letting him get back to enjoying his weekly quiet time. A slight smile crept onto his face as he watched her go, but it quickly turned into a worried frown as he went back to reading the paper. The Japanese had been fighting the Chinese for almost a year. The Russians, Soviets, or whatever it was they called themselves had been fighting the Central Coalition since last November. And now the British and South Americans were shooting at each other, too.

M.L. didn't really care who killed who in other parts of the world, but the South Americans were using religion as a basis, which meant it would spread and be vicious. Most of South America had left the League of Nations to create the Organization of American States, their wing of the Catholic Entente. Now he wondered how long it would be before the Protestant nations of northern Europe left the League to join the Central Coalition. He doubted they'd jump into bed with the British, there were just too many hard feelings towards Britain. Either way, there wouldn't be enough countries left in the League to make economic sanctions work. And that meant that the good ole U.S. of A. might not be able to stay out of the fighting this time around. And with British Canada to the north, and a very Catholic Mexico to the south, that fighting might be a lot closer to home than Europe. Hell, even without Mexico and Canada, the Catholics here in America were protesting the League sanctions on the OAS. Would the country even be united when the shooting started?

M.L. sighed as he folded up his paper and set it on the end-table before eating the last of his wife's red velvet birthday cake. Nelle, their oldest, had baked it for Monday's birthday dinner. Their other two married daughters, Francis and Doris, had pitched in to make a fried chicken dinner that had left the gaggle of kids, grandkids, sons-in-law, and friends stuffed and feeling content. Hell, Jewel had even brought her latest beau, Dwayne Williams. At least she'd learned from Doris and made it past fifteen without getting pregnant. Rita had fit in between Betty and little Eddie well enough, but M.L. was getting too damn old to take on another youngster. Janice and Harry Jamison, Philip and Courtney Lucas, and a dozen other friends and their families had made it by. Leila had been tickled pink with the turnout and that she didn't have to do any cooking or cleaning.

The only dim spot had been that their second oldest, Albert, and his family were in North Carolina and couldn't make it, though they did call. He was in the Army and his unit was getting ready to ship out somewhere. Albert couldn't or wouldn't say where, but M.L. thought it might be to Panama based on what the paper said. The Organization of American States was over-running Colombia, and the government was more than a little concerned about the safety of the Panama Canal. Just one more thing to drive up prices and make things scarce. M.L. finished off his coffee and set the cup on his now empty plate. He got a notepad and pencil out of the end-table. Time to make a list of things they bought that might get scarce but wouldn't go bad.

They'd finally made it to the Piggly Wiggly and M.L. left the women to do the grocery shopping while he led the men into the Lowe's next door. It had taken almost two hours before the kids had finished their chores and cleaned up enough for the trip to Spartanburg. M.L. had used the time taking inventory of their household and hunting supplies while Leila had done a quick check on their kitchen goods. A stop by the bank had fattened his wallet and her purse with some extra cash from their savings.

The store was more crowded than it usually was, and it took M.L. almost half an hour to find everything on his list. Several things, especially the shotgun and rifle shells, seemed to be running low. Apparently, he wasn't the only one who thought that the ability to hunt your own food might be an advantage in the near future. He was just approaching the checkout line when Harry Jamison came in with his sons, Andrew and Zachery. M.L. thought about it for a moment and decided that if the Lowe's was this busy, the Piggly Wiggly probably was, too. He got out of line and made sure Junior and Eddie followed him as he set off to intercept his neighbors. As he approached them from behind, he noticed that Harry had a list, too.

"Hey Harry."

"Hey, M.L. You out stocking up, too?"

"Yep. Leila's over at the Piggly Wiggly."

"Same with Janice."

"Whatcha getting'?"

"Nails, shells, and a couple of new saws. You?"

"That and a few other things. Oil and gas got scarce during the Great War, so I figured I'd get a half a case of oil for the truck and a couple of gas cans to store some extra. I was going to get an extra battery too, but they're sold out."

"Seems like the news is getting around and people are getting nervous, unless your name is Andrew." said Harry with an eye roll towards his oldest son.

"Thinks the military sounds exciting, eh?"

"He thinks anything that gets him out of town sounds exciting, but he wants to be a fighter pilot."

M.L. knew that Andrew had been working for Francis' husband, Buck, at his crop-dusting business but he didn't know if Andrew had done any of the flying.

"Has Buck let him do any of the flying? That'd give him a leg up on the competition."

"Nothing solo yet, but Buck has let him copilot and do everything but land his plane. Where do you think he got the damn-fool idea?"

M.L. just smiled and shrugged. He knew that Harry was against military service in general. His father had died in the Spanish-American war when he was just a baby and his mother had expressed her opinion of the military often enough that Harry grew up considering it to be a less than honorable profession. It was not a tenet that M.L. shared. Wilburns had been involved in every war America had been in and were quite proud of their service. Buck had even mentioned that he might try to join the Army Air Corps if war broke out. That made M.L. wonder just who would do the crop-dusting if both Buck and Andrew went off to the military? He filed that question away for later and decided it was probably best to change the subject.

"Sara and Lucille were looking quite fetching on Monday. You haven't had any trouble with the local boys chasing them around, have you?" M.L. glanced out of the corner of his eye to see Junior turning a bright pink and taking a sudden interest in a display of fishing lures. He was sweet on Sara, while Lucille was all doe-eyed over him. It made for some entertaining situations when the three of them were together. Harry's grin indicated he found it all amusing, too.

"Nothing to worry about, just yet. As far as I can tell. Sara has been keeping the boys in line. It's Lucille I'm worried about. She wants more of the attention that's directed at Sara and she's liable to get herself in trouble trying to get it."

M.L. nodded his understanding and decided he'd have another talk with Junior tonight, just to make sure. Sara and Lucille were two years apart and Junior was smack dab between them. The likelihood of Lucille raising her skirt to attract Junior's attention was pretty high. That kind of rivalry with an older girl was how Doris had ended up a mom at fifteen, a fact that Harry knew too well.

"I'm sure the men have had chats with their sons, but it might not hurt to reinforce those words of wisdom."

"Appreciate it," Harry said with a slight smile.

Junior turned even brighter pink and his fascination with the fishing lures became all-consuming. Eddie looked like he was losing interest and trying to find something to play with, never a good combination between a five-year-old and a hardware store. Time to get moving.

"I guess we oughtta get going. Be seeing ya."

"Catcha later."

M.L. corralled his sons and headed back to the register to check out, while Harry gathered his sons and went back to shopping with a slightly expanded list.

It was another fifteen minutes before M.L. had paid for his supplies and gotten them stowed in his truck. He was just pulling in to the Piggly Wiggly's parking lot when Leila and his daughters came out trailed by two bagboys carrying her purchases. He waved and maneuvered the truck to bring it around. Once he pulled up to the front of the store, he, Junior, and Eddie jumped out to lend a hand. A couple minutes, and some grateful smiles from the bagboys later, and the family was headed south back to Cross Anchor.

Leila and M.L. rode in companionable silence for a few minutes with the kids riding in the bed and trading their bits of gossip. The wind blowing in through the windows had a calming effect on M.L. but it wasn't long before that calm gave way to his concerns about the future and he turned to his wife.

"Did you get everything you wanted?"

"Yep. I also got an earful from Janice."

"About their girls and Junior or Andrew and the military?"

"Both. I guess you ran into Harry and got your own ears talked off."

"Yep. Might be a good idea to have a chat with Jewel. If her latest beau joins the military, there'll probably be pressure to give him a going away present."

"You're probably right. I'll chat with her while we're making breakfast tomorrow. And again, if I hear anything about Dwayne enlisting." Leila paused for a moment before broaching the next subject.

"Phil and Courtney haven't been here but a couple of years. I wonder if they'll be okay if meat gets hard to come by."

M.L. thought for a moment before replying. The young couple was in their mid-twenties and had moved down from Ohio two years ago. He worked in a factory in Cincinnati but had always wanted to be a farmer. Courtney's uncle lived in Union, and he convinced them that area was so nice they moved down and bought a twenty-acre farm.

"We'll need to make sure they know we can help them on that count. We'll also need to make sure they know when we grind corn so they can join in if they want to."

"If they aren't at the church, we could stop by their house and give them a heads-up on all this."

"Sounds good."

Leila's slight smile as she turned back to enjoying the scenery meant M.L. had properly read her mind again. He wasn't sure if she'd thought about the cornmeal, but it didn't really matter. She was happy, so he was happy. He had checked the mill he'd rigged up to be powered by his truck before going to Spartanburg and everything seemed to be in working order there. It was just a pain in the ass to hook the truck up to it, so it wasn't something he did very often.

They rode south in companionable silence. Both were concerned about where things were going, but both knew they would face it like they'd faced every other challenge – together.

EARLY JUNE 1938

The Chancellery, Berlin, Germany

Oberst Ernst Weber opens the door and Otto Woyke, my bodyguard and friend, enters before I do. Even here in the heart of our capital, security must be observed. War has broken out between France and the United Kingdom. The League of Nations is sanctioning both sides and we must walk a tightrope while we fight the Soviet Union in the east. People who remember the deprivations of the Great War are hoarding everything and creating the very shortages they fear. The question is whether we can resolve the eastern conflict before the western one merges with it.

There's no call to attention like there would have been during my military days, but the assembled generals and their staffs stand as I enter the briefing room. There are multiple maps hung on the east wall that show most of the world. A gap in their middle provides space for a speaker's podium. The north wall is adorned with three maps showing different sections of the eastern front. Ernst and I take our seats at the center of the west side of the large conference table while Otto takes his usual position behind me. Nineteen other people in the room also take seats. The twentieth, Generalfeldmarschall Werner von Blomberg, heads to the podium.

"Good afternoon, Chancellor Manstein. The coded message we picked up from the French yesterday, was apparently the go signal for

Entente operations against the British. Our embassy in London reports that the French ambassador delivered the declaration to the British at 6:55 this morning, Greenwich Mean Time. Active operations appear to have started five minutes later.

"There are reports from both the United Kingdom and France of air raids on the Channel ports and air bases near them. We don't have any reports of heavy bombers being used yet, but we expect that to change tonight. There are also reports from the United Kingdom of sabotage at multiple oil storage facilities.

"The map on my far-right shows locations in the Atlantic where British merchant ships have been attacked. The Entente seems to be concentrating on oil tankers, though there have been a few other merchant ships sunk. Reports indicate that these attacks are being carried out by submarines, light cruisers, and smaller craft.

"The map to my immediate right shows the situation in the Mediterranean. The major French surface combatants appear to be concentrated in the western Med and are shelling Gibraltar. The Italian fleet was last reported in the eastern Med with a French carrier providing air cover. It appears to be there to counter the British fleet based in Egypt. Entente ports around the Med are crowded with their merchant ships. We aren't sure if this is to keep them away from the initial naval exchanges or if they plan on moving them in convoys to protect against British submarines."

Blomberg stops for a moment to sip from a glass of water on the podium before waving towards his left and continuing.

"The map on my immediate left shows the situation in Africa and the Middle East. As we expected, this appears to be where the Entente is making its major ground push. There are reports of attacks into Transjordan and Iraq from Syria, a drive into Egypt from Libya, and an attack on British Somaliland from Italian East Africa. In western Africa, combat is reported in Gambia Colony, Sierra Leone, Gold Coast, and Nigeria. Northern and Southern Rhodesia as well as Nyasaland are under attack from forces based in Mozambique, Angola, and the Belgian Congo.

"The map on my far left shows the general situation in the Pacific. We don't have any reports of fighting there but expect the British to move on the French possessions in the area. French Indochina and New Caledonia are expected to be the primary targets of the British once they start reacting. There are two French light-cruisers and several smaller ships that may make life interesting for the British merchants in the area, but we don't expect any major action in that theater.

"The maps on the north wall show the situation on the Russian fronts. The ground is finally drying out there and offensive operations will resume soon."

Blomberg stops for another sip of water before looking at me and asking. "Questions?"

I think for a moment before responding. Unless I want a continual parade back and forth to the podium, I'll need to organize my questions.

"Thank you, Generalfeldmarschall. I know this is broad, but what are our best estimates of the forces involved in active operations and what each country still has in reserve?"

Blomberg turns to his right and an Oberst hands him a binder. He opens it and scans its first page before setting it on the podium.

"Just the British and Entente for the second part, or all the major powers?"

"Might as well hit them all while you're at the podium." I reply.

Blomberg grins and gives me a sharp nod of appreciation. He too, would prefer to avoid the podium dance.

"Since I started with the Atlantic, I'll start my answer with the naval situation there. We believe the United Kingdom has thirteen battleships, ten battlecruisers, seven aircraft carriers, thirty-five heavy cruisers, and ten submarines. The Entente has about a dozen light cruisers and about one hundred submarines there. The Americans have twelve battleships, twenty heavy cruisers, two aircraft carriers and ten submarines. We have ten battleships, eight heavy cruisers, two aircraft carriers, and forty submarines.

"The situation is reversed in the Mediterranean, where there are only five British battleships, two aircraft carriers, five heavy cruisers, and twenty submarines. The Entente has concentrated their fleets in the Med and has twenty battleships, twenty-four heavy cruisers, three aircraft carriers, and forty submarines. The Austrians have four older battleships and six heavy cruisers, not really enough to influence things even if they choose to try.

"The British also have their Eastern Fleet in the Indian Ocean. It has five battleships, ten heavy cruisers, two aircraft carriers, and five submarines. It could influence the battle in the Med if it's committed that way."

Blomberg pauses for a moment as he sips again on his water and looks at me questioningly. I smile back and nod slightly. He's hitting the highlights I want.

"On the ground side, things in the African theater are limited by supply constraints. The French have built up a major supply base in the Levant and we believe they have one panzer and nine infantry divisions there. The Italians have a panzer and around fifteen infantry divisions in Libya, while the British have a panzer and five infantry divisions in Egypt. Each of those groups has around two hundred aircraft in support.

"Our intelligence for the rest of Africa is less reliable. We believe the Entente has around thirty divisions in French West Africa, ten in Italian East Africa, and ten in the equatorial regions. Opposing them, the British have a couple of divisions in South Africa and they've been moving troops from India, but we don't know where they're ending up. Most of their protectorates have small militias but their quality is dubious at best.

"On the Eastern Front, we continue to have a near parity with the Russians in ground troops. They have about twice as many tanks and planes as we do but their equipment quality and troop training are poor. Turkey is shifting five divisions from its Levant border to the front which should help stabilize things in their area.

"The USGA army fields about ninety divisions, five of them panzer. Italy has around seventy divisions, one panzer, in country. The French have around ninety divisions, eight panzer, in country. The United Kingdom has around thirty divisions, two panzer, in country.

"The USGA has around one thousand combat aircraft. Italy has around seven hundred in country. The French have around two thousand in country. And the UK has around fifteen hundred.

"We have sixty infantry and two panzer divisions, as well as twelve hundred aircraft in country. Half of those infantry divisions are reserve units that are being upgraded. The panzer divisions are equipped with older models. We're expanding our panzer and aircraft production, but we'll impact the economy heavily if we expand the Wehrmacht too quickly. We have set up production facilities for our latest panzer and aircraft in Poland, the Ukraine, and Turkey to help expand and standardize the Coalition's capabilities."

Blomberg takes another sip while I scan the overview sheet for his briefing. Things don't look great, but they aren't too bad. I look up from the paper to address my greatest worry, "What are our greatest security threats right now?"

"First, war on two, or more, fronts. The fact that the Entente is at war with the British works in our favor and it's in our interest to keep the British from being defeated. The stronger the British are, the less likely France is to attack us. The recent intervention in Macedonia by the USGA, with League approval, marks them as another potential adversary. If the Entente attack, we will have to decide how much we are willing to thin our defenses on the Austrian border. We don't see the Austrians attacking on their own, but they've demonstrated an opportunistic approach to international relations.

"Second, internal sabotage. There has been a three hundred percent increase in the amount of rejected munitions that we've received in the last six months. Reports have been sent to the Ministry of Justice and several people have been arrested. All were refugees from the 1932 Protestant Exodus from France and Italy. We know Minister Gürtner has people working on the issue, but when you add in the sabotage of petroleum facilities in the UK, we must be concerned about the possibility of serious supply disruptions if we go to war with the Entente.

"Third, we are behind in the quality of our weapons of war. Generallieutnant Kurt Liese will address this issue." Blomberg looks to his right and says, "Generallieutnant Kurt Liese."

The head of Wehrmacht Research and Development stands and takes his place at the podium while Blomberg returns to his seat.

"Sir. The biggest issue we have right now is the French qualitative advantage in both panzer and air forces. The BF 109E is a good match for the French D.520, but the French fighter has more firepower, and we know they're working on improvements. We should have the up-gunned model F out next year. The same is true with the Panzer IVE and the French G1. We're working on another upgrade for the IVE's gun and an assault gun based on the Panzer III chassis.

"The Russians recently introduced a heavy tank that has armor that's thicker than the G1. Luckily, there aren't too many of them and they're mechanically unreliable. The measures we've been working on to deal with the G1, specifically the use of flak guns in the anti-tank role, have proven adequate to deal with them. Russian aircraft continue to be several years behind ours and we enjoy a twelve-to-one kill ratio in the air.

"The Italians and Austrians have both introduced planes and panzers that are close matches of our own, though the Italian panzers are more lightly armored.

"Our efforts to find ways to defeat the G1, and its expected improvements, should allow us to deal with any possible foe. The Uranium Club continues to make progress and Einstein is hopeful that there will be a useful outcome in the next several years. Similarly, Braun reports progress on the rocket development program, though he expects usable results in the next year.

"Questions?"

"Is there any way to improve our ammunition that would allow our older equipment to defeat the new French and Russian tanks?"

"We are working on new munitions, but they are more expensive and slower to manufacture. We will continue to work on them even as we upgrade our panzers' main guns. They would provide a bridge of effectiveness if significantly tougher tanks are introduced by the French or Russians."

Liese looks at me for a moment and heads back to his seat when I nod. Blomberg returns to the podium and looks across the room at me.

"Would you like to hear from the head of any of those development programs?"

"Assuming they agree with Liese's summary, no thanks. Their technical details go over my head."

"Then I'll close this briefing with our recommendations. We need to push for a resolution to the Russian war as soon as practical. We need to work to make sure that the United Kingdom is not defeated, even at the risk of going to war with the Entente. We need to speed up the modernization of our equipment if possible. And we need to expand the size of the Wehrmacht if the war with Russia continues."

"Thank you, Generalfeldmarschall."

I leave the weekly military briefing, accompanied by my small entourage. We detour to the Ministry of Justice to see if Minister Franz Gürtner can fit me into his schedule. I get lucky and he immediately invites us in. Three men I recognize only as his deputies stand and line the far wall so we'll have seats. They look a little annoyed when only Ernst and I sit while Otto takes a position where he can watch them.

"Great timing, Erich. We were just discussing how far we should go to find any French spies in our country. I'm guessing that Werner brought up the issue in your briefing and that's why you're here."

Franz was always smart and direct. He also insists on using first names. I think he probably does it to make sure people know his

Ministry is separate from the military, even if they work closely with them.

"Got it in one, Franz. Just how bad is the problem?

"That's the big question. It's been six years since the Exodus and the Frenchmen have mixed into our society pretty well. Quite a few of them have just disappeared. The couple we've caught have had German papers, German names, and no accent that would betray them. The only way we'll be able to find them is by checking on everyone who's moved in the last six years. And that assumes that none of the spies found loners whose identity they could assume after killing them."

"I'm worried about that possibility too. There's also the issue of public morale. It's a massive task if we start checking every single person. It will also make everyone suspicious of everyone else and you have to wonder how many people will make things up about people they don't like. Our society may fracture back into the Confederation days or worse."

"What do you want to do, Erich? How far should we go?"

"I really don't know. I need to talk to the Kaiser and the heads of the major political parties to get their input. We also have to think about how any crackdown we enact will play in Paris. Can you send me what details and any estimates you have on just how big the problem is or could be?"

"We're working on it and I'll send the information along as we update things."

I thank Franz and we head back to my office. Ernst makes a comment about being glad that it's not his job while Otto seems to be even more alert to our surroundings than usual. A sadness grips me as I realize the suspicion is already spreading.

Amman, Jordan

Général de Brigade Roger Noiret enjoyed the feeling of being in a tank again, even if he wasn't at the front of the battle. The British had concentrated against the French in Syria. Four infantry divisions had been identified by the French forces pushing south from Syria and Lebanon. They had stationed an armored division on their open eastern flank. That same eastern flank was the point of attack for his division. It was definitely not an encounter that the heretics enjoyed.

Even down four battalions of tanks, the French 1st Armored Division seemed to outnumber their British counterpart. Roger wasn't sure if that was really the case or if the enemy tanks just weren't concentrated. Either way, their tanks were garbage. Their Matilda had decent armor but was only armed with machine guns. Their Cruiser had a serviceable main gun, but its armor was so thin that his tanks had to use high explosive instead of armor-piercing shells on them. There were over a hundred claimed tank kills by his men for the loss of four S36 cavalry tanks and one G1 medium tank out of commission. Now came the interesting part.

Sunset was approaching and Roger's command was behind enemy lines with a local population of unknown loyalties. His men had overrun what looked like two division headquarters and their artillery when they'd entered Amman. The captured food, water, ammunition, and petroleum were welcome boons that would also seriously impair the enemy's ability to keep his units supplied. The rest of the Levant Corp was grinding forward through the positions the British had prepared. There was little they would be able to do to aid Roger's isolated men if the counterattack he expected materialized. After all, his men were sitting on the supply line for, and the retreat path of, the British troops fighting at the Syrian border. But that was the job of armored forces. Penetrate the line and force the enemy out of their established positions.

Roger had left his second battalion of light tanks along with the regiment from the 8th Motorized Division to continue guarding the main attack's eastern flank. That left him with three battalions of G1s and two of the lighter S36s along with his motorized regiment. He posted his G1 battalions to the areas where he expected any possible counterattack. The 103rd guarded the northern approaches, the 104th guarded the west, and the 105th screened the south. He posted the 106th battalion of S36s to the east. That left him the 107th S36 battalion and the 14th Motorized Infantry Regiment in reserve. The reserve units were busy moving and dispensing the captured supplies. Everyone was digging in while the interpreters they'd brought along tried to convince the local population to stay out of the fray. Now it was time to try to sleep, something that eluded Roger as his mind kept running through potential attacks.

It was just past five in the morning when the counterattack finally came. The sky was brightening in the east as dawn approached when Roger awoke to the sound of nearby artillery. About fifty British tanks and a large number of infantrymen were attacking from the west along the old road to Jerusalem. The darkness had hidden them until they were only a couple of hundred meters from his men. Scouts reported the approach of enemy troops and a star shell had been launched to see what could be seen. Unfortunately, both sides saw, and soon the shells were flying.

The initial artillery salvos from the British were close to their targets. The French guns were slow to adjust to the range since they were less familiar with the terrain. Commandant Jacques Jeannin's 104th Armored Battalion was dug in on that side of Amman and Roger trusted his judgement.

Roger was just issuing orders to move part of his reserve to Jeannin's aid when his men north of Amman came under artillery fire, too. Great. Roger thought for a moment and modified his orders. He sent a company of S36s and a battalion of motorized infantry to each of the northern and western fronts. That left him with the same sized force in reserve. If two, why not more?

Sergent Jean Martin yelled from across the room. "Sir! Commandant Martin reports tanks and infantry in numbers moving on his positions to the north of town."

"Get on the radio with HQ and let Général Juin know what's going on. Either we badly underestimated the British strength in the area, or some of the troops that had been on the border are down here now. Air support would be useful, too."

Roger threw that last one in more out of hope than expectation. Général de Niort had made it clear that ground support was down on the priority list for his planes. All he could do now was wait. Sergent Martin bent to his radio while Roger studied his map of the area.

It was only moments before an area about a kilometer south of their headquarters came under a furious artillery bombardment. Roger looked across the room at Lieutenant-Colonel Henri Dubois who at least had the manners to look sheepish. Dubois had wanted to set up their temporary HQ where the Brits had set up theirs. Roger had overruled him on the grounds that while it might already be set up for their purposes, it was a spot well known to the enemy. A spot that was about a kilometer south of where they currently stood.

"Sir! Général Juin acknowledges and will press the attack at the border. He'll also see what he can pry loose from de Niort, even if it's just reconnaissance."

"Send my thanks and wish him good hunting."

"Yes, Sir."

It was almost six when the first enemy aircraft appeared in the skies. Roger started to curse Général de Niort when French fighters appeared too. It looked like both sides were evenly matched with around fifty fighters. Roger stood just outside the bank he'd commandeered for his headquarters and watched what he could of the airborne melee. The streaks from tracer rounds and smoke from fatally wounded aircraft made him think of fireworks shows he'd seen.

More planes showed up after about ten minutes. About thirty were British, fifty were French. These were the bombers that did their best to be ignored by the fighters buzzing overhead. At least they were dropping their bombs around Amman rather than in it. Roger didn't want to find out how the locals would act under indiscriminate bombing, though he wished his men weren't getting hit either. Roger's curiosity was aroused when he noticed that about a dozen of the French bombers didn't commit to the attacks on the ground troops, but kept circling north of Amman.

The British broke off after another ten minutes or so and headed west towards Jerusalem with the French fighters harassing them as they went. The circling French bombers followed, too. Understanding dawned for Roger as he realized the bombers were intended to strike the airbase of the returning British fighters. He'd counted twenty-three fighters and eight bombers fall smoking from the skies in their brief fight. The worrisome thing was that he didn't know how many were foes or how many were friends. He headed back into the bank.

Sergent Martin had one earphone of his radio pressed to his left ear while he wrote on a notepad with his right. Colonel Philippe de Hauteclocque, Roger's executive officer, sat at the map table and was sifting through a small pile of papers that looked like they'd come from Sergent Martin's notepad. Dubois was studying the map. Philippe looked up as Roger entered.

"The perimeter is holding, Sir, though reinforcements would be appreciated. The bombing runs seem to have done more damage to the Brits than our men..."

"Sir!" Roger turned to Sergent Martin and suspected the enlisted man liked his power to interrupt officers whenever he wanted to. Regardless, he still got Roger's immediate attention.

"Message from command. No enemy troop concentrations spotted east or south of Amman. No large reserves spotted on the north or west."

"That's good news, Martin. Maybe we can get more help to our men who are fighting."

"Général Noiret?" Dubois was still looking at the map even while trying to get Roger's attention.

"Yes, Henri?" Roger headed over to the map table.

"There are a few small roads that lead from the south side of Amman to the right rear of the enemy line. Maybe we can cut them off from Jerusalem."

Roger studied the area that Dubois was pointing out for a moment before answering.

"That looks interesting, but even the main roads around here aren't the best. Any blockage or hold-up would take a flanking force out of the attack for hours."

Dubois looked unhappy as he gave a resigned "Yes, Sir."

"I didn't say it was a bad idea. Send one company of the 106th and the remaining company of the 107th to the southern flank to replace the 105th. That will give us two companies of S36s on the eastern and southern flanks. Once that's done, the 105th and remaining battalion of the 14th will rest and load up with extra gas and ammunition. All commanders should study the routes south of Amman and towards Be'er Sheva. Philippe, you'll command that force if we can make it happen."

"Thank you, Sir!"

"So, a deeper envelopment?" Dubois looked both hopeful and concerned.

"If we can. Martin, tell command that we need to know as soon as the British start withdrawing. Also, let them know that we could use the units we left to guard their flank as soon as they can release them."

"Yes, Sir!"

Dubois smiled and bent back to the map he'd been studying. After a moment, he looked back up at his commander. "You plan on using the faster AMX38s to catch up with and reinforce the flanking force?"

"Along with the S36s on the eastern and southern flanks. If we can block the road to Aqaba and the Italian navy comes through, we may be able to end this campaign quickly."

Roger paused for a moment before quietly muttering, "And if it doesn't work, we may end our division quickly."

It was just after one when the message came through from Général Juin. The British were withdrawing southwest, and the rest of his tanks were headed his way. It was going to be dicey, but Roger issued the order to go and Colonel Philippe de Hauteclocque headed south with the 105th Tank Battalion and a battalion of motorized infantry. Lieutenant-Colonel Henri Dubois would follow with two companies of S36s and a dozen supply trucks in fifteen minutes. They would rendezvous just west of the Dead Sea, on the main road to Aqaba. Phillipe would then head to Be'er Sheva while Henri held the road for Lieutenant-Colonel Claude Durand and his regiment of the 8th Motorized Division. Durand would continue on to reinforce Phillipe's exposed force.

That was the best Roger could do. His forces north and west of Amman were exhausted and there was no way they would be going anywhere today. The flanking units were fresh and the retreating British units would be tired and disorganized. At least that was the theory.

100 Miles East of Georgetown, British Guiana

Vice Admiral Sir Geoffrey Blake and Commodore John Moore studied the maps of the north coast of South America. He was in a tricky position and he didn't like it. The war with the Catholic Entente had begun but the Organization of American States was still technically neutral. Everyone knew it was a ruse but he had to keep up appearances until the League of Nations decided which way they would jump if they jumped at all. If Hoover had still been President of the United States, the British would have simply ignored the League and its do-nothing policies. But Roosevelt had been trying to reassert League influence by pushing for a more active role in the world.

Now, the OAS had picked a fight and then screamed that they were the victims when the British had responded. The Entente had used that as a pretext for declaring war even while the OAS stayed neutral. The Entente puppet organization was probably trying to convince the League to stay out of the war or protect its remaining naval assets from

Sir Geoffrey's marauding 1ˢᵗ Battlecruiser Squadron. Either way, an annoyed Sir Geoffrey was once again operating with his hands tied and dangerous seas all around.

A rating came in and handed a sheet of paper to the Captain of the *Marlborough*.

"Scouts report no enemy ships within a hundred miles, Sir. Island stations report no sign of Entente or OAS surface vessels in their vicinity."

"That matches the reports we've gotten that the Venezuelan navy is providing fire support in Colombia. Any updates on the arrival of the *Vanguard*, *Temeraire*, and *Ark Royal*?"

"They're still expected to meet us at Georgetown tomorrow."

Sir Geoffrey simply harrumphed as he went back to studying the maps. He'd left the *Hood,* the *Tiger*, and the *Indefatigable* with five heavy cruisers based in the Falklands to keep an eye on the Brazilian battleships they'd damaged near Montevideo while the *Repulse* was on its way back to England for repairs. The *Ark Royal* was slightly smaller than the *Indefatigable* but the two new battleships made up for the firepower he'd lost. All four of his capital ships were bigger than the Venezuelan ships. Destroying them should be easy if he could catch them.

After that, all the Admiralty wanted him to do was keep the Caribbean possessions and shipping safe from French raiders while also protecting them from reprisals by the OAS. And could Sir Geoffrey please maintain enough of a show of force that the League of Nations wouldn't side with the Papists to further its territorial ambitions. Yeah, no problem.

They had shelled the port facilities at Cayenne in French Guiana on their way to Georgetown. It would be months before the French could use it for resupply again. They had not been authorized to give a similar treatment to the OAS ports they'd cruised past. So, when the OAS decided to quit playing victim, the French would have access to numerous ports. That was one of the reasons a reinforced Marine regiment was being sent to British Guiana along with two squadrons of

Hurricanes. It would hurt the British ability to control the waters on the north coast of South America if they lost Georgetown.

Lieutenant Gregory Everett knocked on the open door. When Sir Geoffrey looked up, he noticed a strange, almost fearful look on his young flag lieutenant's face.

"Message from the Admiralty, Sir."

Sir Geoffrey simply nodded and held out his hand, his concerns mounting when Everett was hesitant about giving him the message. When he read it, he understood. He passed the message to Commodore Moore and waited while he read it. Lieutenant Everett moved to a position beside the door and did his best to disappear into the background. Moore looked stunned when he finally looked up.

"The entire 2nd Battle Division?"

"Gone. All five of its *Queen Elizabeth*-class battleships were sunk. There aren't a lot of details, but this is the blackest day for us since Great Yarmouth. At least Admiral Pound dished out some punishment before he went down."

The message said the entire Italian battlefleet had caught up with Admiral Sir Dudley Pound about fifty miles west of Haifa, in the eastern Med. Sir Geoffrey had no idea what they were doing that far away from the Canal, but nine Italian battleships had engaged them. Pound sank the old *Andrea Doria* and *Caio Duilio*. He also heavily damaged three of the new *Littorio*-class battleships. The damaged ships headed back to Taranto for repairs, but were intercepted by a British submarine. It sank the *Napoli*, but the damaged *Roma* and *Vittorio Emanuele* escaped. That meant the Italians still had four operational battleships they could use to either harass the coast of the Middle East or move west to join with the French fleet that was blockading Gibraltar.

The 4th Battle Division, all five of the *King George V* class battleships had been moved to reinforce the 2nd Battlecruiser Squadron stationed west of Gibraltar. That gave them parity with the French, but things would get dicey if the Italians headed that way. Sir Geoffrey voiced his concern.

"If the Italians move west, we can expect the *Vanguard* and *Temeraire* to be redeployed to the Mediterranean, too. We can also expect the OAS to be active if that happens."

"There's also the possibility that we'll be sent to West Africa to provide fire support for our forces there. The French seem to be committed to kicking us out of the region."

"Can we get stretched any thinner? With the redeployment of the 5th Battle Division, Home Fleet is already smaller than the German navy. If nothing else, they and the Americans will be more willing to flex their muscles to influence our policies."

Sir Geoffrey sighed and rubbed his chin in deep thought.

"Signal the *Vanguard* and *Temeraire*. They can expect a quick turnaround once the convoy reaches Georgetown. We will proceed west to find the Venezuelan battleships and deal with them while we have the advantage."

"Should we wait until the Hurricanes are operational, Sir?"

"No. The *Ark Royal* has almost as many Gladiators as the Venezuelans have MS.406s. She's loaded with a fighter-heavy complement and the OAS has very few modern bombers, so I don't think there'll be any problems from the air. Submarines will be a bigger problem and the land-based air assets we have will be our best defense there. The sooner we can deal with the French battleships the Venezuelans acquired, the better our chances of keeping the Atlantic open for our shipping."

"Aye, Sir."

Commodore Moore understood his boss's desire to deal with the battleships as quickly as possible, but he was worried about how well they would coordinate with the new additions to their squadron. Battle was never the best place to work out kinks.

Dire Dawa, Italian East Africa

Colonnello Guido Nobili sat at his desk studying his map of British Somaliland. The Italian East Africa Army under Generale di Corpo d'Armata Guglielmo Ciro Nasi was attacking it from two directions. The 1ˢᵗ Corps was advancing down the coast of the Gulf of Aden. It had an Italian and two Ethiopian infantry divisions along with the 18ᵗʰ Tankette Battalion. The 2ⁿᵈ Corps had two Italian and one Ethiopian infantry divisions and was supported by the 52ⁿᵈ Tank Battalion and its new L6/38 tanks. It was attacking east from Dire Dawa towards Hargeysa. Both forces were supposed to meet up at Berbera, the territory's main port. Generale Nasi's remaining five Ethiopian infantry divisions were scattered around on border patrol duties.

Unlike Generale Nasi, Guido actually believed in reserves. He'd committed four of his fighter squadrons and four of his bomber squadrons to support the attacks. That left him two of each in reserve to deal with whatever surprises the British might have up their sleeves. One hundred and twenty modern fighters and bombers were pounding the British forces which only had eight to ten old biplanes to defend them. Guido still fretted about supplies and possible losses to pilots, some of whom he'd come to regard as friends. The first sorties of the war should be over their targets right now, and Guido was bothered by the fact that he wasn't flying with his men. He stood and looked out his office window to the east with a tightness in his chest no different than when he'd flown into combat in Spain.

It felt like hours, but it was only about fifteen minutes before the first details reached his desk. The British had concentrated their limited resources on the coastal attack. Eight Gladiators had engaged the mixed group of sixty French and Italian planes attacking the British defenses. Two French D.520s and four of the enemy Gladiators were shot down before the British fighters tried to break off. The remaining four Gladiators were hounded as they retreated and taken down with no further loss. One of the French pilots bailed out and had been rescued. Commandant Claude Lefebvre would feel the loss of the other pilot, but he could be proud of the performance his men had given. Guido still waited on the report of damage suffered by the attacking bombers, but things looked good. He breathed a sigh of relief just as another young Ethiopian Caporale knocked at his open door.

"Yes?"

"Reconnaissance reports, Sir. Nothing in the lower Red Sea, but there are two British cruisers and four destroyers in the Gulf of Aden. They're about eighty kilometers east of Saylac and headed west."

"Tell Maggiore Francesco Rossi to load the reserves for ships and sortie them as soon as possible."

"Yes, Sir."

The Caporale trotted down the hall to pass on the orders while Guido drummed his fingers on the desk.

An hour passed before the strike was armed and in the air. Another thirty minutes went by before the sortie reached its targets. Twelve Z.1007s approached from the south, while another twelve approached from the west. Each group had eighteen G.51s escorting them and trying to suppress anti-aircraft fire from the British ships. Rossi had elected to load the bombers with lighter torpedoes so each plane could carry two. Forty-eight torpedoes had crisscrossed through the British ships. Things had gone well, but attacking ships was never an easy task. Both of the cruisers and two of the destroyers had been sunk. Four fighters and one of the bombers had joined them in their rest beneath the waves.

Guido sat at his desk going through the initial sortie reports. Between the attack on Somaliland and the British ships, six fighters and one bomber had been lost. Four more fighters and three bombers had been damaged but had returned safely. He'd started the day with one hundred and sixty combat aircraft and lost almost ten percent of them in the opening hours of the fighting. Things shouldn't be as bad going forward, but the scale of the losses was worrying. He hoped British Somaliland would fall quickly.

Guido stood at the lectern in the briefing room. Three days. That's how long the British had held out. Three days and eleven more aircraft. Four more G.51s, three D.520s, one of the Z.1007s, and three of the French MB.175s. All the damaged planes were back in action, but there was no way to replace the eighteen aircraft he'd lost.

Now, his men faced their toughest challenge. The remnants of the Mediterranean Fleet were headed south through the Red Sea. Ten destroyers, five heavy cruisers, five light cruisers, and one aircraft carrier were making a break for India and the Eastern Fleet, and it was up to his men to stop them. He looked at the room of assembled pilots and aircrew.

"The strike launches in two hours. The British are running at about twenty-five knots, and we should catch them as they enter the Bab al-Mandab Strait. They'll have less room to maneuver but that means their anti-aircraft fire will be more concentrated. Based on our encounter with the light cruisers last week, fighter pilots are reminded not to get too close to their targets when strafing. You are there to drive off the British fighters, protect our bombers, and distract the enemy gunners if you can.

"Italian bombers, don't waste time hunting for the perfect shot. Get in, lay down the crisscross torpedo pattern, and get out. The French bombers will be dropping bombs on the diagonals through the enemy formation. The idea is to not give the British a safe direction to turn away from the threats.

"Reconnaissance shows the Eastern Fleet is headed into the Gulf of Aden and their planes should be able to provide air cover to our targets in five or six hours. Right now, we have a decided edge in the air. Let's make the most of it.

"Any questions?"

A hand went up from a French pilot in the third row. He stood when Guido pointed at him.

"Will we need to worry about Italian submarines in the area?"

"No. There are four of them in the Gulf. They will try to finish off anything we damage. They'll do what they can if the Eastern Fleet sails too far in our direction, but they just don't have the speed to catch the surface ships.

"Anything else?"

There was a gentle murmur but no questions. Guido felt the cross between anticipation and tension coursing through the room. Sentiments he shared.

"Good luck, and good hunting."

The attack went off three hours later. Two more hours went by before Guido's staff had their final results and they assembled in one of the conference rooms. The initial reports had been good and Guido was encouraged by the smiles his men wore.

"Tarcisio?"

Tenente Colonnello Tarcisio Fagnani was Guido's second-in-command. Two years ago, Fagnani had been Guido's boss. That was before the Spanish Civil War and Guido becoming the only ace in that brief conflict. Fagnani nodded and consulted a sheet of paper.

"I'll give you the results of our attack and then each of the wing commanders will list their losses, Sir. Based on the pilots' reports and what our coastal spotters could confirm, we sank the *Courageous*, two heavy cruisers, and five destroyers. One heavy cruiser and three light cruisers were damaged but not slowed significantly. Maggiore Ross?"

Maggiore Francesco Ross was the wing commander for the Italian fighters. He had always been a bit nervous when he did formal reports, but he could fly like a hawk.

"We had forty-six G.51s available for the operation. We shot down twenty-two of the enemy aircraft with no losses. We also made two strafing passes before returning to base. Seven planes were heavily damaged but will be back in action in two to three days. Eleven were lightly damaged and will be available tomorrow. Commandant Lefebvre?"

Ross smiled and turned to his French counterpart.

"We had forty-nine D.520s available. We shot down the other twenty-six planes from the *Courageous* for the loss of five of our own. We also made two strafing passes. Four planes should take a couple of days to be repaired. The remaining forty will be available for operations tomorrow. Commandant Durand?"

Commandant Emmanuel Durand was the wing commander for the French bombers. The blunt Frenchman twirled his large moustache before making his simple report.

"Thirty-three planes went out, bombed the crap of the Brits, and everybody came home safe and sound. Maggiore Fiore?"

Maggiore Stefano Fiore was the wing commander for the Italian bombers. He wore the only pained look in the group.

"We had thirty-four planes available, each loaded with two torpedoes, and each plane made two attack runs. My wing was responsible for almost all of the damage done to the British squadron. It also took the most damage. Ross and Lefebvre did an admirable job in keeping the enemy fighters at bay, but they couldn't totally suppress the anti-aircraft gunners. Nine planes were shot down and twelve were lightly damaged. They should be available tomorrow if needed."

Guido looked a little baffled for a moment and then asked, "There weren't any Z.1007s that were heavily damaged?"

Maggiore Fiore shook his head. "Any of them that took very much damage tended to come apart in the air. The crews have given them a new nickname - 'widow makers'."

Cross Anchor, South Carolina, USA

Manly Lee Wilburn trundled up Highway 56 towards Spartanburg and work. It was a trip he'd made hundreds of times, but this Monday would bring a change. He turned left in the early morning fog, just south of Starnes Road. The old Dixon place had been unoccupied for nearly three months since George had passed on. It was good to see lights on at the house again.

M.L. rattled to a stop and was trying to decide if he should go knock on the door or just honk when the front door opened. Cardy Bravo opened the screen door before turning back and kissing his wife. She handed him a lunch box and he headed out to M.L.'s truck as she waved. M.L. had met Heather and their kids at church yesterday, but there hadn't been much of a chance to talk with all the work to be done around their new house. Leila had invited them over for dinner on Wednesday, both to give Heather a break and get a chance to chat.

Jim Deeson had hired Cardy as the new mechanic the shop so desperately needed. M.L. met him last week and suggested they ride to work together when he found out the Bravos had bought the Dixon place. Cardy crunched his way across the gravel driveway and opened the door with a smile. He was talking before he was in the truck. M.L. had wondered if the dusky man was nervous when they met or if Cardy just liked wagging his tongue. Time would tell.

"Hey M.L. How's it going today?"

"Mornin' Cardy. One of the better Mondays in a while. I've got someone to help with my work backlog."

They both grinned for a moment before M.L. pulled the truck back out on the highway and Cardy started jawing in earnest.

"I guess I don't have to worry about being late to work since I'm riding with my boss. Is this a '36? She's a beauty."

"'35 Model 67."

"Wow, she's in great shape. I've got a '33. Have you done anything to her? I rebuilt mine's carburetor. She gets better gas mileage now..."

Cardy kept going all the way to work, with M.L. only making the occasional contribution. It was a nice change from his talks with Leila. His wife seemed to think there was a finite number of words she could say before she ran out. So, she saved 'em like she was low on ammunition.

On the half-hour trip to work, M.L. found out that Cardy's father was from the Philippines and had been in the US Navy just like Cardy had. His mother's folks were from Norfolk, his wife's were from Tampa. He and Heather had two kids, Acadia and Cannon. Acadia was twenty-one and was going to be the new schoolteacher that M.L. had been hearing about. Cannon was twelve and interested in cars and guns, just like his dad.

Cardy and M.L. put in a long day at the yards and there wasn't much time for talking about anything but work until the day was done. On the ride home, they chatted amiably about work projects for the first few minutes. Things got a little more interesting when M.L. asked Cardy how they'd ended up in South Carolina.

"Well, after twenty years in the navy, Heather wanted us to move away from the water. I think she's afraid they'd pull me back in with all the fuss that's been going on at the naval base. There was a teaching job for Acadia and there's always a job out there for a mechanic, so it seemed like a good combination. Things closer to Spartanburg are a bit more than we wanted to pay. This house was the right size at a good price and, since it's between our two jobs, we decided to take it."

"Glad to have you here. Did you say things were changing at the naval base?"

"Yeah. Norfolk is busier than it has been in years. I don't know if they're shipping stuff to our guys in Colombia or if it's headed to Europe, but there's definitely more ships coming and going than there used to be."

"I can understand why your wife might want to get you out of the area. I bet the navy or merchant marines would try to get you back on the water. Both of those are paths where there's shooting going on."

"Maybe, but I've had enough of that life. I'm not going back unless they make me. And if I'm working in an important industry, the odds of them trying go down."

"True." M.L. paused for a moment before continuing, "Did you say Colombia? My eldest boy is with the 5th Cavalry down there. We got a letter from him but there weren't a lot of details. Did you hear anything before you left?"

"Just rumors. We're down there to protect the Panama Canal, but a lot of Colombia has been overrun. They're even talking about splitting it up. The OAS would divvy up most of the country and maybe a quarter would be given to Panama. My guess is that we will end up keeping troops there for years. Regardless, the League seems to be sitting on its hands while the British and South Americans shoot at each other."

"Damnation. I voted for Roosevelt because Hoover wasn't doing anything. I was hoping he'd do something before things got out of hand, but it sure don't look like he will."

"I think he's trying, but the Catholics are trying, too. And right now, it looks like religion is winning."

"I've got too many kin who could end up being in the middle of that fight to be happy. Things were messy when it was state against state. How bad will it be when it's neighbor against neighbor?"

For once, Cardy didn't have anything to say. He and M.L. rode the rest of the way in silence, both of them lost in their worries.

LATE JUNE 1938

Berlin, Germany

I hold the door for Edna as we leave the restaurant, something I haven't been allowed to do for a long time. I glance behind her to see Otto wearing an indulgent smile. He's trying his best to let us enjoy the night out for our first anniversary. I smile back in appreciation. The night is warm, Berlin is bright, and Edna makes me feel like the luckiest man alive. A fact that would be borne out in the next few seconds.

I reach to take Edna's arm in mine and knock her clutch from her grasp. I gallantly pick it up and return it to her, stealing a kiss in the process. The lingering taste of chocolate and strawberries makes me slow in parting from her.

"GUN!"

The shouted command from Otto has me yanking Edna behind me as I turn toward the street. I briefly see a man in the crowd pulling something from his pocket before my view is obstructed by Otto's back. The shots that ring out are deafening in the confined entryway, then I watch in slow-motion as Otto wheels to tackle us. The shooting has stopped, but I understand and try to help as we all fall in a heap towards the concrete walk. I desperately try to shield Edna's head as we go down, her startled look shows her fear.

The grenade goes off before we hit the ground. I get my hand behind Edna's head as we are tossed into the unyielding wall. Pain explodes in my mind. I'm not sure if I've been hit by shrapnel or it's the knowledge that Edna is being crushed as both Otto and I are blown into her.

Old battlefield reflexes kick in and I push against Otto to clear space so I can fight. My shove catches Otto by surprise as he tries to stand and he staggers as he rises. The only people moving are me and my security detail. Everyone else seems to be stuck in molasses. We search for threats, but the fight is over. At least a dozen people are down in bloody heaps both outside and inside the restaurant. The glass doors had exploded and sent shards flying through the patrons and workers.

Edna is still down and blood drips on her face from my left hand as I kneel to check on her. My ears register sirens blaring as I find the area near her left temple that's already swelling. The damage to my left hand means I got it behind her head, but it wasn't enough. My wedding ring is squashed out of shape, and I wonder if that's what damaged her head. I feel I've failed her.

Hands gently but firmly pull me to my feet and out of the way. Another member of my security detail helps an older doctor kneel beside Edna. A third checks Otto's multiple cuts and his right arm which hangs limply.

"Status." I command.

"One assailant, dead, along with several bystanders. Us and one other guard injured. Eight men in an expanded perimeter but the area is NOT secure. We need to move."

We both turn to the doctor as he probes the swollen spot on Edna's forehead, a dachshund sitting by his side.

"Can she be moved?"

He takes a second before nodding his head and the three guards pick my wife up as delicately as possible. Moments later, we're in the front security limousine, heading to the hospital with police cars leading the way. The dachshund whimpers once or twice before peeing in the car. My would-be assassin had spoiled his and the doctor's nightly walk. Otto leans forward in his seat; a piece of shrapnel is embedded in his arm just below his right shoulder. The doctor looks at Otto and receives a glare before turning back to Edna.

The drive to the hospital is short, though it seems to take ages to complete. It seems like there are police and security men everywhere. The doctor works at this hospital in the ER, and luck has placed him in our path. Edna is put on a gurney and wheeled away with the doctor shouting orders as they hurry down the hall. Otto and I watch her disappear as we're maneuvered into the emergency room, both of us dripping blood on the tile floor.

"Chancellor. ... Chancellor!"

The nurse's calls get past my stunned ears, and we turn around to another swarm of medical professionals trying to get us to sit down so they can examine us. It's going to be a long night.

The next day is Friday and I had the day off. I wanted a long weekend with Edna, but she's still comatose in the hospital and I want answers. A cute, blonde woman announces that Oberst Ernst Weber is here. Something inside me wails at the stark reminder that Edna isn't here. Ernst doesn't look like he slept last night. Join the club. He comes into my office carrying a folder which he lays on my desk and opens, a task that the heavy bandaging on my left hand would have made difficult for me.

"Preliminary report is that the assassin was a Welsh communist. He emigrated in March of '31, when the English economy was recovering slower than ours was. He worked in a coal mine near Szczecin where he joined a communist group trying to unionize last year. Justice knows of the group but didn't think they were dangerous."

He stops and looks at me for a moment. The pain medication and lack of sleep are making my brain dull and I close my eyes for a moment to gather my thoughts. When I open them, Ernst is looking at me with his head cocked to one side.

"Just the pain drugs or do you think something is off?"

My jumbled thoughts coalesce and my hindbrain finally gets its call of 'bullshit' to the front.

"It's too pat. Under any other circumstances, Otto would have had him dead to rights and he wouldn't have gotten close to me. He had to have pulled the pin on the grenade before he got anywhere near us. So why go on a suicide mission when you don't expect to succeed? Things don't add up. Dig deeper. Confirm that he is who we think he is. And do it quietly."

"You think this is a covert op by the Entente?"

"I don't know. But a suicide attack by someone with apparent ties to both the Soviet Union and England makes me suspicious. It's almost as if someone wants us to stay at war with the Russians and not help the British. If it isn't an op, then Christmas has come early for de Gaulle."

"I'll talk to Gürtner to see what Justice can find out. They should already have a team looking into it."

Ernst leaves and Otto comes in followed by two of his men. They set up a cot in my office while he watches them and me. He points left-handed at it when they're done. His right arm is cradled in a sling.

"Lay down."

"I need to..."

"You need to rest. The wheels are in motion and there's nothing you can do for now. You weren't even supposed to be in today. Lay down and rest. Edna will need your strength in the coming days."

"And I'll need yours."

"They already set a cot up for me out front. I'll be in it once you are in yours."

The report will wait. Ernst wouldn't have left anything important out. I get up awkwardly and head to the cot. The security men partially undress me and help me down, removing my shoes as I lay back. I'm asleep before they make it out of the room.

I'm jostled from a dreamless sleep and grunt in pain as I inadvertently flex my left hand. Most of the skin on its back was scraped off, three fingers were dislocated, and the wrist was sprained. It does not like being moved. Another sensation gets through the fog as I try to focus.

"Let's get you up and cleaned up, Sir. The ambassador from the United Kingdom will be here in ten minutes. I've got soap, towels, and a change of clothes. Let's get you to the bathroom."

One guard helps me strip while another one gathers my soggy pants and puts them on the equally soggy cot. Lots of coffee and drug-induced sleep are rarely a good combination. By the time I emerge from the bathroom, the only remaining evidence is a drying patch on the marble floor. My nursemaid / valet helps me get situated at my desk before he salutes and exits without a word. A steaming cup of coffee and a big piece of Beatrice's apple strudel await me on my desk. My stomach growls and I dig into it.

Otto either knows how long it takes a hungry me to eat that much strudel or he listened for the end of the sounds of my fork scraping on the plate. Either way, it's about fifteen seconds after I finish that he knocks on the door and shows Sir Nevile Meyrick Henderson into my office. There is no offer of refreshment and Otto doesn't leave. Instead, he closes the door and takes up a position off to the side of my desk, his hand resting on the holstered gun now sitting on his left hip.

Sir Nevile doesn't move towards the seat opposite my desk, nor does he give me a haughty look when I do not stand to greet him. He simply looks at me with sadness in his eyes. I glare back.

"We had nothing to do with this, Erich."

I take a shuddering breath before responding and waive him to the seat.

"Forgive me if we choose to determine that on our own. And before you say it, I know all about the Štip Incident and how Entente spies tried to start a war between us and the League of Nations. But much like that fiasco, the papers have already released the name of the assassin and the people are out for blood. We are trying to contain things, but I'd suggest..."

"DAD! DAD!"

Yelling from the outer office interrupts my train of thought and Brent bursts into the room. He's wearing training fatigues and must have come here straight from the Military Academy in Lichterfelde. He's halfway to my desk when he recognizes my guest, and his eyes go wild.

"You son of a bitch!"

He grabs Sir Nevile by his coat and yanks him out of his chair.

"Attention!"

My command cuts through his anger and he releases the unresistant ambassador and snaps to attention. His security detail arrives panting at my door.

"It may not have been them. We will find out who did it and they will pay. Do not make yourself easy prey for a trap. At ease."

My son takes a deep breath and looks over me and Otto before turning back to Sir Nevile. Anger masks his face as he grinds out, "My apologies, Sir."

"None needed. I understand and share your anger."

My son turns back to me, "The paper said it was a Welsh spy..." He stops and tears come to his eyes, "I didn't find out until this morning. How are you? How's Edna?"

"We'll survive." My self-control almost breaks as I continue, "Hopefully she will too."

I send Brent and the security detail he'd outrun to sit with Edna. He hugs me and salutes Otto before leaving. I turn back to Sir Nevile after he's gone.

"Most Germans won't stop at a simple command. Stay in your embassy and we'll provide extra security. Things are going to get ugly."

Sir Nevile rises and expresses his hope for a speedy recovery for all of us. As he leaves, a frazzled looking Franz Gürtner enters and takes a seat.

"How bad is it, Franz?"

"Bad, Erich. I think we need to let the people know that we have evidence that the assassin acted alone."

"We do?"

"Not yet, but I think things will get a lot worse if we don't. If he was working for the British, the backlash that's already begun will escalate and I don't see how we could avoid war with them. If he was an Entente agent, then he was deep undercover, and we end up with everyone suspecting anyone they haven't personally known for ten years. We may end up with roaming vigilante bands who claim to be protecting the Fatherland while they settle old scores."

I sit back in my chair lost in the visions of my country turning on itself. I wonder if war with the British would be much better. I hate that I will be lying to my people. I take a deep breath, "Do it. Make sure he had some kind of personal vendetta against me, or no one will believe it."

Franz stares at me for a long moment before he gives me an almost imperceptible nod of his head. "Yes, Chancellor."

10 Kilometers East of Suez, Egypt

Général de Brigade Roger Noiret woke with a start for the third straight night. The Battle of Be'er Sheva had been an ugly, murderous brawl and Roger wasn't the only person having trouble sleeping because of it. Roger sat up in his cot and the weight of his countrymen's deaths settled on his shoulders once more.

Their best estimate was that they'd killed around eight thousand British with thousands more wounded. The 1st Armored had five hundred and eighty-three dead, with another twenty-five hundred wounded. They rested and regrouped the day after Be'er Sheva, sending scouts forward to make sure the town was clear and see what help they could render to its inhabitants. Hundreds of Be'er Sheva's citizens had been killed or wounded and nearly a thousand British wounded had been left behind.

The 3rd Colonial Division arrived that night to help secure the area and Roger did his best to get his division ready for the next advance. Général Juin ordered Roger's men south to Aqaba before turning west across the Sinai towards Suez. There was little resistance and the division advanced five hundred kilometers in ten days. Most of the wounded were back in fighting shape, though almost a thousand were still in local hospitals or headed back to France.

The tanks and trucks were another matter. They were showing the wear and tear of the fighting and the desert. The maintenance battalion was working through the nights and sleeping in the trucks by day. Three tank battalions had been left in Aqaba, partly to protect it, mostly so their equipment could be used for spare parts. Some of their men were used to fill out the ranks of the battalions that were still advancing. The rest were building a runway so the needed replacements of both men and equipment could be airlifted to them.

The 1st Armored Division had boasted four hundred and five tanks in nine armored battalions before the campaign began. A third of those had gone to Iraq. Another third was either damaged or sitting at Aqaba. That left just three armored battalions to continue the advance. The 101st was now a mix of AMX38s and S36s. The 105th and 106th were G1s. The 14th and 83rd Motorized Regiments had been fleshed out and would support the one hundred and thirty-five remaining tanks. Roger prayed it was enough.

The British were still fighting a dogged rear-guard action along the coast road to Port Said. The plan was that the 1st Armored would once again push around the enemy flank to establish a blocking position south of Cairo. One battalion of the 83rd Regiment of the 8th Motorized would be left to hold Suez.

Roger's executive officer from the Spanish campaign, Lieutenant-Colonel Roger Olleris, and his armored regiment had been loaned to the Italians. Now he was leading the Italian Tenth Army forward as he pushed the Italian drive on El Alamein against light opposition. The British forces in the Middle East would be bottled up in the Nile Delta if the encirclement worked. Then they would see if they could get the British to surrender or they would have to go in and dig them out.

Roger thought back to how he'd anticipated taking the fight to the misguided Protestants before the fighting started and shook his head. He should have known better than to think a battle against Satan and his minions would be easy. He hoped the British would choose the path of salvation and return to the righteous path. He closed his eyes and prayed they would surrender and return to God's grace. He also prayed that his men would make it across the Suez Canal in good order. He opened his eyes and got to work on the task he could actually influence.

The Anglo-Egyptian Treaty of 1936 had not been overly popular with the Egyptians. Demonstrations against it had turned ugly at times. French Intelligence had found fertile ground to plant its seeds of full Egyptian independence and the removal of British forces from the Middle East. One of those rebellious groups controlled many of the ferries across the Suez Canal. They had been hindering the movement of British troops and supplies across it since the fighting began. Now it was time to see if they would help get his men and equipment across the waterway. Intelligence said they would. Général Juin had sent rafts and skilled sailors in case they wouldn't.

They reached the Canal the next day. While there wasn't a welcoming committee, there also wasn't anyone shooting at them from the far bank. A ferry near Ma'diyah was their target and two companies crossed that night. Roger stood pensively on the east bank of the Canal, scanning the far bank with binoculars for the first sign of resistance. None came. By midnight, three barges were tied up on the east bank, loading tanks. Their Captains complained bitterly about how terrible it was to be forced to work with the French. All the while, their crews smiled and the French infantry on board stood with their guns slung over their shoulders.

By dawn, a company of G1s was across and a perimeter had been established. Three more barges were rounded up and the crossing continued against sporadic opposition. The locals pointed out four British attempts to set up mortars to disrupt the crossing and things proceeded smoothly throughout the day. Roger's biggest worries, intervention by the RAF or the Royal Navy, never materialized.

Roger felt the bridgehead was secure enough by the next day that he sent the 105th Tank Battalion and the 831st Motorized Battalion south to seize Suez itself. The British were better prepared there. Harbor equipment was damaged and many of Roger's troops were tied up fighting a large fire in the warehouse district. Both were actions that slowed the advance of the 1st Armored Division but gained favor for the French in the eyes of the Egyptians.

It took two days to complete the crossing. By then, Roger had advance elements ten kilometers west of the Canal. It was one hundred and fifty kilometers to their objective of Bidsah on the Nile. There they would do their best to prevent the British from withdrawing south and their supplies from moving north.

50 Miles North of Aruba

To say that Vice Admiral Sir Geoffrey Blake was annoyed would be an understatement. He paced back and forth on the bridge like a caged lion, much like the British lion was currently caged. They had spotted the Venezuelan battleships off the coast of Colombia three days ago. They'd also spotted and been spotted by an American fleet in the western Carribean.

You might think the Yanks would be happy to help get rid of the Venezuelans, but no. It was the Brazilians that had sunk an American ship, not the Venezuelans. Who cares if the countries were part of the same alliance and they had coordinated their attacks on Argentina and Colombia. Damn, stupid, bloody Yanks. Until this particular group of the OAS shot at them, they were happy to work with them, and unhappy with European powers interfering with them. He stopped his pacing and stared out at the beautiful view of the placid Caribbean. It didn't help his mood.

"Bloody Yanks."

Commodore John Moore looked up, "Sir?"

"Nothing. I'm just frustrated that the Yanks won't let us deal with the Venezuelans."

"I agree, Sir. But at least we've cleaned out the Lesser Antilles. The Hurricanes in Georgetown are up and running and the Royal Marines are settled in. Venezuela has been effectively closed off to French ships even if their battleships are still operational."

"Surface ships, not submarines. And if the Venezuelans and Yanks keep this farce going, there won't be a thing we can do about French submarines attacking our shipping."

"I know, Sir, but I don't see any way around it. We have a squadron of light cruisers and a flotilla of destroyers based in Jamaica. They'll be able to protect our commerce from anything short of those battleships. And if you can take the Americans at their word, they will deal with the Venezuelans if they join the war against us."

"Depending on the country that screwed us in the Great War is a recipe for disaster."

"It doesn't make me happy either, Sir, but the orders from the Admiralty don't leave any wiggle room. The *Vanguard* and *Temeraire* are ordered to rejoin the Med Fleet at the Azores and we are to move the entire command to St. Helena."

"I know, John. That doesn't mean I like it. Take us as close to Venezuelan waters as you can get without violating their territorial waters too much. If they react, standing orders say we can defend our ships, and I intend to defend them vigorously."

Commodore Moore's smiled in hopeful anticipation as he acknowledged and carried out the command. Sir Geoffrey held little hope that the ploy would bear fruit. Someone was keeping the OAS on a short leash and Sir Geoffrey was willing to bet that the leash holder was French.

The Venezuelans kept an almost constant aerial surveillance on his ships as they headed east. Their planes made uncoded radio reports that indicated they carried American observers and carefully avoided anything that might be considered provocative. Sir Geoffrey was also quite sure they laughed at him the whole time. The only bright spot was that the move to St. Helena coupled with retaining the *Ark Royal* meant that he would probably get to engage the Catholic Entente troops driving down the west coast of Africa.

Even that little bit of light was snuffed out when they returned to Georgetown. There he received a message from his daughter in Cambridge. Jean, his beloved wife of twenty-seven years, had been shopping in Portsmouth when the French had bombed its port. She had been killed by falling masonry. Sir Geoffrey prayed for the soul of the woman he had come to think of as the other half of himself. He also prayed that God would give him the chance to make her killers pay for their actions.

Dire Dawa, Italian East Africa

Colonnello Guido Nobili watched his forty-three G.51s head east into the morning sun. They would catch up to the sixty-nine bombers and forty-seven D.520s that were already headed towards the British Eastern Fleet. The Levant Corps had broken though the British lines in Transjordan and were heading towards the Suez Canal. It looked like the British Navy was going to try to either stop them or make the Canal unusable, the very thing Guido and his men were here to prevent.

A squadron of SM.79s had flown in from Libya to replace the Italian bomber losses. The SM.79 was a little faster and a little more durable than the Z.1007, but it could only carry one torpedo. Odds were that they would need to make multiple strikes to discourage the British. Guido hoped the new tactics they'd come up with would leave him enough planes to do so.

Guido still couldn't believe that the Italian bombers had flown low over some of the British destroyer pickets before launching their torpedoes. They'd also attacked in small groups, usually three at a time. No wonder the losses had been ugly. Hopefully, this time would be different.

The British were heading west in the Gulf of Aden and his planes would meet them head-on. The squadron of SM.79s would come in from due west while the two squadrons of Z.1007s would come in from the west-northwest and the west-southwest. They would be fanned out and try to launch as close to simultaneously as possible. They were NOT supposed to get within a kilometer of the approaching ships. Ammunition he had. Spare planes and crews were in short supply. He headed back to his office with a grim look on his face.

Ninety minutes later, Guido sat at his desk staring at the same page of a report that hadn't changed in at least fifteen minutes. There were paragraphs on this page that he'd read at least six times but he had yet to make it to the end of the page before his concentration wandered. He was drumming his fingers on his desk again when his thoughts, or lack thereof, were interrupted by someone running down the hallway.

"Colonnello! Colonnello!"

Guido's confusion didn't stop him from appearing to teleport to his doorway as Tenente Corrado Ricci came sliding to a stop just outside.

"What the hell?"

Guido's wingman held up one finger for a moment as he caught his breath.

"British planes to the southwest, Sir."

"What the devil?"

"A local man in Negele spotted eighteen British airplanes headed northeast. That was about twenty minutes ago. The aircrews are prepping our planes right now."

"Where the hell is Negele?"

"About four hundred kilometers south of Addis Ababa."

Guido paused for only a moment before he started jogging towards the flight line. His mind raced as they went. Eighteen enemy planes and there were precisely two fighters left to defend the base.

"Has Generale Nasi been informed?"

An air raid siren started to wail and Ricci just kind of waived at the noise. Generale Nasi commanded the Italian East Africa Army which was headquartered here at Dire Dawa. His men would man the antiaircraft guns that were scattered around the base.

"It's got to be bombers only. Their fighters don't have the range to reach us or Addis Ababa. I don't know how they coordinated it, but this has to be a response to our strike on their fleet."

Guido approached the Battle from below. The British light bomber was only armed with one machine gun pointing out the front and one in a rear turret on top. He pressed the firing stud and felt only the hammer of his two machine guns answer. His firepower was drastically reduced now that his twenty-millimeter cannon was out of ammunition. He sprayed the undercarriage of the enemy plane, trying to concentrate on the wing joints and engine before rolling left to limit how long he was exposed to the back gunner's fire. A gratifying puff of smoke from the enemy's engine told Guido his aim had been true and he pushed the throttle home to gain some distance and prepare for his next run on the light bombers. He might be able to get another one if his ammo held out.

Ricci was already circling the British formation impotently. He'd shot down three of them before he'd spent his last shell. The bomber that was smoking and slowly losing altitude was Guido's fifth. The British were doing their best to make things difficult, but loaded bombers are not known for their maneuverability. Guido lined up his sixth target and started his attack pass. When he pressed his firing stud this time, the staccato hammer of his guns only answered for a moment before falling silent. Guido dove and headed off to join Ricci watching the enemy bombers head to their airbase. Guido picked up his microphone.

"Dire Dawa, Nobili here."

"Go ahead, Colonnello."

"Ten Battles still headed your way. Altitude, two hundred meters. Speed, three hundred. I figure we're about five minutes southwest of you."

"Generale Nasi conveys his thanks for thinning them and says he will do his best to make sure you have a place to land."

"Any news from the strike on the fleet?"

"We've lost seven bombers and twelve fighters. Our fighters claim forty-two Gladiators destroyed. Multiple hits on enemy ships reported. The D.520s are heading back from the Gulf of Aden at speed to try to catch the rest of the British bombers. Recon is headed out to assess the damage and British reaction."

Guido did some quick calculations in his head. "It's too far. Have the D.520s slow to cruising speed. They aren't going to catch the bombers and they may need to conserve fuel."

"Roger."

Guido knew that it was almost impossible for the French fighters to catch up to the Battles and it might be very important to be able to loiter before they had to land. Regardless, the enemy would have already unloaded their bombs on his airfield. Now it was a question of how much damage they would do and whether his planes could stay airborne long enough that they had a place to land.

Guido held his breath as he eased his fighter down onto the runway. It bounced and bucked as he found repairs that weren't anywhere near perfect. Ricci had insisted on landing first and had warned Guido of the potholes on the working runway. The other runway was crowded with men, shovels, and flying dirt. Guido thanked God that it wasn't raining.

Guido quickly joined Tenente Ricci on the runway, pointing out the areas that needed the most work. As long as one of the runways was working, they could land everybody. Launching a second strike would need both runways to properly coordinate.

Generale Nasi joined him on the flight line. It was a measure of the situation that the Generale didn't get prickly when Guido failed to come to attention and salute his superior.

"What do you need from my men, Colonnello?"

"We need the patches as hard packed and smooth as we can get them and we have about fifteen minutes before my men start returning. Most of the planes should be able to loiter for a while, but there's no telling how long the damaged planes will be able to wait before landing. Sir."

Generale Nasi grunted at the remembered honorific.

"They'll be the ones who need the runway in the best condition, won't they?"

"Yes, Sir. And we will be well and truly screwed if any of them crash on landing. It might help if you can detail some men to help the flight line crew in case that happens. Even if everyone gets down safely, we need that second runway as soon as possible if we're going to hit the British again. Any chance we can get your flak crews out here helping?"

Generale Nasi gave Guido a dubious glare.

"And if another set of bombers show up?"

"I'm willing to bet we just saw everything they have that can reach us. And with the three you shot down, there are only seven of them left. Regardless, the returning D.520s will be able to fly cover for us. Will that satisfy you, Sir?"

Generale Nasi looked up and down the runways for a moment before turning back to Guido. "Do it." was all he said before striding off towards a group of his officers. Guido turned and jogged towards the control tower.

Two hours later, weary pilots sat in the briefing room as Guido addressed them.

"We launch in fifteen minutes. Once you're on the runway, don't wait for clearance, just go. Squadrons will form up in the air, then head towards the Bab al-Mandab Strait. The submarines we have in the area will attack in the Straits with the hope of slowing the British down for us. We'll launch in reverse speed order so you'll have a chance to join up before we get to the targets. Battleships and carriers are the priority. Press the attack. If the British shut down the Canal, our whole campaign could be jeopardy. Good hunting."

The weary pilots filed out. Guido was most concerned about the French fighter pilots. They'd gotten the least rest of the group and would be most likely to make fatal mistakes. Those that noticed, gave him strange looks as he followed them out to the flight line. The looks turned to grins as he approached his fighter and they realized that he would be joining them.

It was just past four when the East Africa Air Fleet sighted the British Eastern Fleet and Guido noted the excited chatter of his men. Between their earlier losses and damaged planes, they were down to twenty-six torpedo planes, thirty of the French bombers, and eighty-five fighters. The British were down to nine destroyers, two light cruisers, seven heavy cruisers, five battleships, and two aircraft carriers. Guido didn't like the odds but added a few comments to the bravado on the radio.

It was a French voice that first noted the odd British formation. There were only two destroyers on the south side of the fleet. The rest, and both of the light cruisers were north of the fleet. It looked like the submarines had done their job and Guido felt a bit of hope creep into his thoughts.

It was an Italian voice that first spotted the thirty-six enemy Gladiators diving towards his bombers. Forty-five French fighters dove to intercept them while the Italians enviously remained vigilant. Within seconds, a group of nineteen more British fighters were diving after the D.520s. Twenty-two G.51s joined the chain of pursuing aircraft. That left Guido and seventeen other G.51s flying cover, watching the aerial combat both longingly and nervously.

Three Gladiators made it down to the torpedo planes. Each took down one of the attacking aircraft before they were dispatched in turn. Two more destroyed heavily laden French bombers before they too, fell from the sky. The fighters still battled as the torpedo planes closed to two hundred meters before launching their deadly payload. The Frenchmen showed their courage was just as great as they flew over the enemy ships at barely one hundred meters, trying to make every bomb count.

The whole orgy of destruction was over in less than five minutes. Both enemy carriers were on fire, and one was listing heavily to port. One heavy cruiser had capsized, while two more were sinking fast. Four of the five battleships were smoking from various wounds, though it didn't look like they were in danger of sinking. Guido and his men turned back for home, shouting their curses at the enemy and trying not to notice how many friends were missing.

Guido felt almost ashamed that his squadron hadn't gotten into the fight, but it had been the right call. The aerial fighting was well below him by the time he decided no more enemy planes would show up. He'd counted fifty-five Gladiators in the defense. None had survived, but they had managed to take down six G.51s and nineteen D.520s. His bombers had fared even worse. Between the enemy fighters and anti-aircraft fire, sixteen MB.175s, two SM.79s, and every single one of his fourteen Z.1007s were missing from the return trip.

The East Africa Air Fleet had started with one hundred and eight fighters and seventy-two bombers. Twelve more bombers had joined them from Libya. By Guido's count, it could now boast sixty fighters and a grand total of twenty-four bombers. Eighty-four operational airplanes out of one hundred and ninety-two. There would be a lot of drinking tonight. Guido just hoped that he could keep himself and his pilots from getting too drunk to function tomorrow if they were needed.

Cross Anchor, South Carolina, USA

Manly Lee Wilburn sat on the front steps of the Cross Anchor Yarborough United Methodist Church. Most of the congregation was out back of the church keeping an eye on the kids and catching up on the local gossip. M.L. had enjoyed the Father's Day breakfast his daughters had prepared but now he wanted some time alone to sit and think.

Things were quiet for a few minutes and M.L. watched the traffic go by. The New Hope Baptist Church was just down the road and nearly everyone in the area went to one of the two churches. As far as M.L. knew, the nearest Catholic church was over near Woodruff. There was also one in Spartanburg and yesterday's paper said there had already been 'incidents'.

The Catholics had been pushing the evils of all Protestants since the Pope had called it heresy back in '33. They'd stepped it up since the shooting had started with Britain and some of the locals hadn't taken it very well. So far, they'd only painted some derogatory comments on the church, but M.L. wondered how long it would be before the pot boiled over. Damn, damn, damn, damn, damn.

Ralph Griffin, Doris' husband, came around the corner of the church with two glasses of iced tea in his hands. He handed one to his father-in-law and took a swig from his own before he broke the silence.

"Thought I might find you here. Everything OK?"

"Yeah, just worrying about what kind of world our kids will grow up in."

"Are you talking about the war, the church being defaced in Spartanburg, the talk of conscription, or what the combination is doing to prices at the stores?"

M.L.'s simple response of "Yep" was greeted by a grunt and a smirk from Ralph.

"If you're going to worry, might as well do it big."

Cardy and Buck, Francis' husband, came around the corner of the church to join the two men. Buck spoke up when they got to the front steps.

"Hey M.L., you worried about some of us gettin' sent off to war?"

"Among other things."

"Andrew and I are smack dab in the prime range for getting drafted, so we decided we're going to volunteer for the Army Air Corps at the beginning of July. I'm training Zach on the crop dusting, but odds are that they'll scoop him up next year. Francis and Bobby Lee should be okay, but I'm going to have to ask you to keep an eye on them for me, if you would."

M.L. simply nodded at his son-in-law. Harry Jamison would probably be hot under the collar about his oldest joining the army, even if it was what Andrew wanted.

"Not a problem, son. We may have to watch out for Doris and Ralph, Jr., too. Phil might get caught up too, so Courtney might need some lookin' after."

M.L. looked up and down the road wistfully before continuing, "We really should sit down with everyone after church next Sunday to see who might be caught up by conscription and what we can do to help their families. Prices on everything will go up since they're expanding the military, so we should also figure out what we can supply each other with when things get scarce."

He paused for a moment, looking like he'd sucked on a lemon. "And I hate to say this, but we need to figure out if there are any Catholics in the area. We need to make sure they don't cause any trouble and that no one goes after them."

The small group nodded somberly at the thought of their neighbors being harassed or causing trouble. Ralph was the first to break the gloomy reverie. "I'll talk to Pastor Bailey about announcing something next week. Maybe we can have a get-together with the Baptists so we all work together. In the meantime, let's spread the word so people will be prepared."

The group headed around to the back of the church and scattered on its mission. M.L.'s gloomy mood wasn't helped by it being the anniversary of little David's death in '14. He'd only been three months old when he died of whooping cough.

EARLY JULY 1938

The Chancellery, Berlin, Germany

We enter the briefing room as we have every week since I took office. The usual maps of the world hang on the east wall, though they now have thick lines on them and several countries in Africa are shaded differently. Three maps of the eastern front still occupy the north wall. They too have been updated to show our progress and losses. Ernst and I take our usual seats on the west side of the conference table while Generalfeldmarschall Werner von Blomberg heads to the podium. He launches into his briefing without any prelude.

"We are pushing forward on the eastern front. The newer panzer models are proving effective. We have liquidated the troops we encircled at Minsk and have another large pocket at Pskov that we're reducing. The Ukrainians have taken Bryansk. We plan on converging drives from there and Pskov towards Smolensk. The Poles are twenty kilometers south of Tallinn and the Ukrainians are approaching Oryol, though they have lost some ground near Rostov. The Turks continue to grind forward towards Baku while the Russians slowly push towards Tblisi.

"We continue to be on good terms with the League of Nations. The trade with them has not been impacted by the Anglo-Entente war. As agreed, the USGA has established an airbase in Greece for non-combat aircraft. Our advisors there report that things are running smoothly.

"The Entente is advancing through Africa against light opposition and the Suez Canal is currently closed. The destruction of the British battle fleet in the eastern Mediterranean leaves the Entente with free reign in the area. They are pushing through western Africa and advancing in Kenya and Uganda. Most of their raiding surface vessels in the Atlantic have been hunted down, but their submarines are still taking a toll on British merchant shipping.

"The United Kingdom seems to be concentrating its efforts around drives north from South Africa and have invaded Angola, Mozambique, and Madagascar. They are rationing oil and having issues with their supplies of raw materials. They have been trading air raids with the French but seem to be losing ground. They have approached us about partitioning Iran. We believe this is an effort to support their operations in Iraq and gain access to more oil.

"The rebellion in Quebec has cut off most of the trade between Canada and the United Kingdom. Everything from their western provinces is being shipped through the United States to bypass Quebec. There hasn't been a lot of fighting yet, but both sides are calling up their reserves and the United States has moved troops to the border.

"The OAS is slowly advancing in Argentina. Their advance in Colombia has stalled because the United States has intervened with troops. They claim it's to set up a protective zone around the Panama Canal and we see no reason to doubt that claim. We do have evidence that the OAS isn't happy about the intervention.

"The Japanese advance in central China has stalled for the moment. The Nationalist forces broke the dikes on the Yellow River and flooded thousands of square kilometers of their own land to stop the Japanese advance. We estimate they killed hundreds of thousands of their own people. It allowed the Chinese to trap and destroy two Japanese divisions.

"The Turks are asking for more help and the Navy believes that selling the three *Bayern*-class battleships to them would placate both them and the British while causing more headaches for the Russians and the Entente.

"We suggest we continue our current operations and expand our efforts to modernize the Army. Supply usage on the eastern front continues to be above expectations and we need to increase production of munitions if we want to maintain the current pace of operations. Building tank and airplane production facilities in Poland, Ukraine, and Turkey has helped standardize our weapons and ease some supply issues. We may be forced to enact at least a partial mobilization to keep pace with personnel demands for new units and replacements for units in combat."

Blomberg stops and looks up from his notes expectantly. The idea of selling the older battleships had been brought up earlier in the week and it seemed like a reasonable idea. Then again, he doesn't know that we are covering up our findings about the assassination attempt on me.

"Thank you, Generalfeldmarschall. I'll submit your request for production expansion to the Reichstag and give them your recommendation on the sale of the battleships. I'll also warn them about the possible need for a partial mobilization. How are our hospitals handling the increase in patients from the fighting?"

Blomberg flips a couple of pages in his notes before answering. "Their capacity is sufficient for now, but there is a definite trend down in the number of empty beds."

"I'll recommend we increase both staff and facilities to prepare for future needs. There's always a long lead time on those things and the sooner we get started, the less likely we are to get caught unprepared."

The briefing wraps up quickly and ten minutes later I arrive outside the door to the Ministry of Justice. Franz Gürtner is waiting for me and stands as I enter his office. As far as I know, Franz, Ernst, Otto, and I are the only ones who know about the real results from the probe into the attack on me. I know there are people on Franz's payroll who know, but I have no idea of who or how many there are. He waives us to seats, but Otto opts to stand.

"Good to see you without the sling, Otto."

Otto bows slightly in acknowledgment and unconsciously flexes his recently released arm. Franz turns back to me.

"And how is your hand doing, Erich? It looks like the bandages are smaller than they were last week."

"They are, and it hurts and itches more each day."

"Hopefully that means things are healing."

Franz pauses for a moment and his normally jovial expression takes on a serious cast.

"How's Edna?"

"She's doing better, though she frets about what she calls her Frankenstein hairdo. The left side is still very short and the wound from where they cut into her skull is still plainly visible."

The quick reactions of the doctor who'd been walking his dog kept her swelling brain from doing any permanent damage and Edna's struggle to return to health had become a national story. There had been an outpouring of sympathy and concern for her. The lie that the assassin had met her years ago and developed a fantasy love for her had kept those emotions from turning to anger and hatred.

"She's planning on coming back to work next week. She's going to work half-days while she builds her strength back up."

I pause before continuing. Whether or not I want to know, I need to know how the investigation is going. "Any progress on tracing Edna's family tree?"

Family histories have long been a hobby for Franz, and we decided to use it as a cover for our meetings and his checking into the past. Even here, all references are circumspect.

"It's weird. A lot of the younger people I've checked with identify that picture you gave me as her great uncle, Fredrick. A number of the older generation say it looks like him but it definitely isn't him. The hospital records say he was born near Stuttgart, but there are bible records that say he was from the Hamburg area. All of the information is contradictory, so I can't say anything for sure. But I'll keep digging when I get the time."

"Thanks, Franz. Just keep me informed. I can't wait to surprise Edna when you find out. We can have a celebratory dinner."

I stand and shake his hand before leaving. So, there are official documents that link the assassin to France, but there are personal ones that link him to the English. Great.

I head back to my office to start the ball rolling for the military's needs. The Reichstag has gotten more generous of late where the military is concerned. I don't think there will be any problems getting the funding from them. The question may be one of how long it takes to build the increased capacity they need.

Bidsah, Egypt

Général de Brigade Roger Noiret walked into the classroom in the high school in Bidsah, south of Cairo. Classes were out for the summer, and it seemed like the best place to set up his division's headquarters. The seating might be terrible, but the layout was good for briefings. The cafeteria also eased the job of feeding his men.

They had been here for ten days and things were settling down into a routine. The British had made two attempts to break out through his lines. Both had been costly failures. Roger had just returned from one of his daily tours of his unit's positions and the men were in good spirits. As he approached the teacher's desk he'd commandeered, he noticed that there was an addition to his usual pile of briefing folders. A letter had been placed front and center on it. The pile of folders on the left side of the desk was thicker than normal which made him wonder if his routine was about to change. He sighed before turning his attention back to the letter that could only be from his beloved Catherine. He sat and tenderly picked up the letter from his wife, closing his eyes for a moment as the longing for the woman he loved washed over him. He carefully opened it.

Junior was disappointed that Roger hadn't been able to come home for his birthday, but he understood why his dad couldn't make it. At least his friend, Pierre Moreau, had been cleared of the heresy charge. The same couldn't be said of Pierre's parents. They had been packed up and shipped off to who knew where. Pierre had moved into Guy's old room since Guy was off at basic training. Only Roger's status in the Warriors for Christ and his family's willingness to take in Pierre, had kept the boy from getting shipped off with his parents. Roger prayed that his wife and youngest son would be a good influence on Pierre.

Guy was doing well at training and intended to get his wings. That made Roger smile. Maybe his son would be watching over him from the skies one day, kind of like his own guardian angel. Catherine said their eldest had made references to a girl, but she'd been unsuccessful in getting more details out of Guy about her.

Catherine was keeping busy running the house and doing volunteer work at church. So far, the economic sanctions from the League hadn't had a big effect, though the sanctions and the demands from the military had made prices go up on just about everything. It wasn't affecting Roger's family too much, but many of the poor were having difficulties making ends meet, and most of Catherine's work at their church was directed at helping them through the tough times. Junior and Pierre helped where they could. It was worse for his countrymen living near the Channel coast. The British navy had been shelling ports during the day while their air force had raided them at night. At least their navy was paying a price for their raids. Six of their cruisers had been sunk in the raids and they were slowing in frequency.

Roger removed the last letter he'd received from his wife from his left breast pocket. The new letter replaced it and the older one went into a file where he kept them all. He bent his head and offered up a prayer for the continued safety of his family, the protection of his countrymen in harm's way, and the souls of those who had wandered from the path of righteousness. He lifted his head and opened his eyes. It was time to get back to the business of separating the United Kingdom from the foreign resources that fueled its furnaces.

Général Noiret picked up the first folder on his stack. As usual, Sergent Jean Martin had organized the stack from general to specific. This folder was a report on the campaign progress. Both Alexandria and Port Said had fallen, and the Suez Canal was open to traffic. British naval units had withdrawn from the Red Sea and supplies were once again reaching Italian East Africa. They now had an agreement with the Egyptians that would allow Entente forces to base in the region. The Egyptians would provide some unspecified help in clearing the Nile delta and the Entente would provide at least four divisions to help the Egyptians clear out the British forces in Sudan.

The second folder contained the directives for the next part of the campaign and the role the 1st Armored Division would play in it. The 3rd Colonial Division, nicknamed 'The Gravediggers' for their part in the clean-up of Be'er Sheva, would arrive over the next three days to take control of the southern section of the Entente line surrounding the Nile delta. The 1st Armored would move back to Suez and board ships bound for Mogadishu. They would join up with two Italian and three Ethiopian divisions of the Italian East Africa Army commanded by Italian Generale di Corpo d'Armata Guglielmo Ciro Nasi. Entente forces in the Congo were advancing into western Uganda and Tanzania. The African Expeditionary Corps would attack from the east and sandwich the defending forces.

The folder also contained the orders for the move. Sergent Martin had included a proposed timetable as well as routes and sequence suggestions, all created by Colonel Philippe de Hauteclocque. His executive officer had been busy, only Roger's signature was missing. It looked like Roger might get to actually relax once the move was underway.

The third folder dashed that hope and replaced it with a new one. Once the move was underway, Roger was ordered to fly to Paris to meet with Marshal Charles Delestraint, commander of France's military.

Marshal Delestraint had been one of the main reasons France had pushed armored warfare. Maybe the memos Roger sent about the force mix of his division hadn't disappeared into the labyrinth of the halls of power. Regardless of the reason for the trip, Roger hoped there would be time for a visit home. He felt a little guilty when he closed his eyes and prayed for the chance, one the rest of his men wouldn't get.

Next on the pile were orders that permanently transferred the three loaned armored battalions to the 8th Motorized Division and the 83rd Motorized Regiment to the 1st Armored Division. The 83rd was being redesignated as the 13th in accordance with the Army's numbering system. It was one of the recommendations Roger had sent up the chain of command, so he was happy to see that his suspicions were confirmed.

The rest of the folders dealt with the day-to-day issues of the division. The supply, maintenance, and troop readiness reports were routine. The report on discipline issues showed a slow but worrisome upward trend. Roger signed it and added a note for Martin to have Father Louis Lobau, the division chaplain, report. Maybe Lobau could add something to his next sermon to help reduce the tension in his men. Nothing had boiled over onto the civilian population, but that was a possibility that could turn things into a nightmare going forward.

Roger arrived in Paris three days later. A waiting staff car took him to the Army Command Post in the Château de Vincennes. He was allowed to freshen up before being escorted into a large conference room for the early afternoon meeting. Marshal Delestraint sat at the head of a table where there were enough shoulder board stars in the room to fill the night sky. A number of aides and secretaries sat around the edges of the room. Roger came to a rigid attention as Marshal Delestraint looked him over.

"At ease, Général Noiret. Please take a seat."

Roger nodded and took the one empty seat at the foot of the conference table. A briefing packet lay closed on the table in front of his seat. Similar packets lay in front of each of the fourteen other generals seated around the table. Based on their thickness, Roger guessed that a copy of every memo he'd sent up the chain was in each folder. He wondered how many enemies he'd made with those notes as he waited for Marshal Delestraint to begin the meeting.

"First and foremost, Général Noiret, thank you for your service and suggestions. You've achieved some spectacular results with the 1st Armored so we want to pick your brain on tactics, force balance, and development of the next generation of tanks. We've been using your data from the Spanish Civil War, but some new issues have cropped up."

Marshal Delestraint opened his folder, so Roger did too. The folder contained groups of pages paper-clipped together. The first one had a cover sheet that simply asked, 'FEWER TANKS IS BETTER?!?' Roger smiled a little at that notion.

"As you can see, the first item is not one that anyone here expected. Could you explain why you requested we look at the balance of equipment in our armored divisions?"

"Yes, Sir. It's not that fewer tanks are better, it's that more infantry to support those tanks is. Even on open ground, tanks and their commanders are vulnerable to close assault and ambushes. I believe more infantry in our armored divisions would improve their combat effectiveness at a lower cost than simply adding more tanks. And once it comes to defending the ground taken, the infantry becomes even more important.

"When we moved on Amman, I did so with the equivalent of two armored regiments and one of motorized infantry. The few tanks we lost were destroyed by short range shots from concealed anti-tank guns. All of those guns were in places where we suspected there might be enemy units, but we simply didn't have enough infantry available to check.

"Once we got to Amman, things would have been a lot messier if the local population had been armed and actively resisting. As it was, we lost a dozen tank commanders or drivers to snipers. That may not sound like much, but it temporarily put five percent of our tanks out of commission. And that was without a resisting population.

"The story was similar when we had to defend Amman. The firepower of the extra tanks was very useful, but the limits to their mobility also made them easier targets. Extra infantry would have been almost as effective at a cheaper cost in both material and supplies. They would also have been more resilient. When you lose a tank, you lose four or five men, an artillery piece, and two machine guns. If it's infantry, you have a decent chance of getting those guns back in action."

Marshal Delestraint nodded in understanding, "And how does that compare with the Battle of Be'er Sheva?"

"Colonel Philippe de Hauteclocque had a battalion each of G1s and infantry to start that fight. He also had some room to maneuver so he could use the tanks as a screening element while his infantry prepared defensive positions. The British were a bit disorganized and missing a good chunk of their artillery. He was still hard pressed before I arrived with another tank battalion and a regiment of infantry. His balanced force composition is probably what allowed him to hold the ground."

Roger thought for a moment before continuing, "One of the things I observed at both Amman and Be'er Sheva was the problems the British had when attacking with motorized infantry. If a truck got within a kilometer of the fighting, it would be raked by machine gun fire, usually destroying it and killing any men it was transporting. Similarly, when trying to withdraw, their infantry was ground bound until they could get a good distance away from the fighting. I think we need some kind of light armored vehicle like the Citroën company has built. It would improve the ability of the infantry to both get to and away from the fight quickly."

Roger stopped as Marshal Delestraint raised his left hand slightly.

"That's information our weapons development group will be glad to hear. They're working on a partially tracked armored transport similar to ones being produced in Germany and the United States. It sounds like we need to push the development and deployment."

Marshal Delestraint looked around the room to see if anyone had any more questions or comments before flipping the first packet over. Roger joined the rest of the room in following his lead.

"On to the second packet. Why did you decided to leave half of your armored element at Aqaba?"

"Logistics and maintenance, Sir. My maintenance company had been working their butts off trying to keep up with the simple mechanical issues that arise when you drive trucks and tanks five hundred kilometers across the desert. Have them fight a couple of battles and those issues multiply. Between parts wearing out or being damaged and filters getting clogged, we only had about seventy percent of our vehicles in good running order. We had another six hundred kilometers to advance and it didn't look like the equipment would last. Either we needed to leave some vehicles behind, or we would end up leaving disabled equipment strewn along our path. We took the vehicles that were in the best shape and virtually all of our spare parts forward. We also took about eighty percent of our remaining munitions and fuel.

"Doing so allowed me to leave my wounded in decent quarters at a location that could get resupply by land, sea, and air. It also let me give my mechanics a little bit of a break. Even with only semi-functional equipment, I felt the force I left in Aqaba would be large enough to discourage any hostile action until it could be refitted."

Delestraint looked around the table before turning back to Roger, "Do you have any recommendations to prevent these problems in future operations?"

"A few, Sir. First and foremost, we need to expand the maintenance element to at least a company per regiment or a battalion for the division. The battalion would probably be better, centralized maintenance would better serve the division's needs.

"Second, increase the spare parts that battalion is supplied with by at least a factor of two. That means that if my division had a maintenance battalion with three companies, it would have been stocked with six times as many spare parts. A twenty-five-ton tank that can't go anywhere because of a clogged air filter is just a big, expensive paperweight. From the reports I've seen, we captured almost a fifth of the British armored vehicles. They had been abandoned due to mechanical breakdowns.

"Third, more fuel. My tanks burned through it at an alarming rate. Part of that was due to maintenance issues reducing the tanks' efficiency, part of it was that the tanks had to return to depots for refueling. The farther the tanks got from the roads, the shorter the time they could stay at the front. A partially tracked armored tanker might help. The wheeled trucks we have now can't handle anything off-road and are prime targets any time they're near the fighting.

"Finally, more cross-training of our men. When we set out for Aqaba from Be'er Sheva, I started rotating some of the motorized infantry into the second and third echelon tanks. This gave the men some basic familiarity with the tanks, which let me get the tanks back in action quickly when a crewmember was killed or wounded. The same applied to the trucks. Less than a quarter of my infantry could drive one if the need arose."

Marshal Delestraint checked his assembled staff for questions and comments before moving on to the rest of the packets. Most were questions about equipment, supplies, and the morale of his men. There was one about how the Arabs reacted to the removal of the British. Roger pointed out that the only place he'd stayed long enough to form an opinion was Bidsah in Egypt. There, the people seemed to go from indifferent to hopeful, as long as they weren't in the line of fire.

Two hours passed before the briefing was finished. Marshal Delestraint then took Roger and several staff members to an early dinner. Roger was surprised by the number of people dining. His previous experience in Paris was that the evening meal was enjoyed later in the day. Even the civilians seemed to be in good spirits and the city was bustling.

The mood seemed to change as dusk approached and everyone began to fade from the streets. The City of Light faded as well, and the night encroached. When he asked about the change, Marshal Delestraint said that it was a security measure to protect against night-time bombing by the British and that they were working on something called 'radar' to help intercept the enemy bombers. Roger also found out he'd be spending the night at the Château de Vincennes for the same security reasons.

Roger flew to Toulouse the next day where he was greeted by Catherine, Junior, and Pierre Moreau. Three glorious days followed where Roger got to reconnect with his family and home. There were no night-time blackouts here and things seemed almost unchanged. On his last night in Toulouse, a small party with their friends was quite festive until Roger was pressed for information and stories from his battles. Roger managed to deflect them for 'security reasons' but the reminders made his mood turn dark. Later that night, Catherine managed to bring the smile back to his lips, but he never fully regained his initial joy.

As he boarded his plane back to the Middle East, Roger was worried about how quickly he seemed to be growing apart from his friends and family. He'd met and married Catherine after the Great War. Roger had never really thought about how much she and the Church had pulled him back from those dark experiences. He had shared those experiences with most of the men in France. Not this time. There might have been an underlying sense of urgency, but Toulouse almost seemed like a city at peace. There were a few more men in uniform around, but the great mobilization had yet to occur.

Even mass at the Basilique Saint-Semon de Toulouse had seemed to distance rather than unite him with his hometown. The sermon had been fiery and spoken to Roger's soul, but for Roger, that fire was tempered by the price he knew was being paid to bring about God's justice. The zeal of the rest of the congregation didn't seem to care about the price and Roger dreaded where that unbridled passion would lead. He bent his head and sought solace in prayer as the plane took off.

10 Miles South of Abidjan, Côte d'Ivoire

Vice Admiral Sir Geoffrey Blake looked dispassionately north as Task Force South Atlantic sailed north towards Abidjan, the economic heart of the French colony of Côte d'Ivoire. The French and their puppets were trying to drive the British out of Africa. Trying hell, they were succeeding in the northern half of the continent. The Empire didn't have the resources to defend all of its colonies and the Catholic Entente now had a fairly secure supply line through the Med.

Sir Geoffrey closed his eyes in disgust and anger. His ships couldn't stop the Papist advances on the land, but they could make them pay for their insolence. And their tactics. If they wanted to bomb cities and kill civilians, he would show them the price they'd have to pay. He opened his eyes again and glared north.

"Execute bombardment plan three."

Commodore John Moore's "Aye. Sir." covered the concern he harbored for his commander's mental state. The Admiralty had ordered him to keep an eye on Sir Geoffrey since his wife's death. This was the first time that John had reason to be concerned.

Plan three called for the longest ranged bombardment of the colony's port. That meant the least accuracy and the most collateral damage to the city and its people. It was a perfectly acceptable option that limited the exposure of the squadron, but John worried that the choice was driven more by a desire to punish those who sided with Jean Blake's killers.

Five minutes later, the *Marlborough* turned to starboard and joined the rest of the squadron hurling mammoth shells north. Commodore Moore wasn't sure if the gleam of satisfaction in Sir Geoffrey's eyes was real or a product of his own imagination.

They cruised east along the African coast from Abidjan to the Gold Coast. Once there, they tried to be more surgical in their attacks on the invaders. Even so, British subjects and homes were caught in the crossfire.

Sir Geoffrey was startled out of his fitful sleep early in the morning by a sharp knock at his door. He sat up and rubbed the sleep from his eyes as the pleasant dream of a vacation with Jean fled from his memories.

"Yes?"

"Message from the Admiralty, Sir."

"Enter."

Lieutenant Gregory Everett came in and gave the report to Sir Geoffrey. He knew the message's contents and that the Vice Admiral would be heading to the bridge, so he gathered things to help Sir Geoffrey get ready. It wasn't in his job description, but it also wasn't the first time he'd stood in as a valet to help. Sir Geoffrey took the proffered pants and began putting them on as he gave the young Lieutenant directions.

"Notify the battlecruiser commanders to be here in one hour. I'll want current status reports on their ships. Get Holland and Lucas. We'll need to know how the carriers and cruisers are doing too. I can finish this, get going."

"Aye, Sir."

The young Lieutenant trotted off towards the bridge.

The flag bridge was crowded with a dozen ship captains and their staff when Sir Geoffrey entered an hour later. The murmured discussions ended abruptly as he advanced through the room.

Lieutenant Everett waved a thick folder in Sir Geoffrey's direction, indicating he had the status reports for the task force. Sir Geoffrey would want to look them over after the meeting, now wasn't the time.

"Men, with the way scuttlebutt is, most of you should know that both Sierra Leone and Gambia Colony have fallen. What this means for us is that more Entente forces will be heading to the Ghana front in the next few days. That includes a significant increase in their air assets and the redeployment of an armored division to the front.

"With their current forces, the enemy has already taken Kumasi, just one hundred and twenty-five miles northwest of Accra. With the additional troops, they are expected to overrun the Gold Coast within two weeks and Nigeria about two weeks after that. We simply don't have the troops to stop them.

"What we will do, is make them pay. We have been ordered to expend munitions down to critical levels. We will be returning to St. Helena in three days. Air and submarine defense will be our main priorities on that run, so they are the only munitions that should be husbanded. I'm looking for any suggestions on how we can do the most damage in the time we have before we pull out."

Two hours of suggestions and debates followed. Captain Holland and the aircraft of the *Indefatigable* and the *Ark Royal* would do their best to keep the enemy airbases in the area as damaged as possible. At the suggestion of Captain Eakes of the *Orion*, Captain Lucas would take the 7th Light Cruiser Squadron east to shell the ports in French Dahomey before returning to the task force. Lieutenant Commander Caldwell suggested they drop off propellant bags at British ports along the way so the port facilities could be wired for demolition as the enemy neared. That idea was expanded to include bridges.

Orders were cut and ships left to complete their tasks. Sir Geoffrey mostly brooded about the fact that they were being driven from west Africa.

Three days later, dawn brought a beautiful sunrise to the task force as it sailed south-southwest towards St. Helena. It also brought Entente airplanes. Sir Geoffrey awoke to the klaxons of the general quarters alarm. Lieutenant Everett looked barely dressed as he burst into the Vice Admiral's quarters and helped Sir Geoffrey dress.

"What the Devil's going on?"

"Aircraft from the northwest, Sir."

Sir Geoffrey started to ask how close when the ships anti-aircraft guns started firing. Apparently, they were that close. They must have taken off pre-dawn to get here and catch him with his pants down, though Everett was pulling them up.

"Shit."

"Yes, Sir."

Sir Gregory fastened his pants as Everett prepared a shoe for the Vice Admiral's foot. Moments later, Sir Gregory was running towards the bridge while his flag lieutenant ran back to his cabin and his own clothes. Both slammed into the walls as the *Marlborough* began a hard turn to port. Sir Geoffrey made it to the bridge just as the radio operator called out "Multiple torpedo hits. Bombs on their way."

Commodore Moore was still fiddling with buttons on his jacket as he acknowledged the report. There was little Sir Geoffrey could do at the moment. His ships would have to rely on their training and plans for now. He picked up the few written reports and scanned them as the alarm klaxons finally fell silent. His eyes jerked back up as more explosions punctuated the staccato sounds of the anti-aircraft guns.

The attack was over within minutes. The damage would take much longer to repair. Sir Geoffrey didn't know if their position had been reported by a submarine or if the Entente had just gotten lucky, but over a hundred aircraft had been in the attack.

The dozen Gladiators in the combat air patrol had faced three times their number of D.520s. The Gladiators took down six of the French fighters and two of their heavy bombers as they were swatted from the sky. A number of the enemy planes were damaged but they could only confirm kills on four of the Italian torpedo planes. Surprise had not been total, but it had been close enough.

Sir Geoffrey grimly read over the damage reports as he prepared his report for the Admiralty. Three destroyers had been sunk, including the *Firedrake*. A near-miss from a bomb had already split open the patch in her hull when Lieutenant Commander Caldwell had once again found his ship to be the only thing between an inbound torpedo and the *Indefatigable*. Most of the crew was successfully evacuated before the ship slipped under the waves.

Two cruisers and the *Renown* had taken torpedo hits but were in no danger of sinking. The *Ark Royal* had also taken a torpedo, but the worst damage had been caused when a low-flying bomber managed to land one on her deck. The internal damage control had been good, but the carrier wouldn't be conducting any flight operations until they could repair her at St. Helena.

Dire Dawa, Italian East Africa

Colonnello Guido Nobili entered the briefing room where his friends sat. He'd never been a stickler for protocol and these men were more like brothers than subordinates. He tossed seven copies of the latest orders in front of them and joined them at the table. The copies were passed around until everyone had one and Guido cleared his throat.

"First, every flyer in our unit is getting the War Cross for Military Valor and an extra month's pay for the Battle of the Gulf of Aden. The French government is cooking up something too, but I don't know what it is. They are crediting us with saving the Suez crossing operation."

The news was greeted with subdued smiles. The multi-man bombers had been slaughtered and even the fighters had taken a heavy beating. Almost three hundred flyers had been lost. Barely one hundred and fifty remained. Add in that all four of the Italian submarines had been sunk and the price had been very high to get the British fleet to turn back.

"Reinforcements are on the way now that the Suez Canal is partially open. Work is almost complete on a new base at some place called Kismayo, near the Kenyan border. We're supposed to set up operations there to cover the next phase of the Africa Campaign. Operations here will continue under the direction of Colonnello Fagnani."

Tenente Colonnello Tarcisio Fagnani smiled at the news he'd been promoted. He'd been Guido's boss and subordinate, now he'd be his equal. The men at the table erupted at the news and Tarcisio accepted their congratulations with a seated bow. Guido knew his men needed things to celebrate and let it go on until things quieted back down.

"Maggiore Fiore and Commandant Lefebvre will come with me to Kismayo. Commandant Durand, Maggiore Volpe and Maggiore Rossi will stay here with Tarcisio. Alonzo, I'll need a recommendation from you on who should run the reconnaissance squadron I'll have down in Kismayo."

Maggiore Volpe simply replied, "Will do, Sir."

"We will take two squadrons of D.520s with us. The recon squadron and three bomber squadrons will ferry down from Egypt. Generale Nasi has moved five divisions down there for a drive on Nairobi. We will support his advance and try to keep the sea supply lines open. Tarcisio, you'll support the efforts to clear Sudan and patrol the sea lanes up here.

"We're going to have a lot of new faces both staying and passing through so let's do what we can to make this go smoothly. Read through the orders and we'll meet again tomorrow for questions and planning, OK?"

Francesco Rossi waved his hand before speaking. "May I suggest we meet tomorrow afternoon, Sir? I think we could all do with a little celebrating and maybe a poker game before we start heading our separate ways."

His comments were greeted with more cheers and laughs. Knowing how much they'd been through together and how much they'd lost, Guido smiled and joined in.

Cross Anchor, South Carolina, USA

Manly Lee Wilburn sat on the front pew of the Yarborough United Methodist Church. Pastor Michael Farley was at the pulpit even though church was over and he was a Baptist. Pastor John Bailey stood nearby, lending his support to his fellow clergyman. Most of the adults around Cross Anchor were crowded into the front of the church, listening to the discussion. The older kids were keeping an eye on the younger ones as they played behind the church.

Pastor Farley was a sharp contrast to Pastor Bailey. Pastor Farley was blonde, wore glasses, had a goatee and mustache, and his relatively thin build reflected his life of austerity and academia. While they were close in height, Pastor Bailey had short gray-brown hair, no glasses, was clean-shaven, and had the stocky build of most men who used to play football. Both men were around M.L.'s age, so while they weren't in the draft pool, they were still able to help their flocks with physical as well as spiritual issues. The visiting pastor answered a question from Phil Lucas, one of the few present who wasn't a member of either church.

"No, Phil, it doesn't matter to us if you or Courtney are a member of either of our churches. We are here to help everyone in the community that's impacted by the coming troubles. Anyone in the area can post on our bulletin boards. List the goods or services you need, or what you can supply. We'll help coordinate with our neighbors to make sure that everyone is fed, clothed, and looked after if they need it."

Pastor Bailey nodded his agreement and added, "There may be loss or hardships, but there will also be comforting friends to help carry those burdens. Most of you have trusted your souls to us. We'd be pretty poor stewards if we didn't also try to tend to your physical needs."

"Thank you, sirs."

Phil sat back down, and Pastor Farley stepped out from behind the pulpit and began to pace back and forth.

"I don't know if any of you have heard the story of Carmen Esperanza. I read it in the New York Times. Her husband was the Spaniard who saved the Pope's life during the Spanish Civil War. At the time, she was working as a housekeeper for several British officers in Gibraltar to make ends meet.

"Now the Catholic Church richly rewarded her for her husband's sacrifice, but she kept working as a housekeeper for those British men. When a reporter asked her why she kept working, she said it was good honest work and so were the men she worked for.

"The reporter pointed out that the British weren't Catholic, and Mrs. Esperanza responded that it wasn't her place to judge them for their beliefs. They had helped her when things were tough during the civil war, and she would help them now. They were her friends.

"Well, when the shooting started, the Spanish laid siege to Gibraltar and began shelling it. They didn't count on the faith of Mrs. Esperanza. She showed up the next morning bright and early for work. The Spanish tried to stop her, but she marched right through their lines and the firing died down from both sides as the lone woman walked across no man's land. That afternoon, she appeared from the British line and walked back across that shell-torn ground as the guns once again grew quiet.

"She's been making that trip every day since the fighting started, and twice a day the guns on both sides fall silent. These days, she comes back from the British line covered in British blood, having acted as a nurse for them during the day."

Pastor Farley stopped and turned to face the assembled people. "Regardless of her beliefs, Mrs. Esperanza sets an example for all of us. How can we do less for each other than she is doing for men her country has named enemy?"

Pastor Bailey's hoarse "Amen, brother." was echoed by every throat in the church. Then he looked at Pastor Farley and said, "Philippians 1:27-28?"

Pastor Farley smiled and bowed to our pastor before quoting the scripture. "Only let your conduct be worthy of the gospel of Christ, so that whether I come and see you or am absent, I may hear of your affairs, that you stand fast in one spirit, with one mind striving together for the faith of the gospel, and not in any way terrified by your adversaries, which is to them a proof of perdition, but to you of salvation, and that from God."

Everyone sat silently for a minute before Harry Jamison stood up. The town meeting droned on for another thirty minutes before it started to break up. Most of the crowd headed out back to collect their kids, but M.L. and half a dozen other men lingered.

The draft had been enacted a week ago and all men aged eighteen to thirty were eligible. "Buck" Edwards and Andrew Jamison had already joined up. They were leaving for training tomorrow. Phil had registered and he got his draft notice yesterday, so had Doris' husband Ralph. They would be heading out on Thursday, which might have something to do with Phil's nervousness about what would happen to his wife. Even if he didn't get injured or killed, getting drafted meant that she'd be on her own for a long time. M.L. put a hand on the young man's shoulder.

"Don't you worry, Phil. You've been here long enough to know that we'll keep an eye out for Courtney. Doris is out back talking to her. Your job will be to give the other guys hell and come back to her in one piece."

The reminder that friends were in the same boat helped Phil. At least Courtney didn't have a baby to take care of. On the other hand, if something happened to him, she might never have that tangible reminder of her husband. He sighed and let the tension he'd been carrying ease.

"It'd be nice if I knew who I was going to be fighting. There've been skirmishes in Colombia with the South Americans, run-ins with the British Navy in the Carribean and French submarines in the Atlantic, and Hawaii and the Philippines are pretty isolated these days."

"At least they shouldn't have any reason to send you to the fighting in Africa, Russia, or China."

M.L.'s attempt at levity drew an eyeroll from the younger man. M.L. raised his hands and shrugged in contrition.

"Sorry. How about you and Courtney come over for dinner tonight and we have a beer or two."

"Make it bourbon and you have a deal."

"Will do, son."

LATE JULY 1938

The Chancellery, Berlin, Germany

Edna gives me a half-hug from behind as I sit at my desk. I place a hand on her arms to get her to linger, but it only lasts a moment. "I'm alive and okay, Erich. I love you, but the country needs you right now. I'll let you know if anyone shows up during your meeting."

She plants a kiss on the top of my head before she heads towards the door. I watch her leave and marvel at her strength. She has become part of our cabal that knows the truth about our would-be assassin. She had to if she was to play her part correctly.

She holds the door open for Otto, Ernst, and Franz, before closing it firmly behind them. My aide and the Minister of Justice take seats. My bodyguard stands. Even in this tight little group, it's what he does. I look at Franz expectantly.

"We have the evidence. His real name was Herbert Fournier. We have no idea what happened to the real Rhys Davies, but it happened in early '33. Fournier had a tooth pulled not long after he came here to escape the persecution in France in '32. The two were very close in appearance and Davies was a loner who didn't speak the language very well. We found Davies' old dentist and compared his records with those from Davies' new dentist. Davies was last seen by his old dentist in January of '33. Fournier passed himself off as Davies to his new dentist in April. The records from the new dentist match the ones from when

Fournier had his tooth pulled. That's also when the government records for Davies began to change. I have more than enough examples to provide a strong case that Davies was actually Fournier. Now what do we do about it?"

I stare at my desk for a moment, torn between making the bastards pay and what it would do to my country. Ernst is the first to respond. "I say we publish it and get the whole damn world to jump on their backs."

I look up at him and slowly shake my head. Franz lets out a breath I didn't know he was holding. "That won't work. The French will deny that they had anything to do with it and there isn't enough proof to get the League to go to war. If we push it hard enough, the Entente will use it as a pretext to attack us, not something I want while we're still fighting in Russia. And don't forget that we have no idea of how many agents are still loose in our country."

"Then we just let them get away with it?"

Otto breaks his silence with a growled "No! We use it against them. Minister Gürtner, you've been having trouble tracking down potential spies because we're trying to do it quietly. Use the cover story. We think they'll be loners, so who says they couldn't have written love letters to Edna, too. If anyone asks, we aren't looking for spies, we're looking for other possible threats like Davies.

"And while we can't prove that Fournier was a French agent, we can prove that he arrived with the Protestants fleeing France in '32. Show the Austrians and maybe the Americans. Let them know that we think he was a plant and warn them to be on their guard for similar threats."

I smile. It is rare for Otto to put his intelligence on display, but he'd started out smart and years of security work had given his mind a devious twistiness.

"I like it, though we might need to include the Scandinavian countries on the warning. I also think we need to get out of the war in Russia. If this was a serious attempt on me, the Entente may have been planning a move against us."

We discuss how to implement our plan for another ten minutes before everyone has to get back to their normal duties. Edna comes in from her lookout duties after they've left to find out what went on. She rolls her eyes at the thought of having more secret admirers but understands the necessity.

I meet with André François-Poncet, the French Ambassador, the next day. It's the weekly meeting we've been having since the fighting broke out. He presents me with a list of contacts for the new governments of Egypt, Sierra Leone, Gold Coast, Gambia Colony, and Malta. The former British colonies are under new management and looking for trading partners.

I thank him and express my hope that the conflict can be resolved soon. He agrees, though I think that resolution looks different in his mind than it does in mine. The meeting is cordial, and I wear my best diplomatic smile as he leaves.

Sir Nevile Meyrick Henderson arrives the next day for his weekly meeting. He expresses his deep concern over the French attacks around the world as well as their bombing of cities in England. He once again pushes for us to unite in common cause against the Entente. I deflect his arguments but assure him that we will do our best to increase our exports to the United Kingdom. He appreciates it and urges us to do more.

After he leaves, Edna comes in and sits across from me.

"That was different, but it was the first time I've seen him since the attack."

My perplexed look gets her to elaborate.

"Ambassador Henderson asked how I was doing and was happy to see me back at my duties. He made a comment about what some people will do in the name of love, so I gave him our cover story about us checking into other potential threats. He said he was glad to hear that we were taking precautions and he wished me a continued speedy recovery."

"Didn't François-Poncet do much the same thing yesterday?"

"Yes, but it seemed like Henderson was glad to hear that we were being cautious about other potential threats. François-Poncet had his usual indulgent smile when he heard."

We sit in silence while we both try to figure out if the subtle difference in reactions means anything.

When Sir Nevile arrived back at the British Embassy, he went to his office to compose his weekly report for the Home Office. He included Edna's comments about their new security measures. He paused for a moment before adding, "Tell Winnie that his figgy pudding went over well and has been completely devoured." He smirked at the thought of how Churchill would react to being called Winnie.

Kismayo, Italian East Africa

Général de Brigade Roger Noiret paced back and forth in the office he'd been given. It was small, hot, and dusty, and Roger had been stuck here for five days. He looked out the lone window of his three-meter by three-meter cell at the airstrip that had been constructed by the African Expeditionary Corps. It looked pathetic compared to what he'd seen elsewhere, but almost a hundred Italian planes managed to call it home. Roger hoped they were enough.

The ships carrying the 1st Armored Division were expected to reach the area in an hour. They had been delayed by the invasion of Malta and the slow clearing of mines in the Red Sea. Generale di Corpo d'Armata Guglielmo Ciro Nasi had taken the rest of the corps overland towards Nairobi five days ago, leaving Roger to study maps and worry. Both Madagascar and Mozambique had been invaded by the British and things might not go well if they got wind of this sea move. Almost the entire Italian battle fleet along with all four of the French *Richelieu's* were protecting the transports carrying his men. Six Italian cruisers had broken off from the fleet and were raiding in the Indian Ocean in an effort to tie down the British Eastern Fleet. Italian land-based planes provided air cover for the eight battleships and their consorts. Still, Roger worried and prayed.

Roger would take one of the local boats out to the fleet to rejoin his men. He would be transferred to a troop transport containing the rest of his staff and he would have two days to catch up with any changes that had been made while he was away. After that, the plans would meet the enemy and they would have to change to deal with reality.

The transports had come with a regiment of Italian marines. They were supposed to make the initial landing at Mombasa and seize the port facilities Roger needed to unload his men. Unlike the Arabs in Egypt and Palestine, the Kenyans were willing members of the British Commonwealth. Even if things went well at sea, there would be urban fighting with an unfriendly populace. Roger felt like he had early in his military career, the decisions of other men controlled his destiny and that of his men. He hoped the Lord would guide them and offered up yet another prayer before gathering his things for his trip to the port.

The ride to his ship had been bumpy. Roger was thankful that he didn't suffer from seasickness, a blessing not shared by all of his men. He and his immediate subordinates sat at a table in the mess hall, gently swaying to the rocking of the ship. Colonel Philippe de Hauteclocque, his XO, sat across the table and looked grim but healthy. Lieutenant-Colonels Henri Dubois and Claude Durand looked fine, as did Commandant Richard Levesque. The same could not be said for his fourth regimental commander, Lieutenant-Colonel Alexandre Thomas. Thomas looked pale and like he'd lost five kilos. A fate shared by close to a quarter of the division's men according to Philippe.

"That many?" Roger couldn't keep the surprise out of his voice.

"Yes, Sir. Most are doing better as they get used to the rocking, but I would expect them to perform like they've been in combat for the last week."

"Any other issues?"

"Nothing immediate, but there may be one we'll have to deal with long-term. Supply by sea may be interrupted when the fleet is given new orders or if the English move against us in strength. Food shouldn't be an issue, but things will get very tight if we have to fly in ammunition and fuel."

Roger thought for a moment before coming to a decision.

"The ops plan calls for us to leave a battalion at Mombasa to guard it. We'll also need to leave some detachments along the railroad to Nairobi. If Thomas and the 12th Regiment take on that role, we can reassign the worst seasickness cases to his unit and move healthier men to the advancing units, like we did at Aqaba."

Colonel Hauteclocque looked around at the regimental commanders to gauge their reactions. Roger watched the interaction and realized that those regimental commanders were looking to Philippe for direct control of the division. Roger was both proud of Philippe's growth and saddened by the knowledge that one of them should soon be moving on.

They all looked at Roger with a mixture of relief and pride on their faces. Philippe responded with a grin. "That was the best recommendation we could come up with, though I will admit that we argued about it for over an hour. We can work out the details over the next two days, but we all want to know what happened in France."

Roger almost laughed at how their eagerness for news from home had warred with their commitment to their duties. He took pity on them and launched into a synopsis of his trip. They were glad to hear that the brass had been interested in their ideas. Roger told them of the reports that England was rationing oil and food while France was not.

He told them of the French conquest of the Channel Islands, Sierra Leone, Gold Coast, and Gambia Colony. They already knew about British Somaliland and Egypt. He also told them of the loss of French Indochina and New Caledonia. The wars between the Central Coalition and the Soviet Union, Japan and China, still raged while the League of Nations dithered. The League had barely done anything about the invasions of Colombia and Argentina, two members of their alliance. The men wondered if it would become one big war if the League finally chose a side, and whether it would drag on like the Great War had.

Philippe and Durand were concerned about the welfare of their families. Both were from the north of France, and were happy to hear that the British coastal raids had eased. Everyone was happy to hear about the support of their countrymen, though Roger kept his worries of zealotry to himself. He presented them with little gifts from the members of his church that lifted spirits and then led them in prayer for their loved ones and their men.

During the prayer, Roger began to wonder where his true home was. Here, among his men, where he felt as if he belonged; or in his hometown, where he felt ever more disconnected from his neighbors. He shook those thoughts from his head. Roger presented the group with his final prize from France, five bottles of wine. He gave one bottle to each of the regimental commanders for them and their staff. The last was split among the six men at the table, both as a celebration of life and an acknowledgement that Death would soon reap his harvest in their fields.

Jamestown, St. Helena

Vice Admiral Sir Geoffrey Blake sat stiffly in the chair. The officer on the other side of the desk was only a Captain, but Sir Geoffrey knew just how much power he wielded. His recommendations would determine if Sir Geoffrey would face formal charges or if the Admiralty would make changes to their standard operating practices. A young Ensign sat at a small desk in one corner of the room, dispassionately waiting to record Sir Geoffrey's answers. Both had given their names during the initial greeting, but Sir Geoffrey had been mentally reviewing his testimony and couldn't recall them if his life depended on it. He hoped it didn't.

"Your action report says that the Entente planes attacked at dawn and overpowered your combat air patrol. Why didn't you have more fighters in the air, Sir?"

"If I'd followed standard operating procedure, I wouldn't have had any in the air." growled Sir Geoffrey. "We were three hundred miles from the coast with no enemy contact for eighteen hours and our scouts had been airborne for an hour."

"Then how did the Entente manage to find you, Sir?"

"That's what I've been wondering about for the last week and it's why I wanted this inquiry. They would have seen the task force if we were heading to South Africa or up to the Canaries. Since they didn't, they had to figure we were heading here. I followed standard procedures for zigzagging to avoid subs and maintained standard cruising speed. And that's where I think the problem is."

"Sir?"

"The Entente knows how we operate and used it to get the jump on us. If you know where someone is, where they're sailing, and how they normally sail, you can figure out roughly where they'll be at any time. This attack hurt, but it could have been a lot worse. And the next one will be worse unless we change how we do things. And I don't mean giving us discretion on our speeds and zigzag patterns, I mean actually ordering us to not use the ones we've been trained on. Otherwise, every other Admiral will do just like I did and use the well-worn ruts our minds have been trained to follow. Ruts the enemy knows about and will use against us."

The Captain and Ensign both blanched at that thought. Good. Maybe Sir Geoffrey had made his point and they would do their best to make the issue to the Sea Lords. Since he requested a formal inquiry, someone would have to read it. Hopefully, they'd be able to do something about it.

The inquiry fizzled out quickly and Sir Geoffrey decided to head back to his ships. A Corporal nearly ran into him as he was leaving. Sir Geoffrey's mood darkened even further when he heard that Malta had fallen.

He headed up Market Street to General Hospital where sixteen of his men were still being treated. Almost a hundred of his men had been released in the last two days. Those that remained would never sail with the Royal Navy again even if they lived. He'd promised himself that he would visit them daily while the task force was in port, and he'd walked up here every day. Their injuries only steeled his resolve to make the Entente pay. A resolve that the delays for supplies and repairs tried to sap and turn into despair.

Kismayo, Italian East Africa

Colonnello Guido Nobili shook his head as he surveyed the new airstrip. At least it would be easy to repair if it got bombed, after all, the two runways were little more than fifteen hundred meters of hard-packed dirt. A bulldozer sat in a camouflaged shed two hundred meters from each end of the runways. The control tower was a ten-by-ten two-story building sitting next to a radio antenna and his men were in tents. Then again, so were his planes. The only actual buildings housed his officers, the munitions for his planes, and a workshop for fixing them.

Guido walked over to the mess tent to get lunch. At least the food was fresher and plentiful, now. Two days ago, several small transports had arrived with supplies. Unlike the first group that had shown up a week ago, this group carried more than just fuel and munitions. He grabbed a tray and went through the line just like everyone else before heading to the table where Maggiore Stefano Fiore and Commandant Claude Lefebvre were already eating. They stopped to acknowledge his arrival but quickly went back to eating. Several minutes went by before Stefano finished his plate.

"What's the news on that fleet that went south yesterday, Sir?"

Guido gave him a dirty look before resigning himself to eating between answering questions. "They're going ashore at Mombasa tomorrow."

Claude perked up at that comment.

"I guess that's why we've been scouring the British airfields in the area. Will we change our operational priorities or do we keep supporting Generale Nasi's advance, Sir?"

"As long as we don't spot anything at sea, we interdict the rail line between Nairobi and Mombasa. Supporting the advance on Garissa comes after that. Any sign of the British navy and we abandon everything else."

Both wing commanders stifled groans at that thought. Another attack against alert ships sounded slightly better than getting disemboweled with a dull knife, but only because the attack would be over quicker.

Claude, Guido's fighter commander, was the first to break from that shared dread. "Do you think there's any chance the brass paid attention to our letter about dive bombers?"

"I sent it up the chain and to my contacts at the design bureau. I know they are more concerned with improving our fighters, but they should know who to pass it to on the bomber development side. I wouldn't hold my breath for anything to happen soon. It looks like we're stuck with flying low and slow over ships that are blazing away at us."

Guido decided to change the subject rather than get stuck in a spiral of despair. "How are the new men fitting in with the old ones?"

The looks he got could have soured a new bottled of wine.

Stefano shook his head, "What old ones? Oh, you mean Claude and his fighter pilots. For my men, it's more like how are the veterans fitting in with the new guys? And the answer is not very well. We've been on a few missions and they've been easy. The new guys think the old guys are just making shit up to try to scare them. I've also caught a couple of them saying our War Crosses weren't deserved and we only got them because you know Mussolini."

"That's something we've got to nip in the bud, Stefano. If we don't, we'll have a totally dysfunctional unit in no time. Claude, do you think your veterans can add any weight to the cautionary tales or do we just trundle along until reality and a wall of flak smack the new kids in the face?"

"I'll check with my men to see if they have any suggestions, but I don't know if it will help. I think we're just going to have to train them up as best we can and hope they survive."

Guido looked down at his tray. What was left didn't look half as appetizing as it had a few minutes ago.

The attack on Mombasa had not gone according to plan. Guido rolled his eyes at that thought as he banked his D.520 to begin another strafing run. There had been close to a regiment of Kenyan troops in Mombasa that no one expected. Guido didn't know if it was bad luck or the Brits had gotten wind of the operation.

The battleships had pounded the crap out of the defenders and they had called on him to provide air support. Guido wasn't sure if it was a bug going around or someone had done something to their food, but three quarters of his men were violently ill. He had cobbled together crews to get anything in the air. A squadron of bombers escorted by ten fighters was all he could send to their aid.

The view from the sky showed the Entente forces had made it off of Mombasa Island and onto the mainland. That was both good and bad. They would be out of range for naval gunfire support soon and would need to rely even more on his scant air support. Guido pressed the firing stud and the D.520 spat bullets and shells at the group of men and vehicles heading southeast towards the fighting. At least they were easy to spot in the tidal wave of people fleeing in the other direction, desperate to get away from battle.

The only bright spot was reconnaissance hadn't spotted any British ships in the area. Guido sighed as he pulled his fighter up and prepared for another pass.

Spartanburg, South Carolina, USA
Manly Lee Wilburn cussed under his breath. The wrench he'd been using had slipped off the worn bolt he'd been tightening. He'd banged

his knuckles on the housing of the train engine he was working on. He felt like a trainee as a trickle of blood ran down two fingers of his left hand.

Cardy's head bobbed up from the other side of the engine. "Everything OK, M.L.?"

"Just skint my fingers not paying attention to what I'm doin'. Damn foolishness."

"Need a band-aid?"

"Two, please."

Cardy headed off to the workshop medicine cabinet while M.L. went to the sink to clean up the cuts and see how bad they were. Cardy came back, already peeling one of the band-aids out of its wrapper. M.L. dried his hands and stuck the first damaged digit out for its covering. He had to wipe more blood off of the second finger before it could be patched. Cardy finished up and gave M.L. a quizzical look.

"We've been at this for more than twelve hours. Don't you think that's enough for a Monday?"

"You're probably right. Lunch was a spell ago and it'll be most of an hour before we get home. Between hungry and tired, I rate to do more damage than I do good."

Cardy laughed, "To you or the engine?"

M.L. grinned back, "Good question. Let's head home."

They locked up and headed out to M.L.'s truck. M.L. wasn't sure when everyone else had headed out. He and Cardy had been too engrossed in the engine overhaul they were working on to notice. They headed south towards home and Cardy kept quiet while they drove through the town traffic. The townies drove like crazed idiots and both he and M.L. had dodged cars, bikes, and people walking over the last few weeks. They both heaved a sigh of relief when they got out of town.

Once Cardy felt the distraction of some conversation wouldn't cause a wreck, he asked, "What do you think has gotten into everyone?"

M.L. glanced at his bandaged fingers and grunted. "The same thing that's gotten into me, I guess. Friends and loved ones drafted. Families split when things look rough. People not sure who they can trust. Hell, half the people on the road are women and kids who are only driving now because the men who used to do it have been drafted."

"Hadn't thought about it that way. Heather learned to drive like I did when we got our first car. But you're right. There's a couple of guys in the shop who brag about how their wives don't need to know how to drive. If any of them get drafted, things won't be easy for their wives."

"People in the city don't look after each other and aren't as independent as we are in the small towns. We're used to having everyone able to help out where they're needed. In Spartanburg, they're getting a bit too used to having other people do things for them. When that happens and you pull out a few pieces, things quit running so smoothly."

"Ain't that the truth."

They rode along in silence for a few minutes. Cardy knew that something was bugging M.L. but he didn't know what. Usually, M.L. would bring it up if he wanted to talk about it, but he was staying quiet today.

"I don't mean to pry, but what's got you distracted enough to bang your knuckles?"

M.L. stared out the windshield for a moment and Cardy wondered if he was just going to ignore the question. But M.L. let out a sigh and shook his head a little. "We get letters every Friday from Al. That is, we used to. We haven't gotten one from him for the last two weeks."

"He's your son who's down in Panama with the Army, right?"

"They were in Panama. You read about us landing troops in Cartagena at the request of the Colombians?"

"Yeah, the paper said that there had been some heavy fighting there. Is that where Al is?"

"Yep. And then Harry got pissy at Jewel's birthday party on Saturday."

"I was wondering why he and his family left so early."

"Zachery was talking with Junior and found out we hadn't heard from Al. He went and told his mom. Janice told Harry and he asked Leila if she was happy now that she'd given one of her sons to feed the imperial ambitions of our government."

Cardy blanched, "I bet that didn't go over very well."

"I thought she was going to slap him. Instead, she stared at him for a moment before telling him that it was pissant little men like him that let dictators rise and forced freedom-loving people to give their lives to stay free."

"Yikes! Is that what the commotion was in the kitchen?"

M.L. nodded and continued, figuring he might as well get it all out. "Harry turned purple. Janice turned red. And Leila just stared down her nose at him, which is hard to do when you're almost a foot shorter than the staree. Harry gathered up his family and left. They dodged us at church yesterday and skedaddled right after the service was over.

"Now Junior is moping because he can't talk with Sara. Jewel is moping because we ruined her party. And Leila and I still don't know if Al is OK. I think it might have been better if Leila had just slapped him."

They rode on in silence for another couple of minutes before Cardy got up the gumption to interrupt M.L.'s brooding. "Let me know if there's anything we can do. And I hope you hear from Al soon."

"Thanks, Cardy. Appreciate it."

EARLY AUGUST 1938

The Chancellery, Berlin, Germany

I watch Edna leave my office and my heart stutters. It's been more than a month since the attack and the nightmares are down to every few days. I'm not sure if it's the lack of sleep or the fear of losing her that's been making me jumpy. Gürtner is coming by this morning with his latest report. Maybe I'll finally have a focus for my anger and frustration. Maybe I'll find out I'm leading Germany into the arms of our assailants.

I close my eyes to gather my thoughts before tackling this morning's reports and paperwork. I pick up the first folder. The deal to sell our three old *Bayern*-class battleships to Turkey has finally been approved by the Reichstag. The deal will move forward once I sign the order, but my doubts about the attempted assassination make me hesitate. The calculating part of my brain points out this deal has been in the works for months and it's endorsed by the Navy. They want the ships sold or retired. It's a bonus if it gives the Entente more things to worry about in the Mediterranean. The fall of Malta has freed up the resources they were using against it. I sign it and move on. The rest of the folders are international updates.

The war with Russia is pushing forward. Estonia has finally been cleared. We now control a line from Lake Peipus to the Gulf of Finland. Russian attacks aimed at Pskov and Bryansk are being contained while our advance on Smolensk is pushing forward. The Ukrainians have been pushed back from Oryol, but are exacting a heavy price from the attackers. The Turks are still trading land in Georgia for land in Azerbaijan at a snail's pace. Parts of that line are starting to look like the western front from the Great War.

Blomberg wants more of everything but says the situation is adequate for now. Hmm. He also wants our iron industry to look into salvaging Russian tanks. He's sure that most of the battle sites have enough destroyed enemy tanks on them to make them richer than our best ore deposits. And if they happen to help push the railways east in the process, so much the better for the Army's supply situation. Definitely something to consider since the British demand for Swedish iron ore is pushing prices through the roof.

The British are rationing almost everything in their Home Islands. The Entente campaign to cut their resources at the source, in addition to at sea, is having a definite impact on their industrial output. They've reached out to the Americans, looking for some kind of territory for war material trade. They're interested in purchasing planes and tanks from us, too. They're also pushing forward with their plans to invade Iran and want to know if Turkey is interested in setting up a protectorate in northwest Iran. I bet they've already floated that idea by Atatürk and he's all for it.

The Catholic Entente is pushing forward in Africa and clearing the Med. They've got troops on Cyprus and it's only a matter of time before Gibraltar falls. In Africa, they continue to push south on a broad front. The British seem to be concentrating their efforts on Mozambique and Madagascar, probably to clear their shipping lanes now that the Med is closed to them.

The British have taken the Entente's Pacific possessions and transferred New Caledonia to the Japanese. I wonder what they got in return?

This is new. The Austrians want to hold a joint military exercise with us. It seems President Broz wants to show a united front with us regardless of what the rest of the League of Nations wants. Broz may have been a metalworker at one time, but he is quickly learning the political ropes and fiercely loyal to his country above all else. I have to wonder if that loyalty would keep him from getting his country involved if we were attacked but he wasn't.

The Canadian Civil War has gotten ugly. The Battle of Montreal was two days of slaughter where both sides suffered more than ten thousand casualties before the loyalists withdrew. Quebec City was shelled by four destroyers, one of which was sunk. Quebec sent an ambassador to the United States asking for recognition and admittance to the League of Nations. So far, they've ignored the request. I'm glad I don't have to worry about that mess.

South America is still a mess. The Organization of American States is slowly grinding through Colombia and Argentina. British Guiana is still holding out. France is interested in purchasing Suriname from the Netherlands. I write a note on this one. Do they want our help or blessing or are they just informing us that they're pursuing this with the Dutch?

And finally, we have the League of Nations, or more specifically, the United States of America. They are displeased with our efforts to circumvent their trade embargo of the United Kingdom. Interesting... No 'stop, or else' comments. Are they condoning it or are they just running low on trading partners? Ah. They are concerned with the war in China and want us to press the British to get the Japanese to ease their attacks. They also thank us for our warning about possible fifth column elements in the Entente refugees from six years ago. There have been several incidents that have been traced back to some of those refugees. Yeah, join the club.

I close the last folder and stand to stretch and move around a bit. My old wounds from the Great War have been acting up since the anniversary attack. Either that, or I'm getting too old to sit at a desk for hours on end. I'm laying across my desk, trying to stretch out my lower back when Edna knocks and enters with Franz Gürtner, Oberst Ernst

Weber, and Otto Woyke in tow. The Minister of Justice looks at me like I'm doing something unnatural with the desk. My Aide smirks while my bodyguard smiles before speaking.

"Good. I'm glad to see you stretching your back out. You need to stay limber enough that you can move fast when you need to."

The sideways reference to the assassination attempt causes a shocked, in-drawn breath from Edna, and Otto looks abashed at his lack of tact. She recovers quickly and unconsciously brushes her fingers through the still-short hair on the left side of her head. She smiles impishly at him.

"It's okay, Otto. There are times I need him to be limber and able to move fast, too."

She does her best flounce out of my office to a chorus of low chuckles at my red-faced expense. I return to my seat while my guests take theirs. I recover quicker than they do.

"And here you are, Franz, suggesting I have weird interests in my desk when I have Edna around."

"I may be the Minister of Justice, but who am I to judge what interests the Chancellor of Germany."

There are more chuckles as I ruefully shake my head. I always end up on the losing side of these exchanges.

"Whatever. What's the latest on your investigation?"

Franz sits up a bit straighter and his face becomes serious.

"We've gone back through everything and followed some new leads. Herbert Fournier was indeed a provocateur embedded in the refugees from France in '32. We've found no evidence that he was given any instructions other than to carry out his task, so we think he was assigned that task before he came here. We were able to trace where his order came from. It was the British Ambassador, Sir Nevile Meyrick Henderson."

All of the mirth drains from my face.

Franz quickly continues, "We don't believe that Henderson had the resources to find out what the order code was or the authority to activate Fournier. Henderson's correspondence did contain a curious request for him to distribute some figgy pudding to his staff the day before Fournier was activated. Two weeks ago, Henderson sent a message that the 'figgy pudding went over well and has been completely devoured.' That was right after Edna said he seemed unusually pleased with our cover story.

"We've checked, and there was no figgy pudding sent to their Embassy in the last two months. The message was addressed to 'Winnie.' Our best guess is that 'Winnie' is Sir Winston Churchill."

"Son of a bitch."

"Remember, Sir, we don't know if the British had any idea what Fournier's mission was. We don't think this was a deliberate attempt to assassinate you."

"Do you have any idea how many other deep agents the British can activate? Or any idea of their targets?"

"No, Sir. But we will keep a closer eye on any unusual messages involving Henderson."

Ernst joined the conversation.

"And François-Poncet. We shouldn't forget that the French are the ones who put these agents in place and more likely than the British to activate them."

"Gee thanks, Ernst. I thought Aides were supposed to help, not give their bosses headaches."

Mombasa, Kenya

Général de Brigade Roger Noiret looked at the list of casualties and swore under his breath. Their intelligence had screwed up. The drive on Nairobi by the rest of the African Expeditionary Corps had attracted and pinned down the British forces in Kenya. They should have known that the British were training troops near Mombasa.

The fleet had been spotted on its way south. When the Italian marines stormed ashore, they were greeted by some enthusiastic defenders. The fleet had to shell far more of Mombasa than they had intended. Roger had started landing his division before the port was secure to help the struggling Italians. It had still been dicey. Two transports carrying his men had been sunk on the way to the docks. Snipers had been a constant threat for the first two days.

That was when Roger ordered retaliation. He hated himself for it, but he hadn't seen any other way to stop the seemingly endless array of hidden defensive positions. He ordered the fleet to shell any area that returned fire, areas that often contained houses. He figured they had killed at least ten thousand non-combatants before the resistance had ended. But it had ended.

What was left of the Italian marines and the fleet had pulled out yesterday. The marines had lost over five hundred men, with another three hundred wounded. They wouldn't be back in combat for a while. The 1st Armored had four hundred dead and two hundred wounded, but they had secured Mombasa and were finally pushing towards Nairobi.

Generale Nasi and his men had advanced to Garissa, about three hundred and fifty kilometers east-northeast of Nairobi. They were doing their best to keep the Kenyan army pinned down. The 1st Armored had about four hundred and fifty kilometers to go to make it to the Kenyan capital. Roger detached the light tank battalions from his two armored regiments and assigned them to the 14th Motorized Regiment. The three regiments would leap-frog forward with maintenance and rest every third day.

Roger worried about leaving the 13th Motorized Regiment to hold Mombasa. It had taken the brunt of the casualties and even its commander, Lieutenant-Colonel Claude Durand, had been wounded. The men had a short fuse where the locals were concerned, and Roger didn't want hasty retributions disrupting his supply line. Durand understood the need to keep things quiet, but it didn't seem like he was happy about it. Roger thought wistfully of the days when his concerns were limited to what he could see from the top of his tank.

Roger brought binoculars up to his eyes and peered northwest. Nairobi was less than twenty kilometers away and they still hadn't encountered any real resistance. His men were tired, but it had been an almost pleasant advance. The weather was a lot cooler than he'd expected. The countryside was breathtaking. Damage to the rail line had slowed them more than anything else. Commandant Richard Levesque and the 14th Motorized Regiment were now scattered along the supply line back to Mombasa.

Roger lowered the binoculars and headed back into his command tent. Colonel Philippe de Hauteclocque sat at their makeshift desk, examining reports and maps.

"Give it a rest, Philippe. The pickets are out and there's no evidence the Kenyans have more than a handful of troops in the area."

Philippe shrugged, "I know, Sir, but it's what I do."

"It's what makes you such a good executive officer. But everyone needs a break now and then. We're resting and catching up on maintenance tomorrow. Nairobi can wait a day."

"I just don't like that Nasi is still so far away with the rest of the Corps. He's still over a hundred kilometers away and he says that there's been a significant drop in the number of troops he's facing."

"It won't matter even if they're headed here. They don't have any motorized transport so they have to walk the whole way. They might be able to get back to Nairobi in time, but not if they're lugging any equipment. And they would be exhausted if they did make it."

Philippe stared at the desk for a few moments before folding up the maps and correspondence. "Fine. The roads aren't changing. Tell me more about your time back in France. It seemed like you left things unsaid when you talked with the rest of the staff."

Roger looked at Philippe for a moment, judging whether or not to confide in his friend. Philippe attended services but had always come across as a halfhearted Catholic at best. With a sigh, Roger sat down close to Philippe and lowered his voice.

"It just didn't seem right. I'd always been taught that God gave us free will so we could choose our path to his grace. But things at home are heading more towards mandated religion. I can understand the desire to stamp out heresy, but people are beginning to look down on anyone who isn't Catholic. It's an attitude that the government seems to be pushing. I love the fervor displayed by our people, but I wonder how much of it is driven by fear of reprisals instead of a love for God."

Philippe looked at Roger for a long moment before replying, "You know I'm not a deeply religious man, but what you were noticing is why I go through the motions. I came to the conclusion that if I wanted to defend my country, it would have to see me as a good Catholic. Otherwise, it wouldn't trust me to lead men in its defense. I worry about what lies down the road we've taken, but I will do my best to fight for my country and its people."

"And I respect you for your choice. My problem is that I fear that the ability to choose is being taken away. Without it, we might as well be Calvinists who think being saved is predetermined. Worse, how do I convey my concerns to Father Lobau or my fellow members of The Warriors for Christ without inviting the very censure that would keep the Church from taking my concerns seriously?"

"Very carefully, Roger. Very carefully."

200 Miles Northwest of St. Helena

Vice Admiral Sir Geoffrey Blake stared out at the warm waters of the Atlantic and shook his head. Convoy escort. Really? The 1st Battlecruiser Squadron was reduced to convoy escort? Was it a sign of the Admiralty's displeasure or Great Britain's desperate need for the oil in the tankers they had escorted north?

They had passed the tankers off to the 2nd Battlecruiser Squadron near the equator and taken its convoy under their wing. The big troop convoy was headed to Cape Town with more men and planes to feed into the fighting in Africa. He was supposed to wait there for new orders. Either the Admiralty was cooking up something, or they'd be escorting another convoy. At least the *Ark Royal* had finished its repairs and would join them as they passed St. Helena.

Commodore John Moore joined him at the railing of the *Marlborough*. They stared out at the sea for a few minutes before Sir Geoffrey broke the silence.

"Let me know if you want a transfer, John."

"Why would I want to do that, Sir?"

"If the Admiralty blames me for getting caught by that air raid last month, it may hurt your chances for advancement. And you've acquitted yourself admirably over the last two years. Regardless of what happens to me, I would prefer that the Royal Navy get the benefit of your service for years to come."

"Thank you, Sir. I'd prefer they continue to benefit from your service. Are you that concerned about how the Admiralty will react to your inquiry?"

"You tell me. Our squadron has a sixth of Her Majesty's capital ships and here we are on convoy escort duty."

"True, Sir. But the 2nd Battlecruiser Squadron is on convoy escort, too. I think they're worried about a French breakout from the Mediterranean. Reports from Gibraltar are not good and if it falls, the chances of a French sortie going unnoticed increase dramatically."

"I know, John, I know. It just rankles me that we aren't doing more while the Entente is overrunning Africa."

"Me too, Sir. But I don't know what we can do other than shelling ports and interdicting their sea supply."

"And lone cruisers are easy prey for their land-based planes. Which leaves it up to submarines, which we don't have enough of, or fleet actions, which are hard to hide."

"And which need carriers to protect them from those land-based planes. Otherwise, even large formations are vulnerable if they operate in the same area for too long."

"And the flight operations from the carriers make it even easier to spot us. Which leaves us stuck between a rock and a hard place."

The two officers went back to leaning on the rail, both men wondering how to best use the firepower at their disposal without frittering it away.

Garissa, Kenya

Colonnello Guido Nobili smiled evilly at Maggiore Stefano Fiore as he laid down his cards. "Queens and sevens, eh? I guess my three fives will just have to walk off with the pot then."

Stefano groaned as his boss gathered up the pile of chips on the table.

"You're going to have to promote me if you're going to keep getting lucky. Otherwise, I won't be able to keep playing."

That got a chuckle out of everyone. Without Maggiore Rossi around, the poker games were a lot friendlier and the stakes were relatively small. Guido also won a lot more often without his old poker buddy calling his bluffs. He picked up the cards and started to shuffle when a young Caporale knocked on the doorframe.

"Urgent message, Sir!"

Guido took the message and read it quickly. His expression gave away its content.

"Ships, Sir?"

"Yes, Stefano, ships. The Brits have gotten wind of the big supply convoy headed our way and are out to stop it. One of our submarines reports the Eastern Fleet heading our way."

"Please tell me we're not on our own. We'll get our asses kicked."

"I know the supply convoy is headed to Mombasa, but I don't know many details. I'll see what I can find out. Tomorrow may be a busy day, so get some sleep if you can. Briefing at five."

Guido left a chorus of groans behind him as he headed to the radio room. It was approaching midnight by the time he had a clear picture of what was going on. What sleep he got was filled with nightmares of blazing guns and exploding aircraft.

The aircrews chatted nervously as they filed into the makeshift briefing room the next morning. They'd all enjoyed the relative safety of the ground support missions they'd been running in Kenya. The subdued fighter pilots were veterans of attacking ships while the bomber crews were cocky and boisterous. Guido glanced at Maggiore Fiore and nodded.

"Attention!"

At Fiore's command, the gathered men spun to face their commander and snapped to attention. Guido looked over his men and wondered how many he'd lose this time.

"At ease. Take your seats."

Guido's quiet command was quickly obeyed, and his men looked at him expectantly, wondering what their fate would be.

"Our latest reconnaissance says the Eastern Fleet has turned southwest and is currently headed towards the Seychelles. Another group of large ships was spotted off the northeast coast of Madagascar, heading north. Intelligence believes that it's the 1st Battlecruiser Squadron. The two forces appear to be linking up and we can expect them to attack the convoy on the day after tomorrow.

"We will be shifting back to our old base at Kismayo starting in two hours. All planes will carry full weapons loads since we didn't leave much there. Fuel and ordinance are already on their way from Dire Dawa to both Kismayo and Mogadishu. Fagnani will take his wing to Mogadishu. We will coordinate with Fagnani on the air defense of the convoy and any attacks we make on the enemy.

"The combined British force will have ten capital ships and four carriers with over two hundred aircraft. With Fagnani, we will have one hundred and ninety-two planes to support the convoy's ten battleships. We're working on our battle plan. I will let you know what it is as soon as I can. This is going to be messy and painful. It may also determine the outcome of the war.

"Questions?"

Guido stopped and looked around the room. Even the new aircrews were looking concerned about the information. There was a low buzz of conversation, but no one had a question for Guido. Maggiore Fiore broke the tension.

"Attention! Poker game in the mess tent after dinner. Let's get moving, people. Dismissed!"

Cross Anchor, South Carolina, USA

Manly Lee Wilburn rose with the rest of the congregation to sing "How Great Thou Art." He knew his voice wasn't the best, but he threw his whole heart into it today. They'd gotten a letter from Al yesterday and his soul truly sang today. Leila noticed his extra enthusiasm and joined it as she reached for his hand. She didn't let it go for the rest of the sermon.

They'd told Pastor John Bailey about the good news before church, and Pastor Bailey added to the sermon he'd prepared. He reminded everyone of God's mercy, love, and forgiveness of our transgressions. That got a hard squeeze out of Leila's hand. M.L. guessed it was time to try to mend the fences with Harry. Time would tell if he was in the same mood.

They made a bee line for the door when Pastor Bailey wrapped up and stood waiting at the bottom of the stairs for the Jamison's to come out. Leila stood with her arms akimbo, facing the church and M.L. began to wonder what his wife was going to do. He found out when their neighbors made it to the top of the stairs, and she raised her voice.

"Harry and Janice! I'd like a word with you!"

Harry looked ready to spit nails, while Janice wore the same expression of dread that M.L. felt creeping over his own features. The rest of the congregation grew silent and formed a ring around the two combatants. Harry matched Leila's stance before he responded.

"I have nothing to say to you, Leila."

"Too bad, I have something to say to you... I'm sorry."

The air went out of the crowd and Pastor Bailey breathed an audible sigh of relief along with M.L. and Janice. Harry looked confused while Leila bowed her head briefly.

"I'm sorry for my harsh words. I was worried about Al and lashed out at you. It wasn't Christian of me, and I ask you to forgive me."

Harry stood there for a moment, still looking madder than a cat whose tail had been stepped on. M.L. smiled at his wife's cunning. She had apologized in front of everyone who had been at Jewel's party, the rest of the congregation, and Pastor Bailey. There was no way he could refuse to forgive her without making himself out to be a petty and spiteful man. And if he brought up her insult in the future, people would think the same thing after such a public abasement. Yep. Harry was trapped and he knew it.

Harry put on his best smile and bowed back to Leila, though the daggers from his eyes could have mowed down a regiment in the Great War. "I forgive you and hope you'll forgive me for any of my actions that may have caused you pain. I hope we can forget this trouble and renew our friendship. To that end, we'd like to invite you over for dinner next Saturday."

Leila nodded and mounted the stairs, where she gave Harry a hug. M.L. looked around and decided that a lot of the crowd shared his doubts about either of them forgetting anything. He was pretty sure they didn't share his doubts about what would be in their food next Saturday.

Cardy was in a good mood when M.L. picked him up for work the next day. M.L. had to ask why when he got in the truck. "What's got you smiling and whistling this early on a Monday morning?"

"Things are good at home and I'm just happy for you. Al is okay and your tiff with Harry is over. I'm just looking forward to a busy but uneventful week at work."

Cardy wound down as he noticed the slight giggling and look of incredulity from M.L.

"What?"

"You think things are fixed? Feuds have started over lesser insults. Leila's public apology made her stature rise and painted Harry into a corner. He can't take any reprisal for his public humiliation without vindicating Leila's original insult."

"Really?"

"Yep. It's kinda like what the Catholics are doing to England in Africa. The Entente is cutting off the resources the English need to fight the war, while making them appear to be the bad guys by 'freeing' the colonies they conquer."

"Even though they're keeping enough troops in them to ensure they're free in the right direction."

"That's the jist of it. People, countries, and politicians do it all the time, but most people don't pay too much attention to how they're being led around. Once you start lookin' for it, you see it everywhere."

LATE AUGUST 1938

The Chancellery, Berlin, Germany

I follow Oberst Ernst Weber, Franz Gürtner, and Otto Woyke to the conference room where the leaders of the Reichstag await. Edna holds on to my left arm as we walk down the empty corridor. Her look of worry mirrors my own. I do not look forward to this briefing, but I'm legally and ethically bound to do it.

Otto stops in the doorway and surveys the room. It only takes a moment, but it's long enough to be noticed by the Representatives. We enter and take our seats while Otto closes the door and takes station there.

"Alright, Chancellor, what the hell is going on?"

I'm not surprised that Alfred Hugenberg takes the lead. The distinguished businessman still has dark hair on his head, though his mustache has gone white. He commands a room, and the German National People's Party, as well as any general I know. His conservatives control almost half the seats in the Reichstag.

"This information is extremely sensitive. I hope I can rely on your discretion and concern for our people as we decide what to do with it."

Ernst passes a folder to each of the four Representatives while I open my own. I pensively wait for them to finish reading through our findings on the assassination attempt. Ernst Thälmann is the first to look up. The leader of the Communist Party looks at me questioningly before looking over at Edna. Whatever he sees on her face seems to shock him.

Hugenberg finishes at about the same time as Otto Wels, the leader of the Social Democratic Party. They both look up at me before sitting back in their seats wearing concerned expressions. Ludwig Kaas, Roman Catholic priest and head of the Centre Party, finishes his second pass through the information and starts on a third.

"Kaas."

He looks up and shrugs apologetically.

"I apologize for not bringing this to you sooner. Gürtner and two very trusted members of the Ministry of Justice have been working on this. They are the only people outside of this room who have access to this information. The question is, what now?"

Hugenberg growls, "We publish this and nail their asses to the wall."

"And how many innocent Germans will join them, nailed to a wall or hanging from a tree?"

At least Kaas sees the implications. To be fair, Hugenberg probably does too. He just tends to think in black and white. Gray shows a lack of will.

Wels slowly shakes his head as he lets out a small sigh.

"And how far will we go in violating the peoples' rights to find the enemy agents that may or may not be there? It says the message to activate came in the mail. Are we going to read all of the mail in the country?"

Thälmann glances at Edna before joining the conversation.

"Or are you suggesting a secret police force to try to track the thousands of refugees who sought a new life, here?"

The four party leaders look at me, wondering what kind of monster I'll choose to be. I look back sourly. Only Hugenberg has expressed an opinion, the others seem to be glad it's not their decision.

"I'm not sure that will help. The spy who attacked us was living the life of an innocent man. It was pure luck that we were able to trace him back to his arrival. I don't see any way to tackle this problem without fundamentally changing who we are. And I don't think we would like what it does to our country.

"I do know that we've done similar things in the past and I presume we have agents in the field ready to do them now. We will review our protocols to make sure they're hard to fake, though changing things would be a good way to identify our agents to our potential adversaries. Security wonders if that wasn't the entire point of this exercise.

"What I think we need to do is run a careful propaganda campaign. Let the German people know that there's been a rise in mistakes and accidents that impact how well we can fight the war with Russia. Tired minds and bodies make errors, so we ask them to keep an eye on each other to help our men at the front."

None of them look very fond of my solution, though the only one to comment is Thälmann. "So, you want the workers to spy on each other? I guess that's better than the state doing it."

"It may not do anything, but enemy agents might be reluctant to do things if they think other people are watching. My guess is that Justice will need a department just to weed through the reports. Hopefully, the people will see this as an effort to crack down on the inept, not one to find saboteurs.

"This is the best compromise we could come up with, but we're open to suggestions if you have any. Regardless, I hope we can count on your discretion going forward."

Their nods of assent are reluctant, but they do agree.

Kampala, Uganda

Général de Brigade Roger Noiret sadly looked out the window of his makeshift headquarters at the beauty of Lake Victoria. He and his men were exhausted. Their equipment was in desperate need of maintenance. The 11th Armored Regiment had arrived at the capital of Uganda the day before. He left the 12th at Nairobi to await Generale Nasi and the rest of the Corps.

After they cut off Nairobi, Roger had been unsure how to proceed. The Kenyans had answered the question for him when they offered to surrender. They didn't want their capital to be bombarded the way Mombasa had been. Panic and hunger were already gripping Nairobi and the Kenyans knew they had been beaten. Roger hadn't realized how much of the food for the city moved up the Mombasa-Nairobi railway. That also explained why the Kenyans hadn't damaged the railway during their retreat.

The situation had been almost identical as they advanced on Kampala. The Ugandan forces were engaged with the Belgians advancing from the Congo and Roger's men were advancing up the supply line the Ugandans needed to feed their army and their people.

The Ugandans had surrendered, and the Belgians were expected to arrive tomorrow. Roger had wondered at the relief that seemed to overcome the Ugandans. The Belgians had so abused the peoples of the Congo. Philippe found out why. His executive officer had been working out some of the surrender details when he was asked how he could work with the Butcher of Mombasa. The reprisals Roger ordered for the ambushes had grown in the telling and now he was viewed as a murderous thug.

Roger turned away from the view of Lake Victoria and went back to his desk. He mentally reviewed the choices he'd made but couldn't figure out any other way he could have handled the situation. Butcher of Mombasa, not exactly a desired epithet for a Warrior of Christ. What would Catherine or his sons think of him when they heard it? How about the Army or Father Lobau? He bent his head in prayer.

Colonel Philippe de Hauteclocque knocked on the door frame and closed the door behind him as he entered.

"Are you okay, Sir?"

Roger wore a sour expression when he looked up and watched Philippe take a seat. "It was the right decision. It saved lives at the time and it has kept guerrilla resistance to a minimum."

Philippe stopped for a moment to try to gauge Roger's state of mind. He had been there when Roger learned of his British nickname. He had seen the shock and despair flash across Roger's face. "Your nickname? How many more French, Kenyans, and Ugandans would be dead if you hadn't ordered the reprisals? If they want to turn you into a boogeyman, use it for good. We aren't here to subjugate these people, we're here to free them from the British yoke."

Roger sighed and nodded his head slightly. "I know. But I wonder what will happen the next time I make it home. How much will the tale have grown by the time it reaches their ears. I was already feeling disconnected from them. Will my family and friends shun me as some terrible monster?"

"I doubt that will happen. One side's monster is the other side's champion. I don't doubt that you'll be hailed by the French press and become a favorite of de Gaulle. Just keep winning."

"That's the plan. I prefer not to die, and I don't think I'll like what happens if I get captured."

The Belgians arrived the next day and relieved his weary men. The trains were already running again, and his men boarded for the long ride back to Mombasa. The Italians were in charge of the railway security in Kenya and his scattered division was being reassembled for the next phase of the campaign. Reinforcements had flown into Nairobi and Mombasa to replace the losses they'd suffered, though there weren't any replacements for lost tanks.

Roger took the opportunity to have several chats with Father Lobau and found that Philippe's views were right. Father Lobau praised Roger for his work in the Lord's service. Lobau pointed out that one of Lucifer's tricks as the great deceiver was to use doubt to get the righteous to stray from the path of glory. They prayed together and Roger's faith was reaffirmed. He would do his best to use his skills in God's service.

50 Miles East of Mogadishu, Italian East Africa

Vice Admiral Sir Geoffrey Blake raised his binoculars and stared to the west as the sun rose behind him. The orders at Cape Town had directed him to link up with Vice Admiral Alexander Ramsay and the 1st Battle Division to double the strength of the Eastern Fleet. Vice Admiral Ramsay would be in charge and for once, the Royal Navy wouldn't be at a disadvantage in the coming battle.

There was no doubt that both sides were aware of each other since scouts from both fleets had been sparring for the last two days. Sir Geoffrey ran through their intelligence in his head. There are six Italian battleships and four French ones in the opposing fleet while the Eastern Fleet has five battleships and five battlecruisers. The Entente has ten heavy cruisers to our eight, but we have fifteen light cruisers to their five and thirty destroyers to their fifteen. The Entente also has sixty transports full of troops and supplies that could change the course of the battle for Africa that raged to their south.

Vice Admiral Ramsay wanted to launch an early morning air attack on the Entente fleet but Sir Geoffrey convinced him to wait. If the land-based Entente air attacked their fleet, it would probably be early. That would allow them to launch a second strike later in the day. An initial heavy air defense would provide better protection for their planes and ships. Their planes could then rearm and strike at the Entente fleet while the enemy planes were making longer trips back to their airbases.

The inquiry Sir Geoffrey had demanded apparently did some good, Vice Admiral Ramsay had been flying heavy combat air patrols for the last two days. It wasn't long after dawn when the air raid warning went off. Time to see if the preparations would pay off. Returning to the bridge, Sir Geoffrey heard the radioman call out the first battle orders for the combined fleet.

"Fleet will proceed northwest at twenty knots while aircraft scramble."

Commodore John Moore acknowledged the order and the *Marlborough* turned to starboard. It would be another couple of minutes before the enemy aircraft got close enough to count or fire at. There wasn't a whole lot to do at the moment. The men had been at their battle stations for the last hour, checking their equipment and making whatever peace they could with their maker. John looked over at Sir Geoffrey.

"It looks like you were right, Sir."

"I just hope it's enough. That looks like a lot of planes headed our way."

"Yes it does, Sir. Yes it does."

Commodore Moore looked on with a concerned eye as the approaching swarm of enemy planes appeared. The fleet's anti-aircraft guns began to hammer as their assembled fighters moved to engage. More Gladiators rose from the carriers to join the fray and both of the senior naval officers quickly realized that their ship was not a primary target.

The approaching planes veered south around the formation before turning back to the north. It wasn't long before they were headed back to the west and dropped altitude to launch their torpedoes at the carriers and the light cruisers surrounding them.

The launch was made at long range and was over in minutes. The filers on both sides paid a steep price for the attack. Once the enemy bombers launched, their planes were faster than the carriers' Gladiators. The Entente fighters enjoyed a speed advantage throughout the fight.

Seventy-two Gladiators had gotten into the fray against over a hundred and fifty Entente planes. Twenty-two of the Gladiators had been shot down. Nine enemy fighters and nineteen of their bombers had been knocked from the sky by the air defense and fighters. Three destroyers and one light cruiser were sinking from torpedo hits. The rest of the fleet continued northwest as the carriers launched their strike aircraft to attack the Entente fleet.

The fleet cruised southwest for the next hour as the carrier strike paid a visit to the enemy ships. The Entente escorts were spread out more as they tried to cover their transports in addition to their battle fleet. Thirty to forty Entente fighters faced the fifty-four Gladiators and seventy-two Swordfish torpedo bombers of the British strike. Only twelve of those Entente fighters were left when the British fliers headed home. That also happened to be the number of Swordfish that returned. An additional seventeen Gladiators were also lost. The slow-flying Swordfish had sent a wave of destruction through the transports as they were driven from the skies. The men and material in twenty-three of those transports joined the fliers in the salty waters.

It was a cold calculation, but both of the British admirals considered it a win. They knew the Entente would take time to replace those transports, time the Empire desperately needed. A need that demanded they close with the enemy and do their best to exterminate him.

The air attack had two effects on the Entente fleet. The first was that the transports they were escorting headed to Mogadishu and the comparative safety near their airbases. The second was that the fleet turned northeast to engage its antagonists.

For the second time in his career, Sir Geoffrey found himself in a line of battle, heading south at fifteen knots while the French and Italian ships headed southeast at the same speed. This time, however, Sir Geoffrey was not free to act as he wanted. It was Vice Admiral Ramsay who called the shots and decided their maneuvers. Those maneuvers had placed the *Renown* on the southern tip of their line, closest to the enemy battleships. The *Hood* and *Tiger* were next in line. Then came the *Marlborough*, followed by the *Benbow*. Ramsay was on the *Royal Oak*, second in his line of five battleships. Sir Geoffrey's three most lightly armored ships were closest to the enemy. His protest had been noted and ignored.

The radioman announced the orders.

"Firing will begin in one minute at assigned targets. For King and country, good luck."

Every pair of ships had a primary target. The first six were to fire at the front three French battleships, while the last four would fire at the two Italian battleships at the rear of the enemy line. All ships were to match speeds with their targets and fire at it until it was out of action. Targeting would move towards the center of the enemy formation as their ships were neutralized. The seconds slowly ticked by, and Commodore Moore prepared to issue the order so their shots would stagger with those of the *Tiger*.

The guns from five ships fired almost simultaneously. Two seconds later, the *Marlborough* and the four other ships belched forth their fury. That was when the plan went to shit.

The four French battleships leading the enemy line were *Richelieu*'s. They had all eight of their main guns mounted in two turrets on the bow of their ships. They turned towards the British line-of-battle and increased their speed. The six Italian battleships fired broadsides at the center of the British line and also increased their speed. Sir Geoffrey reacted immediately.

"Request permission to break formation. Enemy will either outflank us or split us under current orders."

"Maintain formation and accelerate to twenty knots."

"Request orders for when the enemy exceeds twenty knots."

If the anger in Sir Geoffrey eyes could be used as weapons, the enemy fleet would have sunk in minutes. Commodore Moore met his gaze and shared his anger as the *Marlborough* sent another salvo at her inbound target.

"Does Ramsay think they don't know that his ships have a top speed of twenty-one knots?"

"I think he's trying to figure out what to do."

Sir Geoffrey turned to the radio operator.

"Order the 6th Destroyer Flotilla and the 7th Cruiser Squadron to accelerate to maximum speed and prepare to launch torpedoes beyond the *Renown*. Copy that to Ramsay and note that the enemy may be doing something similar."

"You think they're copying the tactics we used against the *São Paulo*?"

"I think they know exactly how fast the old *Revenge* class can go and where they can lead us."

The radio operator announced, "Orders to Fleet. All ships are to maintain formation. All ships concentrate fire on the closing battleships."

Sir Geoffrey responded, "Check with the scout planes for cruisers and destroyers that were behind the enemy battleships and may have launched torpedoes. All planes and ships are to keep watch for possible inbound torpedoes on both sides of the French battleships."

"Message from Ramsay. He is in command. One more act of insubordination and you will be relieved, Sir."

Sir Geoffrey and Commodore Moore shared a look of barely controlled fury and frustration. It looked like Vice Admiral Ramsay intended to fight their ships for them.

"Italian battleships have settled in at twenty knots."

"And I bet Ramsay thinks that's a good thing."

Commodore Moore looked a warning at his squadron commander. Any comments from Sir Geoffrey might be used against him if there was an after-action inquiry. Sir Geoffrey's look soured, but he held his tongue.

Time seemed to crawl by. The *Richelieu*'s were pounding away at the *Benbow* and the *Revenge* in the center of the line while taking a beating from the British warships. The Italians had shifted fire to the three lead battlecruisers and scored multiple hits.

"Message from scouts. Many torpedoes in the water, both north and south of the French battleships. Range two miles to battle line."

Sir Geoffrey stared at Commodore Moore for a moment.

"It's Great Yarmouth all over again."

The naval battle from the Great War had turned into a mess when German submarines had disrupted the British line of battle. What would

Ramsay do? Fifteen precious seconds ticked by before Sir Geoffrey could wait no longer.

"Blake to Fleet. Line of battle will come port to one hundred and ten degrees. Light cruisers and destroyers will prepare torpedo launch."

Commodore Moore ordered the turn as Sir Geoffrey stared to the west.

"Ramsay to Fleet. Ignore that order. Blake is relieved of command."

"Lucas reports he's beginning his run, Sir."

Sir Geoffrey simply nodded. He'd hoped the young Captain would ignore the orders from Ramsay, but any attempt to confirm it would have brought attention to Lucas' insubordination. As it was, he could claim he didn't receive the 'maintain formation' order.

Every ship in the 1st Battlecruiser Squadron followed Sir Geoffrey's order, none of the battleships of the 1st Battle Division did. The 7th Cruiser Squadron and 6th Destroyer Flotilla came into view as they rounded the *Renown*. They launched just as the world seemed to explode.

The northern French battleship, the *Jean Bart,* was rocked by a massive explosion that blew both of her turrets fifty feet in the air and gaping holes in her hull. Seconds later, a great gout of flame shot up from the *Hood* and as she exploded and broke in half. The Entente torpedoes arrived just as the two halves of the stricken ship slammed back into the water. The battlecruisers escaped relatively unharmed, only the *Tiger* was hit. She had damage to one of her propellers which would reduce her top speed, but her fighting capacity was undiminished.

The battleships of the 1st Battle Division did not fare so well. All five of them were hit by at least four torpedoes. Their lead ship, the *Revenge*, had already taken a pounding and became the third ship to explode in a span of twenty seconds. All of the other battleships quickly lost speed as they settled in the ocean waters.

Sir Geoffrey turned back from the scene of carnage.

"Blake to battlecruisers, return to heading one eight zero. Reduce speed to fifteen knots. Concentrate fire on the *Richelieu*. 2nd Destroyer

Flotilla and 1ˢᵗ Light Cruiser Squadron will begin torpedo attack on remaining French battleships."

His ships began their maneuvers with Lucas dodging his smaller ships back behind the battle line. Two good things came from the explosions. First, Ramsay was either injured or stunned into silence. Second, the Italians were distracted enough to slow their reaction to the torpedoes launched at them.

The nine destroyers and five light cruisers had launched over a hundred torpedoes at the six Italian battleships. They had just started to turn away from the inbound threat when it arrived. Each of them suffered multiple hits. They did not turn back to the fight and continued southwest behind a cloud of smoke laid down by their destroyers.

The remaining French battleships fought on alone and the *Royal Oak* joined them as they slid under the waves. Sir Geoffrey looked at the battered condition of the Eastern Fleet and chose not to pursue. They had lost *Hood*, *Royal Oak*, and *Revenge*. None of his remaining battleships could do better than fifteen knots. The *Benbow*, *Tiger*, and *Renown* had all taken heavy damage. Each had a turret that was out of action. They'd also lost almost half of their aircraft. Only the *Marlborough* was relatively unscathed. Hits had been scored on the Italians, but the condition of their ships was unknown.

Sir Geoffrey sat down to write up the after-action report, including Vice Admiral Ramsay relieving him of command. The Admiralty would find out about it one way or another, so there was no use in trying to hide it. Despite the risks, they had stayed in the area to pick up survivors. They rescued almost four thousand men after the battle, including just under two thousand French sailors. Some of the prisoners ranked high enough to be worth questioning.

He sent the damaged battleships back to the base at Colombo, while his squadron limped back to Cape Town. Using both repair facilities would get the ships back in fighting trim more quickly. Technically, the battle had been a win. There was still the question of how the Admiralty would view his actions.

Mombasa, Kenya

Colonnello Guido Nobili sat at the desk in his quarters and pulled his wife's letter from his pocket. It arrived this morning along with the replacement men and planes. Thirty of his planes had fallen from the sky during the Battle of Mogadishu. Their loss would have been less painful if there hadn't been a munitions mix-up. The torpedoes that he and Tenente Colonnello Tarcisio Fagnani needed for a second strike on the British fleet had arrived four hours late. Guido shook his head in disgust at the lost opportunity.

The pain was compounded by the loss of Guido's wingman, Tenente Corrado Ricci. Ricci had been with Guido for two years and they could almost read each other's mind when in the air. Guido closed his eyes for a short prayer, both for Ricci and himself, before opening the letter from Aurora.

Dearest Guido,

I was fearful when I saw the length of the casualty list from the Battle of Mogadishu but was so relieved when your name was not on it. I know that the loss of Ricci and the other men under your command weighs heavily on your soul. I wish I could be there to help you through your grief. All I can offer is the knowledge that the efforts of you and your men are appreciated and praised here in Rome. Your unit will receive another medal and the newspapers write of your courage and perseverance.

Mother has come up and is staying with me. I'm usually exhausted after work and too tired to cook, clean, or shop. She's been a great help. Every night, she places a hand on my stomach and sings to our unborn child. I don't know if our child can hear her, but it soothes me and helps me sleep peacefully.

Father comes up after work on Saturdays and goes home on Sunday night. My sister Astra has been cooking for him while he's on his own. He complains about her cooking, but I haven't noticed him losing any weight. I think he does it just to make sure that Mother knows he misses her. He's working long hours at the shipyard and his back is bothering him, but he's looking forward to another grandchild.

My boss has asked about you. He thinks we should find some reason to bring you home. I think I may have been overly dramatic in my concern for you. He also mentioned how nice it would be to be a godparent.

Stay safe and come back to me.
Love always,
Aurora

Guido folded the letter up and put it back in its envelope. Il Duce wanted to be a godparent. Wouldn't that be something. More importantly, he could be getting off this godforsaken continent. Guido stopped and stared into the distance for a moment. Could he leave his men here? Ground units were rotated out of the line for rest and recuperation. Why weren't air units? And his unit had learned some costly lessons that the rest of the Regia Aeronautica could benefit from.

Guido got out a pen and some paper. If Mussolini couldn't come up with a reason to bring his exhausted men home, Guido could.

Maggiore Stefano Fiore and Commandant Claude Lefebvre were confused when Guido kept the replacement men and aircraft as separate squadrons. The new planes were paired up with veterans so they could learn how the squadron operated but they weren't actually assigned to fill out Guido's depleted units. They had done quick run-throughs with previous replacements. This time, Guido had his men spend an entire day working with the new guys.

When they ran their first missions against Dar Es Salaam the next day, the replacements flew as separate squadrons. Fiore and Lefebvre were ordered to observe their performance but to not correct any mistakes they made. Both men were quick to find Guido's office after the flight. Lefebvre was the fastest to ask for answers.

"Okay, Sir. We're back. Will you tell us what's going on?"

"How did the new fliers do?"

Fiore and Lefebvre rolled their eyes at each other, and Fiore responded.

"They did reasonably well. A few minor formation errors and a couple of pilots fell back into basic training habits."

"What happened when they screwed up?"

"Men in their squadron corrected them."

Guido's smiling response of "Excellent" drew exasperated looks from his subordinates.

"What are you up to, Sir?"

Guido spread his hands in surrender.

"Fine. Every group of replacements we get shows up wanting to make the same mistakes we used to make. I want to change that. We did combat training with the men before the war started, but it was a slow process because only a few of us had actual combat experience. I want to use the veterans we have in our unit as a training cadre. We can spend a couple of days with an air unit to try to bring them up to speed before they're ever sent into combat. I think it'll improve their performance and help them survive longer. It would also get us a break from getting shot at."

Cross Anchor, South Carolina, USA

Manly Lee Wilburn folded up the Spartanburg Herald-Journal and put it down. He'd never been that keen on international politics until they might put sons and neighbors in harm's way. It sure looked like the country would end up involved in this war. M.L. didn't think the question was if, but which side, the country and the rest of the League of Nations would join.

Roosevelt had signed the treaty of Bogotá with the OAS on Tuesday. The treaty split Colombia between Venezuela, Brazil, Peru, Ecuador, and Panama. But on Thursday, he'd approved the sale of the five old *Nevada*-class battleships to the USGA. That was a direct challenge to the Catholic Entente's domination of the Mediterranean Sea. The fall of Cyprus and Gibraltar had effectively turned it into an Entente lake. Things might be more clear-cut if the US didn't support China against the invasion by Japan, Britain's ally. At least the Germans were keeping their heads down and beating on the commies. Things were getting tricky.

The paper said that the Entente claimed Sweden and Norway were shipping restricted goods straight to Britain. M.L. didn't doubt it, since his boss said that there was extra train traffic going to Canada. It didn't look like everyone was honoring the trade restrictions put in place after the fighting broke out. M.L. knew there were protests against that, and some of them had turned violent. He'd never had to repair bullet holes in trains before this summer. What worried him was that no one knew who was behind some of the attacks or what they would lead to.

He was still deep in thought when Leila, Jewel, and Courtney Lucas came into the parlor from the kitchen. His wife wore a smug smile.

"M.L., you remember how I've been saying something was off with Phil and Courtney?"

M.L. nodded and leaned back as he noticed the twinkle in Jewel's eyes and the worry in Courtney's. He turned to Courtney.

"Congratulations, when are you due?"

"Around Thanksgiving."

"That makes Phil's anxiety about leaving you alone make more sense. Make sure he knows that we'll be here to help you with whatever you need. I'm sure Francis still has a lot of the things you can use from Bobby Lee's birth last year."

"Thank you. I'll let him know. My uncle has offered to let me stay with him, but I don't want to abandon what Phil and I have started."

For once, Leila didn't go through her usual routine of making M.L. figure out what she wanted. Either because it was her area of expertise or because Courtney wouldn't understand their way of addressing Leila's concerns.

"Don't you worry about that. Junior and some of the other boys will take turns helping in the fields. I'll set something up. And you should come to Eddie's birthday party on Labor Day. Most of the local kids will be here with their mothers in tow. You can start figuring out who you want your young'un hanging out with and learning from."

That got a shocked look from Courtney, but there were smiles all around as the women traipsed back into the kitchen. M.L.'s smile stopped after a moment when he wondered if Jewel would get any fool notions about having her own kid.

EARLY SEPTEMBER 1938

Manstein Residence, Berlin, Germany

Ipush back from the table, overstuffed but contemplating the rest of the chocolate cake sitting in the middle of the table. At the other end of the table, Edna clears her throat and gives me the 'You don't need that' look. My sigh of defeat as I lean back in my chair is greeted by low chuckles from Brent and Peter. Otto knows better.

"One day, it'll happen to you, too."

"But not today, Dad. Not today."

My son pulls the cake from the center of the table and adds a slice to the already chocolate-covered plates in front of both him and Peter. My look of condescension bounces off their smug smiles and gets a giggle out of Edna. We both still have the occasional nightmare, but we're returning to normal. I raise my voice and call out to the kitchen.

"Beatrice, I hope you bought enough groceries for these two. I'd rather not find out what happens if they get hungry."

My long-time cook appears in the doorway with a smile on her lips and a twinkle in her eyes. She points at the eighteen-year-old boys.

"These four? I remember how much they eat."

"Four?"

"At their age, you count legs, not mouths."

She smiles and disappears back into the kitchen. She's gotten more comfortable with us since Edna moved in. And she's been downright motherly since the assassination attempt. Edna has that effect on people. My smile at Edna is returned in full force and I feel my tensions drain away.

We eventually pull ourselves away from the table, and I sit down next to Edna on the couch in the living room. Our glasses have been topped off with schnapps and Beatrice has headed home. Peter has learned from Brent and managed to keep his earlier conversation to 'safe' subjects while Beatrice was here. Not because we don't trust her, but because she doesn't want to know. She worries about us all enough as is. Peter and Brent exchange conspiratorial glances as they sip their schnapps. Brent tilts his head in my direction and Peter turns to me.

"Chancellor..." Peter stops at the dirty look I give him and looks guilty. "Fine. Mr. Manstein, we think you should know that no one is buying the story about the assassin being obsessed with Edna. At least, not at Lichterfelde."

The boys only recently started their second year at the Military Academy, but apparently, they'd returned to a buzz of questions and speculation. My glance at Brent isn't met. For once, he's watching Edna, not me. I look back at Peter as he smiles.

"He looked at you" Peter proudly proclaims.

"She looked at him" is Brent's answering response.

It seems they're at least learning about tactics at school.

Brent grimly looks at me. "We'll keep digging if you don't tell us. And we'd prefer not to mess things up. So, what actually happened?"

I consider them for a moment. "First, tell me why you don't believe the official story."

Peter proudly smiles, "Brent has talked about Edna a lot, and I didn't remember anything in her background where she might have met Rhys Davies. So, I pestered him about it. We didn't have the time or access to check it out, so we got in touch with our old art teacher. He checked into things as discreetly as possible, and things don't add up."

Great, one of my own intelligence analysts is digging into things on behalf of my son. Otto, Edna, and I exchange worried glances. Mr. Hitler is good at making connections.

"And what did he have to say?"

Brent begins to look a little worried.

"He found some evidence that linked Davies and Edna, but he was fairly certain it was recently created, and done to support the official story. He says there's evidence that Rhys Davies had been replaced by a Frenchman who came over with the refugees in '32. He thinks he was a spy, just like so many people were worried might be hiding among the actual refugees."

"Anything else?"

"Yes. He said it didn't make sense. If we know of one spy, there are probably more. And if you go to the trouble of planting saboteurs or assassins, you would coordinate their attacks for maximum impact. So, why did only one spy carry out his mission? Mr. Hitler thinks he was either accidentally triggered, or he was activated by another government in an attempt to move public opinion. He gives it about four-to-one odds that the guy was triggered by the British based on the need for a cover story."

Trust the guy with the twisty mind to ferret out the truth while missing a lot of the evidence. My face goes deadly serious.

"Hitler's right, but you two will point out to anyone who asks that you've seen pictures of Rhys and Edna, and that you've read some of the letters he sent her. Edna will show them to you later. This is an order, NOT a request. We'll talk to Hitler on Monday.

"There are probably only a dozen people who know what actually happened. We do not want the general population to find out. There will be chaos if everyone starts suspecting everyone else of being a French spy."

Brent looks at me suspiciously for a moment, "That's why you came up with the Efficiency Initiative, isn't it? It's a way to get the people to look out for spies without actually telling them what they're doing. Mr. Hitler wondered about the timing on that, too."

"It was the best compromise we could come up with that doesn't cause the same kind of damage we're trying to prevent."

Brent and Peter sit back for a moment and look thoughtful. I drain half my glass of schnapps in one swig and look around to see my tension mirrored by Otto and Edna. Brent looks back at me with a hate in his eyes that I've only seen once before.

"Did the British Ambassador have anything to do with activating the agent. And if he did, did he know what the agent would do?"

Crap. He remembered Sir Nevile's visit and denial right after the assassination attempt. I don't see any reason to lie, and all it would do is get him and Peter digging into things again. "Yes, and we don't think so."

Peter whistles softly while Brent just stares at me. He takes a deep breath and lets it out slowly.

"I will make sure you know when I'm coming to visit you in the future. Please make sure that son of a bitch isn't there or there WILL be an international incident."

I shrug. "Will do, son. Trust me, every time he comes by, and I have to wear my plastic smile, I feel like I need a shower after he leaves. If there was ANY evidence that he knew the agent would try to kill us, there would have been an incident already."

Edna clears her throat. "It's being handled, Brent. It won't be forgotten." She waits for him to nod his head in acknowledgment before continuing. "How are things going at the Academy?"

We all breathe a sigh of relief as Peter pipes up and takes us away from the volatile subject.

"We're both near the top of our class. It's the usual university stuff with extra military history and tactics and strategy classes thrown in.

Some of the instructors have started an after-hours discussion of the various wars going on. Brent and I like to go because there isn't a lot to do when you aren't studying."

Edna giggles, "Ah, I understand. No members of the fairer sex to distract you."

Peter turns red while Brent just rolls his eyes. I decide it's time to step in to save Peter from more of my wife's teasing.

"Has the group come up with any interesting ideas?"

Peter grabs the change of subject and runs from talking about girls with Edna.

"A few, Sir. We know that our sale of three battleships to Turkey had been in the works for a while, but Brent correctly guessed that the USA would sell its old battleships to the USGA."

Brent interjects, "Mr. Hitler had pointed out that the USA was planning on decommissioning them last May. I just figured the League might find a better use for them if they sold them to the Austrians."

Peter looks at Brent derisively. "I was there when Mr. Hitler brought that up, too. The thought of sending them to the Austrians never crossed my mind. Quit being too modest."

Peter looks back at me with his own eye roll before continuing. "Anyway, a number of people figured the British would reinforce their Eastern Fleet to try to slow the Entente advance through Africa. About half the group expected the British move into Iran, and pretty much everyone was expecting the fall of Colombia and Argentina."

"Not bad. Are there any predictions for the near future?"

"A couple. One of the guys thinks the Catholics in North America will form their own branch, kind of like the Anglican Church. It's been five years since Papal primacy was renounced and he thinks they'll do it to remove any association with the Pope and the Entente."

I hold up my hand as I think about that for a moment.

"That might be worth suggesting to the Americans. They might be able to draw the OAS into it and pry them away from the Entente."

Peter just stares at me for a moment while Brent chuckles.

"My dad doesn't care where ideas come from, but he does like to run with them. Like the other stuff, we are to keep our mouths shut about that possibility."

Otto chimes in, "The best way to make sure something doesn't happen is to break security and start rumors about it,"

Peter nods and turns to Brent, "Don't forget your latest."

Brent smiles and turns to me, "Have you heard about the Battle of Lake Khasan?"

I dredge through my memory of the myriad reports I've read.

"Wasn't that early last month, on the Korea-Russia border?"

"Got it in one. It was basically a stalemate and both sides have quit shooting at each other. It's the first time since the Russo-Japanese War that the Russians managed to fight the Japanese to a standstill."

"And what do you think will happen now?"

"I think there's a small chance that the Russians will push the issue in another disputed border region. They outnumber the Japanese and may try to expand their influence past Mongolia and western China. I think it's more likely that the Japanese will make a move to put the Russians in their place. The only place they could get the extra troops they would need to do this is from China. And the only way they would do that is if they were getting help in China from their one and only ally, the British."

"And why would the British go into China?"

"The land and resources are part of it, but the biggest thing the Japanese have right now that the British are short of, is ships. The Battle of Mogadishu crippled both the Italian and British fleets in the area. The Entente is using land-based air to cover their supply convoys and the British can't push through it, but that's not the case if they can get help from the Japanese. They have a lot of mostly idle battleships and aircraft carriers that would wildly alter the naval balance around Africa."

I stare at my son for a moment, and he watches my forehead crinkle as I add another load of coal onto the burning pile of my worries.

"I'm sorry, Dad" he says as his own face saddens.

Mombasa, Kenya

Général de Brigade Roger Noiret was going through the morning reports when Sergent Jean Martin entered his office. The arrival of his clerk barely registered on Roger's conscious thoughts. He read another paragraph of the report on the plans for the advance into Tanganyika before he realized that Martin was just standing there in the doorway, a folder clutched in his hands. When Roger finally looked up at his clerk, he noticed the smile on Martin's face and the sounds of feet shifting in the hallway.

Puzzled, Roger held out his hand for the folder. Martin gave it to him and returned to his position in the doorway. Curiouser and curiouser. Roger stared at Martin for a moment before he opened the folder to read its contents.

The message inside was from Army Command. A new command staff for the 1st Armored Division was arriving tomorrow. He was to leave for Paris in three days. He could take up to ten members of his staff with him. And he was being promoted to Général de Division. Roger was so intent as he reread the brief orders that would change so much in his life, that he didn't notice the rise in the ambient noise level. He finally looked up to see that Martin had been joined by a small crowd in the doorway. There were smiling faces all around, except for that of Colonel Philippe de Hauteclocque. His was almost somber, though he did have a bottle of wine in his hand.

"Congratulations!"

The bellowed shout and cheers of approval brought a smile to Roger's lips and pride to his heart. He basked in the moment before his face went serious again.

"Attention!"

There was a minor amount of chaos in the doorway as men who had been leaning in to watch tried to come to attention without losing their view of what was going on. Roger stood and came to attention. He held the pose for a moment before slowly bringing his right hand up to salute the people who had made this possible. He snapped his hand down.

His order of "At ease!" was greeted by more cheers as his friends came in to offer their hands and individual words of joy. Philippe managed to distribute a glass of wine to everyone so they could toast their commander's good fortune. It was only a few moments before Roger's mood turned somber and he looked over at Philippe. His executive officer gave him a rueful smile as Roger understood his reaction. The division had been through a lot in the last three months and some of them would be left behind as Roger moved forward.

"OK, break it up. This means we have more work to do, not less. It's been an honor to work with each and every one of you. Figure out if you want to stay here or come with me. If you want to come with me, I'll need recommendations for replacements for the new division commander. The orders don't say what I'll be doing, but I think the promotion and the option to bring some of you with me means a command somewhere. I'll call people in starting this afternoon to talk. Now, get back to work you bums."

The jovial group dispersed, and Roger went back to his desk. His mind was torn between trying to figure out what lay ahead, the current operations preparations, and the pile of information he would need to give to his successor. One thought quickly came to the forefront. He was about to shout when Martin came into his office carrying a pile of folders. Roger let out a soft chuckle and smiled at his Sergent as he placed the folders on Roger's desk and turned to go.

"Martin."

The bespectacled clerk turned back with a "Yes, Sir?"

"You're first. I may command this division, but you're the oil that makes it run smoothly. I'd be happy to have you join me on this new assignment. Take your time and think about it. Either way, I hope you know that I wish you only the best."

Martin stood still for a moment before reaching up to wipe a tear from his eye. He straightened to attention and saluted. "I'm honored, Sir, and will happily follow where you lead."

Roger stood and returned the salute before extending his hand. They shook hands and Martin simply smiled before turning to leave. He looked back over his shoulder. "Lots to do, Sir. Let me know who and when you want to see people. Everyone is hoping to go with you."

The time flew by. Roger greeted the new commander for the 1st Armored Division. It was Général de Brigade Jean Ris, former commander of the 3rd Colonial Infantry Division. His alpine and desert experience would be useful to Generale Nasi as the African Expeditionary Corps pushed forward in Tanganyika.

There was an introduction / going-away party that night. Roger and those going with him were toasted, presented with various made-up medals (what the heck were the Order of the Scratched Goggles and the Ribbon for Sightseeing?), and told how much they'd be missed.

The next day, a great sadness gripped Roger as they boarded their plane to Cairo. Endings were always hard, even when they led to beginnings.

Naval Base Simon's Town, South Africa

Vice Admiral Sir Geoffrey Blake stared out over the waters of False Bay from the bluffs behind Simon's Town. The Admiralty had congratulated him on the victory at Mogadishu and then confirmed him as acting Commander of the Eastern Fleet. They also sent an Admiral to discuss the current situation in the Indian Ocean. He would arrive this afternoon, along with a major supply convoy. Both had left England two days after Sir Geoffrey's report on the Battle of Mogadishu had arrived.

Sir Geoffrey clasped his hands behind his back and closed his eyes. He enjoyed the brisk morning air on his face and his service coat kept the rest of him warm and dry, despite the cool, misty wind coming off the water. He had little doubt that he would be chewed out for disobeying orders. The question was, would he be formally relieved of command? He'd run through his actions hundreds of times in his own mind and with Commodore John Moore. Both of them were convinced that he'd done the right thing.

Sir Geoffrey opened his eyes. Damn, he'd miss the sea if they cashiered him. He looked down at the dockyards where the *Benbow* and *Renown* were being worked on. The *Renown* had replaced the *Tiger* in the slips two days ago. Yesterday's dispatch from the Royal Naval Dockyard at Trincomalee, said the three remaining battleships of the 1st Battle Division should be fully repaired in three days. That was two days ahead of schedule, and four days ahead of when his own ships would be finished.

The biggest problem he had was airplanes. He'd virtually stripped the *Ark Royal* and *Indefatigable* to bring the *Formidable* and *Indomitable* up to strength. The carriers of the 1st Battle Division were more likely to need them sooner, and less likely to receive replacements than his own carriers. The expected convoy was supposed to have those replacements. Time would tell.

A glint of reflected light drew Sir Geoffrey's gaze to the south. Dozens of ships had rounded the Cape of Good Hope and were headed into the bay. One of them was a battlecruiser. It looked like the *Lion* or the *Princess Royal.* Maybe the losses they'd inflicted on the Entente navies had let the Admiralty free up a replacement for the 1st Battlecruiser Squadron. He turned back for one more long look at the waters he called home before heading down to the Naval Base and his fate.

Admiral Sir Martin Eric Dunbar-Nasmith, Second Sea Lord and Chief of Naval Personnel, looked up from his desk as Sir Geoffrey entered the room. Sir Geoffrey marched stiffly to the front of the desk and saluted.

"Vice Admiral Blake, reporting as ordered, Sir."

"At ease, Geoffrey. Have a seat and call me Martin."

"Yes, Sir."

The Second Sea Lord gave Sir Geoffrey an indulgent smile before continuing. "First and foremost, you're not in trouble. There were already concerns about Ramsay's handling of the 1st Battle Division. He was a good administrator, but the board was split on his ability to handle ships in combat. We've reviewed the after-action reports and come to the conclusion that your orders kept Mogadishu from being an ugly defeat. We do have one request. You set a dangerous precedent, and the Board asks that you think about what you'll do when a subordinate disobeys one of your orders."

Sir Geoffrey looked thoughtful for a moment before clearing his throat and responding, "Yes, Martin."

"Now, on to other issues. You may have noticed the *Lion* is with us. She will replace the *Hood* in the 1st Battlecruiser Squadron. Commodore John Moore is promoted to Rear Admiral and will take over the 1st Battlecruiser Squadron. You are being promoted to Admiral and will command the Eastern Fleet."

Sir Geoffrey's surprised look made the Second Sea Lord smile. Martin waited for a moment as it finally dawned on Sir Geoffrey why Martin had insisted on first names.

"Thank you, Martin."

"Congratulations. It was overdue, and the fact that you have the most recent combat experience doesn't hurt.

"Back to your information. The convoy contains the first five squadrons of Fulmars in the Navy. They are faster, longer ranged, and have twice the firepower of the Gladiators you've been using. We hope this will keep us from losing so many ships and pilots to the land-based Entente air power. There are also three squadrons of replacement Gladiators. Sorry, but we weren't able to make them all Fulmars."

"I think it'll be okay. The Gladiators do reasonably well when the enemy has to come to them."

"Still, we'll work on getting them all replaced as soon as possible. We're working on an upgrade to the Swordfish, but that won't be ready until next year. Instead, we managed to convince the Japanese to sell us eight squadrons of their carrier-based bombers. We think you'll like them."

"How did you manage that? And will our pilots be able to fly them?"

Martin chuckled, "We've been working more closely with the Japanese since Egypt fell, and the loss of Gibraltar means we'll need their help more than ever. We've been supplying them with Asian resources. In return, they've been helping us expand the industrial base in India and Australia. It's helped reduce the strain on our shipping, both of resources and manufactured goods. It's also helped with our fuel problems."

Sir Geoffrey couldn't help but ask, "How bad is it?"

"Bad. The Entente has been concentrating on oil tankers since the start of the war. We've had to use convoys to get them through and that cuts our imports by about twenty percent. There have been two successful bombings of fuel depots, and five that were unsuccessful. The military and the railways have fuel for now, just about everything else is moving by foot or bicycle."

"How are the people doing?"

"Oh, stiff upper lip and all that. They're pitching in where they can with drives for everything from blood to metals. A lot of them have sent their children to the countryside to avoid the bombings around the cities. The air raids are getting to be more one sided as we try to conserve fuel and the RAF gets worn down. The old Gauntlets were getting massacred, so they were pulled out of the front-line defenses. The only saving grace is that the Entente is limited to French and Belgian bases, so we know where we need to concentrate our defenses. Unfortunately, the same applies for our raids on them."

Sir Geoffrey turned somber at the talk of Entente air raids. The loss of his wife still haunted him. Martin quickly moved on as he realized the distress his comments had caused.

"Anyway, there are some other projects where we're coordinating with the Japanese that you'll learn about if they come to fruition. Their planes are supposed to arrive at our base at Trincomalee either today or tomorrow. And they're supposed to have English labels on everything. The Japanese are sending a maintenance group, flight instructors, and translators. Our pilots should have about a week of training with them before your fleet is ready for operations again."

"That should get them at least proficient with the Japanese planes. I presume they're better than the Swordfish."

"Just a little. There are four squadrons of their B5N torpedo bombers. We've code named them Kate. They're almost a hundred miles per hour faster than the Swordfish and they have a range of around six hundred miles."

Sir Geoffrey sat back and let out a low whistle.

Martin continued, "There are also four squadrons of their D3A dive bombers. We're calling them Vals. They'll be the hardest for our men to get used to since we don't operate dive bombers at the moment. It's almost as fast as the Fulmar, can carry over seven hundred pounds of bombs, and has a range of over eight hundred miles."

"Holy... I'm glad we don't have to face those. Are we getting the plans for them, or are we going to rip a couple apart?"

"We've got the plans and we're using them to improve the designs for our next generation of planes."

"Great. We've got new planes, and the battle fleet is mostly repaired. What does the Admiralty want me to do with them?"

"Defend the Indian Ocean against Entente raiders and submarines, provide support for our forces in Iran, interdict the Entente sea supply lines, and sink as many of their ships as possible. Or, at least, more of theirs than they sink of ours."

"I'll do my best."

"That's been pretty good so far. Keep it up."

Mombasa, Kenya

Colonnello Guido Nobili sat at his desk and stared at the orders he'd received. So many different emotions clamored for release that he froze for almost thirty seconds. Across the desk from him, Tenente Colonnello Tarcisio Fagnani smirked.

"What's the matter, Guido? You're getting what you want. You'll be in Rome for your child's birth. You're being inducted to the Military Order of Savoy as a Knight for being Italy's first double-ace. You'll get to train our new pilots, and no one will be shooting at you. Can't you think of anything to say?"

Guido sadly looked at his mentor and friend. "You know how much I want this for myself and my men. I just wish that it had happened earlier and there was some way to get you off the front-line, too."

"I miss Ricci, too. But if you set a good precedent, then I'll get out of here in a couple months and get to enjoy some cooler days, food worth eating, and wine worth drinking."

Guido brightened at Tarcisio's comments, though the sadness lingered around his eyes. "Then I'll do my best to pave a smooth landing strip for your journey home."

Tarcisio saluted, "Here, here!"

It took almost a week to get Tarcisio's command transferred to the base at Mombasa. Supplies were getting spotty the further they advanced down the African continent. That week was fraught with worry and restless nights for Guido. They were still supporting the ground operations in Tanganyika and there was the ever-present possibility of a naval raid that carried far more risk than the ground support missions.

Guido split each command in half and paired them with their opposite numbers in Tarcisio's command. Each day, one group would go on the assigned missions or do practice sorties. When they got back, the pilots would write down the advice they'd given or been given. The other group would attend classes where Guido and his men tried to instill the hard-won knowledge they had paid for. Evenings were spent showing the new fliers the best local spots for everything from women to local food. The nightly poker games were large and boisterous.

During the first four days, Guido's men coached, cajoled, and swore at Tarcisio's men to get their points across. Both groups had incidents where the new fliers nearly got themselves or squadron-mates killed. Over a dozen planes came back with holes in them that shouldn't have been there and could have been fatal.

During the sorties on the last two days, Guido's men let the new fliers correct each other. Only once, when a new bomber went in for a low-level attack run against a well concealed anti-aircraft battery, did Guido's men need to break their silence to save the new fliers.

All too soon, and yet nowhere near soon enough, Guido found himself on the flight line, embracing and saluting Tarcisio. He presented Tarcisio with a folder.

Tarcisio looked puzzled for a moment, "What's this?"

"I compiled and organized the reports from the pilots into what I hope is a useful format. I have a copy with me and plan to make copies for the groups we work with. Maybe I can even get the training schools to use it. If you come across things to add to it, do so. Then send me a letter about what you added or changed. With a little luck, maybe we can get more of our boys to make it home."

"Will do. It's been an honor, Sir."

Guido looked fondly at the man who had been so influential in his career and life, "I had a good teacher."

For Guido, it felt as if a great weight had been lifted from his shoulders as he turned and followed his men onto the waiting transport. The need to order his men to put their lives on the line for their country would come again, but for now, Guido could simply enjoy their company without worrying who wouldn't return from carrying out his orders. He was asleep within minutes of the plane taking off. His men lowered their voices as they babbled excitedly about returning to Italy. They took a little longer to decompress from the stress of the front. Within fifteen minutes, the only sound from the passengers was those few snores that were louder than the drone of the engines.

Cross Anchor, South Carolina, USA

Manly Lee Wilburn finished the front section of the Spartanburg Herald-Journal and tossed it across the room to his oldest son. It fluttered as all papers do when thrown, but Al still managed to catch it out of the air. The two men shared a grin for a moment before Al set down the sports section and began his perusal of the front section. M.L. simply watched him for a few minutes, taking in how his son had changed.

Al had lost the extra fat he used to carry around his waist and there was a haunted look around his eyes. Noises from other parts of the house drew a predatory glance and a cocked head until he determined what they were. His tan was a little darker and he didn't slouch like he used to. He also didn't laugh like he used to.

A loud bang from the kitchen followed by a baby crying meant that one of the kids had dropped something and startled Al's youngest, Gloria. Al looked concerned and turned to his father.

M.L. held up a hand, "If anyone was hurt, there'd be sharp words and scattering kids coming from the kitchen."

Al stifled a snicker, "Momma always did have a sharp tongue." He went back to reading as M.L. took a sip of his coffee.

Al, Vera, and their kids had gotten in late last night. The partition of Colombia had cut down on the number of troops the U.S. was keeping there. Al got a two week leave when the 5th Cavalry had been rotated home. They had driven down from Burlington, North Carolina yesterday to join in the celebration that was planned for this afternoon.

Buck, Andrew, Ralph, and Philip were all back from their basic training and Cross Anchor was throwing them a party. Al and Vera decided to make the drive down to see everyone since they'd already be gathered. But Al seemed to be jumpy since they'd arrived. It made M.L. wonder if Al's combat experience was part of the reason he'd had made the trip. Was he, let's call it concerned, about whether they would all be around for the next gathering?

Al finished the front section of the paper and looked up to see his father eyeing him. He drew a deep breath and released it before he half-turned to face M.L., "I presume you want to know why we were delayed?"

"That'd be nice, since there's nothing in the paper."

"Everything was fine until we got to Charlotte. We ran into a traffic jam downtown that turned ugly when shots were fired. We were trapped. I waited a couple of minutes, then went to see what was going on. Vera didn't like that, but I thought it was the only way we were going to get here.

"Anyway, there were three fender-benders where people had panicked and tried to move their cars when they had no place to go. Everyone was scared and a lot of them were angry. Some of the people were yelling curses at Catholics in general and the Jesuits in particular.

"After a half a mile, I came to an area that looked like some of the skirmishes I'd seen in Colombia. There were a lot of cops and two groups of civilians. The bleeding and the dead were scattered on the street between the civilians. Some Jesuits had been proselytizing downtown when a couple dozen people showed up to chase them off. Fighting broke out and the cops fired some warning shots in the air to break things up.

"I've had some basic medical training, so I helped tend to the wounded. It took a while to get the traffic straightened out and moving again."

Al looked down at the floor for a moment before he continued, "Dad, there were at least five people killed and it was early enough in the day. Why isn't there anything about it in the paper?"

M.L. shook his head, "Probably the same reason I haven't seen anything about trains getting shot up even though I've been repairing bullet-holes for the last month or two. There were reports of clashes back in June, but they stopped by July. I think the government put a lid on stories about the anti-Catholic violence. The question is whether they're doing it to keep from inciting more, or if they're just trying to cover up how much of it there is.

"Did you notice that the war reports refer to France and Italy as 'the Entente' and not 'the Catholic Entente'?"

Al sat back with a grunt, his look of concern mirroring that of his father.

The whole town turned out for the party at the Yarborough United Methodist Church that afternoon. After hugs of greeting for the returned members of the town, Pastors Bailey and Farley prayed for the safety of Cross Anchor's sons and peace and tolerance in general. M.L. wondered if they had other sources of information about anti-Catholic violence or if it was just a general prayer.

Now that the festivities were formally started, tables were set up in the yard and a buffet was created. Everyone loaded plates while the women kept a careful eye on whose offerings were the quickest to go. Pride might be a sin, but it was definitely on display among the cooks. People ate and joked, slowly gravitating into smaller groups.

Leila and the slightly bulging Courtney joined Vera and Francis as they took care of the small ones in the shade of the church. Gloria and Bobby Lee were both nearing the one-year mark and the women commiserated about the pains and joys that Courtney could expect.

The kids under ten were running around the churchyard, playing everything from cowboys and Indians to tag. M.L. was just happy they were spending all that energy here.

Most of the teenagers had split into groups by sex, though a few couples were meandering around under the watchful eyes of parents and pastors alike. The girls seemed to be paying extra attention to Andrew even if he wasn't in uniform. It made the other boys jealous and Harry unhappy.

Buck, Ralph, and Phil had joined the group of men hanging out near the back of the church when Andrew and Zach peeled off from the boys and headed towards the girls. Buck chuckled and said, "I guess Andrew's using his little brother as his wingman. I wonder which one of the girls he's set his sights on?"

Harry blew his top. He waggled his finger in Buck's face, "You will NOT drag another of my boys off to die in some God-forsaken war to keep our coffee cheap or England's king on his throne!"

Most of the people turned to see what the commotion was, and Harry threw a haymaker at Buck. Buck reacted with newly acquired skills, dodging the punch and dislocating Harry's shoulder before his brain caught up. The scream of pain got the attention of everybody else and people came running as Harry hit the ground.

Buck stood over Harry, torn between trying to help and wanting to pull back from what he'd done, mumbling, "I'm sorry" over and over. Doc Wadley jogged over to check out Harry. Al bent to help him as M.L. pulled his son-in-law away from the scene. Janice arrived, looking embarrassed more than anything else. Harry found his voice again and started cussing out Buck.

Janice closed her eyes and shouted, "SHUT UP, HARRY!"

The crowd was stunned into silence at the outburst from the usually meek Janice. Harry looked up at her with a combination of shock and anger.

Janice stared him down before continuing, "Some pacifist you are. Throwing a punch at anyone goes against everything you claim to stand for. Throwing it at someone who just finished basic training just shows how stupid you can be sometimes. Now stand up and apologize to Buck and everyone here." She glared down at her husband as her rage-fueled breathing became the only sound in the shocked pool of silence.

The anger drained from Harry's face, and he sheepishly started to get up when Doc Wadley stopped him with, "Just a second. Al?"

Al helped popped the shoulder back into place which caused another cry of pain from Harry. Then they helped him to his feet, where he stood cradling his arm. He looked both disgusted and ashamed. His sons approached him while his daughters moved to flank his wife.

It was Andrew who broke the silence. "Dad, if we do go to war, we'd rather go as pilots than as infantrymen. We'll get paid more and have a better chance of surviving."

Zach added his two cents, "And we'll get more girls."

Andrew gave him a dirty look while the crowd snickered. "Buck isn't trying to drag us into the war. He is trying to give us skills that will help us survive it if we do go."

Harry closed his eyes and gave a barely perceptible nod before wrapping his boys in a one-armed hug. He looked up while he held them close and found Buck in the crowd, "You keep him safe."

"I'll do my best" was Buck's reply.

It wasn't long before the kids were back playing. The adults were somber for the rest of the afternoon.

LATE SEPTEMBER 1938

The Chancellery, Berlin, Germany

I wearily open my eyes to read the message a second time. The idea of separating the Catholics of the Americas from Rome is going nowhere. Roosevelt thought it was a good idea, but the Archbishop of Baltimore refused to even consider it. I find the quote again, "How can I claim the authority to separate my flock from the very source of my authority?" Roosevelt's expression of disappointment mirrors my own. My chat with Ludwig Kaas about separating from the Vatican met with a similar fate.

A knock at the door is followed by Edna poking her head into my office. "Five minutes until Sir Nevile."

I smile wistfully and sigh before responding, "Thanks."

Edna's eye roll becomes an impish smile on her face, and she closes the door. Visits by the British Ambassador have become more strained for us since we learned of his involvement in the attempt on our lives.

I skim through a couple more reports before he arrives. The division we sent to Austria is nearing the end of its two-week deployment on the Italian border. The division they sent us has been staring at Belgium. Everything has gone smoothly and I write a reminder to send an appropriate message to President Broz. I clear my desk and await my 'guest'.

I stand to receive Sir Nevile Henderson when he arrives. Our relationship had been improving before he activated the French assassin. I put a smile on my face, even though I'd prefer to strangle him. After all, it's the last time I plan on seeing him.

"Good morning, Ambassador Henderson. Please have a seat. Is there anything Edna can get for you?" Greeting, seat, and the offer of refreshment, the ritual helps keep me in control.

"Good morning to you, too, Chancellor Manstein. A spot of tea would be greatly appreciated. I believe that your delightful secretary knows how I like it." His response and the presentation of his tea by Edna follow our ingrained habits. His smile seems more genuine since he 'got away with' triggering the spy. It turns my stomach. At least I know that today will be different.

"What can I do for you today?"

Sir Nevile is surprised by my direct leap into business. He looks concerned but pushes forward. "We would like your help in getting more resources from the Americas. The amount of oil and other material we've been getting has dropped lately. We know that Germany is trying to increase its reserves, but we are actively fighting a war and desperately need those imports."

I stare at him for a moment before replying, "In case you've forgotten, we're fighting a war, too. Our men are doing better in Russia than your men are on their various fronts, but why should we hamstring our efforts for you?"

"Really, Erich? You know that the Entente has their sights set on Germany, too. Yet here you are, shipping them resources they use to fuel their war production."

"And buying time for my country to resolve the Russian war and prepare for what comes after that."

"You think de Gaulle will honor his non-aggression pact with you any longer than it benefits him? Don't you remember how quickly he tossed aside the Non-Intervention Treaty in Spain?"

"He, and everyone else, too."

Sir Nevile looks annoyed and cocks his head to one side, "You know we've been dealing with French saboteurs since the fighting started. Do you think England is the only place their spies are hiding?"

I give him my first genuine smile in months. It does not convey warmth and a look of concern creeps up his face.

"We're quite certain that there are Entente spies in Germany, just like they know there are German spies in Entente territory. The big difference is that neither of us has activated any of those spies. That's partially because they tend to be one-shot attacks, and partially from concern about what the reprisals would be."

"I'm glad your country has escaped their terrorism. Mine has been suffering their attacks and bombings for four months."

"Oh, I didn't say we hadn't been attacked by their spies. Just that they weren't the ones who tried to feed us figgy pudding."

Sir Nevile freezes. I lean forward.

"Yes, Sir Nevile. We know it was the British who activated Herbert Fournier and what roll you played in it. We've known for a while. The French know that we know, and they know that we have agents in their country. Guess what? We have some in your country, too. We have reached a gentleman's agreement that the agents on both sides will remain inactive. I expect that agreement to hold unless one of us is about to lose a war against the other. The United Kingdom might want to consider whether it would like one of those agreements, too."

I lean back and look coldly at the man who almost killed Edna. He seems to tremble slightly. Good.

"The ranking members of the Reichstag have decided that information will be made public tomorrow. I trust that you will be out of the country by then. If you aren't, I can guarantee that my countrymen will not bring you to justice... I will."

Sir Nevile swallows nervously as he looks into my eyes and slowly rises from his seat. He backs to the door and opens it without taking his eyes off of me. He is surprised when Otto grabs him by his neck and spins him around. Edna delivers a slap to his face that leaves a red welt. She brushes her injury-shortened hair back from her head and spits in his face. I rise to follow his departure. Otto's grip never wavers as he pushes the British Ambassador down the halls. My staff lines those halls and watches with silent hatred as Sir Nevile is removed from the building.

Otto makes only one comment as he releases his charge at the front doors, "Please stay. It would bring joy to more people than you can guess."

Sir Nevile Henderson tries to regain his normally haughty composure, but his suppressed trembling makes him stumble as he heads down the stairs of the Chancellery.

André François-Poncet calls to request a meeting within minutes of Sir Nevile's exit. I make the French Ambassador wait. Edna, Otto, and I want some time to let our long-suppressed rage subside. Lunch helps, but we are still wound up and know there is more to this drama.

André arrives at two. I stand to receive him and direct him to a chair. He notices my annoyed look and lack of greeting as he sits and opens the conversation, "So, Ambassador Henderson isn't the only one you are displeased with."

He returns my blank stare for a few seconds before he looks away. I stare for an extra moment before responding, "It was your spy who almost killed my wife. Henderson was just the one who was stupid enough to say, 'Go.'"

André nods once, "I would say malicious, not stupid. They hoped to foster enmity between our countries."

"Good thing there isn't enough of that already."

"That and plenty of distrust. I do not know all of the spies we have in your country. Nor do I know what tasks they have been assigned or how to activate them. I have contacted my superiors and been told that we have no plans to use them."

"And we have no plans to use ours. I told Henderson that we had an agreement with you that our agents will remain inactive. I expect confirmation from your government that there actually is such an agreement."

"Of course, Chancellor."

"The story will be in the papers tomorrow. The story will point out that while the agent was yours, it was the British who sent him on his mission. We will also admit that we have similar agents in both England and France, and that we have all agreed to refrain from employing these assets. Even with that, we expect there to be a surge of anger towards both of your countries. Be careful. We will try to keep our people in line."

"I understand. Edna's injuries and recovery have endeared her to the German people. That we were involved, even if we didn't do it, means there will be anger and resentment directed our way. Unless there's anything else, I think I should get you that confirmation as soon as possible."

We both stand and he extends his hand. I glare at him for a moment before reluctantly shaking it. André heads off and I wait until he's around the corner before I wipe my hand on my trouser leg. It still feels slimy.

Oberst Ernst Weber comes in carrying a bottle of schnapps and four glasses. Otto and Edna aren't too far behind, closing the door after they enter. Ernst pours and we all raise our glasses silently. I take a heavy swig and lower my glass. Edna's is the only other glass that still has any schnapps in it.

Otto makes a face, "The nasty taste is still there."

Edna's giggles a little before responding, "Yeah, but if we drink enough to make the taste go away, we'll need someone with a wheelbarrow to get us home." We all chuckle bitterly at the shared truth.

I look back down at the remains of my drink. "The other major countries will know the details by tomorrow, as will our own people. Even the party leaders don't know how their members will react. We enter a new era tomorrow and I have no idea who will control the rudder of our ship-of-state."

When I look back up, Edna is staring at me. She says, "You will, Erich. The ship may get tossed around in the storm, but your hand on the tiller will guide us through it."

Nasiriyah, Iraq

Général de Division Roger Noiret drained his glass of water and placed it back on the conference table. He looked around at his assembled staff as they studied the maps he'd passed out. It was apparent that he wasn't the only one suffering in the heat of southern Iraq. How bad was it for his men in the field? He closed his eyes and offered a brief prayer for their comfort and well-being. He opened them, stood, and began to pace. He wondered how many of the men who followed him from Africa were wondering if they'd made the right choice. Time to get things started.

"The liberation of Iraq was a great success partly because the British didn't have a land route to reinforce their troops. Now they do. That leaves us outnumbered, outgunned, and at the long end of a tenuous supply line.

"We've identified four Indian infantry divisions on the line between us and Basra, and a fifth division in Kuwait. Intelligence says they have at least one more division in reserve at Basra. They also have Royal Navy cruisers prowling the coast and gunboats on the waterways. With the latest reinforcements, we're up to three divisions, the 8th Motorized, 14th Infantry, and 11th Armored. Two Iraqi security divisions guard the border from Amarah north. If we just sit here, they'll build up enough strength to overwhelm us. So how do we kick the Brits back into Iran?"

Général de Brigade Auguste Alaurent, commander of the 14th Infantry, rubbed his chin for a moment before responding. "My men just got here and relieved the 8th on the line. We need time to get used to this ungodly heat before we can really contribute to offensive operations."

Roger simply nodded in acknowledgment. The 14th arrived at the same time he did, and the thought of marching through this heat was almost enough to make him long for the oven-like confines of his tank. Almost.

Colonel Robert Olleris, commander of the newly formed 11th Armored, studied the maps arrayed around the table. "We could either drive south and east from Nasiriyah to Basra, or we could drive straight down from Amarah. It's their supply hub for the area. If we take or threaten it, they should withdraw their forward units back towards Iran."

Roger looked at the maps and shook his head. It was a step in the right direction, but it didn't go far enough. "That's assuming they don't simply stand and try to cut off our spearhead. And even if it does work, we're still stuck with six enemy divisions that are getting reinforced faster than we are."

He turned to the commander of the 8th Motorized, Général de Brigade Marie Joseph Edmond Welvert. "Général Welvert, you've been dealing with the Indian troops for over three months. What's your assessment of them?"

"They're tough in a fight and they're getting more of the fifty-seven-millimeter anti-tank guns to replace their older, forty-millimeter guns. That will make our tanks more vulnerable. Their guns are horse-drawn as are most of their supplies. They may lack mobility, but do not doubt their courage. Any attempt to simply go through them will be costly."

Roger simply nodded and smiled.

Welvert looked puzzled for a moment before he smiled, too. "We go around them?" He grabbed the map from the table and began examining the area east of their lines. Olleris joined him.

Roger leaned across the table to tap the map. "11th Armored attacks from Amarah towards Ahvaz, then it pushes down to the coast. 8th Motorized works as a reserve with a regiment here, one at Amarah, and one at Ahvaz. They have interior lines, but we'll be able to react to their moves since they're walking. The terrain also breaks up their possible axes of advance so no attack can be directly supported by another.

"We've got four fighter and four bomber squadrons now, so we should be able to achieve air superiority. We push a company east down each of the railways headed to India, destroying them as they go. Even if we can't hold the perimeter, their supply line should be so screwed up they'll have to depend on the sea to keep them going."

Welvert's grin was almost an evil sneer. "And they know how vulnerable that is. That's why they went through Iran."

It had taken three days, but the attack had gone off without a hitch. Olleris drove to Ahvaz against light opposition and took it in two days. He left one of his motorized infantry regiments there along with a battalion of light tanks and headed for the coast with the rest of his division.

Roger hoped the British commander would panic, but that didn't happen. Instead, he launched an attack up the road from Basra to Nasiriyah while he sent his reserve division at Basra east on a collision course with the 11th Armored. He also pulled a division out of the line facing Amarah and most of the men out of Kuwait to form a large force at Basra. Air battles whittled away at the British air force while both sides strafed the ground troops when they could.

The British attack on Nasiriyah ended on the third day. The attacking division had been driven back with heavy casualties, but it kept Roger from moving the 8th Motorized east. Olleris and the 11th Armored collided with the reserve Indian division about five kilometers from the coast in a slugfest that left the Indian division shattered and the battered French holding the coast road.

Roger and acting Général de Brigade Philippe de Hauteclocque studied the reports as they came into the new headquarters in Amarah. Sergent-chef Jean Martin brought in the latest batch along with a jug of water. He refilled the sweat-soaked officers' empty glasses and left almost before his presence was even noted. Roger called out, "Thanks, Martin" as he left the room, and Roger picked up his glass. Roger drained half of it with a sigh and held the slightly cool glass to his forehead before putting it back on the table.

"Drink, Philippe. I can't have you keeling over from heat stroke on me."

The newly minted general raised his glass in a mock salute before taking a healthy swallow. He put it down and passed the message he'd been reading to Roger. "Recon says the British are pulling their artillery out. It looks like an orderly withdrawal."

"Damn." Roger drummed his fingers on the tabletop. "Alaurent says the 14th only has one regiment ready to move forward and Welvert says that the regiment he sent to reinforce Alaurent's right flank is tired and low on ammunition."

Philippe looked grim. "Don't forget that Olleris lost a couple ammo trucks to strafing on his drive to the coast. I don't think we can put enough pressure on them to keep them from wrecking the 11th Armored in a couple of days. If they stay organized, they'll just have too much artillery."

"I know." Roger pulled a map over and looked at the rail lines in southern Iran. "What do you think of pulling the 11th north about five kilometers? It'll give the British a choice, attack our men or escape."

Philippe rubbed his chin. "They'll probably do both. An attack to push us back while the rest of their forces withdraw. Are you trying to give them an escape route?"

"Yes. They can make one if they concentrate, so let's give them a path that maximizes the damage we do to them, while minimizing what they do to us."

Philippe grinned. "I think it's the best we can do, Sir. I'll get the orders written up for Olleris." Philippe grabbed a pencil and notepad and began writing.

"And have Welvert's regiment in Ahvaz take over its defense so Olleris can move the rest of his men forward. Any extra ammo they have should go with Olleris' men. The 14ᵗʰ will advance cautiously. We want to encourage the British to leave, not to turn around and fight."

Roger went back to reading dispatches and studying his maps while Philippe finished up the orders. Roger started to call for Martin to take the orders over to the communications tent, but Philippe stopped him.

"I need to stretch my legs and I'm hungry. I'll drop them off on my way to the mess tent. You should get something to eat too."

"I'll head over in a couple of minutes. Save me a seat. Oh, and tell Martin he can go too."

He was still studying the maps, trying to figure out what the British would do, when the sounds of sporadic gunfire picked up in the distance. He was too engrossed to react until the nearby anti-aircraft guns started hammering away. Had the British figured out where he was or were they just raiding Amarah because it was where the French attack had come from? He dove under his desk as the whistling of an incoming bomb grew louder and louder.

For the second time in his military career, Roger's world went black.

The Persian Gulf

Admiral Sir Geoffrey Blake wore a satisfied look as he stood on the bridge of the *Marlborough*. He could see the planes from the first air strike returning to their carriers. It felt like the first win they'd had since May when they put the Brazilians in their place. Sir Geoffrey had wanted somewhere to test out the new pilots and planes. The isolated Entente forces in Iraq had given him the opportunity. They had flanked the Indian forces holding Basra and cut them off. The Eastern Fleet had come to their aid.

His carriers' planes had teamed up with their land-based air in Basra to finally hand the Entente a defeat in the air. The Fulmars and Hurricanes had outnumbered the D.520s almost two-to-one in the initial raid on Amarah. Thirty-six of the French fighters had fallen from the sky, while the British had lost four Hurricanes, ten Fulmars, six Blenheims, and two of the Val dive-bombers. They had also bombed the crap out of the supply route for the Entente forces in Iran.

He turned to Rear Admiral John Moore. "Send a 'Well done' and proceed to second target."

"Aye, Sir."

A call from the radio operator broke the good mood. "Planes reported over Nasiriyah, heading towards Basra."

Sir Geoffrey thought for a moment, "Send the combat air patrol to assist."

The radio operator began relaying both sets of orders.

"Think they'll make it in time?"

"It'll be close. A lot depends on how long the bastards spend over Basra."

Fifteen minutes later, the thirty-six Gladiators of the combat air patrol arrived in the sky over Basra. The Entente fighters were engaged with the defending Hurricanes, while enemy bombers approached the air base. For once, the Gladiators got a crack at the loaded French bombers without being harassed by enemy fighters and they took a heavy toll. Over half of the MB.175s were shot down before they dropped their bombs and fled. But the raid had done its damage. The airbase in Basra was left a smoking, pock-marked mess. The remaining Hurricanes headed south towards Kuwait City while the Entente planes headed northwest.

Sir Geoffrey received the reports with a grim calm and was about to order the strike on Ahvaz, when his scouts spotted a submarine in the Strait of Hormuz. This had always been a raid. The one thing Sir Geoffrey didn't want to have happen was getting caught in the Gulf at night by enemy submarines. He turned to Moore.

"Any bright ideas?"

"None that don't risk the carriers, Sir."

"Me either. Time to head home. Launch the attack on Ahvaz. Once the strike is off, the Fleet will head southeast at thirty knots. Send our regrets to the Eighth Army that we can't enjoy their company anymore."

"Aye, Sir."

The raid on Ahvaz had gone off without a hitch, and Sir Geoffrey was reading the after-action reports in his cabin. In the combined fighting, the British aviators had shot down forty-two of the French fighters and twenty-three of their bombers. They'd lost fourteen more Hurricanes in the dogfights above Basra, which brought their total to thirty-six planes lost. The almost two-to-one kill ration was the first time they had done more damage than they'd taken. Hopefully, it would throw a spanner into whatever plans the Entente had in the area. Now it was time to get his exposed ships back out to the Indian Ocean where they could maneuver.

Rear Admiral John Moore knocked on the wall as he entered the cabin. Smiling, he handed a piece of paper to Sir Geoffrey.

"We got a report from one of our men in Amarah that the French Corps commander is in the hospital, Sir. It appears Davis wasn't making it up when he said he planted his bomb on a tent with a general's stars outside."

"I just might have to present him with a bottle from my personal supply."

"I think you'll want to, Sir. The report says it was their new commander, General Noiret."

"The Butcher of Mombasa?"

"One and the same. When he got here from Tanganyika is anybody's guess. Their current offensive does reek of his tactics, though. Our agent said that Entente men were showing up in numbers and then cut off."

"Let's hope he stays safe. What's the word on the ground?"

"The Eighth Army is pulling back into Iran. We may have hurt the French ability to control the air, but they damaged the rail lines for almost sixty miles east of the border."

Sir Geoffrey sighed, "And with Operation Boxer 2 in the works, we don't have enough transports to keep them supplied by sea."

"And we won't for some time."

"It'd be nice to have a clear victory every once in a while."

"We did our part, Sir. The Eighth is sure they would be taking a lot more damage as they withdraw if we hadn't stomped on the Entente air. And if we got Noiret, there will be a lot of cheering on Whitehall."

"We can hope, John. We can hope."

Practica di Mare Air Base, Pomezia, Italy

Colonnello Guido Nobili got off the transport plane with the rest of his men. Like them, he was slightly hungover from celebrating the previous night. Unlike them, he would not be staying at their new air base southwest of Rome. A car was waiting to whisk him the forty-five kilometers to Aurora's bedside. She'd gone into labor when Guido was in Italian East Africa. By the time he made it to Libya, he was a father. Both Aurora and Dawn were doing well.

The party for his daughter's birth had turned into a long night of release for everyone as they celebrated survival and mourned their fallen. Only the fact that they would soon be reporting to Practica di Mare had kept them from drinking through the night. The flight from Libya was quieter than any Guido could remember as they all tried to recover.

The young Caporale who drove him to Rome tried to be chatty. He gave up when all he received was taciturn responses. Guido enjoyed the view of the passing farms and villages, drifting off to sleep after the first few kilometers.

They were well into Testaccio, the 20th rione of Rome, before the traffic noises roused the new father. He stared out the window and marveled at the bustle of the capital for a few minutes before he was fully awake. As a pilot, Guido had barely noticed the enlisted men who didn't work on his airplane. As he'd gained more responsibility, he'd become aware of just how critical those 'unimportant' people were to making things run. He dug in the carryall he had with him and produced his last cigar. He leaned forward and extended it to his driver.

"Sorry about earlier, Caporale. I'm just very tired. We were celebrating the birth of my daughter last night and things got a little carried away. Do you want a cigar?"

Guido's fumbling attempt at an apology almost cost him his life. He didn't know that the Caporale had won the right to drive the Air Force hero in a straw drawing contest that had twenty-two entrants. The eager driver half-turned to accept the cigar just as another car changed into their lane, cutting them off. Guido blurted 'Gah' as the Caporale jammed on the brakes and the horn. The driver did his best imitation of a fighter pilot surrounded by enemies while Guido clutched the back of the seat. It was only a moment before they were sedately driving down the road again.

Then Guido snorted, which turned into a giggle and quickly progressed to a full belly-laugh that lasted until tears leaked from the corners of his eyes. The Caporale added nervous glances at his passenger to the things he was constantly checking.

Guido looked down at the now bent and mangled cigar in his hand and shook his head. He waited until they were stopped at a red light before disturbing the young man again.

"Let me know if you ever want to be a fighter pilot. Those were some impressive evasive maneuvers you pulled back there. I'm sorry if I startled you."

"Not your fault, Sir. Things would have been fine if more of the civilians on the road had any idea how to actually drive a car." He paused for a moment before continuing, "If you don't mind me asking, what was all the laughter about, Sir?"

"After all I've been through, the thought of being killed by a bad driver in Rome just struck me as a silly way to go."

The Caporale looked visibly shaken and Guido realized his misinterpretation. "Not you, Caporale. The idiot who tried to hit us. You did an amazing job dodging him. That's why I asked if you had any interest in being a fighter pilot. That kind of situational awareness is hard to teach."

"Thank you, Sir. I'll keep that in mind, but I don't think I'm any better at it than the other men in the motor pool."

"Hmm, maybe we should be looking for fighter pilots in places we don't normally look."

Guido was very awake for the rest of the drive. He chatted amiably with the Caporale, though only when they were stopped. He got the Caporale's name, Giovanni Barcaro, and shook his hand when they arrived at his house.

"Don't forget what I said about being a pilot."

"I won't, Sir. And thank you."

Guido grabbed his bag and headed towards his door. Dawn was suckling greedily at Aurora's breast when he went inside. The dark circles around his wife's eyes showed how tired she was. She smiled up at him and tilted her head up for a kiss. He then kissed his daughter on the top of her head. Dawn fussed and waved an arm, apparently not happy with having her meal interrupted. Guido put his bag down and sat next to his wife. They quietly shared proud smiles over their daughter's head.

The reverie lasted for a good five seconds before Aurora's mother came into the room. "Welcome home, Guido. Dawn just started and you smell worse than a fisherman. Maybe you should go clean up."

Guido's exasperated smile at Aurora was met by a smirk and gentle nod. "Yes ma'am. And thank you for all your help."

"I'm happy to help... as long as I can smell the difference between the adults and used diapers."

The repentant Guido rose and bowed to his mother-in-law before blowing a kiss to Aurora. Once it was returned, he picked up his bag and headed off to his bathroom to try to remove days of accumulated sweat and dirt.

He dressed in non-military attire for the first time in months and spent the afternoon getting to know his daughter. He even got instructions on how to carry and care for her. His first diaper change was carried out under four watchful eyes that critiqued his every move. Dinner that night was tasty, but Guido had no idea of what he'd eaten, Aurora and Dawn chased all other thoughts from his head.

Dawn ate after they did, and Guido got to burp her when she was done. The little bit of spit-up was caught by a strategically placed towel on Guido's shoulder. He put his daughter into her crib and hugged his wife from behind as they cooed the baby to sleep. The tune was the one Aurora's mother had been singing to the unborn child each night. It seemed to have a remarkably calming effect on Dawn.

When she finally fell asleep, Guido nuzzled his wife's neck and gently kissed its nape.

"None of that for a while" whispered his mother-in-law from the doorway. "She needs all the rest she can get."

Aurora turned in his arms and looked up into his eyes apologetically before turning her head and leaning it against his chest. Her yawn was quiet, but Guido didn't miss it. He picked her up and started for their bedroom when her mother hissed at him.

"The girl will be up every hour or two to nurse and you look almost as tired as she is. Put her on the bed next to the crib."

Guido reluctantly obeyed and caught the soft sounds of Aurora snoring as they closed the door to the nursery.

The next morning, he got to spend a little more time with his family. All too soon, a car arrived to take him back to Pomezia. Their first students would arrive next week, and they had to get everything organized. Saturday morning would bring another trip to Quirinal Palace where Mussolini would induct him into the Military Order of Savoy.

Dawn would be christened on Sunday after mass. Benito Mussolini and Donna Rachele would stand as godparents. Luckily, Guido didn't have to do anything other than show up for those ceremonies.

It was mid-morning when Guido finally got to the air base that would be his new station. He was surprised to be greeted by most of his men. His driver made off with his bag, while his men herded him towards one of the hangers as they questioned him about his family and Rome.

They had him hemmed in against the hanger doors when Capitano Guillermo Bianchi rapped smartly on the tin doors. His men had found the mysterious hanger the previous day and been rebuffed by its inhabitants. They were told it would only be opened for Colonnello Nobili and his pilots weren't overly interested in waiting any longer to find out what was inside.

Guido turned around as the doors opened slightly, and a Frenchman stuck his head out.

"Ah, Colonnello Nobili. Please come in."

Guido wasn't sure, but he thought the Frenchman was one of the people he'd worked with in Paris when they were designing the G.51. The doors rolled back, and the Italian fliers gawked at the plane within.

It looked like a French D.520 but it was a little larger and sleeker. The Frenchman turned back to him.

"May I present the D.530. We wish to give you the honor of being the first non-Frenchman and only the fourth pilot to fly our new fighter."

Guido cheerfully accepted the honor and headed off to get his flight suit as his men did their best to examine the airplane without being allowed to touch it.

Spartanburg, South Carolina, USA

Manly Lee Wilburn and Cardy Bravo looked over the locomotive in their shop. Bullet holes riddled one side and the front of the cab. Dried blood on the floor of the cab said the engineer and fireman had not escaped unscathed.

Cardy whistled softly, "Damn. Where does it say this one came from?"

M.L. checked the paperwork, "It was pulling freight to Norfolk when it was attacked." M.L. paused for a moment. Cardy's family lived in Norfolk, and he'd been stationed there before he got out of the navy. "Do you want to check on people? I can check with Jim, but I don't think there'll be a problem."

Cardy thought for a moment, "When did this happen?"

"Paperwork says three days ago."

"I'll wait 'til lunch then. They're either okay, or there's nothing I can do about it."

"Then let's get her pulled apart and checked out. We'll need to check everything on the surface inside and trace any holes we find. There's no telling what's been damaged."

The two men spent the morning pulling the engine apart. The damage was mostly superficial. The gauges and some tubing would need to be replaced, but the larger parts were made of sturdier materials.

Still, there was enough damage to make Cardy wonder if the ambushers had a machine gun. M.L. pointed out the different sized holes, "It's more likely that there were several people with hunting rifles. Probably at least a dozen of them."

Cardy's softly whispered "Damn" generated a lingering silence as they worked to repair the damage. They took a break around ten and M.L. went to check with their boss about the long-distance call for Cardy. Jim agreed to it, as long as he got to hear what the news was.

M.L. and Cardy had just finished laying out the new parts for the engine when Jim joined them in the workshop. "It's about that time, Cardy. Why don't y'all come up to the office, it's quieter in there. You can use my phone and there are seats for all of us. We can eat lunch after the call and chew on whatever tidbits you get."

They washed up and grabbed their lunch pails. Once they were settled around Jim's desk, Cardy made the call to his family. As the call went on, the usually animated Cardy got quieter and quieter. Jim and M.L. exchanged worried glances.

Only ten minutes had passed when Cardy hung up the phone. From the half of the conversation they'd heard, Jim and M.L. didn't think things were going well. They waited patiently while he gathered his thoughts.

"My folks are fine, and they said this wasn't the first attack. The track and road that runs southwest from Norfolk to Suffolk has been the sight of attacks on trains and trucks for almost a month. The group that attacked this engine was caught and lynched. There were eight of them, including two sixteen-year-old kids. All of them were members of St. Mary's Catholic Church and claimed they were doing God's work. The next day, a train was derailed by another group from the same church. Two of them were shot and killed. The other three are in jail along with the church's pastor. The church was burned to the ground last night. The fire department made sure the fire didn't spread, but they didn't make any effort to save the church itself."

Jim sat back and M.L. softly swore before restarting the conversation. "I bet there isn't a peep about this in Saturday's paper."

Jim looked thoughtful, "You think they'll cover it up?"

"Would you want to give people ideas about sabotage or mob justice? I bet Roosevelt has another one of his fireside chats, too, calling for unity and tolerance."

Cardy glumly lifted his head, "My mom and family are fine, but my dad is a die-hard Catholic. Don't get me wrong, he loves America, but mom's worried that someone will decide he's a threat because of his religious beliefs. The other parishioners at his church have already reported incidents that have them all nervous."

Jim just shook his head before commenting, "What in the hell has the Entente unleashed?"

M.L. quietly added, "And will we survive it?"

EARLY OCTOBER 1938

The Chancellery, Berlin, Germany

I drum my fingers on my desk, torn between my happiness at seeing an old friend and my loathing at having to deal with anyone from the United Kingdom. The thought hits me that my disgust probably mirrors how Ambassador Bernstorff felt all those years ago when I showed up on his doorstep in America. I take a deep breath and let it out. I will try to remember that Sir Phipps was not personally responsible for his government's actions.

It's almost five past ten when Edna knocks on my door and opens it. She ushers him in with a, "Sir Phipps to see you."

Sir Eric Clare Edmund Phipps had been the ambassador from Britain for four years before Sir Nevile replaced him. We had been on good terms when he left and he'd always been friendly. He'd also always been punctual. He already has a cup of tea and his eyes are moist and red. I glance at Edna and she gives me a brief smile. I guess he wanted to talk to her before he came in. If she can be accepting, then that's the least I can do. I stand and extend my hand, saying "Good to see you, Sir Phipps" as Edna closes the door.

Sir Phipps hesitates a moment before he takes it while staring into my eyes. "No, it's not, Manstein. I'm here because my predecessor and my government screwed up so royally that I'm their only hope of repairing our relationship. I apologize for what happened. Not because

Downing Street wants me to, but because I'm ashamed of what my countrymen did."

I close my eyes and nod briefly before giving his hand one vigorous shake which rattles the teacup in his other hand. I open my eyes and release his hand, "Take a seat."

We both sit and Sir Phipps takes a sip of what I suspect is lukewarm tea. He puts the cup and saucer down and tilts his head slightly, "I'm supposed to spin you tales of how my government had no part in what happened to you and Edna. How we need to stick together to stop the Entente and keep the world safe from fascism." He stops for a moment and his eyes unfocus, like he's staring at something far away. I sit back and wait while he gathers his thoughts.

With a little shake of his head, he continues, "Someone very highly placed authorized triggering the French spy. They're still trying to figure out exactly who it was. But it doesn't really matter for us. They are high enough up that they can make decisions about our policies, so the action was effectively sanctioned by my government.

"The extra sanctions that you and the League have put into place are totally justified, but I need to know if there's any way we can get them lifted. Things have gone downhill quickly in the last two weeks. The League is still shipping food, but they've stopped everything else and we're having to choose between distributing that food to our people and flying our planes to protect them from French bombing raids. Our factories are only running part time, even though we desperately need the weapons they turn out to replace our losses. If things don't change, we expect thousands to freeze this winter and I don't know how long we'll be able to continue the war."

Sir Phipps stops with a shrug. I lean forward and clasp my hands on my desk before responding, "And what would you have Germany do?"

He smiles despondently, "Forgive us if you can. Take pity on our people if you can't. Act as a mediator for peace, if you can't extend the pity we don't deserve. Try to imagine what may happen if the Home Islands fall."

"That last point is the only reason the Reichstag was willing to let you into the country. Edna and I know you, and don't blame you for what happened, but we've had more time to come to grips with the attack than the German people have had. They are not in a forgiving mood right now, and I doubt that will change any time soon. Members of the Reichstag are trying to keep those flames of hatred burning to increase their power. They're also using it to push for more military spending, something I fully support.

"I'm sorry, Sir Phipps, but forgiveness will be a long time coming. Pity for the plight of your people will come sooner, but I doubt it will be soon enough to help this winter. I doubt I can even get the Reichstag to let us act as a mediator, I expect them to send you to the League."

Sir Phipps finishes his tea and heaves himself to his feet. He looks like he's aged ten years in the past few minutes and there is a deep sadness in his eyes as he stands, and I rise. He extends his hand and breaks our old convention of not using our shared first name, "Thank you, Erich."

I take his hand and his sadness leeches into my soul. "I wish things were better between our countries, Eric."

He drops my hand and lets himself out. I watch him leave, wondering what the future will bring.

My weekly briefing is anything but brief. My meeting with the Reichstag leaders isn't either. Hugenberg and Wels say their constituents are out for blood and would support a declaration of war on Britain, France, or both of them. Thälmann and the Communist Party would support it too but think we should get out of Russia first. Kaas says the Centre Party is all for war with Britain, but not France. He also points out that a lot of his constituents are being harassed. The backlash I had feared seems to be coming home to roost.

I look around the table at them, "I know our people are angry, but going to war with either side right now is a really bad idea. Our best equipment is several hundred kilometers inside Russia, and it's stuck there because of the mud. Hitting France would get a lot of our men killed and make us more vulnerable. Attacking the British would leave us less vulnerable, but it helps the French."

Hugenberg leans forward, "I'm not sure the German people care. They want blood and it's going to get nasty if they don't get it. I think our only way out of this without more shooting is if you and Edna make some kind of grand gesture with the bastards."

Wels interrupts, "Do we really have spies out there just waiting for their orders to assassinate the leaders of France and the United Kingdom?"

The room goes quiet as they all wait for my answer. "We have deep cover operatives in most countries that could be given orders to take out enemy leaders. We don't have anyone whose only task is to do so."

"So, a lie."

I concede the point, "No, a half-truth. And one that's truer now than it used to be. We've had deep-cover men in both countries ask if they could return the favor. We're trying to make sure that none of them decide to take matters into their own hands."

Hugenberg looks at his fellow political leaders, each giving a slight nod as he polls them. When he turns back to me, it's with a seething anger boiling just below the surface.

"The Reichstag will vote to increase the military budget by fifty percent with a tax increase to pay for it. We will formally request meetings with the League of Nations, and specifically the USGA, about mutual defense agreements. We will request that a delegation be sent to Sweden to try to get the Russians to come to the peace table. Finally, we will recommend a cessation of all trade with both the United Kingdom and the Catholic Entente."

I look around the table before responding, "That will put us in violation of our non-aggression treaty with the Entente."

Hugenberg shakes his head, "No. Part of that bill will be our view that the Entente abrogated the treaty when their agent was used in the assassination attempt. How they react will determine our future course."

"So, you want to slap them in the face for what they've done and see if they apologize or rattle their saber."

"Exactly, Chancellor."

Basra, Iraq

Général de Division Roger Noiret sat at his desk for the first time in almost two weeks. OK, it wasn't really his desk, it was a narrow table that Sergent-chef Jean Martin had placed over the long cast on his right leg. The leg was propped up in a chair on the far side of the table while his crutches were leaning on the wall behind him. His bruised ribs and sprained wrist had healed enough that he could finally use the crutches to get around.

Amarah had been another Mombasa. The Iraqis had been confined to their houses as the French offensive rolled through. Radio signals from a Sunni area had been detected and the area had been cordoned off. The Sunni minority had been placed in power by the British, while France worked with the Shiite majority. Inquiries were met with stony silence,

The mixed Iraqi-French security troops were still deciding what to do when the air raid had hit. Another broadcast was detected from the four-block area right after the attack and the commanders on the ground reacted with a righteous vengeance. No one was allowed out and nothing was left standing. Roger had offered up a single prayer for those in the area that had been too young to know what their parents did. The rest could enjoy their time in Purgatory.

Roger scanned the situation report that had been prepared by Général de Brigade Philippe de Hauteclocque, Philippe's promotion had been confirmed while Roger was in the hospital. Troops and equipment were pouring in. The Iraqi Corps had doubled in size. Another motorized and two more infantry divisions had been added to his command. The airbases in Kuwait and around Basra were being expanded to handle an increasing number of planes. The Iraqi security forces were being expanded, too. They were even building a new oil pipeline from Kirkuk to Beirut at a frantic pace.

The British 8th Army had pulled back into Iran. It seemed to be intent on defending the Gachsaran oil field that was about three hundred kilometers east of the Iran-Iraq border. Roger's men occupied about fifty kilometers of Iran. Between the two forces was the largest no-man's land Roger had ever seen. The 8th Army had ripped up the railways as they'd retreated east, finishing the job the French raiders had started.

Philippe came into the room with a smile. "Good to see you up and about, Sir."

Roger eyed his ever-dapper executive officer before responding, "I'm not sure why I bothered. You've got everything in hand, and we seem to be in a stalemate with the British. Unless we plan on attacking Saudi Arabia, there doesn't seem to be a lot to do."

Philippe pulled a chair up next to Roger's exposed toes and sat. "I don't see that happening any time soon. And I don't think we're going to push deep into Iran, either." He scratched his chin. "There were a couple of days of excitement, but after the constant grind through Africa, this almost seems like we've been put out to pasture."

Roger glumly nodded, "I'm not sure which itches more, my cast and stitches, or my desire to be doing something. How are things going with the Iraqi population?"

"The Shiites are happy to finally be in charge of their own country. The Sunnis are keeping their heads down. I'm not sure if it's because of Amarah or their desire to stay out of the Shiites' way. The Sunnis threw their weight around a lot when the British put them in charge."

"Is there anything we need to do?"

"I don't think so. There were a few incidents early on where Sunnis who had abused their power were arrested and executed, but things have settled down in the last week. I'm more worried about what our men will do. I'm trying to keep them busy, but men sitting around near cities full of women has always been the bane of discipline."

"Even if those women are covered from head-to-toe."

"Even then."

The two generals sat in silence for a few moments before Roger gave an exasperated sigh. "Well, this isn't helping. Grab my crutches and help me up, if you would. I'm going to hobble around a bit before I push High Command for some kind of direction."

It was two days before Roger got new orders from France. They were happy that things had stabilized in southern Iraq but as expected, pushing into or through Iran was not something they thought was feasible. There would be a buildup of forces in the region. Général de Brigade Marie Joseph Edmond Welvert, commander of the 8th Motorized Division, would be promoted to Général de Division and take over the Iraqi Corps. Roger and Philippe were to report to the Army Command Post in Paris for their next assignment. Once again, Roger was allowed to bring as much of his staff as he wanted.

Roger gathered them in a conference room in Basra and read his orders to them. "It sounds like I'll get a new command, but I have no idea what or where it will be. Things should be quiet here for a while. There will be no censure of anyone who wants to stay and recuperate a bit, but I would be proud to have each of you accompany me wherever I am sent. You have two days to make a decision."

The response was immediate and gratifying to Roger. With one exception, they wanted to follow him on the next leg of his journey. Lieutenant-Colonel Alexandre Thomas was quiet while the others babbled excitedly about returning to France.

Roger held up a restraining hand to ask for quiet and the conversations died down. "Thomas?"

The dependable regiment commander cocked his head to one side, "If Olleris goes with you, Sir, who will take over 11th Armored?"

Roger smiled with a slight head nod, "Someone chosen by me and Welvert. I can't see him objecting if you want the job."

Thomas looked down at the table for a moment and rubbed his fingers on it in a small circle. He looked back up with a heavy sigh, "Then I'll stay here to learn the business of running a division, as long as you keep me in mind down the road."

"I discussed these orders with Welvert, yesterday. He wanted me to leave at least one of the armored commanders here. We wondered if I would have to push someone to stay and help him. I'm glad that you're interested in the job, Colonel Thomas."

Whoops of congratulations for the promotion quickly died down, as the tight knit group realized they would be leaving their friend behind. They were replaced by murmured comments of good luck and that he'd be missed.

As it quieted down, Roger and Thomas locked eyes. A sad but proud Roger offered some final advice. "Learn from Welvert and train your replacement so you'll be available when I call."

"Will do, Sir."

1000 Miles East of Mombasa, Kenya

Admiral Sir Geoffrey Blake gazed at the placid Indian Ocean from the railing of the *Marlborough*. Rear Admiral John Moore stood next to him with a death grip on the railing. Sir Geoffrey smirked and said, "Annoying, isn't it?"

John heaved a heavy sigh, "Was it this bad for you?"

"You get used to it. It helps if you understand that your control of the *Marlborough* wasn't as absolute as you think it was. You think you gave orders and everybody jumped. In reality, you gave orders that were passed down through the chain of command until they got to the right person, who jumped. Having to work through your squadron's captains is no different than working with your department heads."

The new commander of the 1ˢᵗ Battlecruiser Squadron shrugged, "My mind knows that's true, but my heart feels like it did when my son left home to join the Army."

"Give it time, and the whole squadron will take its place."

They cruised on in companionable silence for a few minutes. John started back into the bridge several times. Each time, Sir Geoffrey grunted and held up a restraining hand. Eventually, Sir Geoffrey looked at his watch and said, "Reports should be in soon. Getting there too early will make Glennie think you're either nervous or don't trust him."

"And if both are true?"

"They usually are, but his performance, and the ship's, will suffer if you let him know."

John stared at his mentor and remembered the times he'd left John on the bridge while Sir Geoffrey stood at this very railing. And he remembered the desire to justify the trust that Sir Geoffrey displayed by leaving him to run his ship. Had Sir Geoffrey been as nervous as he was? A bare smile came to John's lips and he gave a single curt nod. Sir Geoffrey's smile was that of a proud father. They turned and headed inside.

Commodore Irvine Glennie was new to the ship and crew, but he was doing well at remembering crewmen names and duties. He gave a nod of recognition to the admirals and went back to reading reports. He shuffled what he was reading to the back of the pile he held and looked up. Apparently, he'd come to the end of them.

John looked at Sir Geoffrey, expecting him to lead the conversation. Sir Geoffrey casually looked everywhere else. John took the hint. The chain of command said that the conversation was his, not Sir Geoffrey's. He tried to remember the casual way Sir Geoffrey had when they weren't in battle.

"What's the situation, Glennie?"

"All's quiet at the moment, Sir. But I don't like some of the reports from our shore bases. Trincomalee reports a drop in submarine activity over the last month, while Cape Town reports an increase."

"You think the Entente is concentrating them around South Africa?"

"It would make their intercepts easier, Sir."

"Recommendations?"

"I think we need to get to work clearing them out of the convoy's path as soon as possible, Sir."

John gave an approving nod and turned to find an attentive Sir Geoffrey standing with his hands clasped behind his back. "Request permission to take my squadron and the *Ark Royal* south-southwest at twenty-five knots, Sir. We'll begin anti-submarine operations south of Madagascar and sweep southwest along the convoy's intended route."

Sir Geoffrey considered the proposal for a moment before responding, "Take *Formidable* instead. You can use the land-based scouts to supplement your search patterns. We'll need the extra planes the *Ark Royal* carries to keep up an effective patrol on the way. I'll transfer to the *Resolution* and stay with the convoy. We'll be a couple of days behind you, so take your time as you clear the path for us."

While the Eastern Fleet escorted its convoy to Cape Town, the Entente ran its own convoy down the east coast of Africa. Sir Geoffrey would have loved to intercept it, but the sixty tankers in the convoy he guarded carried oil that was desperately needed in the British Isles. There was no way he would take chances with its protection.

Six days later, the convoy arrived at Cape Town. There had been no major incidents and three enemy submarines had been sunk. The 2nd Battlecruiser Squadron claimed two more as they escorted the return convoy that was headed to India.

They exchanged their charges for the supply and equipment convoy headed back to India. Once they left the African continent, Sir Geoffrey had them cruise east for an extra five hundred miles. The merchant captains asked why they were going out of their way and Sir Geoffrey replied, "Security." There was a lot of grumbling, but the merchants didn't have a lot of options and followed where their escorts led.

Four days later, they were well east of Madagascar and Sir Geoffrey was pleased that they hadn't encountered anything on their way back to India. He was back at the railing outside of the bridge on the *Marlborough* when John came out to join him. When his second-in-command didn't join him at the rail, Sir Geoffrey turned from the sea to find out why. The cold anger of John's eyes and the report in his hand made Sir Geoffrey close his eyes and pinch his nose in fear.

"Please tell me it's not the tankers" he half pleaded.

"Sorry, Sir. I was there when you reminded Rear Admiral McHugh to be careful and alter his course on his return trip. He followed the letter of your orders. His return course was a grand total of five miles west of his course to Cape Town. Two different groups of six submarines hit the convoy. McHugh claims they sank eight of them."

"And how many tankers went down?"

"Forty-three, Sir."

Sir Geoffrey finally opened his now watery eyes and looked back up at John. "I'll push for formal charges on dereliction of duty, but I'm not sure what good it will do. England needed that oil to keep the RAF and Navy running. And it needs those tankers to have a chance to keep the oil flowing."

Sir Geoffrey turned back to the sea, "It's going to be a cold and perilous winter for our countrymen."

Practica di Mare Air Base, Pomezia, Italy

Colonnello Guido Nobili slipped and pulled into a tight turn. He enjoyed the feel of the open cockpit and grace of the CR.42. He was also thankful that he didn't have to go into combat in one. The CR.42 had been intended as the successor to the CR.32 he flown in Spain. It was faster than the Gladiator fighters the British had been using on their carriers for over two years. The Gladiators that his men had been slaughtering.

The British were replacing the Gladiator with the Fulmar, and while the Fulmar might carry more guns, it was just as slow and maneuverable as the CR.42. That's why he and his men were flying them in today's fleet attack training exercise. Almost all of the CR.42s produced were now based at Practica for his training exercises. Unfortunately, this set of pilots were just as predictable as the first ones who had come through last week.

Commandant Claude Lefebvre and his squadron of French pilots were less familiar with the Italian biplanes, so they were tasked with attacking the inbound bombers. Many of Guido's men had flown CR.32s for years. Their squadron engaged the fighters assigned to protect those bombers. This week, the trainees were flying the MS.406. It was the front-line French fighter two years ago. Now, the French were phasing them out. Guido shook his head at the thought that these fighters were gladly accepted by the Regia Aeronautica. They were still an improvement over the older Italian fighters. He wondered how many of his countrymen would die because of poor equipment if war broke out on the continent.

Guido came back to the present task with a vengeance. If Italian pilots died, it wouldn't be because he hadn't tried his best. He ordered, "A Squadron, go!"

His eighteen planes dove towards the thirty-six torpedo bombers that were advancing on the cruisers and destroyers that were playing today's target. The CR.42s picked up speed as they dove and it was only a few seconds before Guido was rewarded with Lefebvre's voice on the radio, "Enemy moving to engage. B Squadron, go!"

B Squadron began its dive towards the torpedo planes and kept an eye on A Squadron's tail. The MS.406s were steadily gaining on Guido's fighters. It was barely a minute before the next call came over the radio.

"Pivot in three..., two..., one..., now!"

Guido's squadron pulled out of their dives and turned their aircraft as tightly as they could, racing back up at the intercepting trainees.

The trainees were thrown into chaos as they dodged their suddenly approaching targets and the massed guns now pointing in their direction.

The trainees did a good job of regrouping and engaging Guido's fighters. They had claimed six of Guido's pilots and only lost two of their own when Lefebvre's voice came over the general channel. "Splash eighteen. Moving to engage the rest."

Guido chuckled and joined Lefebvre on the general channel. "Mission complete. All aircraft return to base."

Thirty minutes later, Guido walked onto the auditorium stage and looked out over the assembled pilots. His men lazed in the back while the trainees crowded the front. Guido stopped and came to parade rest, waiting for the murmured conversations to die down.

"Capitano Romano, while observing from the ground, what did you see?" Romano was one of the two fighter squadron commanders who had watched this morning's exercise from the coast. He and the rest of group two would get their chance in this afternoon's session.

Romano stood, "Sir, your fighters peeled off to go after group one's bombers and Capitano D'Angelo pursued to protect them. When Commandant Lefebvre's fighters headed into the fray, I thought it was to provide cover for your group. And it looked like D'Angelo had done his job when your men turned to engage him. I wasn't sure what your lesson was until Lefebvre's fighters dove right past the fight and kept going towards the bombers."

Guido tried his best to look stern, but a slight smile crept onto his face. Romano was honest enough to admit that the maneuver had surprised him, something last week's Capitano refused to do. "This was a tactic the British carrier-based fighters surprised us with on our first encounter. Luckily, we had more fighters than they did, and Lefebvre held his men back from the initial British intercept. When the second group of Gladiators dove, Lefebvre moved to intercept them and pursued them past the area of the initial dogfight.

"You don't have the luxury of outnumbering us. I want you all to get together and decide how you should handle the exercise. I look forward to this afternoon's engagement."

Guido was about to dismiss them when one of the group one pilots stood up with a "Sir?"

"Yes?"

"I understand your point, but I'm pretty sure we would have gotten all of you and your men." The young pilot sat back down.

"Almost guaranteed, Tenente. And we would have taken down a number of your fighters. We would have also taken down all of your bombers. We lose eighteen planes; you lose forty to forty-five. Our eighteen fighters carry eighteen trained aircrew. The forty planes you would have lost carry around two hundred trained aircrew. And each of the fighters is cheaper to make than the bombers are. Add in that any of the bombers that get through can sink a ship, killing dozens or hundreds more. If that ship happens to be our carrier, our planes will end up in the water, whether or not you shot us down.

"At Dire Dawa, we launched a successful raid against the British navy. Unfortunately, the British countered with a long-range raid on our airbase. It was close, but we managed to get one of our airstrips operational before our raid returned. If we hadn't, we would have lost most of our wing to crash landings. What I'm about to say applies to your fellow airmen, your mechanics, the men on the ground defending your base, the ships defending it from the sea, even the people who supply and feed you."

Guido paused for a moment, then began pacing back and forth on the stage. The pain of the men he'd lost, and Ricci's sacrifice to save Guido came back like a tremendous weight. Tears came to his eyes, and he stopped. He tensely turned back to the trainees, "Every one of you needs to understand this. We are at war. Each and every one of us is expendable. It is almost guaranteed that people in this room will die in battle. Our job is to make sure that those who do die, don't die in vain.

That their loss costs the enemy as much as possible, both in men and weapons.

"If you don't consider your fellow military men as brothers now, you certainly will once you've been in combat. There may come a time when you have to decide whether it's you who will die, or one or more of them. Your brothers will notice what you choose and if you put more emphasis on personal glory than their lives. When it comes time for them to make that decision, do you think they'll be willing to die for you? Will they risk themselves for you? Do you think they'll even follow your orders?"

The auditorium went quiet, and Guido let them think for a few moments before asking for any other comments or questions. When the somber crowd stayed quiet, Guido said, "Group two, you're up at two o'clock. You'll be on your own after the exercise. I want all of you to figure out what you did right and what you screwed up today. We'll meet in the auditorium tomorrow morning to discuss things. Dismissed."

The afternoon session went about as Guido expected. Half of the trainee fighters held back when Guido's squadron dove to engage, waiting for Lefebvre's fighters to commit. Lefebvre dove and the trainees pounced, proud of their discipline and refusal to repeat group one's mistakes. They weren't expecting it when both Guido and Lefebvre had their men stop their dives and turn to face their pursuers. Both trainee squadrons scattered in disarray.

Both of Guido's squadrons continued their tight turns, nosing back into dives for speed as they slammed their throttles home. By the time the trainees had recovered from their evasive maneuvers, Lefebvre was closing to engage Guido's pursuers while Guido's men were closing on the loaded bombers. It was Lefebvre's men who would have died this time, but the end result was the same.

Guido was pleased when the returning pilots were clustered in groups, trying to figure out how to combat his instructors. Tomorrow the lessons would extend to the bombers.

Cross Anchor, South Carolina, USA

Manly Lee Wilburn and Cardy Bravo wearily climbed into M.L.'s truck at the Piggly Wiggly. This was the second straight six-day work week with ten-to-twelve-hour shifts, and it didn't look like things would ease up any time soon. Jim was trying to find more help, but so was everyone else. The draft left holes in the very workforce the Army needed to build their weapons and supply them.

M.L. sighed, "How'd you do here?"

Cardy looked over the list he'd gotten back from the grocery store before answering, "All of what we needed, but only about two-thirds of the extra stuff that Heather wanted."

"Same here. At least we did better at Lowe's."

"Yeah, but how long will that last?"

M.L. rubbed his chin and cranked up the truck, "I think Lowe's will keep up as long as there isn't any hoarding. Same goes for the Piggly Wiggly, at least for the staples. I don't think they'll cut too much into the basics. The government understands that people need to be able to eat and get to work. Otherwise, they can't produce the weapons the army needs. I do kinda wonder if they won't start rationing things though."

M.L. pulled out of the parking lot and they headed south. Traffic was worse on Saturday evening than it was during the week and Cardy kept quiet until they were out of town.

Once things had settled down, he went back to yakking, "My mom said they've already started rationing things in Norfolk. People were scared after the incidents last month and started hoarding everything they could get their hands on."

"Makes sense that the bigger cities would have problems sooner. We don't have rationing here, but Harry said the stores've put limits on how much you can buy. That's probably why Lowe's and the Piggly Wiggly started their pick-up service. It lets them fill the orders without having to argue about how many of an item you can get. It also cuts down on how much shelf restocking they have to do."

"All I know is it means I can get our shopping done without forcing Heather to make extra trips up here. Things are closed by the time we get off work during the week. And there's no way we could go through the stores after work on Saturdays before they close."

"It was a tad busy back there. I wonder how many of the city-folk are in the same boat?"

Cardy shrugged, "At least the extra hours at work are paying for the extra cost of everything, but how long will they? I think we need to talk to Jim about pay raises."

M.L. nodded his head, "I think you're right. Things are going to get worse before they get better. Leila is worried that the money we have saved is losing value and won't be enough for any emergencies if prices keep rising."

"Heather said the same thing to me, but she also pointed out that our mortgage payment is taking a smaller bite out of our budget than it used to."

"Aren't you glad you aren't looking for a house now?"

"You better believe it. My folks are on the other end of the stick. Dad isn't working much. They live off his retirement from the Navy and their savings. With prices going up, they're going through those savings a lot faster than they used to. Mom is looking for odd jobs to help, but I'm worried about what'll happen to them."

"Is your dad still getting grief for being Catholic?"

"Some. He thinks that's why people aren't hiring him for work. His auto shop used to be pretty busy. You'd think business would pick up with things getting harder to replace. But his business has actually slowed down. He said he only sees about half of the people he used to think of as regular customers. My brother said he checked around and all the other shops in the area are backed up, just not my Dad's."

M.L. shook his head in disgust. "And he served this country for forty years. People."

"It's the other veterans and men in the military who are keeping him open. It's the civilians who've abandoned him. Mom's not happy with a bunch of people from church, but Dad says he understands. Until things settle down, they need to look after themselves. We all just hope that things settle down before they run out of savings."

They rode on in silence for a few miles and M.L. began to understand just how worried his chatty friend must be. He decided to try to get Cardy onto a different subject. They had listened to the Georgia Tech – Notre Dame football game on the radio this afternoon while working. "How'd you like today's football game?"

Cardy perked back up, "It was a lot closer than I thought it would be. If Beinor hadn't recovered that fumble in the third quarter, things would have been even tighter."

"Do you think he'll win the Heisman this year?"

"An offensive lineman? Not a chance. They always give it to a quarterback or running back. I doubt he'll get any votes, even though he's the reason their running game works so well. That boy can sure knock a hole in defenses..."

M.L. sat back and enjoyed it as Cardy chattered excitedly about his favorite sport. He wasn't sure where Cardy had developed his passion for college football, but talking about it was something that seemed to cheer him up. It made things seem to be closer to normal, at least for a while.

LATE OCTOBER 1938

The Reichstag, Berlin, Germany

I pace back and forth, more nervous than I've been in years. Edna is heading to the podium to address the assembled Reichstag and, through the numerous microphones and cameramen, the German people. This is not what she signed up for when she married me, but she knows how important it is.

Edna places her speech on the podium and looks around at the assembled crowd. She brushes her fingers through the hair over her left ear, a new habit of nervousness that reminds those attending of her injuries. Flashing lights startle her and she quickly drops her hand. But the unconscious moment was caught and will be memorialized in tomorrow's papers.

"Members of the Reichstag, Bundesrat, and people of Germany, thank you for letting me speak with you at this time of peril for our beloved country. I am not a politician, nor have I sought notoriety, but I find myself at the center of a test of our way of life. A test we cannot afford to fail.

"It has been four months since the attack on my husband and me. Four months of painful recovery. Four months of digging for the truth. Four months of trying to figure out what to do once we found the truth. Four months of joy at your outpouring of support. Because of your support, I am fully recovered from my injuries. Now I ask for your continued support as our nation tries to heal.

"One of the things we feared would happen, was that the action of a few would be reflected on so many. My attacker was a French Catholic spy, but he was sent on his mission by a British Protestant diplomat. The actions of the men involved do not indict everyone who shares their religion or nationality. If it did, we would have to empty all of the churches."

That gets a nervous chuckle from the assembled crowd, and I begin to hope that this will work.

"The actions of the men involved indict only themselves and the governments that triggered them. We must not, we cannot, turn on our neighbors purely based on their religious beliefs or where they used to live. Many of you want to do something, to strike back at those who colluded in this attack. I, and our government, appreciate your fervor. But you need to report your suspicions to us rather than act on them yourselves. There are some who see this as an opportunity to settle old scores, and whisper lies to fan your anger. Some of those whispering may actually be friends of the dead assassin, trying to sow discord and suspicion to weaken our will.

"I ask that you stay vigilant, but report what you see rather than act as our enemies wish. Come together and support our neighbors, our military, and our country so that Germany will stay strong and retain her place as a leader among nations. Thank you."

I'm not sure how much of the applause is political theater to encourage those listening, but it is definitely thunderous. Edna waves once and places her right hand over her heart for a moment before turning to leave the stage. Her eyes are wide and amazed as she nears me.

I beam with pride as she hugs me, and we turn to go. Security is airtight as Otto leads us to our waiting car and we head back to the Chancellery. Edna turns to me, "Is that what it's like when you give a speech?"

"I wish. When I give one, there's usually almost half of the people who are dead set against what I'm saying. I've never gotten them all to agree with me, let alone gotten their enthusiastic support. You were great."

"I hope it makes a difference. I don't want our child to grow up in a country that's consumed by hate."

My brain stops and nothing seems to work for a moment before I stammer out, "You're pregnant?"

Edna smiles and leans in for a kiss, transferring her smile to me. I grab her hand, sit back and mutter, "I'll be damned." That gets a laugh from the front seat.

Otto turns his head and says, "She finally told you?"

Edna gives him a dirty look, but I just sigh, "How long have you known?"

"I've suspected for a couple of weeks and been certain for one."

Edna looks exasperated. "How?"

Otto actually looks a little embarrassed as he replies, "Everything comes through Security, ma'am. Everything that comes in, and everything that goes out. Even the trash."

"And I'm normally as regular as clockwork."

"Yes, you are. I presume the doctor confirmed it at your check-up yesterday?"

"She did."

We ride home with Edna snuggled up against me. I proudly drift along, happier than I've been in years.

It takes a few days, but Edna's appeal seems to calm things down. The incidence of targeted violence drops, and the German people return to a friendlier public demeanor. Franz Gürtner says that the anger is still there, but everyone is trying to suppress it. It's the best we can hope for at the moment, but another big incident could set things off like a volcano.

The French take a cue from Edna's speech and Charles de Gaulle issues a formal apology for their part in the attempt on my life. The next day, the Reichstag votes to resume trade with them. Neville Chamberlain follows suit, but it falls flat when they place the blame squarely at the feet of the French. The Reichstag is still debating a resumption of trade with them when news of the British invasion of China gets out. The discussion is ended with a near unanimous vote against it.

I get Brent to come home for the weekend so we can tell him the good news. Peter Hipper comes with him. He's been like a brother to Brent and a son to me for years. Both of them congratulate us and rub Edna's belly, though Brent does defiantly assert that he's not changing any diapers. We overeat with joy as Beatrice does her best to make us explode. We even manage to get her to join us in a toast to Edna's pregnancy.

It's fairly late by the time Beatrice heads home and the rest of us gather in the living room. Edna is cuddled up next to me on the couch, half asleep. Her pregnancy seems to be tiring her out already. My arm is around Edna's shoulders, but my eyes are on Brent. My son takes a sip of his schnapps and looks at me sheepishly.

"I know today should just be about Edna and the baby, but we don't get to talk that often. Is it okay to discuss…", he waves his empty hand around and finishes plaintively, "things?"

Edna's eyes open all the way, and she sighs sourly, "Where could you have possibly gotten this obsession with work?" Her poke in my ribs startles me and makes her laugh. She removes my arm from her shoulders, sits up, and turns expectantly back to Brent with a smile.

Peter chuckles as Brent shrugs guiltily. "Is the oil situation in England as bad as it seems to be? Our logistics class has been running the numbers and they don't look good."

I try to be non-committal, "I think that most people would agree with you. It has been the cornerstone of the Entente strategy since the beginning of the war."

"I'm trying to read more newspapers like Mr. Hitler does, but I just don't have enough time. I did see an article in a French paper about a convoy attack in the South Atlantic where they lost six submarines. It struck me as odd that they reported it as a successful attack with that many losses. They claimed fifty-one enemy ships sunk, but they didn't list any warships. It made me wonder. How big was the convoy escort that it managed to sink six submarines? And what was so valuable that the French had that many submarines out hunting it? I can't see the British sending more troops to the home islands, and the only other thing that's that valuable is oil. I didn't bring this up in class, but if I'm right, things in England are going to grind to a halt."

"Intelligence has reported on that convoy, though the British claim they sank eight submarines and lost forty-three of sixty merchant ships. It was escorted by their 2nd Battlecruiser Squadron. Its admiral has been relieved of command, so yes, the convoy was very important."

Brent sits back, concern and calculations running across his face. "That's still too many. Will the British be able to keep things running? And if they can't, what do we do?"

"Your logistics class isn't the only one squeezing the numbers. And you aren't the only one wondering what we should do to use the situation to our advantage."

Brent's "Damn" is simultaneous with Peter's "I'll get more schnapps."

Edna looks up at me, "I think we're going to have to increase the schnapps budget."

"I think you're right" I reply ruefully.

Paris, France

Général de Division Roger Noiret and his staff arrived in Paris on Monday afternoon. The flights from Iraq had been long and tiring. Roger was in worse shape than his men. They had been able to walk around and stretch on the plane. They had even taken turns helping him hobble up and down the aisles, but it didn't keep Roger's muscles from tightening into painful knots. So, while his men got to enjoy the City of Light for a few hours, Roger was handed over to an invalid therapist for stretches and massage.

When they gathered for a late dinner, Roger asked how their sortie into the capital had gone. Almost everyone gushed over the peace and friendliness of the Parisians. Only his executive officer demurred. Général de Brigade Philippe de Hauteclocque had spent time in Paris before the war and noticed a number of changes.

When Roger pushed for more information, Philippe responded, "The civilians are more overtly religious. Jewelry is more common and based on Catholic symbolism. The friendliness that the others noticed was directed at those in uniform or wearing identifying jewelry. People who didn't fall into one of those two categories were avoided and ignored. Conversations always contained a blessing of some variety, and a praise to God greeted good news."

Roger cocked his head to one side, "And are those bad things?"

"Not necessarily. It just seems more formal and strained. Like they are trying to prove their faithfulness. The easy-going Parisian attitude is gone."

"Maybe it's strain from the war."

"Maybe, but that doesn't fit with the workers' reactions as they closed down for the evening. All of them seemed to relax as if a great weight had been lifted, or another test had been passed."

Roger nodded uneasily at his friend's comments. Faith and love of God should be joyous and come from the heart. Fear of the Lord should come from sure knowledge of his judgment. This sounded more like feigned joy because of fear of those in power. It also sounded a lot like what Roger had observed the last time he was in Paris. He decided he needed to talk with the elder Warriors of Christ to see what their take was on his and Philippe's shared experiences.

The next day, Philippe came by Roger's room to push him to the front of their hotel. It was time for their trip to the Army Command Post in the Château de Vincennes. Philippe gave him the morning paper and pointed to a story on the front page. Roger read while Philippe pushed.

The British had joined the Japanese in China. There was a drive from Hanoi in Indochina to the northeast and a drive from Hong Kong going west. British and Japanese bombers based in Hanoi were flattening the industries in southern China. The Chinese thought they were safe due to their distance behind the front lines with Japan. Chinese resistance was negligible, the areas had been stripped to strengthen the troops fighting the Japanese.

Roger folded the paper and spoke over his shoulder, "Do you think we'll be pulled into the discussion about this, or will our appointment be delayed?"

"I expect us to be shuffled off somewhere else this morning. But I think they'll either want our input or us out of the way this afternoon."

"Makes sense. We can mull over the implications, but I think it's mostly a waste of time until we get more information."

Roger and Philippe joined his men as they waited for their ride. They passed the paper and the men speculated on where they'd go. A bus arrived and its driver was surprised when the gathered men wanted to know their destination. His response of, "L'École Militaire" was greeted with haughty smiles by the three men who had guessed correctly. As they got off at the military academy, Roger said, "See you after lunch." The confused driver simply shrugged.

They were greeted by Commandant Petit who guided them through the hallways towards the parade grounds of the school.

"My apologies, Sirs. We expected you this afternoon and were only informed of the change in schedule an hour ago."

Roger simply chuckled, "Don't worry, Commandant, we are not surprised by the change in our schedule. Anyway, my men and I are probably not the best targets for flowery presentation. Months of combat has roughened our edges. We will try to keep your babysitting duties as boring as possible."

Now it was Petit's turn to chuckle. "There were supposed to be a few speeches, but there is a reason for you to be here." They exited into the morning sun and Petit waived his hand theatrically, "Behold!"

Five armored fighting vehicles sat in the center of the grounds. Petit took over pushing Roger so Philippe could join the others as the eager men jogged over to get a better look. Roger got Petit to confirm that these were the new models that the French Army had under development. His men were looking over and through them by the time he arrived. Roger's limited mobility meant he was stuck outside of them, trying to gauge things from the ground and reading the manuals Petit gave him.

A big version of the G1 was labeled a B2 Heavy Tank. The forty-ton monster had one hundred millimeters of armor on its sloped front. The side armor was eighty millimeters, while the rear was sixty. It sported a ninety-millimeter main gun and a semi-automatic loader to reduce the time between shots.

Next was the G2. The major differences between it and the current G1 were twenty extra millimeters of armor on the front and the same larger gun carried by the B2. A quick scan through the specs showed changes to the internal layout. Most of his men's complaints about the G1's performance had been fixed. Roger liked everything except that the tank was now a solid thirty tons.

Then came the S39 Cavalry Tank. It also sported more armor, though it was only ten more millimeters. The barrel of its main gun had been lengthened and it now sported the same gun used on the G1. That gun was fed by a five-shot magazine like the one they'd put in the AMX38. A new engine got the tank's top speed up to fifty kilometers-per-hour.

The last two vehicles were totally new. The PD90 was called an assault gun. It looked like the chassis of the new G2, but instead of a turret, a ninety-millimeter gun protruded straight from the middle of the front armor. The barrel was over a meter longer than the one on the

B2 and G2, so it would have better range and penetration. Roger would have to think about how best to use it.

Finally, there was the AK1, which looked like the ugly child of a truck and a tank. Named for Adolphe Kégresse, it was intended for transport of men and material in combat conditions. Its fifteen-millimeter armor would stop rifle and machine gun fire but not anti-tank shells. It could move a squad quickly while providing some protection.

They were all still going over the vehicles and manuals when they were called to lunch three hours later. The students were respectful, but they still slowed down the visiting officers' eating pace. Roger sat back when he finally finished and examined his pique. When had he forgotten the art of conversation or the joy of a relaxing meal?

They were taken to the Château de Vincennes after lunch. Roger and his men cheerily greeted their morning bus driver. He welcomed them back with amazed deference. He'd only learned he was to pick them up a half an hour earlier. When they said they would see him this evening, the bus driver simply shrugged at the probability they would be right again.

The group was taken to one of the largest conference rooms in the château. Marshal Charles Delestraint, commander of France's military, welcomed them and ran the meeting. Roger sat as the spokesperson for his men.

"I'm sorry for the delay, but there have been developments that require our attention. Are you aware of the British incursion in China?"

"Yes, Sir."

"We are working on the ramifications of that action, so I will keep this brief. You were brought here to get your reaction to our new equipment and for Operation Fog Bank.

"You've had a chance to look over the new vehicles. When this meeting is over, members of our design team will return to L'École Militaire with you to go over the vehicles. The 1st Armored Division is back in France and some of its men will meet you there to operate the vehicles and help provide feedback. You will join the 1st Armored at the test grounds tomorrow for live fire trials. There is room for some minor modifications to the designs, but not much. We want you to rank any changes by importance and note how they will impact the fighting ability of the tanks.

"Thursday will be a day of leave for you, though you will need to stay in Paris. On Friday, you will report to Calais. There you will report to Général de Corps d'Armée Juin. He will fill you in on Fog Bank and the role he wants you to play. Operational security about Fog Bank and your movement to Calais will be maintained. There will be no discussion of it outside these grounds."

There wasn't a question, but Roger understood the need for an acknowledgment, "Yes, Sir."

"Very well, Général, dismissed."

Roger's men rose and left the room while everyone else stayed. Once outside, they began a hushed discussion as they headed for their waiting transport. It was quickly decided that a group of ground combat leaders secretly going to Calais could only mean one thing, a visit to England.

Trincomalee, Ceylon

Admiral Sir Geoffrey Blake, Rear Admiral John Moore, and Vice Admiral Sir Ralph Leatham prowled the halls of His Majesty's Naval Dockyard, Trincomalee. The three admirals were looking for a fourth, Vice Admiral Sir James Somerville, Commander of the Dockyard. They found him in the records room.

Most of the merchant ships from their last convoy run had scattered around southeast India. Half a dozen of them had stayed here to unload their cargo. They contained more Fulmars for his carriers and munitions for his ships. At least a dozen of the merchants carried equipment for building factories. They went to the mainland.

The Entente was harrying England's supply lines enough that she was being forced to move the factories out of the Home Islands. It would be a couple of weeks before another convoy could be assembled and Sir Geoffrey wanted, or was it needed, something to do while they waited.

Somerville made them wait for a few minutes as he and an assistant dug through filing cabinets and pulled out folders. Sir Geoffrey was beginning to get agitated when Somerville finally finished and led his guests back to his office. They took their seats while Somerville scanned through the folders he'd retrieved. An aide got drinks for everybody while they waited. Somerville looked up when Sir Geoffrey began drumming his fingers on Somerville's desk.

"Sorry, Sir, but the Admiralty wants this information as soon as I can get it to them."

That made Sir Geoffrey pause before responding, "What is it, and why is the Admiralty concerned?"

"It's details on our iron stocks and our capacity for repairing ships if we don't receive material from Great Britain. And they want it is because this convoy contained about half of the plates it was supposed to. If we have another battle with damage like the Battle of Mogadishu, we would only be able to repair two of your big ships. We can handle about a dozen of the ships with less armor, depending on how bad the damage is. After that, we're not fixing anything major."

Sir Ralph looked concerned, while John let out a low whistle. Sir Geoffrey rubbed his chin worriedly, "What about Cape Town?"

"My understanding is that they're in a similar state. We've always depended on the Home Isles to provide the large items we need for ship repairs, but they're having trouble keeping the mills running. That's one of the reasons this convoy had so much manufacturing equipment. We need to be able to make the parts rather than shipping them in. Unfortunately, the expansion of the Indian Army and Air Force are already straining our resources. Even if they weren't, it will be close to a year before we can get things set up to make our own parts.

"The Japanese are supposed to send us some material, but the Admiralty isn't sure when it will arrive. They also don't know what its quality will be, or how much work we'll have to do on it to fit our needs. That deal was one of the major reasons we went into China."

"Great. I came looking for something to do and find out I should keep my ships out of harm's way."

"That about sums it up, Sir. Hunt submarines, stop any raiders, and keep your ships in good working order. The Entente is using Mogadishu as a base for their subs and raiders. They don't have enough of them to impact the big convoys, but they've been sinking a few merchants in the Andaman Sea and the Bay of Bengal."

Sir Geoffrey's dry chuckle interrupted the Station Master. "Don't think they can't hit the big convoys. Their attack on our last convoy shows they can. It's more a matter of getting the slow submarines into position and a belief that the target is worth putting them in danger."

Somerville's despondent look conceded the point. "The Admiralty is also trying to get the Japanese to sell us some of their tankers, but it doesn't look promising. They're close to capacity just supplying their own needs. They have agreed to build more tankers to improve the situation.

"And right when things are getting tight, some diplomat gets caught activating a bloody French spy who tries to kill the German Chancellor. Sweden, Norway, and Denmark had been funneling imports to Britain. That's all stopped since Germany went public with their evidence."

The four admirals sat quietly exchanging looks of dread, as they tried to find some reason for hope. Somerville went back to compiling his report. It looked like the Eastern Fleet wouldn't be doing much for the next few weeks. Hunting subs and training with the new aircraft seemed like a poor use of his men and ships. Sir Geoffrey brooded over the impotence.

Rome, Italy

Colonnello Guido Nobili carried the pile of baby and picnic supplies into his house. Aurora's parents, Maria and Giuseppe, descended on their daughter and grandchild as soon as they entered. He couldn't blame them, but a little help would have been nice. Aurora deftly passed Dawn off to her mother and came to Guido's rescue. He smiled gratefully. Trust someone in Intelligence to notice things. She grabbed a couple of the things he was loaded down with and got the door closed. He headed into the living room and dropped everything else.

His mother-in-law bounced Dawn in her arms but took the time to give him a disproving tsk. "Wearing your dirty shoes inside, Guido? I thought you knew better."

Guido's sigh was exasperated. "Yes, Maria, I know better. It's just really hard to take your shoes off when your hands are full."

"Why didn't you say something? We could have helped."

Aurora arrived from their bedroom. "Mama, Guido could have arrived in a tank and you and Papa wouldn't have noticed. If Dawn is in the room, the rest of the world goes away." She stopped and sniffed for a moment. "Like whatever is burning in the kitchen."

Aurora dashed off to rescue whatever was in the oven as Guido chuckled and took off his shoes. It was his first weekend off since Dawn arrived, and they had gone to the park for a picnic. He closed his eyes and tried to dwell on the peace he'd felt. Maria was making dinner for them, so they had enjoyed the day.

Maria had helped with the lunch basket while he and Aurora gathered everything they could think of that they might need. His mother-in-law had chuckled at the mountain of stuff they'd packed into the car. They'd driven to a local park and found a peaceful spot to just laze the day away. It had settled Guido's soul to just ignore the world and spend time with the woman he loved and their daughter.

Dawn was asleep and Aurora was sitting on their blanket. Guido was sprawled on it with his head in her lap, just watching clouds go by. Aurora caressed his brow and he relaxed more completely than he had in months. Guido might not have been asleep, but his mind was definitely off when the first couple interrupted them. The couple recognized Guido and Aurora from their pictures in the paper.

Guido hadn't thought about the photographer at Dawn's christening, but having Mussolini as a godparent meant it would be in the paper. Guido's record had been brandished for publicity and to instill national pride. Now Guido was apparently a walking recruitment poster. He smiled at the couple and returned the salutes from their young boys. He also heaved a heavy sigh when they finally left.

Guido decided it was time to give up when the fifth couple brought their child over to meet the 'war hero'. Aurora thought the salutes from young children were adorable but noticed the slow darkening of her husband's mood.

"What's the matter, Guido? Don't you think they're cute?"

Guido fidgeted for a moment before responding, "That's the problem, they are cute. They also remind me of some of the young pilots I've served with and commanded. Men who went where I told them and didn't come back. And me? I get people introducing me to their children with the hope that they'll be just like me, while I pray that they won't."

Aurora hugged him and looked up into his eyes. "That you care is what I love about you. It's also what makes you a good commander. It's why you're trying to teach the young pilots how to survive and make it home."

There was a deep sadness in his eyes as he looked down at her. "It was also a way to be near you and Dawn. That it got my men away from flying bullets had little to do with it. Honest."

Aurora did the best she could to provide the comfort her husband needed. She buried her face in his chest as she pulled him closer.

Guido was startled when his wife kissed him on the cheek. Whether or not the afternoon had included some painful thoughts, it had relaxed him enough that he'd fallen asleep on the couch.

Aurora smirked at him and pointed down, "You still need to take that one off and wash up before you come to the table."

Guido looked down and found he'd only gotten one of his shoes off before he'd succumbed to the weariness that was far more mental than physical. He looked back up at his wife and snapped off a salute with a "Ma'am, yes ma'am."

She laughed, "And I thought new mothers were the ones who were supposed to be exhausted all of the time."

Guido bent to his task as she headed back to the kitchen. Everyone was sitting at the table by the time he'd cleaned up and gotten to the dining room. He took his seat and reached for his in-laws' hands. They bowed their heads and Maria said grace. The food was excellent and the conversation was light. They talked about what Dawn had been doing and the local gossip. Guido was a little surprised they didn't ask how the picnic had gone, but decided they'd probably discussed it with Aurora while he was snoozing.

His suspicions were confirmed when they were finished with dinner. He tried to help with the cleanup, but Maria and Aurora shooed him out of the kitchen. He went to the living room where he found his father-in-law with a snifter of brandy in his hand. The bottle and a second snifter, already poured, sat in front of him on the coffee table.

Giuseppe waved a hand at the glass, "Sit. Let's talk."

Guido picked up the glass and sat in his chair. Giuseppe took a sip and waited for Guido to do the same. Then his face went very serious and he let out a barely audible sigh.

"I don't talk about my time in the Great War very often. Those that were there don't want to remember it. Those that weren't, have no reference to understand it. Seeing the death of dozens, or hundreds of men you think of as brothers. Sometimes being the one who gave the order that caused their death. Sometimes knowing a stupid order will kill them for no reason, and not being able to do anything to stop it."

Giuseppe's eyes had gotten a distant look to them as his mind replayed scenes from twenty years earlier. He took a healthy swig of the brandy before continuing, "We share that bond now. That it bothers you is good. It's why men will follow where you lead. But whatever you do, don't let the fact that you care about your men keep you from making the tough decisions. Even if those decisions mean that some of your men may die.

"I was at Caporetto, near the area where the poison gas was spread, and mines were blown. Many men died. A few stayed and manned the defenses. Far too many ran. Land that had cost the lives of tens of thousands was lost in a matter of days. In a month, three hundred thousand Italians were killed, missing, or wounded.

"Would things have been different if our men hadn't run? I like to think so, but I'll never know. The men who ran doomed so many." Giuseppe stopped and shook his head sadly. Another sip of brandy seemed to bring him back to here and now, "In the air, it is harder for you to see the men that hold the line with you, but they are there. Whatever you think your reasons are for coming back to Italy to train our pilots, you are giving them better odds of surviving, of holding that line for their brothers-in-arms so disaster doesn't strike.

"Remember, just because something benefits you, doesn't automatically mean that it's bad. Is there any other group of pilots that has the combat experience that yours has? If you were still in Africa, you would be able to influence your section of the line. Here, you can influence all of it."

Giuseppe wound down and finished off his drink. Guido raised his glass and found it was already empty, though he only remembered taking the initial sip. When he looked back up, the older man had the bottle in his hand and tilted it towards Guido's unresisting snifter. He then refilled his own and put the bottle back on the table.

When Giuseppe looked back at Guido, Guido gave him a small smile. Both men understood that Guido's quiet, "Thank you, sir" was for more than just the brandy.

Cross Anchor, South Carolina, USA

Manly Lee Wilburn and Leila loaded the kids up in their truck. Jewel, Junior, and Sybil rode in the truck bed with the supplies for the party. Eddie, Rita, and Betty rode in the back seat where the parents could keep an eye on the fidgeting kids. M.L. was in a good mood. Like almost everyone else in the country, work had shut down early so people could get home in time to celebrate Halloween. The excuse for a party would help the people feel like things were more normal.

It was a good thing that the school and its gymnasium weren't too far away. The older kids mostly dressed themselves, though Sybil had needed some help with her vampire make-up. Jewel's nurse and Junior's soldier outfits seemed to be more about catching the attention of the opposite sex than celebrating Halloween. Then again, M.L. had been doing the same thing at that age. Rita's ghost was the only costume that was easy. Betty needed a lot of help getting into her skeleton outfit and Eddie had wanted to copy his 'bubba', so Leila had made him a little uniform.

M.L. pulled into the school parking lot and joined the dozens of cars already there. The older kids had disappeared by the time they'd unloaded the youngsters, so it looked like unloading the truck would be up to him. Leila was losing her tug-of-war with the little ones as they pulled her towards the sounds of music and laughter coming from the gym.

M.L. grinned at his apologetic wife. "Go on, I've got this."

She smiled sheepishly. "Love you. See ya inside." Leila had always enjoyed a party, even if she was supposed to be a chaperon. She allowed herself to be towed into the fray as Pastor John Bailey came out. Pastor Farley would still be inside. Their presence helped keep these parties from getting too rowdy.

He greeted the rest of the family as he passed them on the way to M.L., "Need a hand?"

M.L. chuckled, "Or three or four. Thanks. It seems I always get stuck carting the supplies in at these things."

Pastor Bailey looked over the pile of apples, candy, and drinks before turning back towards the gym. He'd just started to whistle when Frankenstein's monster came jogging out. Pastor Bailey smiled at M.L., "Now that's what I call service. God will provide."

It was Dwayne, Jewel's boyfriend. God may have had a hand in it, but Jewel knew how much stuff they'd brought and sent her boyfriend to lend a hand. M.L. wondered if she was being helpful to him or if she was trying to show him that Dwayne was a good guy. It was probably a bit of both.

The three of them managed to carry everything inside in one trip. Dwayne put his load down near the tables that had been set up and tried to be helpful. He was a good kid so M.L. only got him to do a little more before releasing him back to the party. Dwayne let out his best monster groan, held his arms out in front of him, and plodded back into the fray.

A group at the far end was doing their best to provide music and a lot of the older kids were dancing near them. This end of the gym had food and games. M.L. watched it all as he loaded the table. He whispered, "We needed this", and was surprised out of his reverie when Pastor Bailey responded, "Amen, brother."

Nelle's husband, Guy, joined them. Nelle and the other women with small children had claimed a corner of the gym as far from the musicians as possible. They still had a good view of the festivities but could keep the toddlers and crawling babies out of the chaos. M.L. thought his son-in-law was an overly serious man and Guy proved it by promptly launching into a diatribe about the state of the world after he greeted them.

He hadn't gotten more than a sentence into things when M.L. held up his hand, "Guy, please, not now. Let's enjoy ourselves without worrying so much about what the rest of the world is doing and what might happen tomorrow."

Guy looked like he'd sucked on a lemon, "That's how you end up on the path to Hell."

Pastor Bailey jumped in to diffuse the situation. "True, but if you don't put your faith in the Lord, you'll end up there, too. Let's go pray about your worries and see if we can't lift your spirits." He turned to M.L., "Can you handle things by yourself for a few?"

"No problem."

Pastor Bailey put his arm on Guy's shoulder and herded him towards the door outside. He turned back to M.L. with a grin. M.L. mouthed, "Thank you" and turned back to the crowd.

M.L. tried to lose himself in the party again, but Guy had broken the mood. He was distracted enough that he was startled when a pair of arms encircled his waist from behind.

Leila's voice came from just behind his shoulder blades, "Everything okay, Honey?"

He sighed happily, "Yes, m'Love. Just Guy trying to ruin the mood."

"I can fix that." Leila started swaying to the music and soon had M.L. back into a celebratory mood. They switched places after a few minutes and Leila's gyrations quickly had M.L. in a totally different mood.

Leila gave one final twitch of her hips and said, "Now you feel like you're at a school dance." Then she walked away with a mischievous snicker, leaving M.L. feeling like some awkward teenager trying to hide his interest in the opposite sex. He sat at the chair next to the table and was glad no one wanted anything for the next few minutes. Damn, foolish woman. She'd pay for that later tonight, or so he hoped.

Foolish or not, M.L. was back in the spirit of things and even got out on the dance floor once his shift at the table was done. He danced with Leila, Heather, and even Courtney and Acadia. But it was the dance with his daughter Jewel that brought reality back into the evening.

He was a little worried when she asked him to dance, and it must have shown on his face. Jewel looked at him for a moment before letting out a heavy sigh, "No, Daddy, I'm not pregnant." His relief must have been just as apparent since she reacted with what Junior had come to call her 'stink-eye face'.

"That doesn't mean I don't want to be. Dwayne wants to get married now, so we can start a family and get settled before he gets drafted. And we know it's not guaranteed that he will, but we think things are going to get worse before they get better."

M.L. looked down at his daughter, "What makes you think things will get worse?"

"We read the papers and listen to the radio, too. England is teetering, and with what they pulled in Germany, no one is willing to help them. And the OAS has been making noises about the British territories in the Caribbean now that they've taken British Guiana. Roosevelt has already said we would stop them if they went after any of those territories. We don't think anything will stop the Catholic Entente except brute force, and that means an even larger military."

M.L. nodded despondently as Jewel continued, "And then you have the British helping the Japanese in China. Another League of Nations country is now isolated and rates to fall. Does that mean the Japanese will help the British against the Catholics, or are they trying to free up the Japanese for something else? Either way, we're going to have to pick a side soon or we'll be on our own."

"And that makes you want to get married?"

"Oh, we were going to get married at some point. It makes us want to get married and start a family now. Dwayne wants a chance to see his child before he goes off to war. And I want a part of him here in case he doesn't come back. His folks have that house out back where his grandmother used to live. We can clean it up and live there, while we help on their farm and finish school. It's only a half a mile away."

"Y'all have put some thought into this, haven't you?"

Jewel simply nodded and stared into his eyes. Confounded women and their ability to wrap him around their fingers. He simply nodded. Jewel hugged him tightly and buried her head in his chest.

They finished the dance and headed off the floor towards Leila. M.L. was pretty sure she'd already known. She confirmed it when Jewel headed off to kiss Dwayne and Leila simply said, "Better than another one out of wedlock." M.L. couldn't argue with that sentiment, so he hugged her and kissed the top of her head.

EARLY NOVEMBER 1938

The Chancellery, Berlin, Germany

I drum my fingers on my desk as I wait for Oberst Ernst Weber to get back. My aide is checking with the party leaders in the Reichstag to see how they feel about my proposals for Germany's reaction to a French invasion of England. I sent the information to them on Monday, and they said they'd give me their reactions today. But lunch has come and gone, and the afternoon sun is nearing the horizon.

I scan through the status reports again to see if they look like they will interrupt my weekend. The mud in Russia is freezing, and Blomberg expects operations to pick up again. The Russians are out of the Caucasus Mountains and nearing Tblisi, the capital of Georgia. The attackers seem to be solidly Russian now. I wonder if the Finns have been pulled back because they took so many casualties. Or are they moving to another sector of the front where their skill with skis will give us headaches? That's Blomberg's problem, not mine.

The USGA is deliberating our defense proposal, though the USA has been pushing for a closer relationship with our Coalition. I think they understand the possibility and danger of a surrender by the United Kingdom. The question is whether it's safer to have a defense agreement with us, or to maintain the official League neutrality.

The British are losing ground in southern Africa, but the French may be reaching the end of their supply lines. It looks like the French are doing their best to build a rail net to supply their troops. Maybe something good will come out of this for the people of Africa when the fighting ends.

China... It looks like the British and Japanese have totally cut them off from League shipments. The Russians may be sending some equipment, but whatever they send over is just as likely to be shot back at them by the Chinese.

Wilhelm III is on his way to Warsaw. He's doing a morale and solidarity trip. He'll give a speech there tomorrow, and one in Kyiv on Sunday. As long as no one tries to kill him, I may actually have a quiet weekend. One where it looks like I'll be reading the Reichstag's responses and trying to figure out compromises that they'll at least consider.

I put my head in my hands and sigh. Sometimes I dream of how much easier things would have been if I'd kept my mouth shut so long ago. They might have been easier for me, but I bet we'd still be looking at another war, there's always another war. And I wouldn't have met Brenda or Edna, or fathered Brent, or met any of the people I now call friends. Maybe things would have been better for other people, but I doubt they could have been better for me. Sometimes I have to remind myself just how good things are. It's frightening just how many people I care about are depending on me to keep them that way. It's a weight, but it's a weight that I wouldn't trust someone else to carry. A weight that they've entrusted to me. I strive not to let them down and am buoyed by their faith in me.

I raise my head from my hands with a deep breath and a slight smile. My smile grows when I see Edna standing in the doorway, watching me. She smiles and says, "Welcome back." Maybe I was doing some actual dreaming. I hope I didn't snore.

"Ernst called and said he'll be here in ten. There's a pile of paper in the responses and they only gave him one copy. He jumped at the chance when I asked him if he wanted to spend the weekend with us so you could go through things together."

"Thanks."

Beatrice is back to her old, reserved self with an intruder in the house. Dinner is still excellent, but she's quieter than she's been since Edna moved into my house. I like the chattier version of Beatrice. I hope she returns when Ernst leaves.

We lounge in the study after dinner, but Ernst doesn't wait long to pull out the pile of papers he brought. He has yet to learn the value of taking a break from things, probably because he's younger and not pregnant. I expected this, but a sigh still escapes when I sit forward to receive my share.

Ernst hands them over, "Sorry, Erich."

"I just miss my Friday night schnapps. We can have some when we finish going through these."

"I hope it's just to relax and not because we need it."

"Time will tell."

We start going through our scenarios and the Reichstag responses. Ernst and I write our comments on notepads. Otto reads a book in his chair, while Edna works on a crocheted gift for Christmas. She's listening to something on the radio, but I'm too deep in my work to notice it. We've been staying in a lot more since the attack. I hope we're not getting too isolated to connect with our people.

Ernst finishes his half before I finish mine, and Otto beats Edna to the kitchen for a snack break. They return with milk and cookies while Ernst and I are still stretching out the kinks from sitting in the same position for too long. It's a sad reminder that neither of us is young.

"Eat. Take a break and rest your eyes before you go back to it." Otto adds a little of his security command voice to the suggestion and I shrug in surrender.

Between mouthfuls, Edna asks Ernst how his family is doing. My internal reaction is 'Good wife. Keep him busy so I can get more of the cookies.' Otto's smiling eyebrow waggle says he agrees with my sentiment. That keeps me from feeling guilty as a grab another cookie from the dwindling supply.

"Gertrude and the kids are fine; I think she's happy to have me out of the house for the weekend. Tom wants to join Brent and Peter at Lichterfelde. Terri is doing well in high school. Her boyfriend, another Peter, has plans for them after they graduate, but Terri wants to become a teacher. How are your folks?"

I'm sure he really wants to know, but he definitely had ulterior motives based on how quickly he grabbed the last cookie from the plate . That and the guilty but don't care look I get when I smirk at him.

"My folks are fine, though Dad's right leg is bothering him. It usually acts up when it starts getting colder. Rick was promoted to regional manager for Mercedes-Benz, so he and Wanda get to drive their kids around in the latest and greatest the company has to offer."

She looks down at the plate. There had been a dozen big chocolate chip cookies on it, and now it's empty. She looks at her hand where the remains of her first and only cookie look small and lonely. We at least try to look ashamed when she mutters, "How gentlemanly. Taking food from the pregnant lady." She stuffs the last bite of her cookie in her mouth and stands with a sniff. She grabs the plate and tromps into the kitchen with a sigh of exasperation. It's only a moment before she's back, carrying another plate of cookies. "Good thing Beatrice knows about you three, and I know where she hid the extras."

We all knew there were more cookies, but the little bit of theater helps lift our mood. Ernst and I eventually go back to reading and taking notes, careful to keep melted chocolate from smearing our progress.

It's nearly midnight when we finish. Otto and Edna have already turned in when Ernst and I trade our notepads. We read through each other's notes before calling it a night. Time to see what our brains can come up with while we sleep. Ernst heads off to the cold blankets in the guest room, while I get to snuggle into pre-warmed ones.

Saturday is bright and crisp. Apple strudel is presented and demolished. Beatrice shakes her head despondently at the need to make more cookies and heads off to the market. I'd feel bad if I hadn't seen the smile she tried to hide. It's nice to have a cook who enjoys her job, but if she keeps making extra treats for Edna, my waistline will expand as fast as Edna's does.

We convene back in the study, though Otto and Edna are paying attention this time. I pick up my notes from last night and start our little brainstorming session.

"We broke down Blomberg's estimate and sent off our possible scenarios for what could happen in Great Britain to the Reichstag. Here are their responses.

"Scenario One – Great Britain carries on with no French invasion. The Reichstag thinks this is the most likely scenario and what we should base our plans on. Despite our logistics numbers, they don't think the British production will fall as much as our numbers say they will. They generated some more optimistic numbers that keep the British fighting for at least another year. More than enough time to negotiate things with the League, the Russians, the Entente, and the British.

"Ernst, check with intelligence on Monday to see if we can get hard data from our assets in Britain. Maybe we can learn which projection is more accurate. Also, get logistics to run the Reichstag's numbers to find out when they would bottom out. Either way, we should start working on those negotiations. The longer we wait, the stronger the Entente position gets. Any other ideas?" I look at Otto and Edna.

Otto cocks his head to one side, "We could check with the League to see what their sources say about the situation. They have embargoed a number of things, but their ships are still delivering the basics to British ports. They may have a better read on the supply situation than we do."

I hear Ernst jotting notes as Edna develops a look of surprise, "We could always just ask Sir Phipps. He's been pretty forthcoming about their situation."

"True, but will the Reichstag believe what he says?" We all ponder that for a moment before I continue, "Either way, it can't hurt to ask him.

"Scenario Two – the Entente launches a full-scale invasion. They agree with our assessment that this is unlikely but not what the likely outcome would be. They think the losses would be so heavy that the invasion would fail and both sides would want to negotiate. Blomberg thinks the French would be able to secure the Channel and pump enough men ashore to grind their way up the island. Either way, it's expected that there will be enough damage to the fleets that we'd be able to keep our sea lanes open to the League. The Reichstag does like the idea of trying to get the Americans to station a fleet in Norway. Anything?"

Otto gets a far-off look in his eyes, "What would happen to the rest of their empire? If they keep fighting, would they align themselves with local powers, or stay coordinated as the Empire? Would they go neutral, or join the League?"

"That's a question we haven't investigated. On to Scenario Three – England caves on the religious issue. The Reichstag rejects this as a possibility, even though the Church of England is a cross between Catholicism and most Protestants. I don't put a lot of stock in this option either, but we should see if our agents notice any change in the mood of their sermons. That will be a tough one to pull off, but it could keep us from getting blind-sided. It would leave us in a very isolated position if the British came to an accord with the Entente."

More silence and I move on.

"Scenario Four – the Entente negotiates a 'Peace in Place' with the British. Another one that the Reichstag doesn't take seriously. I might agree with them if it wasn't what we're trying to do with Russia. If the Entente can beat the English down enough that they're willing to take territory losses for a respite, then the Entente would be able to turn their whole focus on us or the League. At least the Reichstag sees the benefit of strengthening relations with the League. If this happened right now, I don't know if the League would come to our aid, or if we would go to theirs."

Edna chimes in, "Maybe we could invite President Broz for a visit or go visit him. A little bit of smiling and handshaking might get the people to think of the USGA as close friends."

I nod, "And if we can get a new trade agreement, even if it's just a slight modification of an existing one, we can push it as demonstrating how important they are as a trading partner."

Otto breaks in, "The same thing would probably work if we looked north. We've always worked well with the Scandinavian countries; it wouldn't hurt to remind people of their importance."

"Very true. Looks like it's past time for some State dinners. Lastly, Scenario Five – Outside intervention. We, the League, or the Japanese come to the British aid. The Reichstag says it won't be us and they're pretty emphatic about that. There isn't a lot of history of cooperation with the League, either. That leaves the Japanese, and here the Reichstag agrees with our assessment that it's likely. They agree that the primary reason for the British intervention in China was to get something from the Japanese. The unanswered question is whether that will be just production assistance or whether there will be military aid, too. We just don't have enough people over there to guess what they'll do."

Ernst looks up, "Didn't I write down Dutch? Their people in the East Indies may have some ideas about what's going on. It couldn't hurt to check with them."

"Put it on the list. In the meantime, let's mull things over while we relax and enjoy the weekend. If you come up with something, write it down, and we can discuss it when Beatrice isn't around."

Calais, France

Général de Division Roger Noiret limped around the conference room. His cast had been removed yesterday and he was still getting used to walking normally. He wasn't sure if he was more grateful for finally feeling clean, or not having a constant itch he couldn't scratch. Either way, being able to get around on his own was a close third.

There was an exasperate sigh, "Sit down, Roger."

Roger looked up to see Général de Corps d'Armée Alphonse Pierre Juin looking at him from his seat at the head of the conference table. "Sorry, Sir."

There was a gentle chuckle from Roger's staff at the table and from Juin, "I know you're happy to be mobile again, but it is a little distracting."

An abashed Roger sat down and looked over the maps piled on the conference table again. At least he finally understood why they wanted him in charge of the main landing. His landing under fire at Mombasa meant that he was the only French commander with that kind of experience. He hoped he wouldn't have to experience it again.

Juin continued, "Operation Fog Bank is scheduled for tomorrow night. Our Air Force has been bombing the Channel ports and British airbases every day the weather's been clear. The British have moved their fleet and fighters north to preserve them. This means there shouldn't be any surface ships in the area."

"But a submarine could ruin our day."

"True, but it would have to be very lucky to be in the right place at the right time. We think it's highly unlikely considering the British don't have many of them. The few they do have get sent to the Mediterranean to harass our shipping.

"The British started bombing our Channel ports at night when hostilities began. That has tapered off since July as they've moved on to other, more valuable targets. They still come calling occasionally but they know we don't have any major targets for them. That's why you won't have an escort. It would attract attention and put you in more danger, not less.

"We didn't start bombing at night until August. That was more a lack of bombers that could perform the mission than restraint on our part. The night-time bombings are nowhere near as effective as daylight raids, but they have disrupted lives and created new routines. We hope to take advantage of those routines."

The conference droned on as Juin made sure that everyone knew their role.

Roger did his best to project confidence to the men around him. The Channel was fitful tonight. The French Marines tried their best not to chuckle at their commander's green tinge. A lurch from the dancing waters made Roger clutch the AMX38 that occupied most of this landing craft. The second group of bombers passed over their heads and it wasn't long before he thought he could hear the air raid sirens going off in Dover. He knew they were still too far away for that. Anyway, the sirens would have been blaring since before the bombers left France. The bomber groups were spaced a couple of minutes apart so that fires could help guide subsequent groups to the target. That would also keep most of the people in Dover cooped up in the air raid shelters of Dover Castle.

Thirty landing craft had been secretly assembled in Calais for this operation. Five of them should land on the east edge of Dover in the next few minutes. Two hundred French commandos would split up for their assigned tasks. One hundred would push down the Eastern Arm to Dover Port Control. Their job was to clear the way into the harbor for the rest of the landing craft. The rest of the commandos would head inland to Swingate and its Chain Home radar station, the objective of this whole operation.

Time seemed to crawl as they bounced across the Channel, but they eventually saw their target. A hooded green light shone in their direction. The commandos had taken control of the building. The remaining landing craft chugged into the harbor as the last bombers dropped their payloads on the town. Roger mounted his light tank as they turned towards the docks.

They had just started offloading when the all-clear siren went off. It was followed almost immediately by multiple short bursts from the sirens. It looked like they'd been discovered. Since no one was shooting at them, Roger guessed it was the attack at Swingate. He turned on his radio as three hundred Marines fanned out towards their objectives.

Roger kept his communication brief, there might be someone listening in. "Okay everyone, let's do this like we planned."

Général de Brigade Philippe de Hauteclocque took his company to the west end of the docks. Roger headed north towards Swingate, making sure the five trucks they'd brought followed his tanks. Lieutenant-Colonel Jacques Jeannin took up a blocking position east of Dover Castle.

Roger had just left Dover when the Swingate assault group checked in. "Fog Bank One reports situation overcast as of five minutes ago."

"Roger, situation overcast." That meant they'd taken the Chain Home station, but the defenders had gotten a message out. That meshed with what he'd suspected. "Transport inbound, five minutes."

Roger dropped two of his tanks off to watch a road that headed west towards old Fort Burgoyne while the trucks headed east on that road. He took the other three tanks north to cover the next crossing.

Things were relatively quiet for the next ten minutes as the commandos of Fog Bank One loaded the trucks with everything they could pry from the radar station. Philippe and Jacques reported probes by a couple of patrols from Dover Castle, but nothing serious. Roger pensively scanned his surroundings, unsure of what might lurk in the shadows caused by the pale moonlight.

The report of "Fog Bank One ready to move" eased his tension for just a moment before he realized the growing rumble wasn't just coming from the radar station. Three British tanks were heading cross-country from the north and a couple of trucks were headed down the road. Because of the goofy British roads, Fog Bank One would have to drive north towards the advancing enemy before they could turn back towards Dover.

Roger tapped his gunner's shoulder as he ordered, "Fog Bank One, hold position." The light tank's main gun was smaller than the G1's, but it sounded just as loud. At barely a hundred-and-fifty-meters range, the forty-seven-millimeter shell tore through the Cruiser tank and it exploded in a ball of fire. The driver opened up on the lead truck with his machine gun while the turret slewed slightly. The British tanks stopped to return fire and a second one blew up before they could get their turrets around. They hadn't encountered the quick-fire capability of the magazine-fed AMX38. The last Cruiser tank shot just as Roger's gunner fired his third round. The embankment five meters to Roger's left fountained into the air as the last Cruiser tank joined its brothers in lighting the countryside.

Roger radioed, "Fog Bank One, you are clear to move" just as fire erupted from his other tanks. The trucks began their dash north as explosions north and west of his position punctuated the night. Roger directed fire at movement north of the burning tanks but was frustrated when only the driver's machine gun responded. His gunner was changing out the ammo magazine which took another ten seconds to finish. Ten seconds that cost him a truck and its cargo.

The other trucks stopped, and Roger had to order them to get moving. His tank's main gun finally roared again and silenced the British machine gun. Roger ordered his other tanks to fall back to the rest of the company while he took his own tank down the berm to the burning truck that was barely fifty meters away. Four men were able to climb onto his tank and ride south. The rest were either dead or too badly hurt to move.

The tricky part was getting back on the transports. Someone at Dover Castle had set up a couple of mortars that were lobbing shells into town. The commandos guarded the perimeter before running for their boats, ending their short vacation in the British Isles. The transports headed back to Calais as their nervous cargo hoped the sea wouldn't be able to do what the British hadn't.

Roger's crew had quickly exited the tank once it was on the ship. They milled about and the Marines proclaimed them all honorary Marines now. Their laughs were a little too forced as everyone slowly came down from the adrenaline of combat. They were nearing Calais when Roger's driver mustered his courage and asked him a question.

"Sir, where do you think the British troops came from? I thought there weren't supposed to be any in the area."

Roger replied flatly, "There weren't. Considering the response time, I'm fairly sure they came from the Duke of York's Royal Military School which was west of our position."

Roger watched his driver swallow as he concluded that what he'd feared had actually happened. "So, they were kids?"

Roger nodded, "I suspect the instructors led the way, but it's almost guaranteed that some of the soldiers we shot and killed were older cadets."

The tank driver sagged against his tank and Roger put a hand on his shoulder. "They would have killed us if they could have. They did kill some of the commandos. You should never feel good about killing your fellow man, nor should you shy away from it when it's required. There will be wine tonight and we can talk more then if you wish. I know I'll be praying for our fallen as well as those we killed."

A dejected nod was the only response Roger got. He made a mental note to talk to the battalion Chaplain.

600 Miles East of Mombasa, Kenya

Admiral Sir Geoffrey Blake gazed at the placid Indian Ocean from the railing of the *Marlborough*. Rear Admiral John Moore stood next to him with a more comfortable look than he'd sported since he took over the 1st Battlecruiser Squadron. It was good to see him settling in. Sir Geoffrey just wished the circumstances were better.

"How are things going with Glennie?"

Commodore Irvine Glennie had taken over as Captain of the *Marlborough* when John was promoted to command of the squadron. He had been Commander-in-Chief of the New Zealand Division before the Admiralty had sent him their way. He seemed solid and competent, but Sir Geoffrey suspected that the main reason he was here was because he spoke Japanese fluently.

"We're working things through, Sir. It's been a while since he had to work with a local commander. I'm still working on thinking squadron and not ship."

"That's one of the reasons for this sweep. It gives us all a chance to work on our command process. Hopefully it improves our coordination for Operation Clear Decks."

"I thought that was supposed to be in January."

"The Admiralty wants the timetable moved up. Things are not good in the Home Islands. The hope it will get the Entente to move planes away from that front."

John shook his head slightly, "They've got plenty of planes back home, but they don't have the fuel to fly them. We've got all the fuel we can use, but not enough planes. Somebody in logistics isn't doing their job worth a damn."

"It's more likely that someone on the other side is paying attention. And McHugh sure didn't help."

"That's one hearing that didn't last long."

Rear Admiral McHugh had been in charge of the 2nd Battlecruiser Squadron when it escorted a large convoy of oil tankers to Great Britain. He lost almost three-quarters of those tankers to a submarine ambush. His court martial had lasted less than an hour and he was now a very despised civilian. There were rumors that he was being investigated for treason.

"At least we're making progress in China. Wavell's weekly bulletin said that Hainan, Guangzhou, and Nanning have all fallen. And the Japanese have finally taken Wuhan."

Sir Geoffrey drummed his fingers on the railing before continuing the conversation. "It's like the planes. We have plenty of Indian troops. Getting them into action against the Entente has been the problem. We just can't get through their land-based air to get our troops ashore."

"Clear Decks should help with that, Sir. But I see a bigger problem that no one seems to want to discuss." John waited a moment, but Sir Geoffrey continued to stare out to sea. "What do we do if England falls?"

The cold look of hatred John got from Sir Geoffrey made him cringe. Had he overstepped?

Sir Geoffrey closed his eyes and turned back to the sea. "Damn you for bringing that up, but you're right. No one seems to want to make any contingency plans for that. We practice and plan for so many other remote possibilities, but not that."

"You could ask Wavell."

"I guess I'll have to. General Wavell is technically the Commander-in-Chief of the Middle East, but he's the de facto commander of everything east of Africa. If he hasn't made any plans yet, he needs to. I hope it won't come to that, but if things are as desperate as the Admiralty says they are..."

They both stared at the sea as that bleak possibility ran through their minds. John was still mulling things over when Sir Geoffrey turned to him. "I'll tell you one thing, John. I don't plan on surrendering my command to the Entente. If they want these ships, I'll find someone else who's willing to fight the bastards and join them."

John looked at his boss and friend for a moment. Technically, what Sir Geoffrey had just said could be construed as mutiny or treason if a surrender order ever came. "And I'll be with you, Sir. There's no way..."

"Airplane sighted, Sirs!"

The two admirals turned as Lieutenant Gregory Everett came out to join them. He looked at them innocently as they tried to figure out how much of their conversation he'd heard.

Sir Geoffrey held out his hand for the message and scanned it as Everett gave the basics. A reconnaissance plane had been spotted by the destroyer screen ten miles west of them. It was circling the destroyers. Four Fulmars from the combat air patrol were moving to intercept.

Sir Geoffrey passed the note to John. "Thank you, Everett. Keep us informed."

His flag lieutenant saluted and headed back onto the bridge. John folded the message and put it in his pocket before turning to Sir Geoffrey. "Do you think there's any way we could get one of the *Vanguards*? This would be a lot easier if we had a ship with radar."

"I've already sent that request to the Admiralty. Whether they'll see the sense of it or not is anyone's guess."

The minutes crawled by as the two admirals watched the sea and let their men do their jobs. Everett eventually came back out.

"Message from the *Indefatigable*, Sirs. Italian float plane destroyed. It looked like a Ro.43, one of their ship-based planes. Scouts are being launched to sweep for her home ship."

"Thank you, Everett and our complements to the fighter pilots. Let us know if there are any other developments."

Another salute and Everett was gone again.

John waited a minute before asking, "So, we've gotten them to use planes rather than submarines to picket the Arabian Sea. I guess our plan is working."

"That is why we've been doing this when we aren't guarding a convoy. If we can get them used to us pushing west to the edge of their fighter cover, we have a better chance of catching them napping with Clear Decks."

"We can hope, Sir."

Practica di Mare Air Base, Pomezia, Italy

Colonnello Guido Nobili sat in the middle of the large conference table that he'd come to think of as his. Not today. Today it was the property of Generale di Corpo d'Armata Francesco Pricolo. Generale Pricolo had been instrumental in developing Italy's torpedo bombers. Guido had also worked with him on the fighter improvement project. Guido was deeply honored that he'd decided to have this conference here.

Pricolo paced around the seventeen officers sitting at the table. Guido outranked exactly one of them. That he was sitting in the middle of the table and not at the end was Pricolo's doing, and not appreciated by some of the attendees. They had received the briefing materials last night. Today, the conference table was covered with a model of the port of Fiume in the USGA.

Pricolo stopped across from Guido, "As you can see, the base at Fiume is an excellent anchorage for the Austrian fleet. The shipyards are good and the port is deep. It has two exit channels and is virtually surrounded by land, meaning any approach will likely be spotted. There's an airbase just outside Fiume that currently operates almost two hundred of their new IK-3 fighters. They are comparable to our G.51. The question, gentlemen, is how do we disable their fleet without suffering prohibitive losses?"

There was a general murmur around the table as generals discussed it with their neighbors. Guido noticed that he and the Maggiore at the end of the table were the only people being ignored by their neighbors. Guido sighed in exasperation and looked back at Pricolo who was looking expectantly at him. Guido nodded and Pricolo smiled as he rapped once on the table to get everyone's attention.

"Colonnello Nobili?"

Guido stood and presented his plan, "It will take a significant portion of our air force, but I believe this is our best option. We may not be able to achieve complete surprise, but we should be able to reduce their defense's effectiveness if we hit quickly.

"It's virtually guaranteed that there will be enough warning for their ships to man their defenses, so we should ignore them initially. Their air force will take time to scramble and get that many planes in the air, so they should be our first target. We should hit their airbase with every modern fighter we have..."

A Generale near the head of the table interrupted. "And when more Austrian fighters arrive from other air bases, what will protect our bombers?"

Guido turned to address the speaker, "What bombers? The only bombers in the initial strike will be ten squadrons of MB.174s whose objective will be to make sure that the Fiume airbase is put out of operation. MS.406s will patrol the Adriatic while the initial strike returns and rearms..."

"And their fleet gets underway."

"Yes, their fleet will get underway. But it will be coming out of a port in a hurry. Formations should be ragged at best and anti-submarine measures shouldn't be a priority. We can station a number of submarines outside their harbor defenses to wait for them. I'd place the majority of them on the main channel since it's the quicker path to open water. If the Austrians slow down to deal with our submarines, they'll be easier targets for our second wave. If they don't, they'll be easier targets for our submarines. And if they stay in the harbor, they'll be the easiest targets for our airplanes and still have to run our submarine gauntlet to do anything to us."

The Generale subsided with a harrumph, and Guido turned back to the table and Pricolo, "The second wave will attack the Austrian fleet. It should include every torpedo plane we have, eight to ten squadrons of MB.174s, and at least four squadrons of Br.20Ms or SM.82s. Any SM.86s we have should be included, too.

"If the Austrian fleet is hunting our submarines, their air defense won't be as good. That will make them easier targets for the torpedo planes. If they're ignoring the submarines or are still at dock, they'll be easier targets for the level bombers. The heavy bombers will strike the port facilities to reduce their ability to repair any ships that are damaged. This should force the fleet to leave if it hasn't already. Subsequent strikes would depend on the results of the first two."

A Generale across the table from Guido asked, "And what will happen to our shipping and the Army while you use the entire Air Force on this mission?"

"We will still have several hundred fighters and bombers available for them. They won't be our latest, but they should still provide effective support for the Army. Our shipping will have to depend on reconnaissance and destroyers for protection. I know that leaves them vulnerable, but how vulnerable will they be if nine enemy battleships make it out into the Mediterranean?"

"Your previous reports said that airstrikes on fleets have high casualty rates. What will we do when we've lost half of our Air Force?

"Attacks on fleets that are in formation and have room to maneuver can be high. The Austrian fleet will have limited room to evade torpedoes and their formation should be haphazard. We've also been working with our torpedo squadrons on new tactics based on lessons learned from fighting the British."

"And how will we coordinate these airstrikes? We'll need several air bases for that many planes."

"What else? Practice. I'd suggest using Taranto as a practice target, both for coordinating launches and the airstrikes. I'd also recommend moving the fleet away from the USGA in case they're thinking about doing anything similar to us."

Generale Pricolo joined the conversation at this point. "That's almost identical to my plan, though I had bombers coming in to strike the fleet in the first wave. But I suspect you're right, Colonnello Nobili, on the probability of them not being ready. Let's use your version as a basis and see what we can do to tweak it to our best advantage."

The planning session lasted well into the evening. Guido's eyes were beginning to cross from staring at maps and calculations when Generale Pricolo finally called an end to the meeting. A late dinner in Rome had been arranged for all the visiting brass and Guido was invited to ride with Pricolo to the restaurant.

They rode in silence for a few minutes before Generale Pricolo spoke to Guido. "You have more recent combat experience than anyone else in the room today. Yet most of them dismissed you and your plan until I pointed out how close it was to my own. I think we may need to do something about that, so your ideas aren't dismissed out of hand in the future."

Guido was shocked and excited at the implications of that comment. His reply was a neutral, "I'll do my best to make myself heard, regardless of my station, Sir."

That got a chuckle out of Pricolo. "That's one thing I'm sure of. I've heard about your comments to Il Duce at the end of the Spanish Civil War. Not many people would have made so blunt a comment to him and survived."

Guido smiled sheepishly, "Yes, Sir. Would you believe it was at the suggestion of my base commander? Colonel Sarbonne told me I'd have more influence right after the award ceremony than at any other time in my career. I guess he was right."

Pricolo let out another wry chuckle. "We'll see about that, Colonnello Nobili."

Cross Anchor, South Carolina, USA

Manly Lee Wilburn had Leila packed in the truck as they headed to the Post Office to vote. Senator Ellison Smith was a shoo-in for reelection, but Joe Bryson needed their vote. He was trying to move up from the state Senate to the federal House and the Wilburns were here to support him.

Everything went smoothly and Ray Robinson, the postmaster, took their ballots with a smile. They ran into the Bravos as they were leaving and M.L. said he'd be waiting for Cardy at their house. He drove back home and dropped off his wife before heading up the road to wait. He stood beside his truck and was starting to wonder what was taking so long when the Bravos finally pulled up. His questions got a lot more serious when Cardy got out of their truck. He was sportin' a shiner on his left eye, though he seemed to be in a good mood. Heather and Acadia waved before heading into the house.

"What the heck, Cardy?"

"Harry came in while we were voting and decided he was going to derail things. He grabbed the ballot box and Ray grabbed him. That made Harry start flailing around. I tried to help, and Harry caught me in the eye with an elbow. I stepped back and decked him. Ray thanked me for the help, then I had to hang around 'til the police got our statements."

M.L. shook his head in exasperation. "That dumb ass. At least you seem to be okay. How's everyone else?"

"Everyone but Harry is fine. Ray brought him around with some smelling salts and the police carted him off. I think he's in a world of trouble."

"You can say that again. That's federal stuff they can charge him with. Damn."

Heather came back out carrying Cardy's lunch and a towel wrapped around some ice. She gave him a big kiss after making sure his eye was fine. She turned to M.L., "Could you keep an eye on him for a few days? That's a pretty good shiner and it might interfere with his vision."

"Happy to, Heather. Could you do something for me? Janice will be beside herself. If you could get Leila and take her to visit, it might help settle her down."

"Won't she be chasing off to wherever they took Harry?"

"Was she at the Post Office?"

"We didn't see her there."

"Then she may not even know what's happened. And if Harry was there, he had their car and Janice is stuck at home. She may need you to help her chase down her husband. If nothing else, she'll need a ride to the Post Office to get their car."

She nodded, "I'll call Leila when you leave. She can check with Janice while I take Acadia to school. I'll swing by after that to see what they want to do."

"Thanks, and good luck."

Heather gave Cardy a 'be good' glare before rolling her eyes and turning back to M.L., "You, too. I think you'll need it more than I do."

They shared a chuckle as Cardy did his best to look innocent. Cardy and M.L. piled into his truck and headed up the highway to Spartanburg. They rode in silence for a few minutes as Cardy kept the cold compress on his eye and stared out the window. It wasn't long before M.L. started getting worried.

"All right, Cardy. How bad is it?"

Cardy continued to stare out the window as he responded, "It's fine, M.L."

"No, it ain't. You normally jaw all the way to work. You've been in a fight, even if it was a quick one. I'd expect you to be even more talkative, but here you are, quiet as a church mouse. Something's wrong, and my guess is it's got you worried."

Cardy swallowed and sighed. "It's my vision. It's been kinda blurry since Harry stuck his elbow in my eye."

M.L. sucked in some air, "Just the left one, or is it both?"

"Just the left."

"Well, thank God for that. It might be something in your head if it was both of 'em. Stay in the truck when we get to work. I'll let Jim know what's going on and I'll take you by the doctor's to get checked out."

"It's not that bad."

"Yes, it is, and you know it. If it's anything serious it could keep you from working. Vision problems can be deadly when you're slinging around multi-ton parts on pulleys."

"I know. And if it's serious, I may be out of a job." Cardy went back to looking out the window.

"Won't happen, son. You'll be taken care of one way or another."

Cardy just grunted and M.L. focused on getting them to work as the younger man's pensive mood spread to M.L.

Jim looked over Cardy's swelling eye and got a brief rundown on what happened. He changed out the ice in the towel and sent them on their way. They spent most of that morning at the hospital, waiting between short sessions of people prodding at Cardy's eye. They didn't find anything that looked like permanent damage, just the swelling putting pressure on his eye. The doctor said Cardy's vision should return to normal once the swelling went down. Both Cardy and M.L. breathed a sigh of relief. Cardy got some pills for pain, but they came with a warning. No driving or operating heavy machinery for eight hours if he'd taken one.

Cardy was in a better mood as they headed back to the shop. "Thanks, M.L."

"No problem. Just remember that in the future, you let me know if something is wrong. I don't want you getting yourself or someone else hurt because you're trying to tough it out."

Cardy looked a little chagrined, "Will do."

Jim was glad to hear the doctor's prognosis. When Cardy was adamant about working, Jim found things for him to do that were useful without putting him in harm's way. He even came by and chased the two men off earlier than they'd been staying. M.L. gave him an appreciative grin and a mock salute. Jim returned it and told them to get their asses out of there before he changed his mind. They left with a chuckle.

Cardy's truck was in the front yard of his house when they pulled up. M.L. honked the horn just as Heather came out. She walked up to M.L.'s window as Cardy got out of the other side. "How's he doing?"

"I took him by the doctor to get checked out. Doc said the swelling was messing with his vision, but it should be fine once the swelling goes down. Cardy's got some pain pills that will probably make him sleepy, so if he needs to take one in the morning, he should stay home from work. I did my part, now it's your turn to keep him out of trouble."

"He can be a handful, but I'll do my best. Thanks, M.L." Heather leaned in through the window and gave him a peck on the cheek. She smiled and went to corral her wayward gladiator. M.L. smiled the rest of the way home.

When he got home, Leila wanted all the details about Cardy. Then she made M.L. wait until after dinner for the news on Harry and Janice. M.L. didn't get worried until Leila put him off again. She waited until the dishes were done and the kids were playing outside. When she finally turned to him, she leaned forward and took a deep breath before starting.

"Janice is livid. Harry heard Smith and Bryson on the radio last night talking about how we need to get involved in what's going on around the world."

"Yeah, I thought they were good speeches."

"Me, too. But Harry just started ranting about how they were getting kickbacks to get us into a war so some companies could make a bunch of money. How they were all ready to kill our kids so they could grab more power. How the federal government wanted us in a war so they could take away our rights and do whatever they want to."

A dry snicker escaped M.L. "Sounds like he's in favor of bringing back the Confederacy."

"Some pacifist. He started drinking last night. When he went to bed, he hit Janice and tried to force himself on her. She kicked him in the nethers and went to sleep with Sara and Lucille. He tried to get in their room before he finally passed out. He woke up hung over and in pain. He screamed at all of them, grabbed a bottle of rum and left.

"The police have him in jail in Woodruff and Janice refuses to go get him. She said she doesn't want him back in their house and that he can rot in jail for all she cares."

"Damn. You think she'll calm down?"

"Not likely. Janice said that when Harry was trying to get into the girls' room, he said that if she wouldn't do her wifely duties, Sara or Lucille could."

M.L. sat back and whistled.

Leila leaned back, "You should talk to Harry and get his side of the story. I don't think it matters if Cardy wants to press charges or not. He's in a world of trouble and he's pissed off his family and all of his friends."

M.L. thought for a moment. "I'm sure this will be the talk of school tomorrow. I'll talk with the pastors after work tomorrow to see what we can do for them. Maybe they'll have some idea of what we can do for Harry. Regardless, we can make sure that Janice and the kids don't pay for what he did."

Leila got up and leaned over her husband to plant a kiss on his forehead, the love in her eyes fighting with the sadness. He pulled her down and hugged her fiercely.

LATE NOVEMBER 1938

The Reichstag, Berlin, Germany

It's amazing how much things can change in a couple of weeks. Ernst, Otto, and I make our way through the beautiful halls of the Reichstag. It felt ridiculous to drive the couple of hundred meters to get here, but Otto wouldn't budge. Either the way has been cleared or everyone is taking the day off. Our guide is the only person we see on the way to our emergency meeting with the representatives of our people.

Our guide stops in front of a door and knocks firmly. The door is opened from the inside and our guide bows out of the way. It's a modest-sized conference room. The big four are seated at the table along with four other leaders of minor parties. We take our seats. I wait for them to begin, it's their show after all.

As head of the largest political party, Alfred Hugenberg takes the lead. "Thank you for coming, Chancellor. We wish to discuss the English situation in more depth. Recent events indicate our earlier assessment may have been overly optimistic."

I try to remain as diplomatically impassive as Otto does. Ernst cocks his head to one side and gives them his best 'No. Really?' look. Sometimes it's good to have an aide who can express your feelings for you.

Hugenberg looks at Ernst sourly before he continues. "The reports from the Navy and the League indicate that your original numbers for British production are closer to the truth than our numbers. And the recent French raid on Dover means both of us may have underestimated the possibility of an invasion."

I hold up my hand to interrupt. "Getting a raid in and out is a lot different than the long-term supply commitment of a full-scale invasion."

"We understand that. But if you combine it with the British supply issues, we think that a successful invasion is far more likely than we originally believed."

I nod, happy to concede the point. Hugenberg continues, "We also have the report from the League that the British have approached them about mediating a cease-fire. When you add in that the Dutch report the Japanese navy is very active in the South China Sea, things look grim.

"Chancellor, you sent us five separate scenarios to consider on October thirty-first. Our question to you is, what if they aren't separate? Has the military considered the possibility that all of the scenarios may happen at the same time?"

I close my eyes for a moment before looking at Hugenberg. Then I look around the table at the other representatives, making sure to make eye contact with each of them before moving on. Hugenberg looks nervous when I get back to him. "That was our original assessment, but we didn't think you would take it seriously if we presented it as one big problem."

Hugenberg looks annoyed, "Chancellor, please..."

"How many of those scenarios did this body think were far-fetched or outright reject? Would you have even discussed things if we'd sent it over as a whole?"

I scan the table. At least most of them have the decency to look guilty. "Of anyone here, I have the most reason to hate the British and watch happily as their empire burns to the ground. But I don't think that will be good for our country. We have to decide what we're willing to do for our people, even if it means helping the British.

"The latest reports from the Russian front indicate a general counterattack, using the snow to their advantage. We cannot afford for the Entente military to be freed up while most of our army is engaged in Russia. That situation would be even bleaker if the British, and possibly the Japanese, began actively working with the Entente.

"We've come up with several different responses to the current situation, as well as contingencies for the near future. I'll send them over later today. All I ask is that you consider them as seriously as we have. I will warn you now that all of them involve expanding our military funding."

It's Hugenberg's turn to look around the table, making sure they were all in agreement. He looks back at me, "We will await your proposals and give them our complete attention. Thank you for coming to see us."

"Thank you for wanting this conversation."

We all stand and my contingent heads out the door. The trip back to the Chancellery is quiet. Edna greets us with drinks and joins us in my office to see how things went. We get settled and Ernst breaks the silence. "And how many of those contingencies do we actually have?"

"You know that Blomberg has plans for almost everything. It's what the military does when it's not fighting. The political and economic options have been run; we just need to write up the proposals."

Edna looks a little lost. "Did they connect the dots or did something new come up?"

Ernst snorts, "Oh, they connected the dots. And Erich made sure they saw the not-so-pretty picture it made. They're more willing to listen now. We're supposed to send over proposals this afternoon."

Otto chimes in. "Including economic and military intervention to help the British."

Edna's face goes blank, and I look down at my desk.

"I don't like it either. Unfortunately, it may be the best option to keep our country safe." I look up at her with a sadness that mirrors hers. A sadness tinged with disgust.

Paris, France

Général de Division Roger Noiret and his staff were back at the Army Command Post in the Château de Vincennes. Général Juin sat with them as they waited for Marshal Charles Delestraint to arrive. Folders lay on the table in front of each of the seats. Roger had opened his and found the enclosed page that he expected to be relevant. The Commander of the French Army was a few minutes late, which surprised Roger. They all stood when the Marshal arrived with half-a-dozen generals in tow.

After everyone was situated, Delestraint opened a folder on the table in front of him and looked across the table at Roger and Juin. "Good morning."

Juin replied for the group, "Good morning, Sir."

"First and foremost, well done. The raid was a success despite the loss of one of the trucks. Our scientists are pouring over the equipment you brought back, to see if there's a way to jam their radar or overload it. And to improve our version of it.

"What I need to know is how the landing went. What problems arose and how do we prevent them in the future."

Juin replied, "The broad information is in my after-action report. Général Noiret will go over it and answer any questions you have."

Delestraint turned to Roger and cocked his head to the left.

Roger looked at the open folder in front of him, "Sir, if you'll turn to page five of the report, I'll go over our main points." He waited as everyone found the section on recommendations.

"Since our landing at Mombasa was done under fire, I included information from it as well as the landing at Dover. The landing craft were similar in both cases and opened by dropping the front of the craft. This gets the troops out of the landing craft faster, but it also makes them extremely vulnerable. A lone enemy machine gun would cause heavy casualties. We had the Italian fleet to suppress the enemy at Mombasa. We had surprise at Dover. I don't expect to surprise the British again, so we will need either the Navy or Air Force to provide heavy firepower until our troops are ashore. Either would require the landing be in daylight.

"At both Dover and Mombasa, a significant portion of the landing force was seasick. At a minimum, we need to provide something to the men to combat it. It would be best if we could figure out which men are most likely to suffer from it and keep them out of the initial assault. Not only are seasick soldiers not useful in combat, but they also take up resources needed to treat our wounded.

"It would be useful if our landing craft had some kind of intrinsic firepower that could react quickly to threats. A heavy machine gun, or a couple of mortar tubes should work. And we're going to need a lot of them. Our estimate is around a hundred of them to land a single battalion.

"The commandos and marines did an excellent job of helping us get ashore, but they weren't enough to prevent inland forces from counterattacking. If we want to maintain troop concentration, we will need to land in waves. The larger the invasion force, the longer it will take to unload them and the more vulnerable they'll be. I know we've been training paratroops; I think dropping some inland from the landing site would improve the odds of completing the offload before the enemy can counterattack.

"Finally, there's the issue of supplying the force once it's ashore. We didn't have to worry about this at Dover, but at Mombasa, we had to push the enemy far enough away from the port to protect our supply ships. If we land at a port, the enemy will be able to threaten our supply-line for an extended period of time. If we land on a beach, we will need to use ships similar to the landing craft to bring supplies ashore. Either that or we will need to be able to rapidly build docks.

"In either case, we will need to control the air to prevent enemy raids from stopping our supplies and follow-up troops. The seizure of an airfield would allow us to airlift some of the needed material, but ships are still the best way to provide the amount of supplies needed."

Marshal Delestraint sat back and steepled his fingers, "Your numbers on landing craft needed agree with our estimates. We also think the British have around thirty divisions in Great Britain. Add in that we believe they have a stockpile of chemical weapons, and we think a simple invasion won't happen in the near future. We are doing our best to strangle them economically, but do you have any suggestions on how to make them surrender?"

Roger looked thoughtful as he looked around at Général Juin and his staff. Général de Brigade Philippe de Hauteclocque looked thoughtful, and Roger's gaze settled on him. When Philippe came back to the present, he looked at Roger. Roger rubbed his chin for a moment before whispering, "Supplies?" Philippe nodded. Roger smiled, "Let me know if I miss anything" and turned back towards the assembled generals.

"Supplies, Sir. I know we've been working to cut off their imports, but we also need to work to destroy or make them burn through their existing supplies. Our oil situation is good while theirs isn't. So, we need to move our fleet around to make them chase us. The same goes for their Air Force. And it will work even better if we can get the Italians to help. They've got some longer ranged and heavier bombers than we do. We've been bombing ports and airfields. We need to expand to hitting their factories, too."

Delestraint interrupted Roger. "I'll point out that is almost guaranteed to spill over into the cities. It's one of the things we've been using against them when we deal with the League and Central Powers."

"I know, Sir, but we can rightly claim that we are simply responding in kind. There's a chance that the British will escalate to bombing our cities in earnest, but even that would be a win. They would use up more of their resources for less impact on our fighting capabilities, while annoying their potential allies and galvanizing our people against them."

Marshal Delestraint stared dispassionately at Roger. "That's a very cold-blooded calculation that puts French civilians in the cross hairs of our enemies."

Roger stared back and, with a slight dip of his head, conceded the point.

After a few moments, Delestraint dropped the stare and closed the folder on his desk. He moved it to the side and replaced it with the second one he had. "Are you against going to war with Germany?"

Roger answered almost immediately, "I am at the present time. I think any conflict with Germany will reduce the pressure on the British. And while we have plenty of ground troops, I don't believe we have enough planes. There's also the probability that the League, or at least the USGA, would intervene on their side." Roger paused and scratched his chin before continuing, "Have you thought about getting Germany to help against the United Kingdom?"

"And why would they do that?

"As a buffer, Sir. After the attempt on their Chancellor's life, the German people are pretty pissed at the British. If we invade and take over the British Isles, German and the Scandinavian countries become a lot more vulnerable to being cut off from North America. If we offer them control of something like Manchester north, they would be able to protect their sea lanes better."

"Yes, they would. That's one of the big reasons for invading England."

"I know, Sir, but I think it would actually make their defensive situation worse."

Marshal Delestraint's eyebrows went up with that comment. "Please tell me how?"

"They would have troops and airbases to protect their shipping. But those assets would be relatively isolated. Our interior lines mean we would be able to shift between the English and German front more rapidly than they would and their forces would be more open to defeat in detail. In addition, the Germans would have to spend time and men keeping the British people under control. That's something that might drive a wedge between them and the League."

"That's an interesting point of view. We're working on what your next assignment will be. Enjoy some time in Paris and we'll contact you in the next few days."

Marshal Delestraint rose, and everyone else joined him. He and his staff exited the room. The last general paused and called, "Dismissed" over his shoulder before following Delestraint.

Roger and the other married officers began discussions on how to get their wives to Paris. The single officers began planning their hunt of entertainment. Général Juin paused to remind Roger of their obligations at Notre Dame that evening.

The Warriors for Christ meeting started with a prayer and blessing. There were almost a hundred members in attendance. Most were in the Army, and almost every rank was represented. It wasn't long before Roger found himself in a small group with Marshal Delestraint, Général Juin, a Sergent introduced as Bernard, a Commandant named Henri, and a tall gentleman who went by the name of Charles. Even here, where everyone was expected to be straightforward, people tended to defer to Charles as he steered the conversation between the current world and historical comparisons.

At one point, Charles turned to Roger, "How was your trip to England, Roger?"

"Too brief" Roger chuckled. "Seriously, things went very well with one exception. We had to deal with a half a dozen tanks and a couple of truckloads of infantry that made us all seek solace with the Lord."

Henri piped in, "What did they do that shook you?"

Roger smiled morosely, "They fought and died like good soldiers." Roger continued when Henri looked confused, "They were from a nearby military academy. One of my commanders said that some of them didn't look older than twelve."

Charles nodded somberly, "I can understand why you would want to talk with the Lord to seek His comfort. It's sad when the great deceiver leads ones so young to their death. It's one of the reasons we need to persecute this war to its end. Doing less would fail not just us and God, but also those we leave in Satan's thrall."

Charles put a hand on Roger's shoulder and Roger closed his eyes at the remembered pain. When he opened them, Charles offered his other hand and Roger shook it. He smiled gratefully at the solace offered by his country's leader.

100 Miles East of Madagascar

Ask and ye shall receive thought Admiral Sir Geoffrey Blake. The *Vanguard* wasn't as fast as the *Renown*, but she was as fast as the *Ark Royal*. She wouldn't slow the 1st Battlecruiser Squadron down. The only person happier about this was Rear Admiral John Moore. His squadron was now the second most powerful in the Royal Navy. The Admiralty had also transferred *Formidable* from the 1st Battle Division to the 5th Battle Division. The loss of the aircraft carrier would hurt, but Sir Geoffrey had been expecting it for a while. They got the bigger and newer *Ark Royal* from the 5th Battle Division. It made sense that one of his carriers would go back as a replacement.

The convoy they had dropped off at Cape Town was symbolic of his country's woes. There were plenty of merchants carrying raw materials, but there were only thirty oil tankers. Worse, five of those were conversions that carried barely half of what the regular tankers carried. The situation was bad enough that the Admiralty was converting some of the new light carriers they were building into tankers. Sir Geoffrey's shoulders sagged as he realized that the only times a country converts warships into merchants is when the war is nearly won, or when it's close to being lost.

John joined him outside at the rail. "At least the hand-off went well, and we have the *Vanguard*, Sir. It'll be nice to see what its radar can do for us. I've ordered standard air reconnaissance and patrols until we have a better idea of how well it works."

"Prudent. I just hope this convoy fares better than the last big one we sent home."

"At least we can be sure that they won't be anywhere near the course they took to Cape Town."

"Too bad that it took such a bloody expensive proof to drive our lesson home."

John didn't reply. When Sir Geoffrey got into one of his dark moods, it was best to leave him alone for a while.

They continued cruising almost due north towards the Seychelles. The British had cleaned out the small islands in the Indian Ocean and used them as bases for their own scouts.

Two days had come and gone, along with four Italian scout planes. They were a hundred miles west of the Seychelles and the radar on the *Vanguard* was proving its worth. Sir Geoffrey was sure that all of the enemy planes had gotten off radio reports. They wanted to establish this pattern to lull their enemy into complacency.

Sir Geoffrey was at the rail again, though he was sporting a more predatory look now. John joined him from the bridge. "Radar confirms the kill and no other enemy aircraft in the area, Sir. Scouts have come up empty on any ships or submarines in our path."

"Very good, John. Do you think they'll change things up or just accept the losses as part of the war?"

"That's the big question. We haven't managed to chase down any of the ships that are launching their scouts. I think they'll just keep using them as pickets until something changes."

Sir Geoffrey drummed his fingers on the railing. "My guess is that they put up more scouts about fifty miles west of where we splash one of theirs. That way they can see if we're headed their way or we're just scraping off the scouts we find as we patrol."

"That's what I'd do in their place. Though if I had the ships, I'd put out submarines too. But it would take a lot of submarines to cover our approaches."

"So, you put them on the approaches to the critical areas."

"The Persian Gulf and the Red Sea?"

"I'd have a couple on the approaches to both. And if they have any near the Persian Gulf, they're damn good. We have land-based scouts in that area and haven't spotted them."

"They may simply not be there." John's response got a dirty look from his boss, so he held up his hands in surrender, "I didn't say it was likely or we should plan on it. Just that it's a possibility."

Sir Geoffrey's eye roll showed how low he thought that possibility was. Both men went back to staring at the sea as the sun sank towards the western horizon.

Sir Geoffrey moved with a start as he realized he'd almost fallen asleep standing up. He'd have to try to remember this feeling when he went to his bunk tonight. Sleep had not come easy over the last few months and the relaxation he felt here could do a lot to restore his tired soul. Until then... He turned to John who seemed as far away as Sir Geoffrey had been. "Let's go inside and get this circus turned towards Trincomalee."

The sag in John's shoulders showed that Sir Geoffrey wasn't the only one who had enjoyed the brief respite from the weight of their responsibilities.

Paris, France

Colonnello Guido Nobili had only gotten two hours of sleep last night, but he couldn't have been more awake if he was in battle. He flew up to Paris yesterday. Unlike the scientists on this trip, Guido was allowed to bring his wife and child, Aurora was a Colonnello in Intelligence and had been part of the program to improve Italian fighters, too. The British seemed to have taken exception with the French raid on Dover, and between two bombing raids and his daughter's cries of hunger, sleep had been elusive.

He glanced over at Aurora and was amazed. She looked alert and was following the description of the radar equipment from Dover. Guido knew that everyone was working on radar, but most of the technical details went over his head. He held onto the folder of information he'd been given like it was more precious than gold. It probably was.

Alert or not, Guido had to stifle a yawn. That made him miss whatever was said. It also made both Aurora and the Frenchman who had been doing most of the talking turn to him. "Um, sorry. I missed whatever you just asked. The noise kept us up most of last night."

Aurora gave him her best haughty look. "Good thing you didn't have to nurse or change Dawn, too."

The French scientist, George Richard, couldn't suppress his smile, "Women are far stronger than most men believe."

Guido shrugged. "Not me. I know I can't keep up with her."

Aurora preened for a moment before relenting, "He asked if you understand how radar works."

Guido brightened a bit at getting off the hook so easily. "From what I can tell, radio waves are sent out from a tower and bounce back when they hit something. When the tower gets a return signal, it figures out the location of the object that made the signal bounce back, right?"

George replied, "That's a very simplified view of the process, but it's basically right. Do you have any ideas on how we can reduce its effectiveness?"

"Could we figure out what frequency they're using and simply broadcast on it to blind them?"

"We think that will work up to a point. Returns from actual objects would eventually get stronger than whatever we're broadcasting, but it should be able to reduce their radar's effectiveness."

Guido scratched his head for a moment, "Can their radar tell how big an object is?"

"The strength of the return gives you some idea of the objects size."

Guido looked disappointed, "Oh, well. So much for planes dropping little parachutes to convince them there are a lot of planes where there aren't."

George waved a finger at Guido, "Hold on. Some things reflect the radio waves better than others. We should be able to figure out how well they bounce off airplanes or any other objects. If there's something that gives a much stronger return for its size, we could use small amounts of it to appear to be more planes."

He waved at another Frenchman who wrote something on his notepad. When he finished, he looked up and George turned back to Guido, "Anything else?"

"Well, if you can do that, there might be a way to string up a group of them to be towed by a plane. Then one plane could appear to be a whole squadron. You could even mount some of the material on a small plane to do the towing. It could confuse the enemy about which groups are real."

George signaled at the note taker to write it down and turned back to Guido.

"Can you make the sets small enough to fit on an airplane? I'm sure it would make it easier to intercept those night bombing missions if you had fighters with radar."

"We're already working on that, but it's good to know a pilot thinks it would be useful."

"I presume you're looking at mounting radar on ships." A nod from George and Guido continued. "Do you think a plane with radar would be able to find ships at sea and figure out how big those ships were?"

"Maybe."

"We attacked British fleets at dawn a couple of times. We had to wait until then to be able to pick our targets. It would have been nice if we could have done that in the middle of the night. We wouldn't have had to worry about their carrier-based fighters as much. I bet their anti-aircraft fire wouldn't have been as effective either."

George smiled and his assistant went back to scribbling. When George looked at him again, Guido just shrugged. "Sorry, that's all I've got."

"Don't worry. The insight into how you would like to use it will help us make sure our efforts have a real impact on the war. Let me know if you think of anything else."

"Will do, George. And I'm sorry if it looked like I wasn't paying attention."

George waved his apology off. "It's good. Sometimes it is better to let the subconscious work on things. It will often find things that elude us when we are actively thinking about them."

Aurora snickered, "Then my husband is your man."

Guido gave her a sour look. She would pay for that comment later tonight. Her smirk said she didn't care.

They spent another day in Paris. They'd planned on three more days but decided to cut it short. Their plan to recreate their honeymoon didn't work out. There were two more raids that night. The sounds from falling bombs mixed with anti-aircraft fire kept waking them up. Guido developed a deeper appreciation of what Aurora went through every night with Dawn.

When they went out during the day, they found people packing vehicles for extended stays in the countryside. They didn't see much damage, so the bombing wasn't very effective. What it was doing was disrupting the easy-going Parisian lifestyle. Everyone seemed skittish. Guido couldn't tell whether it was from worry or lack of sleep. Most of the shops had boarded up their windows, either to cover damage or prevent it. It was just generally sad and depressing.

That afternoon, they boarded a train for home. It was packed during the first part of the journey as more Parisians fled for safer pastures. Guido thought back to the planned attack on the USGA and wondered how much of his country would end up like Paris if fighting broke out that close to home. He told Aurora about his concerns when she noticed his worried look. Their sleep was restless for a third night.

Spartanburg, South Carolina, USA

Manly Lee Wilburn joined Cardy Bravo and Jim Deeson at the break room table. Cardy's eye wasn't swollen anymore and his vision was normal. They were back to working together on engine maintenance, but they still weren't keeping up. They ate in silence, as each man tended to his own thoughts.

Jim finished first but waited for Cardy and M.L. before he broke the tranquility. "The company wants us to get more done. I told 'em that we're already scheduled for more than we can handle. They said they'll send up two more men to help. What I'm going to need y'all to do is split up and each take on one of the new guys."

Cardy perked up. "Senior mechanics make more money, don't they?"

Jim sighed, "Yes, they do. You're both going to get a twenty percent pay raise."

M.L. looked at Jim suspiciously. "And how many more hours are they wanting us to put in?"

Jim held up his hands. "None, for once. They're happy with our work and they need to expand. This is one of the cheapest areas where they can do that. They're going to build us a bigger shop. For now, you'll need to figure out how four of you can work in the current shop."

"We'll find a way, and I'll make sure Cardy is ready to lead a crew. He's definitely got the mechanical skills. We'll have to see how he is at handling people, without punching them."

Cardy rolled his eyes, "Jeez, it wasn't my fault."

Jim and M.L. both laughed, "We know."

When they settled down, Jim cocked his head in M.L.'s direction. "How is Harry?"

"The police dropped things down to a drunk and disorderly. He's back at work now, though his wife still won't let him back in the house. He sees Pastor Bailey three times a week and has sworn off alcohol. He apologized to Cardy specifically and everyone else at church last Sunday, but he's got a ways to go."

"How's his family doing?"

"Janice has their car so they can get around. Harry's staying at a hotel about two blocks from where he works, so he can walk. Leila and I go with Janice and Zachary to visit him once a week. We give him a ride to and from church on Sundays. Janice still won't let him near their girls."

Cardy just shook his head. "Heather said if I ever pulled something like that I'd be peeing through a straw for the rest of my life."

M.L. looked surprised. "She'd let you live? I wouldn't see the next sunup."

Jim sighed despondently, "What's the world coming to?"

M.L.'s response was grim. "I hope it's not coming to anything. That would mean whatever happens, happens here. And it sure looks like the wars are going to spread before they die down."

"Tell me about it. The rail lines are humming these days. At least we haven't been getting too many shot-up engines lately."

"True, but is it because the fire's died down or is the pressure building? It could be loud and ugly if that whistle screeches. And even if it doesn't, the rest of the world is going to Hell in a hand basket. If we don't watch it, we're going to be alone fighting the rest of the world."

Jim looked pensive. "Ain't that the truth. Did you see where the OAS formally joined the Catholic Entente and the French purchased Suriname?"

M.L. nodded. "Yeah. That means that the only part of South America they don't own is the rump portion of Colombia that we added to Panama. Wanta bet on when that blows up?"

"Not me. I was surprised when the Brits invaded China. I know they're allied with the Japs, but you'd think they had enough on their plate with fighting the Entente."

"Not if they're thinking down the road. They're working to cut out our trading partners, just like the Entente is doing with England. There's a reason Washington is talking about aligning with the Central Powers. I bet de Gaulle is working on something to try to drive a wedge between us."

Jim sighed, "Divide and conquer."

"I sure as hell hope not."

Cardy usually stayed out of these discussions. Both because they were bleak, and he didn't pay that much attention to the international news. That had begun to change over the last few months. M.L. and Jim were only a little surprised when Cardy broke in. "What do you think we'll do if the OAS goes after the British possessions in the Caribbean?"

Jim recovered first. "Who knows? A better question is what happens if England falls? The French made a successful raid. Will they stay longer the next time they go ashore?"

Cardy got a faraway look in his eyes. "What would the rest of their empire do? And what would happen to their fleet?"

"Their fleet?"

"Yes, their fleet. Remember, I was a Navy man. The British fleet is as big as ours, and ours is split between the Atlantic and the Pacific. We may move a lot of freight by rail, but we move even more by sea. And I'm not sure we have enough ships to guard the coasts if the Entente gets control of the Royal Navy."

M.L. just shook his head in disgust. "Thanks, Cardy. I think I liked it better when you ignored these conversations."

Cardy looked like he'd eaten something disgusting. "I think I did, too."

EARLY DECEMBER 1938

The Chancellery, Berlin, Germany

I'm not sure if I'm happy that they're finally paying attention or annoyed that they don't appear to have read any of the previous reports. I know Generalfeldmarschall Werner von Blomberg is squarely in the annoyed camp. The big four have finally joined us for the weekly military briefing and they keep interrupting him. At least they're letting Alfred Hugenberg do all the talking.

Blomberg looks at the Reichstag leader with the same petulance he usually reserves for Wilhelm III. "If you look at the strength comparisons in Appendix D, Section I, you'll see that we don't believe our units in country are adequate to stop a full-scale Entente attack. We would need to strip the Russian front to stop the French. And that's assuming we have the expected notice of them concentrating their forces.

"Section II shows how quickly we think the Russian front will deteriorate if we do that. Those estimates are based on numbers from last week. As I pointed out earlier, the situation has deteriorated since then. The Russians are counterattacking all along the front, using the snow to their advantage. Two divisions are currently cut off at Novgorod and we're organizing an attack to rescue them."

Hugenberg looks around at his peers to make sure they all follow Blomberg's logic. Ludwig Kaas looks skeptical, but shrugs and

Hugenberg turns back to Blomberg, "Thank you for your patience. Please continue."

Blomberg looks relieved as he goes back to his briefing. "We're outnumbered better than two-to-one in panzers and combat aircraft by the French, though our troop strength is comparable. The latest appropriations will help us address our equipment deficiencies in the coming year, but a ground war right now is not in our interest. We could not sustain offensive operations, so virtually all of the fighting would be done in our country."

Hugenberg checks with his contingent and I decide to head off their questions. "In other words, our navy could disrupt an invasion of England, but the resulting conflict would be fought almost exclusively on our soil. And with the Ruhr so close to the border, our production capacity would be under fire in short order."

"Yes, Sir. We believe we would lose everything west of the Rhine and all our gains on the Russian front. There's also a high probability that Turkey would be invaded from the south."

Hugenberg looks concerned. "How would intervention by the League alter things, both with and without us?"

"If we intervene first, we don't think the League would join us. That might even put us on their restricted trade list which would hurt our ability to prosecute the war. If the League intervenes first, they could supply Great Britain with enough resources to revive their war effort. However, that would open Ireland up as a much softer invasion target which carries its own set of problems."

"Recommendations?"

Blomberg looks at Hugenberg with diminishing patience. His recommendations were on the cover sheet. "Any assistance for the British should be economic at this time. We need to continue the planned expansion and upgrade of our army. We need to work on closer ties to the League. We need to end the war with Russia."

I sit back and watch as the Reichstag politicians huddle around their end of the table. Ernst Weber nudges me and points to them expectantly. I clear my throat, "Gentlemen."

When I have their attention, I begin. "I had meetings with both the French and British ambassadors yesterday. Ernst will provide you with my reports after we finish. Basically, Sir Phipps has asked that we act as intermediaries in negotiations for a cease-fire. François-Poncet asked if we would like to be part of the occupying forces in Great Britain."

That shocks them. "François-Poncet claims they are on target for an invasion by summer, but de Gaulle wants to keep our relationship friendly. They are willing for us to run an enclave that would cover everything north of and including the Liverpool-Manchester-Hull line. They would administer everything south of that line."

They talk in a jumble before I hold up my hands to quiet them. "You're only finding out about it now because both meetings were late yesterday, and we already planned on meeting today. I believe both offers are ploys to get the League and us more involved in the conflict."

Hugenberg takes the lead again. "We understand that, but both proposals give us some advantages. Any assistance we provide to stop the shooting will generate closer ties with the League. The same holds true if we protect part of Britain from French occupation."

"And how would you react if you got this kind of proposal from Thälmann and the Communist party?"

Hugenberg looks at his fellow party leader and chuckles dryly. "I'd wonder what he had up his sleeve."

"So?"

Hugenberg sits back and thinks for a moment. "If we act as intermediaries for cease-fire negotiations, the French will see us as siding with the British. Frustration at any snags or disruptions will be directed at us as well as the British. It might initially improve our stature with the League, but failure, or even slow progress, would undermine our relations with both the Entente and the League."

"And who would control the pace of the negotiations?"

"The French to some extent, but mostly the British."

Thälmann chimes in. "Good to know you think I'm a sneaky bastard."

Hugenberg chuckles again. "Don't take it personally, I expect you to look for hidden hooks in my proposals, too." He turns back to me. "I can see why the French told us about their invasion plans. Real or not, if we pass the information on to the British, they may be more likely to negotiate. It also provides us with a carrot to stay out of the conflict. And if the League finds out we're considering the proposal, they're less likely to work with us."

I lean forward and clasp my hands on my desk. "Don't forget that our occupation zone would include heavily Catholic areas."

Blomberg joins the conversation with, "And our barely adequate defense would be spread even thinner. We would have men and planes stuck at the end of a long and vulnerable supply line."

It's Hugenberg's turn to raise his hands in surrender. He does a quick scan of his contingent. "Okay. Those options join military intervention as non-viable. That leaves us with economic aid. Are we back to shipping things through Norway and Sweden? Are they even willing to do it?"

"I think we need to push it harder than that. I think we need to make the case to the Americans that they need to loosen their sanctions if they don't want to see a radical power shift."

Hugenberg looks at me for a moment. "And what do we do if they don't like our suggestions?"

"I think Blomberg is right. We need to get out of the war in Russia as soon as possible."

"Even if our allies don't like what we agree to?"

"Even then."

Paris, France

Général de Division Roger Noiret sat near the front of the conference table. It was where you sat when almost everyone else at the table outranked you. It meant he got to spend his time looking over his left shoulder to see what Marshal Delestraint presented and then swiveling his head to the right to see how President de Gaulle reacted. de Gaulle sat at the end of the table with a view that meant he wouldn't have a sore neck at the end of the meeting.

Roger had already studied the proposed attack on the Central Coalition. It wasn't long before he started following along by ear while he watched de Gaulle full-time. There were several times when de Gaulle looked dubious. Roger was gratified that they lined up with his own doubts about the plan.

Marshal Delestraint ended his presentation and waited for questions. The President shook his head subtly. "So, the basic plan is to attack from Strasbourg to the sea and see what happens? Really?"

Marshal Delestraint looked a little uncomfortable as he answered. "There will be an effort to encircle the German forces around Metz, but yes, it is a general attack."

"And what reserve would we have to exploit a breakthrough? It looks like everything is already accounted for."

"Eighth Army would move forward from Calais to Namur to act as a reserve for the Belgian front. Fourth Army would act as the reserve for the center once Metz is reduced. Third, Fifth, and Sixth Armies contain four of our six tank divisions. Once Saabrücken is taken, the situation will be reexamined. Our expectation is that we will follow up with an attack towards Frankfurt or Koblenz."

"And the preferred target is?"

"Koblenz, Sir. A crossing there would allow us to push the Germans off the Rhine River and make it into open country."

"And what are our force levels compared to the Germans?"

"They currently have seventy infantry divisions in country, along with three tank divisions that mostly contain older equipment. We have seventy-nine Infantry and six tank divisions. We also outnumber them better than two-to-one in the air."

"And how much of our equipment is outdated?"

"On the ground, roughly a third. In the air, it's more like ten percent."

"We'd also still be engaged with the British air force. And what happens if the League intervenes? Won't we need to reinforce Italy?"

"Probably, Sir. But the League may intervene anyway."

de Gaulle shrugged. "True, but unlikely. They don't like people waging war on civilians, and this winter will be a cold one for the British. Then again, we aren't the ones bombing cities at night. I don't see them declaring war on us unless we expand the war by attacking Germany.

"I'm sorry, Marshal, but I just don't see us successfully invading Germany until after the United Kingdom is dealt with. What's the plan for invading England?"

An assistant changed out the set of maps that Delestraint had been using with maps showing southern England. The Marshal took the opportunity to get a drink of water.

"We don't think it's feasible before March. The weather just isn't stable enough to allow us to supply a large force before then. Our current plan is to feint towards Dover and Plymouth to keep their forces in the southeast and southwest tied down.

"Our initial landing will be by the Ninth Army on the Isle of Wight, from Compton Beach down to Chale. This should limit how quickly they could reinforce the area. We believe we can overrun the island in three to five days. We will then use it as a base to threaten Portsmouth and Southampton. We expect the British to reinforce the area. Our air force will do as much damage as possible to their forces while they're moving in the open.

"We will proceed to the next phase once we have at least three divisions on the Isle of Wight. Tenth Army will land at the border of Devon and Dorset, between Seaton and Charmouth. They will drive towards the Bristol Channel to cut off Devon and Cornwall. The Ninth will cross the Solent when and where it can. Depending on circumstances, The Eighth Army will either land between Dover and Folkestone or move to reinforce the Ninth. Armored divisions would be moved from the Fifth and Sixth Armies to the Eighth and Tenth for the operation."

de Gaulle looked concerned. "I presume we aren't hitting all three areas at the same time because we don't have enough sea lift to move that many troops at the same time. Correct?"

"Yes, Sir. We are getting more landing craft brought in by rail every day, but our facilities on the Mediterranean have a limited production capacity. As it is, a quarter of the landing craft we'll need for this plan will come from Italian construction."

The French President looked unhappy as he scratched his chin. "In other words, if anything goes wrong during the multiple rounds of invasions, everything that comes afterwards is at risk."

"Yes, Sir."

"Meanwhile, Africa and Iran are virtual stalemates, and China is collapsing. We've purchased Suriname from the Dutch, so South America is quiet for now. Russia is making some headway with their counterattacks, but I'm not sure how long they'll keep the Germans tied up. How do things look if we push an invasion out to June?"

Delestraint consulted his notes before responding, "Better. We'll be able to transport two divisions at a time by March, that number goes up to three by June. It also gives us more time to pummel their infrastructure and fleet."

"Stay with the March date for now, and we'll see where things are at the beginning of February. The navy will work on burning the Royal Navy's gas and try to maneuver them into some disadvantageous situations. The air force will work on that pummeling you mentioned. I've requested air assets from Mussolini to help overwhelm the British and we're working on ways to blind their radar network. There are also some political options we are pursuing that might weaken their resolve."

de Gaulle looked thoughtful for a moment before continuing. "Is there anything else?" When the room stayed silent, he rose and with a "Thank you, gentlemen." He and his aides left.

The rest of the attendees rose and began to mill about. Roger made his way over towards Général Juin to see what his immediate boss wanted him to do. When Roger caught up with him, he was in a discussion with Marshal Delestraint. Roger was noticed, but not invited into the discussion. He watched and waited for their discussion to end. It wasn't long before Delestraint extended his hand and shook Juin's. As Delestraint turned to leave he gave Roger an appraising look and smile.

Roger approached Juin. "What was that about, Sir?"

"I've been given Ninth Army at Caan. We'll lead the way into England under the current plan."

"Congratulations, Sir. And do you know why he smiled at me as he left?"

Général Juin smiled, too. "That would be because 1st Armored is being transferred to my command and will be part of your Corps. It's also slated to be the first division with our new tanks."

And finally, the smile spread to Roger.

Trincomalee, Ceylon

Admiral Sir Geoffrey Blake felt truly apprehensive for the first time in his naval career. It wasn't that he was worried about how Clear Decks would go, it was that he felt like the junior partner for the first time. The Japanese First Carrier Striking Force had arrived yesterday. While the two battlecruiser squadrons matched up reasonably well, the Japanese had a decided edge on the carriers.

The Eastern Fleet had three out of four of Britain's largest carriers. The Japanese sent six carriers that were just as big or bigger. Sir Geoffrey's carriers were already using Japanese dive bombers and torpedo planes because they were so much better than the British versions. It appeared the Japanese fighters enjoyed the same type of advantage. The A6M

Hachi was sixty miles-per-hour faster than his new Fulmars, more heavily armed, more maneuverable, and had a longer range. Hell, the damn things were almost a match for the Spitfire. He was glad they were on his side, but the difference in capabilities shook his Royal Navy pride to the core.

"You're awfully quiet, Sir."

Sir Geoffrey was brought back to his surroundings by Rear Admiral John Moore's comment. They sat in a conference room of His Majesty's Naval Dockyard, waiting for their liaison to arrive. As head of the station, Vice Admiral Sir James Somerville and his staff would greet their guests and bring them here.

"Just glad we aren't fighting the Japanese. I think we'd do fine on the surface, but we are definitely outclassed in the air."

"Based on the reports from Boxer 2, I'm not even sure we'd do well in a surface engagement. The reports on the *Yamato* and *Musashi* are hard to believe, Sir."

"They may be hard to believe, but those reports came from veteran sailors who've served on some of our battleships. I think we need to control what our liaison sees and hears if we want the Japanese to keep treating us as partners."

"Maybe we can play on how we're just a far-flung outpost. It's why we needed to get planes from them, after all."

Sir Geoffrey was about to respond when approaching footsteps signaled the arrival of their counterparts. They stood and waited as Somerville brought in the delegation. John made a partial bow, while Sir Geoffrey merely inclined his head slightly. Three of the four Japanese bowed deeply in return. The fourth, a short but fierce-looking Vice Admiral, returned John's half bow.

Sir Geoffrey was taken by surprise when the Vice Admiral finished his bow and stepped forward, extending his hand. "Kaigun-Chūjō Chūichi Nagumo, Sir."

Sir Geoffrey shook it. "Admiral Sir Geoffrey Blake. Welcome to Trincomalee."

Somerville looked stunned. Nagumo turned to him, "I'm sorry if our earlier exchanges were cumbersome, but honor demands that I only respond to Japanese in public. It has been twelve years since I visited your country to study your naval tactics and strategies. Please forgive me if my English is ..."

He stopped for a moment and one of the men behind him prompted, "Rusty, Sir?"

Nagumo nodded. "Yes, rusty. I have been working with Ichiro to improve my skill. I hope it will make it easier to work together." A slight smile flashed across the face of the young Lieutenant behind Nagumo looked pleased, while the other two remained stone-faced.

Sir Geoffrey smiled and waved them to their seats. The joint operation looked like it would be a lot less cumbersome than he had feared. They spread out maps for Operation Clear Decks and started going over the details.

It was almost three hours later that the Japanese contingent headed back towards their ships. The British admirals watched them go before returning to Somerville's office.

Sir Geoffrey looked exasperated even after taking a drink from his teacup. "I don't think we're going to be able to get anything past Nagumo."

Somerville agreed. "At least he has an appreciation for all things British and was impressed by *Vanguard's* radar. He did seem a bit dubious about depending on it, though."

"I understand his hesitancy. Six to ten minutes of warning is useful, but it will still be difficult to coordinate the air defense among this many ships and planes. We may not have to have as many planes in our combat air patrol, but we'll need to keep more fighters ready on our decks to respond to any threats."

"That's your area, not mine. I'm just glad he could promise us more plates for any repair work we need to do. That's been my biggest worry about this operation from the beginning."

Sir Geoffrey agreed. "I was more worried about it before I saw what the Japanese are committing. I think the Entente is in for a rude awakening when we come calling. I just hope it's enough to relieve some of the pressure on England."

"Me too, Sir."

"At least operations in China are proceeding smoothly."

"True. It sounds like the Nationalist army is collapsing, though the Communists are still fighting. I've got reports that they're working with the local warlords to divide China into occupation zones for us, the Japanese, and the Russians."

"That's one headache I'm glad I'm not..."

A knock at the office door stopped the conversation. The duty officer reported that their Japanese interpreter was waiting for them at the docks. Lieutenant Ichiro would be joining them on the *Marlborough* for the operation. Sir Geoffrey understood the logic of the communication redundancy, but he wasn't sure how he felt about having a foreign officer on his bridge.

"Looks like it's time to get things moving." Sir Geoffrey extended his hand as they all stood. "Wish us luck."

Somerville took the proffered hand. "Good hunting, Sir."

Sir Geoffrey enjoyed the view as he and John headed down to the docks. The gathered fleet was magnificent in the evening sun. Nine capital ships lay at anchor with nine aircraft carriers that carried almost six hundred planes. The slow battleships of the 1st Battle Division wouldn't be coming. They were making another anti-submarine sweep in the Arabian Sea.

A coldness crept into Sir Geoffrey's eyes as they walked. Maybe he could take another pound of flesh from the bastards who'd killed his wife.

Brest, France

Colonnello Guido Nobili had only been back in Italy for two days before he was headed to France again. He'd hoped to keep his men out of the fighting for longer, but it was time to return to the fray. They were changing base to Brest to help in the air assault on Britain and interdict any shipping they could find.

The only bright spot was that he would be working under Général de Brigade Jacob Sarbone again. Sarbone had been in charge of flight operations at Figueres, Spain during the Spanish Civil War.

When Guido arrived with his expanded air wing, he reported to Sarbone. He was pleasantly surprised to find another familiar face. He'd been working with Claude Lefebvre for much of the war. Claude had been transferred back to France almost a month ago. Guido happily paused in the doorway for a moment when he saw his friend.

Général Sarbone cleared his throat. "Commandant Lefebvre is not the Pope."

Lefebvre chuckled. Guido had the decency to look embarrassed at the reference to the Spanish Civil War. Guido had spotted the Pope traveling through the Spanish countryside. He'd stared long enough that he almost crashed his plane into His Holiness.

"Colonnello Guido Nobili reporting as ordered, Sir."

"At ease, Nobili." Général Sarbone rose and offered his hand. "It's good to see you again."

Guido shook it with a smile. "You too, Sir. Both of you." He took the vacant chair that Sarbone waved him to and waited for his new commander.

Sarbone grabbed a paper from the left side of his desk and quickly scanned it before looking back up at Guido. "This says you have ninety G.51s, and one hundred and twenty torpedo bombers. How many are veteran aircrews?"

"About a quarter, Sir. But we've been working on tactics with the green crews. Hopefully, we've gotten rid of the bad habits they picked up in their initial training. This will be the first big test to see if it helps."

Sarbone looked dubious. "At least that's something. Have you been working on ground or sea targets?"

"Both, Sir. Based on our experience in Africa, we've been concentrating on sea attacks more than ground. We're trying to cut down on our loss rate for both kinds of missions."

"You can work with Lefebvre to find out how the British are doing things over England. They've got radar and a lot more planes than you dealt with down in Africa. Lefebvre commands our French squadrons. We've got ninety D.520s and sixty MB.174s. There's also ninety MB.152s. Their range is too short for most of our missions, so we use them for air defense. Your torpedo planes will give us the ability to hurt the Royal Navy that we've been missing."

"I thought you were building some proper torpedo planes of your own."

"We are. Just not enough of them. We've been interdicting the British supplies, with an emphasis on their oil. To tighten the squeeze, the brass wants us to make the RAF fly, and the Royal Navy sail, as often as possible. Our fleet will change bases back and forth between Gibraltar and La Rochelle. Our planes will raid England every chance we get."

"And after your raid on Dover last month, the British will have to respond to your fleet movements."

"That's the expectation. If we can catch them at sea without any land-based air cover, we might be able to chew into their numerical advantage."

"Do you know how many carrier aircraft they have?"

"Their Home Fleet has moved down to Hull since the Dover raid. It's got three small carriers with about seventy aircraft, but I doubt we'll have to deal with them. Their Atlantic Fleet is based in the Azores. It's got four carriers with just under two hundred planes. That's our primary naval target."

"Understood. Do your pilots have much experience fighting their Gladiators and Fulmars?"

Lefebvre answered. "Not really. We've been dealing with Hurricanes and Spitfires over England."

"Maybe we could bring up one of the CR.42 squadrons I was working with in Italy. They're slower than the British planes but they're more agile. Some practice missions against them will give your pilots a better feel for what to expect if we strike their fleet."

Sarbone nodded, "I'll see what I can arrange. Now go get settled in. Lefebvre will be by in two hours to take you to the maintenance hangar. You can get to know your counterparts and pass on some of your lessons to our pilots. They'll teach you what we've learned about the RAF."

Guido stood. "Sounds good to me, Sir." He saluted and left when Sarbone responded, "Dismissed."

The hangar was big, but the massed pilots still crowded it. There was food and wine and tales of exploits. Luckily, Lefebvre and Sarbone kept Guido's encounter with the Pope a secret. Guido had worried that the tale was common knowledge.

The groups began to mesh nicely over the next few days. They ran some joint strikes against the southwestern English ports. There were even a couple of practice missions with the CR.42s from Italy before the French Fleet made its dash to La Rochelle. Both Claude and Guido were too nervous to send their pilots out without going along to coordinate the strike. They did promise Général Sarbone that they would stay out of the action. Whether or not Sarbone believed them was open to debate.

They met the British fleet about three hundred kilometers southwest of Brest. The Italian G.51s had a shorter range than the French D.520s, so Guido's fighter pilots led the way. They were met by over a hundred

Fulmars and Gladiators. With his pilots slightly outnumbered, Guido was quickly drawn into the fray. He wasn't supposed to see any action, so he didn't have a wingman. That lack almost cost him his life.

Guido dove after a Fulmar that had one of his men in its sights. He got too focused on his target as he followed the chain of twisting aerial acrobatics started by the lead G.51. He finally got a clean shot on a tight left turn. The long familiar vibration of the guns sent a smile to Guido's face as he pressed the firing stud. Those same ingrained habits made him pull up and away from the now burning enemy plane. That made the enemy's wingman miss his shot, as the fourth plane in the chain was slow to respond to Guido's sudden change of direction. Guido continued his evasive maneuvers while he got back in tune with the air battle as a whole.

The dogfight was still going on when the French fighters joined the fray. The battle quickly went from a grinding Italian edge to a rout. The only problem Guido had with chasing the enemy fighters from the sky, was that they were replaced by anti-aircraft fire from the enemy ships. He called his fighters to return to base. They headed back to Brest, leaving the French to command the skies.

It was less than a minute before they passed over the torpedo bombers that were flying low towards the enemy ships. Two more minutes behind them were the French bombers. They hoped to catch the British fleet holding straight courses to avoid the Italian torpedoes. There was little Guido could do now other than get his men home and wait for the results of their mission. It was a task Guido found more stressful than the actual combat.

Nervous and excited chatter bounced between the returning pilots. Fourteen of their brothers were missing and six of the returning G.51s were damaged, including Guido's. It looked like his escape had been narrower than he thought. That was a detail that would get back to both Sarbone and worse, Aurora. Guido didn't look forward to either one of those conversations.

When he finally got to Sarbone's office, his commander accepted his after-action report and shook his head in exasperation. "At least you saved the skin of one of your pilots. In the future, you will take a wingman with you on any missions. Understood?"

"Yes, Sir. Old habits die hard."

"Just as long as they do die, before they kill you."

Sarbone glared at Guido for a long time before he finally relented. He pulled a bottle of brandy and three glasses from his desk. He had just finished pouring when Lefebvre joined them. His report included the results from the bombers. They'd lost nine Z.1007s and six MB.174s in addition to eight D.520s. Almost all of the enemy fighters had been shot down. Scouts were already over the British fleet, trying to determine how much damage they'd done and what the enemy was doing. If nothing else, tonight's gathering would get to celebrate the air victory to offset their losses.

When the air crews got together, the gathering was more subdued than Guido had expected. It took him a few minutes to understand what the difference was. Unlike Africa, where the big fights were few and far between, tomorrow would bring another big mission for these men. If they didn't launch another strike on the Royal Navy, they would head to England to engage the Royal Air Force. Only the weather would give them a break. Guido would have to make sure that the grind didn't affect his men's morale too much.

The next day was overcast and rainy, but it brought a more joyous mood to the pilots. No one would be flying any missions and they got the results from reconnaissance on yesterday's attack. The British had headed northwest. That would put them in a better position to intercept any landings in England. It would also let them get more aircraft. The scouts reported that there were six destroyers, three light cruisers, and two heavy cruisers missing from the British fleet. Best of all, one of the three smaller carriers had been trailing a huge plume of smoke.

Spartanburg, South Carolina, USA

Manly Lee Wilburn had expected the new mechanics to slow him and Cardy down for at least a little while. He was happy with just how wrong he'd been. Cardy was working with Bill Hawkins. Twenty-eight-year-old Bill was a little taller than M.L. and a bit beefier. He was a Spartanburg native who Jim Deeson had hired away from Sanford's Salvage. Bill was new to working on trains, but he knew his way around a shop and an engine. He was a quick study, and he fit right in once he got used to the size of the tools for the trains.

Andrew Christianson was twenty-seven and had come from Savannah. The Georgia-boy was even taller than Bill and towered over Cardy by a good half a foot. Andrew had been working at a John Deere repair center on some of the larger farm machines. He didn't have the breadth of knowledge that Bill had, but he was actually used to the scale of train engines. Andrew had moved into a boarding house that was near where Bill lived, so they rode in to work together.

Jim called M.L. into his office at the end of the week. "How are the new guys working out, M.L.?"

"I'm happy to report that everything is running as smoothly as it can with eight elbows in a confined space. They're both picking things up quickly, and experience from their previous jobs has helped us rearrange things to make them more efficient. Why? Do we have more changes coming down the pipe?"

Jim chuckled at the suspicion in M.L.'s expression. "Not that I know of. The home office sent me info on five people they could move here, and I picked Bill and Andrew. I just wanted to make sure I hadn't saddled us with dead weight."

"You did fine, boss. They're still in that new-job phase where they're eager to please. Hopefully, that attitude will hang around after the new-job shine has worn off."

"I hope so too. How are things going with Jewel's wedding?"

M.L. let out an exasperated sigh. "Leila is doing her best to make a dress for Jewel, but she isn't happy with the short notice. Jewel just wants 'something simple' but keeps coming up with more things that it would be nice to have. Friends are helping with the decorations and getting the word out. In other words, the usual wedding circus crammed into three weeks. Are you and yours coming?"

"I appreciate the invite, but the family doesn't know anyone in Cross Anchor, and I only know you and Cardy. I'll send a gift for the newlyweds, but we'd just be the outsiders at the wedding. I don't want you keeping an eye on me to make sure I don't feel left out. I want you to concentrate on your daughter's happiness. You can even have a day or two off if you need it."

"You wouldn't be a bother Jim, but I can understand and appreciate the sentiment."

"I might not want to be any trouble, but I would be. Just like I am right now. Cardy's out there waiting on his ride home and here I am keeping you from giving it to him. Now get outta here before I find more work for y'all to do."

M.L. chuckled. "Take it easy, Jim. See ya Monday."

He got Cardy and they headed out to brave the Saturday traffic. As usual, it was full of impatient and angry drivers. They carefully made their way south towards home. Instead of stopping at Cardy's house, M.L. drove straight to church.

He parked next to the half-a-dozen cars already there. Inside, they joined the group that was working on the decorations for the wedding. Heather and Leila quickly chased their husbands to a corner and sat them down. A couple of thick, ham sandwiches and beers appeared in front of the men. Cardy and M.L. smiled as they clinked their bottles together. Pitching in would just have to wait until after lunch.

Everyone was late getting home that night and dinner was leftovers, but M.L. was happy. They'd done this three times before, and what Leila forgot, one of the girls remembered. Even with Christmas a week after the wedding, everything was running smoothly. Leila was in the kitchen, directing the kids on clean-up duty when M.L. walked in. She gave him a suspicious look at his invasion of her domain, but a brewing fight between Sybil and Betty demanded her attention.

M.L. walked up behind his wife and slipped his hands around her waist, hugging her tightly. He nuzzled the back of her head and murmured, "Thanks for everything, m'Love."

He rested his chin on the top of his wife's head and watched the barely controlled chaos of their kids doing the dishes. Her arms slid over his and she leaned back into him, "You're welcome for everything, even me providing a place to rest your chin."

The delivery was so deadpan that it startled a snort out of M.L. and he pulled his head back to kiss the top of hers. The kids were too absorbed with playing while they cleaned to pay much attention to their parents. Leila casually asked, "How are things going?"

That brought another smile to M.L.'s face. Even when they were playing, the kids would notice if their parents whispered something. Normal voices meant normal, boring, adult things and were automatically tuned out. "Work's a little cramped with the new guys, but they're already being useful. Jim said I can have some time off if I need it and that they won't be coming. He felt like they'd be intruding."

"I thought he might. One of these days we'll get him down here to meet people. And the time off?"

"We're swamped, but Jim will make it happen if I ask. We're still getting a few engines with bullet holes in them. We got one sent down from New York that looked like it had been hit by a mortar. Someone doesn't like that we're shipping food to the people in Quebec."

Leila tilted her head slightly and M.L. answered, "The company says they inspect every shipment for war material. Maybe somebody would rather the Catholics starved. Pretty unchristian. Then again, who knows how many more Protestant Canadians will die because we're feeding the rebels."

A shrug from his wife and a squeeze of his trapped hands, signaled the end of her interest. She was like most Americans, far more concerned with what happened around here than the rest of the world. But the thoughts had been released in M.L.'s head. Now, they were running around like chickens being chased by a fox.

Because of the raid into England and the attack on China, Roosevelt refused to lift any sanctions on England or France. He gave a couple of reasons why, but it basically came down to what would happen if they were lifted. Both sides would start shooting at American ships as soon as they started carrying anything that could be considered war material.

The men who were gone because of the army and Jewel's wedding showed the impact the conflict was already having on his town. M.L. knew the changes were being repeated all across the country. It made him wonder how much more things would change when the war finally spread.

LATE DECEMBER 1938

Manstein Residence, Berlin, Germany

It's a week until Christmas and I'm sitting alone at home. Edna, Brent, and Otto are out shopping. I look over the small stack of gifts I just finished wrapping and am sad. I made the list, but it was Ernst who picked them up for me. This is the first year I haven't done my own shopping. I had planned on doing it, but Otto started talking about the security arrangements and I gave up. The gifts I wanted to get came from different stores, and each would have been effectively closed while I was there. That was not a good way to endear myself to the shopkeepers or their customers. So, Ernst went in my stead. And now, Edna is picking up the cuckoo clock for Ernst.

It's been a long, eventful, and scary year. What worries me most is that the coming year may be worse. I no longer think it's a question of if we go to war with the Entente. I'm sure of it and I hope we're ready for it. I'm too isolated to know how the German people feel about the coming war. The only time I interact with them is at staged events with carefully controlled audiences. I get reports from Franz Gürtner at Justice that the people are restless but behind us. Otto checks with the other members of my security detail, and Ernst talks with his friends. They say that the subdued grumbling about higher taxes and the scarcity of goods has died down since we went public with the real story of the attempt on my life. They also say that outright hatred for the French and British is very prevalent. Then again, both Otto's and Ernst's friends are heavily military.

I get up and prowl restlessly around the house. After nibbling one of the cookies that Beatrice left for us, I end up in the library. I pull Clausewitz' *On War* from a shelf and flip through the pages.

I've read it many times and mostly use it to stimulate my thinking. Mussolini and de Gaulle have their people solidly behind them, as does Broz in the USGA. However, the United Kingdom is anything but united. Chamberlain just barely survived a no-confidence vote after the French raid on Dover. Churchill would have probably taken over if he hadn't been involved in the assassination attempt on me. It makes me wonder if I will be able to mobilize the people of Germany when we need it.

I put the book back on the shelf and scan through my collection. I realize that they're almost all about war or politics and shake my head. My interests have become very narrow over the years. Not for the first time, I wonder what I'd be doing if I hadn't run into Ludendorff all those years ago. That thought takes me to my science fiction section. I fondly remember reading Verne and Wells to Brent when he was young. Almost all of them are tales of overcoming adversity to get to a place of hope. I smile at the thought that these fanciful tales still have the power to lift my spirits. I brush past *A Modern Utopia,* select *The World Set Free* and sit down to read. I quickly remember the premise and wonder how close Wells' predictions will match with what Einstein is working on.

I'm about halfway through when my family returns. I happily greet them and listen to the tale of their hunting expedition. The shops were packed, but the other customers were friendly and glad to see Edna out and about. They disappear to stash their hard-won trophies. I miss the time when I could have been with them without involving a wall of bodyguards.

After they come back downstairs, Edna and Otto excuse themselves to work on dinner. They're both pretty good cooks, they just don't normally have the time for it. We watch them leave and Brent turns to me with a questioning look on his face. I think I've been set up.

"Yes?"

"Sorry, Dad. I'm just worried about you. Mom says you've been a little distant lately and she's worried about you, too."

Even Brent calling Edna Mom doesn't break my mood. I look down and scratch at something on the back of my left thumbnail for a moment. I'm stalling and I know it. I look back up at Brent, "I'm just down and keep wondering what I could have done differently. Christmas is coming, but all I see is trouble and conflict in our future."

"I thought so. You rarely dive into the science fiction unless you're looking for encouragement. And I'm sorry if you haven't been getting enough of it. Yes, storm clouds are building, but we are all solidly behind you. And I don't just mean our family.

"Everyone at school, and everyone they know, is glad that you're the person leading us. The consensus is that the Reichstag would still be dithering if you weren't pulling them forward. If we make it through the next few years, it will be because of your actions."

"And if we don't?" The question is out before I can censor it.

"Then it will be our fault for letting you down. I hope you know how proud I am to be your son. Dozens of people stopped us today because they wanted to thank us for what you've done."

"Are you sure they weren't just glad I wasn't there to keep them from shopping?"

"Dad." The annoyed look that goes along with that plaintive comment makes me give him a small shrug in surrender.

"People listen to your radio broadcasts. They trust you to tell them the truth, or to have a good reason not to. You may not be flashy like de Gaulle, but they know you have their best interests at heart. Peter said his pastor even included you in his list of things and people to pray for in his sermon last week."

Brent stops for a moment and stares at me. Then he looks down at my book on the table. When he looks back up, there are tears in his eyes.

"You know how those books always end up with things heading for a brighter future? That's where our people believe you can take us."

I lean forward and give him a hug. "Thanks, son."

Meanwhile, a little voice in my head says, "Yeah, no pressure. No pressure at all." I tell it to shut up.

Toulouse, France

Général de Division Roger Noiret was happier than he'd been in a long time. The war seemed like it had been going on for years, even though it had only been seven months. At least most of it was being fought outside France this time. The damage at the channel ports and around Paris was minor compared to the horrors of the Great War.

Most of the men he'd started the war with were back in France too. It had lifted his spirits to see so many familiar faces that he doubted he'd ever meet again. They'd been happy to see him too, and that was before he showed them the new equipment they were getting.

Now he was on leave in his hometown, surrounded by family and away from his usual burdens of command. Roger brought mementos from his campaigns home as gifts for his family. Most were wrapped under the tree, waiting for Christmas morning. A couple of them had been doled out to increase the anticipation.

Guy, Junior, and Pierre had pushed him after every dinner to tell them of his adventures. Roger had edited things the first night, and the boys had seemed a little too enthusiastic about the prospects of war. Catherine thought he was being gruesome the second night, when he put in the uglier details. The boys had responded with rapt attention and eyes full of anticipation. That lasted until he pointed out that sometimes the flying body parts were from your friends, or even yourself. The boys grew more somber when Roger showed his battle scars, and they realized how close their father had come to not returning home.

That night, Catherine snuggled up to him and fell asleep holding him in her arms. Roger basked in her love but felt a deep sadness at the worry and pain he'd caused her. He wondered how much more he would cause before this war was over. Sleep was elusive. It was only after a long prayer that Roger finally managed to surrender to it.

Toulouse still seemed mostly undisturbed by the war. No bombing raids had penetrated this far south. The paper carried daily stories and photographs of the damage caused by the indiscriminate British bombers further north. That Roger might be somehow responsible was information he kept to himself. At least the people he met didn't seem to be as disconnected from his reality anymore. They were learning that there was a price to be paid for fighting for the Lord.

Roger tried to sleep in during his leave, but never made it past six thirty. The whole family spent one of his precious days at the Basilique Saint-Semon de Toulouse. They helped prepare food for the needy and cleaned up afterwards. The boys were confused by Roger's joy in doing this, and it was Guy who finally asked him about it. "Alright, Dad. Why do you seem to be so happy to serve food and wash dishes for these people?"

Roger kept serving food as he responded. "It's the same thing I do in the army." If anything, Guy looked more confused. Roger chuckled lightly. "We fight for those who can't fight for themselves, to protect them from those who would keep them from living in God's grace. That fight doesn't always involve shooting at people. Sometimes it's about a full belly or a warm bed. It's an old maxim that an army travels on its stomach. The same is true of a country. Besides, a little humility is good for the soul."

Roger looked around at the people still eating, then back at his sons. "I bet you don't realize that half of the men we've fed today are veterans of the Great War. Yes, it didn't turn out the way we would have liked, but it could have been much worse. These men bear scars on their bodies and souls from the fight to keep us free. Those scars can make it difficult to get or hold a job. How can we not honor those who have given so much?"

Guy was silent as he contemplated Roger's words. Junior wasn't. "We've seen the scars on your body, Dad. Do you have them on your soul, too?"

"I'm afraid so, son. But I have you and your mother to help me heal from their pain and remind me why I fight."

In moments, Junior went from being fifteen to being five. Tears welled up in his eyes as he gave his father a fierce hug. In moments, Roger was at the center of a hug knot, as the rest of his family joined in. As they slowly disentangled themselves, they noticed that much of the dining hall was intently watching. Junior whispered to his father and Roger nodded. He turned to the people they'd fed.

"Soldiers, attention!"

About two-thirds of the diners stood and came to attention, the others simply stopped what they were doing.

"Present arms!"

Hands bobbed to heads, not only among the diners, but also among the servers and his family. Roger slowly brought his hand up in salute. "Thank you for your service and for giving us the opportunity to live in a free France. God bless you."

As Roger brought his hand down, the standing men shouted, "Vive la France!" and someone led the crowd in a badly off-key, but oh so sweet-sounding rendition of La Marseillaise.

150 Miles East of the Horn of Africa, Arabian Sea

Admiral Sir Geoffrey Blake and Rear Admiral John Moore were at the rail of the *Marlborough*, watching the sun set. John noticed the apprehensive mood of his boss. It might be pre-operation jitters, but John hadn't seen them in the past.

"Concerns, Sir?"

A heavy sigh escaped Sir Geoffrey, "Something doesn't feel right. We got the Entente scout this afternoon, but we haven't run into any more of them. Something doesn't fit. It's like when you're expecting something for Christmas, but the box under the tree is the wrong shape for what you want."

"Maybe they're running low on scouts. Maybe it's that we have so much riding on this, or that it's the first time we've really worked with the Japanese." John paused for a moment before quietly admitting, "But, yes, I feel it too."

"It's like the change in the air before a storm. Your body notices it before your eyes ever see any clouds."

They watched as the last sliver of the sun slid below the horizon. Sir Geoffrey pulled out his watch to check the time, then snapped it closed. "Either way, it's time."

John followed him back onto the bridge where Sir Geoffrey simply said, "Go for Phase One."

"Go for Phase One, Aye" came the response. Moments later, the *Marlborough* surged ahead as she pushed her speed to thirty knots.

Dawn was still an hour away and the sky was slowly brightening. They were a hundred miles into the Gulf of Aden now and the strike force was preparing to launch. The *Vanguard's* radar detected an Entente scout just after midnight. It flew within ten miles of the fleet before circling and heading west.

Tactical surprise may have been lost, but they outnumbered the defenders of Dire Dawa by almost four to one. The launch began on schedule and Sir Geoffrey could do little more than stand and wait.

Sir Geoffrey and John stood at the rail again. Commodore Glennie was braced on the bridge, trying to stoically wait for news. Only Lieutenants Ichiro and Everett seemed to be immune to the tension in the air. They leaned together discussing something, probably Everett trying to learn more Japanese.

Sir Geoffrey had just rolled his shoulders to relieve his tension when he heard the first commotion from inside. John jerked as his initial reaction was to find out what was going on, but he took a deep breath and settled back at the rail. It was almost a minute before Ichiro and Everett joined them.

"Initial reports were of total surprise at Dire Dawa, Sir. These were quickly followed by no sign of enemy aircraft. The strike force is bombing the base now, but the only resistance appears to be from anti-aircraft batteries around the base. There's a bit of confusion on what to do, Sir."

"Wipe the base and return. Make sure all remaining fighters are ready for launch."

Everett snapped off an "Aye, Sir" before heading back onto the bridge with Ichiro in tow. They returned moments later.

John looked puzzled. "Where the devil are they, Sir?"

"That is the big question. It's likely that their scout saw our ships last night, but the Japanese were twenty miles behind us. Are they just trying to avoid air casualties, or have they sniffed out our plan? If they know the Japanese are with us, they may have figured out that we're going after the Canal. If that's the case, then they're scrounging every fighter they can find to defend it.

"Everett, have them radio our contacts in Egypt. We're still going, but it would be nice to know what we're walking into. Ichiro, see if your people can find any information and make sure they know what my concerns are."

Sir Geoffrey drummed his fingers on the railing as the Lieutenants sped off to relay his orders.

Time crept by as the fleet continued its journey towards the Suez Canal. The strike group came back without incident. The airbase at

Dire Dawa was in flames. Three Kates had been shot down and four Vals had been damaged but would be ready for operations tomorrow.

The tension was palpable as the fleet passed through the Bab al-Mandab Strait that afternoon. They continued their charge north. The Japanese had come a long way for this attack and were against backing down. Sir Geoffrey wondered how much of that was their code of honor, and how much was wanting to know how their pilots stood up to European standards. Every scout sent north was shot down by multiple fighters. It was after midnight when they finally got confirmation that the Entente was gathering planes around Suez. Even Sir Geoffrey had trouble sleeping that night.

The predawn launch was repeated, but there was a certainty of battle this time. Fifty-four fighters were held back for fleet defense. Five hundred and forty-one planes headed north. The question was just how many planes the Entente could scrape together. Regardless of the outcome, nine capital ships, nine aircraft carriers, twelve heavy cruisers, eighteen light cruisers, and forty destroyers were headed north to finish the job. Ten of those destroyers had been rigged as minelayers and would do their best to close the Canal.

Sir Geoffrey was alone at the rail this morning. John was inside in case he needed to coordinate the actions of the 1st Battlecruiser Squadron. Lieutenant Everett came out after a few minutes and waited. Sir Geoffrey finally relented. "It's too early for any reports, so what do you need, Gregory?"

"I just wanted you to know that Ichiro says that Vice Admiral Nagumo is leaning on the railing outside of the bridge on the *Zuikaku*."

That got a chuckle from Sir Geoffrey. "It seems we're not so different after all. Tell Ichiro I said thanks, and it's fine if he informs Nagumo of my actions."

"Aye, Sir."

The burden seemed to ease a bit as Sir Geoffrey understood that his weren't the only shoulders bearing it. He went back to watching the sea.

Half an hour had passed when the sirens for battle stations went off. Sir Geoffrey felt the *Marlborough* change course as the fleet turned into the wind. More fighters joined the combat air patrol in the sky and began heading west. Time to return to the bridge.

John greeted him with the reason. "*Vanguard* reports close to two hundred aircraft approaching from the west. Fifty-four fighters heading west to intercept. I think we found the planes from Dire Dawa."

Everyone had their orders and knew their roles. Once again, Sir Geoffrey had little to do while his men put their lives on the line. All he could do was project calm and coordinate the reaction to the changing situation.

The air battle was over in little more than five minutes. Ninety Italian G.51s had met 36 Hachis and 18 Fulmars. Just over half of the Italian fighters had fallen from the sky, along with almost two dozen of the bombers they were trying to protect. The speed and agility of the Japanese fighters may have surprised the Italians, but the Japanese planes were too lightly armored to take much punishment. His pilots had done well, they were just too heavily outnumbered. Seventy torpedo planes and bombers pressed the attack.

Lieutenant Commander Caldwell and his 2nd Destroyer Flotilla did their duty to protect the carriers. Three of them were sunk, though for once, Caldwell's ship wasn't one of them.

Captain Lucas' 7th Cruiser Squadron was also in the cross hairs. Three of his ships took torpedo hits. The *Neptune* and *Ajax* each took two torpedoes, while Captain Eakes of the *Orion* managed to dodge three out of the four sent his way.

The anti-aircraft fire shot down another two dozen of the attackers, but not before they put two fish into the *Ark Royal* and five each in the *Vanguard* and the *Takao*. The Italian pilots fled the smoking scene as those three ships slowly slid beneath the waves. Sir Geoffrey dispatched ten destroyers to search for survivors while the rest of the fleet continued north.

The loss of the *Vanguard* and its radar meant they were back to relying on scouts for information. It didn't make that much difference though; they didn't have any planes left to commit until the strike got back from Suez. Trying to sneak out of the Red Sea at this point was useless. Sir Geoffrey was determined to at least complete his mission.

It was another thirty minutes before the reports finally started coming in from the strike force. Five hundred and forty-one planes had headed north. The Entente had scraped together close to two hundred fighters, most of them D.520s. Claims were still coming in, but apparently neither group had been willing to disengage. Current estimates were that both sides had lost three-quarters of their fighters. Almost fifty attacking bombers had joined them.

That left him less than a hundred fighters and around two hundred bombers. Suez was ablaze and the Entente airbase there was out of commission. Sir Geoffrey knew that the longer he stayed in this exposed position, the more likely it was that the Entente would bring more planes to bear. Still, the fleet sped north. One way or another, the Suez Canal would be closed.

Brest, France

Colonnello Guido Nobili sat at his desk gripping a cup of coffee. The weather was terrible, so there weren't any missions today. The pilots were relaxing and there was supposed to be a tactics discussion this afternoon. That was for the aircrews that slowly filtered in to replace their losses. The warmth from his cup bled into his chilly hands and he was reluctant to release it to turn the page of the latest report.

A rap at the door pulled his eyes up from the paper. A young French Caporale waited for Guido's acknowledgment before delivering his message. "Général Sarbone would like to see you in his office, Sir."

With Guido's response of "On my way", the Caporale left. Guido wasn't sure what Sarbone wanted, so he grabbed the latest readiness and supply reports and headed down the hall. Ahead of him, Commandant Lefebvre came out of his office and waited for Guido. His shrug showed that he didn't know why they'd been summoned. The papers he carried looked suspiciously like his supply and readiness reports.

They got to Sarbone's office and the Général dismissively waved them to seats as he finished reading something. They settled in and waited.

A page flip and a few extra seconds went by before Sarbone looked up. "It's nothing that directly affects us, but it will probably impact future operations. The Japanese are taking a more active role in the fighting. They sent a task force with four battlecruisers and six carriers to help the Eastern Fleet. The combined group raided up the Red Sea and hit the Suez Canal. We had some advance notice, so we weren't caught napping. There were a couple of big air battles, but they managed to blow Dire Dawa and Suez to pieces. They also mined the Canal, which is expected to be closed for at least two months."

Lefebvre's simple comment of "Shit" barely registered on Guido. When he looked up, Sarbone was staring at him.

"Okay, Guido. How bad is it?"

"I don't know. Sir. It's been a couple of months since I was down there, but most of our supplies for the eastern half of the South African front ran through the Canal. I know they've been building railroads to help. I just don't have a clue how far along they are. A lot depends on how many transports they have on the far side of the Canal and whether they can keep them safe. You said Dire Dawa was attacked?"

"That's right, you were based there at the beginning of the war." Sarbone flipped through his report before continuing. "There was enough warning that they moved to a base near Port Sudan. They're the only ones who did any major damage to the Eastern Fleet. They launched a strike that sank a carrier and a couple of battleships, though it cost them half of their fighters and some bombers. Right now, they're about all that's left of our air assets between Italy and Iraq."

Guido sat back in shock. "I thought you said we had advance warning. How did carriers do that much damage to us?"

"The Japanese carriers are pretty big. Our best estimate is that the combined fleet had close to six hundred planes."

"That would explain why Fagnani bugged out. They would have overwhelmed his exposed force. Still, carrier fighters aren't nearly as good as ground-based ones."

"Apparently the Japanese ones are. Reports are that they are only thirty kilometers per hour slower than our fighters and carry two cannons plus machine guns. They can't take much damage, but they're maneuverable as hell. Fagnani said they held their own against his G.51s."

Guido just shook his head in wonder. Lefebvre leaned forward, "So how could this impact us, Sir?"

"The replacements for the air losses will have to come from somewhere. Command may even want to bolster our garrisons. There's also the question of supplying the South African front. Bombers may be pressed into delivering supplies."

Guido chimed back in, "How bad were the losses and do you know if they went after the air bases in Tanzania?"

"There's nothing in here about Tanzania. We lost about three hundred planes, and our best guess is that we got about two hundred and fifty to three hundred of them. A submarine in the Arabian Sea had the fleet headed east, presumably back to their base in India."

Guido thought for a moment. "We need to find out if the Japanese ships are staying in the Indian Ocean or returning home. We also need an estimate on British air losses. Do we know if the Japanese planes can operate from the remaining British carriers? That would get them back up to fighting strength faster than waiting for replacements from England. And I would appreciate it if I could get a list of casualties for our pilots and the ground crew at Dire Dawa. I had a lot of friends down there."

"I'll see what I can get for you. Command is already working on the other questions. They think this is the payback for sending troops into China, but they aren't sure if it's a long-term effort. A lot will be determined by what happens in China. They're working with the Russians to split it up into occupation zones."

Lefebvre looked dubious. "That's not something I expected out of the Japanese. Maybe the British are pushing it. Hmm, there could be a silver lining to the attack on the Canal."

"Oh, Claude? Please enlighten me."

"Well, the closing of the Canal and cooperation in China will push the League further away from any assistance for the British. It also means that the Italian battle fleet is currently out of a job. Couldn't they combine with our fleet to give the British even more headaches in the Atlantic?"

Sarbone mulled the suggestion over for a moment. "That's worth sending up the chain, in case they haven't thought about it. You're right about the League being even less inclined to work with the British. It probably just drives them further into bed with the Coalition. I can send up a question about assisting the Austrians with their shipping issues, but I don't know how it fits into our long-term strategy.

"Anyway, it looks like you brought your reports, so you might as well leave them with me. We'll keep on our normal bombing schedule until I hear otherwise. Dismissed."

The casualty list contained almost two dozen names that Guido recognized. Half of them were men he thought of as friends. He sent Fagnani a letter of condolence for his losses and congratulations for their success.

Then he sent a telegram to Aurora. Their weekly call was still a few days away; however, the recent losses made him want to make sure she knew how much he missed her. He was disappointed that he would miss Dawn's first Christmas. The basics were still available in Brest, but most of the merchants who sold non-essentials had moved south during the early days of the war. Aurora would have to get gifts for her parents for him. She would also have to pass along his love and appreciation for all their help.

Even a poker game that night failed to catch his interest. Commandant Lefebvre noticed Guido's melancholy and joined him as he meandered around the base. There wasn't a lot of conversation, Claude just wanted to be there for his friend. They eventually ended up at église Saint-Pierre-aux-Liens. The church seemed to beckon to Guido, and they went in. Claude helped Guido light candles for his lost friends and sat quietly while Guido knelt to pray. Claude knew Guido was a good commander because of how much he cared about his men. He tried to emulate Guido's concern with his own men. That meant he understood just how difficult it was to deal with heavy losses.

After about ten minutes, Guido let out a heavy sigh from their pew. Claude nodded and rose, helping Guido to his feet. The withdrawn Italian pilot was easy to guide out of the church and down the road. Guido eventually came back to their surroundings and asked Claude where they were going. Claude's response was simple. "A bar."

Cross Anchor, South Carolina, USA

Manly Lee Wilburn sat in the swing on his wrap-around porch, gently swaying back and forth. His melancholy mood didn't fit Christmas morning, but it wouldn't go away. The kids were playing with their gifts while Leila tried to get them ready for church. He'd tried to pitch in, but Eddie and Rita had used him as a distraction to keep from getting ready. An annoyed look from Leila had chased him from the house, so here he sat while chaos ruled his home.

He'd had almost two months to get used to the idea of Jewel moving out, but it had only been a week since the wedding. Her present sitting under the tree came as a stark reminder that she didn't live there anymore. His other daughters had been married in spring or summer. Maybe that was why their departures hadn't hit him so hard at Christmas.

M.L. picked up a block of wood he'd been working on and pulled out his pocketknife. Whittling often took his mind off his troubles. He shaved a sliver of wood off the block as he mused, waiting for it to tell him what it hid.

The wedding had been nice. Dwayne and his folks were Baptists, so both Pastor Bailey and Pastor Farley did parts of the ceremony. The ceremony was held just after church to take advantage of everyone already being dressed up. Yarborough had been hurriedly decorated after normal services and the ceremony had been joyous. It was the reception where things went out of kilter. The short lead time meant that the usual bounty of wedding gifts was pretty thin. The same applied to the food. Things were out of season, or out of stock at the Piggly Wiggly. Normally, the women brought out their specialties for weddings. They did their best, but their usual variety of offerings was pared down and subdued.

When it came time to do some dancing, the men who were missing quickly became obvious. Jewel and Dwayne only had eyes for each other. Everyone else couldn't help but notice the lonely wives wearing brave faces. M.L. danced with a few of them to get them in the spirit, but they all quickly ended up somber again once the dancing stopped. It wasn't long before they congregated in a corner of gloom that put a damper on the festivities. And then, Harry had shown up.

No one knew if it was that he hadn't been invited to the wedding or that Christmas was approaching, and he still wasn't allowed in his house. He borrowed a car and drove over from Woodruff. Considering how drunk he was when he showed up, it was a miracle he made it at all.

Harry had staggered in and announced his presence with a loud cry of "Janice!" His almost-sobbing apologies turned Janice beet-red and stopped the dancing. He was quickly corralled and walked outside. Pastor Bailey disappeared with the wayward drunk and things just kind of ended. The nervous sense of foreboding that emanated from the lonely wives spread rapidly around the room. People started making excuses to leave. The remaining women tried to console Janice and her kids. The wedding celebration was forgotten.

Leila leaned out of the front door. "They're as ready as they're going to be."

M.L. got up and headed to the truck to load up his slightly smaller family. With Jewel gone, no one had to ride in the truck bed. Junior rode there anyway. It kept him from getting poked and bothered by his younger siblings, so M.L. let him do it. There had already been enough family drama this Christmas.

The sermon had been of hope and renewal. Leila had issued a warning glare to M.L. when she noticed he was doing more looking around the church than paying attention to Pastor Bailey. M.L. didn't know if she thought he was looking out for a Harry arrival or searching for the missing Jewel. Either way, the elbow to his ribs had refocused his attention.

The kids were all enthusiastic in their singing, but last week's hullabaloo seemed to still be bothering the adults. When church was over, they thanked Pastor Bailey and gave him his Christmas gift. For once, it wasn't accompanied by a sweet treat. Pastor Bailey had gotten the word out that his icebox was still packed with leftovers from the wedding.

The ride back home was even stranger than the ride to church. With Buck gone, Junior had left with Francis to help her collect things for the trip to M.L.'s house. Sybil had gone with Doris for the same reason. Leila had invited Janice over and had ridden off with her to help her get what she'd cooked. That left M.L. with just Betty, Rita, and Eddie for the ride home. Even with lots of room, the poking and jawing quickly escalated. M.L. was glad it was a short ride, but still had to resort to threatening their lunch to get them to behave.

Lunch was tasty and filling, though the fact that it was on a Sunday meant they were limited to sandwiches and things that had been previously prepared. M.L. missed the turkey that Leila usually made. He also missed the conversation. The only other adult male present was Guy, and he was more interested in talking religion than dealing with the real world. The arrival of the Baptist Dwayne hadn't helped.

Guy's dander rose at the same rate as his conviction of his own moral superiority.

They exchanged presents with the extended family and began breaking up into groups as they usually did. M.L. slipped out to the front porch and picked up the whittling he'd been working on earlier. He'd barely started in on it when the front door opened, and Jewel leaned out with a "There he is."

She came out and was followed by Dwayne and Janice's son, Zach. M.L. put away his pocketknife and looked at the trio expectantly. They pulled some of the chairs over and Jewel sat next to him on the porch swing.

His daughter took the lead. "Daddy, no one else wants to talk about everything that's going on in the world, but I know you pay attention to it. Can we talk with you?"

M.L. hadn't really thought about how much the world's problems would impact these three. They were still kids in his eyes. Even the wedding hadn't really moved them out of that 'kid' category. Maybe it was time M.L. started viewing them as the adults they were becoming.

"I'm more than happy to talk. Just remember that I don't know all the answers. Hell, I don't even know half of the questions that should be asked. But I'm willing to share my opinions if y'all are willing to share yours. Conversation takes people talking and listening on both sides."

The three seventeen-year-olds exchanged glances before they turned back to M.L. with nods of agreement. A genuine smile crept over M.L.'s face. He said, "Let me get my thinking cap on." He pulled his pocketknife back out and picked up his block of wood again. After a couple of shavings, he asked, "What's on your minds?"

Dwayne took the lead this time. "Well, sir, mostly the future. You know why Jewel and I pushed our wedding date up. That you agreed to it makes us think you expect the war to spread and go on for a while like we do. Zach's dad always said that everything would blow over, but now Zach is wondering if Jewel and I might have the right idea."

It wasn't really a question, and it was territory that might get him into hot water with Janice. M.L. didn't care. It was the type of conversation that he craved.

"There's always a reason to rush into things, just like there's always a reason to take your time. You three were born after the Great War, and just after the Spanish Flu killed millions more. The older kids got to experience that firsthand. But they also got to enjoy the relative peace of the last fifteen years.

"If you expect to serve our country as a fighting man, then there's more reason to do things quickly. If you don't want or expect to be snapped up by the army, take your time and get a job that helps the coming war effort. We just recently hired two more mechanics that are in their twenties. Their work to keep the trains running will have a bigger impact than anything they could do on the field of combat. The government pays attention to things like that."

Jewel looked smug. "See, Zach. If you're worried about getting drafted, stay in school and get a job that's important."

M.L. smirked, "All jobs are important. Even the crop-dusting that Buck taught you is vital for our crop production. It may not be a full-time job, but the government needs to make sure there are enough people to get it done. You could check with the other towns in the area to see if you can expand the business. The more people depending on you to do your job, the less likely you are to be drafted."

Zach nodded sadly, "I know. I just feel like I'm chickening out if I don't go fight."

"Son, a long time ago, almost everyone fought. Once you had a club, you were good to go. But as we've developed better and deadlier weapons, more and more people have been needed to supply each fighting man with what he needs to do his job. People are needed to supply the food, clothes, equipment and ammunition that keep our men fighting. Sometimes, the women step forward to help in the factories, but it's usually men slinging the steel around. Just because you aren't getting shot at doesn't mean you aren't contributing. A big reason the South lost the War Between the States was that we couldn't keep our fighting men fed or clothed."

Dwayne chimed in, "At least you know how to fly. I don't have any special skills so I'm just a replaceable cog wherever I go. There's no reason for them to not draft me."

Jewel reached over and held her new husband's hand. M.L. suddenly realized just how much of this the newlyweds had already hashed out. His respect for their maturity grew.

Zach broke the reverie by asking for M.L.'s opinion on the fighting going on around the world. They discussed everything from the partition of China to the fighting in Canada. M.L. thought about it for a while, but eventually decided to tell them about the damage to the trains. The teenagers were shocked to hear that there was fighting already going on inside the country, and M.L. wondered if he'd been wrong to tell them.

Zach gave him his answer. "Thanks for letting us know about that. Our parents, teachers, and even the government seem to be trying to keep things from us. It's really hard to make good decisions when you don't know what's going on."

M.L. shrugged. "Remember that as you go through life. Nine times outta ten, you won't have all the information when you need to make a decision. Try to learn from it when you screw up but cut yourself some slack. The scary thing is when you realize that this applies to people you work for, or who work for you."

Jewel gave Dwayne a glare that reminded M.L. of Leila. "That means it's best to let each other know what's going on so we can work together to fix it."

M.L. didn't know what that was about and didn't want to. It still made him smile.

JANUARY 1, 1939

Manstein Residence, Berlin, Germany

It's after one in the morning. Edna and Otto have gone to bed, while Brent is still out at a party with his friends. I sit in my library, Wells' *The World Set Free* lies closed in my lap. It may be where Leo Szilard got his idea for Einstein's special project, but I hope Wells wasn't right about much else in his book. The Carolinum he envisioned is little better than regular bombs and is much messier. And getting to his utopia involves everyone surrendering to a world state, something the French seem to be intent on imposing. I take a drink of my schnapps and rub my forehead.

Asia is closer to peace than it's been for decades, though Mao and his Communists continue the guerrilla war against the Japanese, British, and Russians. I'm not sure if the Russians agreed to the Partition of China to free up troops to attack us, or because they expect an attack from the Japanese. The Russians claim to be interested in swapping Georgia for Azerbaijan as part of a peace agreement, but I don't know if I trust them. The rest of the Central Coalition seems to be happy with the proposal, and it would free up our forces. It's in the hands of the Reichstag now, so there's nothing I can do but come up with contingencies for them killing the deal.

At least there have been some cracks in the expansion of the Entente. The mining of the Suez Canal has closed it for at least a month. Their expansion in Africa has ground to a halt. That will probably change as the Entente frantically builds a rail network to supplement their sea supply routes. South Africa is just too isolated to stand alone.

The same could be said of Canada. Quebec has created its own church to distance itself from the Entente, but there's still a lot of bad blood there. The entire country would be starving if the United States wasn't feeding them. If England falls, will Canada fight on as part of the Empire, or will they cozy up to the people who are keeping them alive?

1. And England's fall is looking more and more likely. With the Suez Canal closed, the Italian fleet has joined the French fleet in the Atlantic. Their threats to the British Isles pulled the British Atlantic fleet up to the Irish Sea. The Entente turned around and raided Ponta Delgada in the Azores. That closed the only major British base between England and South Africa. Even the OAS has gotten back into it. They've landed in the Falklands, and it looks like another isolated British garrison is going to be overrun.

Wilhelm III and the Reichstag are still debating on help for the British even while we try to improve our ties with the League. The question of whether the League's 'moral compass' will keep it from doing anything effective still haunts my nightmares. Then again, so does my willingness to compromise my principles for what I think is the good of my people.

I drain my glass and rise to get another. It will be my third since midnight. I don't care, but I do go back by my bookshelves for a new book. I close my eyes and pick something randomly, *Master of the World* by Jules Verne. I quickly put it back and hope it isn't prophetic. Kurd Lasswitz's *On Two Planets* is my next random choice, another one quickly returned to the shelf. I drink my schnapps in one gulp and head to bed. Maybe science fiction isn't always hopeful in the end.

CHARACTERS

Note: Characters marked as **Historical**

are based on actual people from our timeline.

GERMANY

Erich von Manstein – **Historical**

Chancellor of Germany

Born 24 Nov 1887

180 cm tall, dirty blonde hair, proud

Prussian nose, likes an occasional cigar, trim

Edna von Manstein

Wife and secretary

Born   7 Dec 1910

170 cm tall, long blonde hair, shapely

Married 26 Jun 1937

Brent von Manstein

Son of Erich and his first wife, Brenda

Born 19 Jul 1920

185 cm tall, thin, blonde, Prussian nose

Peter Hipper

Brent's best friend. Nephew of Admiral Hipper

Born 13 Apr 1920

Beatrice Schmidt

    Erich's cook since 1925

    Smiling, slightly plump

Otto Woyke

    Bodyguard and Erich's best friend

    Born 11 May 1892

    190 cm tall, blonde, muscular

Oberst (Colonel) Ernst Weber

    Erich's aide

    Born   5 Sep 1895

    175 cm tall, pudgy, black hair

Generalfeldmarschall Werner von Blomberg – **Historical**

    Commander-in-Chief of the Wehrmacht (German army)

Generallieutnant Kurt Liese – **Historical**

    Head of Heereswaffenamt (Research & Development)

Franz Gürtner – **Historical**

    Minister of Justice

Sir Nevile Meyrick Henderson – **Historical**

    UK Ambassador to Germany until October 1938

    Born 10 Jun 1882

    White Supremacist.

Sir Eric Clare Edmund Phipps – **Historical**

    UK Ambassador to Germany 1933 – 1937, October 1938

    Born 27 Oct 1875

André François-Poncet – **Historical**

    French Ambassador to Germany

    Born 13 Jun 1887

Alfred Hugenberg – **Historical**

    Leader of the German National People's Party

Ernst Thälmann – **Historical**

    Leader of the German Communist Party

Otto Wels – **Historical**
> Leader of the German Social Democratic Party

Ludwig Kaas – **Historical**
> Roman Catholic priest.
> Leader of the German Centre Party

FRANCE

Général de Brigade (Brigadier General) Roger Noiret –
> **Historical**
> Commander 1st Armored Division
> Born 10 Aug 1895
> 178 cm tall, dark hair, thin mustache
> Boyish face, looks younger than he is, lives in
> Toulouse
> Warrior for Christ, shoulder injury still bothers him

Catherine Noiret
> Wife of Roger
> Born 19 Nov 1899
> Married 4 Apr. 1920

Guy Noiret
> Son of Roger and Catherine
> Born   7 May 1921

Roger Noiret, Jr.
> Son of Roger and Catherine
> Born   2 Jun 1923

Pierre Moreau
> Friend of Guy, family is Protestant

Sergent (Sergeant) Jean Martin
> Division clerk – 1st Armored Division

Colonel Philippe de Hauteclocque – **Historical**
> Executive officer of the 1st Armored Division
> Born 22 Nov 1902
> 185 cm tall, dark hair, mustache
> Uses a cane due to a riding accident

Aristocrat, back channels for information, non-religious

Commandant (Major) Jacques Jeannin

Battalion commander 1st Armored Division

Lieutenant-Colonel Henri Dubois

Commander 11th Armored Regiment, 1st Armored Division

Lieutenant-Colonel Alexandre Thomas

Commander 12th Armored Regiment, 1st Armored Division

Lieutenant-Colonel Claude Durand

Commander 83rd Regiment, 8th Motorized Division which becomes the 13th Motorized Regiment, 1st Armored Division

Commandant Richard Levesque

Commander 14th Motorized Regiment, 1st Armored Division

Father (Commandant) Louis Lobau

Chaplain 1st Armored Division

Lieutenant-Colonel Robert Olleris

Commander 512th Armored Regiment in Libya. Executive officer for Noiret during the Spanish Civil War

Commander 11th Armored Division

Marshal Charles Delestraint – **Historical**

Commander of the French Army

Born 12 Mar 1899

Proponent of armored forces

THE LEVANT CORPS –

Général de Division (Major General) Alphonse Pierre Juin –

Historical

Corps Commander

Born 16 Dec 1888

Warrior for Christ

Lost use of right arm in Morrocco in 1914

Général de Brigade Marie Joseph Edmond Welvert – **Historical**

Commander 8th Motorized Division

Born 30 Oct 1884.

Général de Brigade Godefroy Louis Pfister – **Historical**

Commander 1st Colonial Infantry Division

Born 16 Sep 1885.

Command experience in the Levant

Général de Brigade Paul Émile Britsch – **Historical**

Commander 2nd Colonial Infantry Division

Born 20 Jan 1879

Command experience in Algeria

Général de Brigade Jean Ris – **Historical**

Commander 3rd Colonial Infantry Division

Born 22 Aug 1883

Alpine operations experience

Général de Brigade Auguste Alaurent – **Historical**

Commander 14th Infantry Division

Born 22 Feb 1883

Infantry / light infantry experience

Général de Brigade Charles Marcel Louis Lucien Trinquand –
Historical

Commander 26th Infantry Division

Born 14 Nov 1888

Infantry experience

Général de Brigade Marie Alexandre Martin Henri Fondi de Niort –
Historical

Air commander for the Levant

Born 29 Jul 1888

Hashim al-Atassi – **Historical**

President of Syria

Born 11 Jan 1875

White hair, mustache and goatee

Damien de Martel – **Historical**

High Commissioner of the Levant
Born 27 Nov 1878
Slightly chubby, black hair, mustache

THE AFRICAN EXPEDITIONARY CORPS –
Generale di Corpo d'Armata Guglielmo Ciro Nasi – **Historical**
Corps Commander
Born 21 Feb 1879

UNITED KINGDOM
Vice Admiral Sir Geoffrey Blake – **Historical**
Commander of the 1st Battlecruiser Squadron and
Task Force South Atlantic
HMS Marlborough flagship
Born 16 Sep 1882
5'9" tall, thin, balding. Lop-sided smile
Wife – Jean St. John Carr
Two daughters – Emily and Faith
Commodore John Moore
Commander of the battlecruiser *HMS Marlborough*
Lieutenant Commander Travis Caldwell
Commander of the destroyer *HMS Firedrake*
Captain Cedric Holland
Commander of the aircraft carrier *HMS Indefatigable*
Captain David Eakes
Commander of the light cruiser *HMS Orion*
Captain Jonathon Lucas
Commander of the 7th Light Cruiser Squadron
HMS Leander flagship
Lieutenant Gregory Everett
Sir Geoffrey's flag lieutenant
Admiral Sir Dudley Pound – **Historical**
Commander-in-Chief, Mediterranean Fleet
HMS Warspite flagship

Born 29 Aug 1877
Lieutenant General Archibald Wavell – **Historical**
    Commander-in-Chief, Middle East
    Born   5 May 1883
Vice Admiral Alexander Ramsay – **Historical**
    Commander of the East Indies Station
    Born 29 May 1881
Commodore Irvine Glennie – **Historical**
    Born 22 Jul 1892
Vice Admiral Sir James Somerville – **Historical**
    Commander of the East Indies Station beginning
    Sept. 1938
    Born 17 Jul 1882
Kaigun-Chūjō (Vice Admiral) Chūichi Nagumo – **Historical**
    Commander of the Japanese First Air Fleet
    Born 25 Mar 1887
    Studied Naval warfare and strategy in England and the
    USA
Lieutenant Ichiro
    Translator on loan from the Imperial Japanese Navy

ITALY
Colonnello (Colonel) Guido Nobili – **Historical**
    Air Commander – Dire Dawa, Italian East Africa
    Born   5 May 1908
    175 cm tall, farm boy from Napoli
    Reads voraciously, shy, black hair, almost pale, trim
    Likes to play poker, ex-liaison for plane improvement
    5 kills in Spanish Civil War, ex- "Fighter School"
    instructor
Colonnello Aurora Esposito
    Intelligence liaison in Rome
    Born 13 Dec 1910
    165 cm tall, athletic figure, black hair

Married to Guido 26 Jun 1937 - just after full moon
Honeymooned in Paris. Pregnant – due Sep 1938
Mother – Maria. Father – Giuseppe

Generale di Brigata (Brigadier General) Attilio Matricardi –
Historical
Base Commander of Dire Dawa

Tenente Colonnello (Lieutenant Colonel) Tarcisio Fagnani
Fighter Commander
175cm tall, trim, outgoing, brown-graying hair, tanned
Outdoorsman who likes soccer

Maggiore (Major) Francesco Rossi
Italian Fighter Wing Commander
Nervous in formal settings

Capitano (Captain) Guillermo Bianchi
Rossi's wing man

Commandant (Major) Claude Lefebvre
French Fighter Wing Commander

Maggiore Stefano Fiore
Italian Bomber Wing Commander

Commandant Emmanuel Durand
French Bomber Wing Commander
Terse. Has a large mustache

Maggiore Alonzo Volpe
Reconnaissance Wing Commander

Tenente Corrado Ricci
Guido's wing man

Général de Brigade Jacob Sarbone
Base Commander of Brest
Worked with Guido during the Spanish Civil War

ITALIAN EAST AFRICA –

Generale di Corpo d'Armata (Lieutenant General) Guglielmo
Ciro Nasi – **Historical**
Commander of the East Africa Army

57th, 58th, 59th Infantry Divisions

1st, 2nd, 3rd, 4th, 5th, 6th, 7th, 8th Ethiopian Infantry
Divisions

XVIII and LII tankette battalions

LIBYA –

Generale di Corpo d'Armata Francesco Guidi – **Historical**
Commander of the Tenth Army

60th, 61st, 62nd, 63rd, 64th Motorized Infantry
Divisions

1st, 2nd Libyan Infantry Divisions

1st, 2nd, 3rd, 4th Blackshirt Infantry Divisions

I, II, XX, XXI, XXII, L, and LI tank battalions

UNITED STATES OF AMERICA

Manly Lee "M.L." Wilburn

Head Mechanic at the Seaboard Air Line depot in
Spartanburg, South Carolina

Born 16 Jan 1887

6'1" tall

One older brother and older sister dead

One older brother, David Hampton "Hampie", still alive

Wilma Leila Harvey Wilburn

Wife of M.L.

Born 23 May 1889

5'2" tall, thin, strong-willed

Nelle Erminer Wilburn

Daughter of M.L. and Leila

Born 6 Jul 1910

Married Guy Thomas Taylor

Two children – Junior (1934), Gladys (1936)

Albert Allison Wilburn

Son of M.L. and Leila

Born 21 Mar 1912

Married Vera Hadden

Two children – Junior (1934), Gloria (1937)
Army Sergeant stationed in North Carolina
Works in the Motor pool
David Wilburn (1913 – 1913)
Son of M.L. and Leila. Died at the age of three months
Mary Doris Wilburn
Daughter of M.L. and Leila
Born 26 Sep 1915
Married Ralph W. Griffith
One son – Junior (1933)
Francis Margaret Wilburn
Daughter of M.L. and Leila
Born 13 Oct 1918
Married Walter Clinton "Buck" Edwards
One son – Robert Lee (1937)
Julia Annette "Jewel" Wilburn
Daughter of M.L. and Leila
Born 23 Jul 1921
Boyfriend Dwayne Williams
Manly Lee Wilburn, Junior
Son of M.L. and Leila
Born 26 Jul 1924
Wants to be a Marine
Aurie Sybil Wilburn
Daughter of M.L. and Leila
Born 11 Apr 1926
Selena Elizabeth "Betty" Wilburn
Daughter of M.L. and Leila
Born 23 Dec 1928
Rita Jean Wilburn
Daughter of Mary Doris Wilburn, raised by M.L. and
Leila
Born 15 Apr 1931
Clarence Edward "Eddie" Wilburn

Son of M.L. and Leila

Born   5 Sep 1933

Jim Deeson

M.L.'s boss at the Seaboard Air Line depot in
Spartanburg

Harry and Janice Jamison

Neighbors of M.L. and Leila

Four Children - Andrew (1920), Zachery (1921),
Sara (1923), and Lucille (1925)

Philip and Courtney Lucas

Neighbors of M.L. and Leila

Moved from Ohio. Philip had been a factory worker

Courtney's uncle lives in Union, South Carolina

Pastor John Bailey

Pastor of the Yarborough United Methodist Church in
Cross Anchor

Short gray-brown hair, clean-shaven

Stocky build, used to play football

Pastor Michael Farley

Pastor of the New Hope Baptist Church in Cross
Anchor

Blonde, wears glasses, has a goatee and mustache

Thin build with an academic look

Cardy and Heather Bravo

New neighbors from Virginia

Cardy retired from the Navy

Senior mechanic at the Seaboard Air Line depot

Daughter Acadia is new teacher in Cross Anchor

Son Cannon is into guns and cars

Bill Hawkins

Mechanic at the Seaboard Air Line depot

Age 28

6'2" tall

Spartanburg, South Carolina native

Worked at Sanford Salvage
Andrew Christianson
Mechanic at the Seaboard Air Line depot
Age 27
6'4" tall
From Savannah, Georgia
Worked for John Deere

EQUIPMENT

AVAILABLE IN MAY 1938
MAJOR SHIPS

GERMAN NAVY

Bayern – Class ship.

> 8 Fifteen-inch guns. Speed: 24 Knots
> Sold to Turkey in August 1938

Baden – *Bayern*-class battleship

> Sold to Turkey in August 1938

Sachen – *Bayern*-class battleship

> Sold to Turkey in August 1938

Scharnhorst – Class ship.

> 6 Fifteen-inch guns. Speed: 30 Knots

Gneisenau – *Scharnhorst*-class battleship

Admiral Scheer – *Scharnhorst*-class battleship

Admiral Graf Spee – *Scharnhorst*-class battleship

Bismark – Class ship.

> 8 Fifteen-inch guns. Speed: 30 Knots

Tirpitz – *Bismark*-class battleship

Hindenburg – *Bismark*-class battleship

Graf Zeppelin – Carrier: 42 aircraft. Speed: 34 Knots

Richtofen – Carrier: 42 aircraft. Speed: 34 Knots

AUSTRIAN NAVY (USGA)

Austria – Class ship.

  12 Fourteen-inch guns. Speed: 21 Knots

Hungary – *Austria*-class battleship

Croatia – *Austria*-class battleship

Bohemia – *Austria*-class battleship

FRENCH NAVY

Richelieu – Class ship.

  8 Fifteen-inch guns. Speed: 32 Knots

  Sunk at the Battle of Mogadishu in August 1938

Jean Bart – *Richelieu*-class battleship

  Sunk at the Battle of Mogadishu in August 1938

Clemenceau – *Richelieu*-class battleship

  Sunk at the Battle of Mogadishu in August 1938

Gascogne – *Richelieu*-class battleship

  Sunk at the Battle of Mogadishu in August 1938

Cherbourg – Class ship.

  9 Fifteen-inch guns. Speed: 31 Knots

Toulon – *Cherbourg*-class battleship

Casablanca – *Cherbourg*-class battleship

Bizerte – *Cherbourg*-class battleship

Dakar – *Cherbourg*-class battleship

Lyon – Class ship.

  9 Sixteen-inch guns. Speed: 30 Knots

Duquesne – *Lyon*-class battleship

Béarn – Carrier: 32 aircraft. Speed: 21 Knots

Joffre – Carrier: 40 aircraft. Speed: 33 Knots

Painlevé – Carrier: 40 aircraft. Speed: 33 Knots

ITALIAN NAVY

Andria Doria – Class ship.

  10 Twelve-inch guns. Speed: 26 Knots

  Sunk at the Battle of Haifa in June 1938

Caio Duilio – *Andria Doria*-class battleship

Sunk at the Battle of Haifa in June 1938

Littorio – Class ship.

9 Fifteen-inch guns. Speed: 30 Knots

Vittorio Veneto – *Littorio*-class battleship

Roma – *Littorio*-class battleship

Napoli – *Littorio*-class battleship

Sunk at the Battle of Haifa in June 1938

Impero – *Littorio*-class battleship

Vittorio Emanuele – *Littorio*-class battleship

Francesco Caracciolo – Class ship.

9 Sixteen-inch guns. Speed: 30 Knots

BRAZILIAN NAVY

Deodoro – Class ship.

Previously, the Italian *Conte di Cavour*.

13 Twelve-inch guns. Speed: 27 Knots

Floriano – *Deodoro*-class battleship

Previously, the Italian *Giulio Cesare*.

Minas Gereas – Class ship.

12 Twelve-inch guns. Speed: 21 Knots

São Paulo – *Minas Gereas*-class battleship

Poor maintenance gave it a top speed of 10 Knots.

Sunk at the Battle of Montevideo in June 1938

VENEZUELAN NAVY

Caracas – Class ship.

Previously, the French *Dunkerque*.

8 Thirteen-inch guns. Speed: 31 Knots

Maracaibo – *Caracas*-class battleship

Previously, the French *Strasbourg*.

ROYAL NAVY (UNITED KINGDOM)
EASTERN FLEET

1st Battle Division

Revenge – Class ship.

    8 Fifteen-inch guns. Speed: 21 Knots

    Sunk at the Battle of Mogadishu in August 1938

Resolution – *Revenge*-class battleship

Royal Oak – *Revenge*-class battleship

    Sunk at the Battle of Mogadishu in August 1938

Royal Sovereign – *Revenge*-class battleship

Ramillies – *Revenge*-class battleship

Indomitable – Carrier: 45 aircraft. Speed: 30 Knots

Formidable – Carrier: 40 aircraft. Speed: 30 Knots

MEDITERRANIAN FLEET

2nd Battle Division

Queen Elizabeth – Class ship.

    8 Fifteen-inch guns. Speed: 24 Knots

    Sunk at the Battle of Haifa in June 1938

Warspite – *Queen Elizabeth*-class battleship

    Sunk at the Battle of Haifa in June 1938

Valiant – *Queen Elizabeth*-class battleship

    Sunk at the Battle of Haifa in June 1938

Barham – *Queen Elizabeth*-class battleship

    Sunk at the Battle of Haifa in June 1938

Malaya – *Queen Elizabeth*-class battleship

    Sunk at the Battle of Haifa in June 1938

Glorious – Carrier: 48 aircraft. Speed: 30 Knots

    Sunk at the Battle of Haifa in June 1938

Courageous – Carrier: 48 aircraft. Speed: 30 Knots

    Sunk at the Battle of the Red Sea in June 1938

2nd Battlecruiser Squadron

Iron Duke – Class ship.

    9 Sixteen-inch guns. Speed: 31 Knots

Emperor of India – *Iron Duke*-class battlecruiser
Lion – *Hood*-class battlecruiser
Princess Royal – *Hood*-class battlecruiser
Repulse – *Renown*-class battlecruiser
Implacable – Carrier: 80 aircraft. Speed: 32 Knots

HOME FLEET

3rd Battle Division

Nelson – Class ship.
 9 Sixteen-inch guns. Speed: 23 Knots
Rodney – *Nelson*-class battleship
Saint Andrew – Class ship.
 9 Eighteen-inch guns. Speed: 23 Knots
Saint George – *Saint Andrew*-class battleship
Saint Patrick – *Saint Andrew*-class battleship
Saint David – *Saint Andrew*-class battleship
Argus – Carrier: 18 aircraft. Speed: 20 Knots
Hermes – Carrier: 20 aircraft. Speed: 25 Knots
Eagle – Carrier: 30 aircraft. Speed: 24 Knots

4th Battle Division

King George V – Class ship.
 9 Sixteen-inch guns. Speed: 28 Knots
Prince of Wales – *King George V*-class battleship
Duke of York – *King George V*-class battleship
Anson – *King George V*-class battleship
Howe – *King George V*-class battleship
Furious – Carrier: 36 aircraft. Speed: 31 Knots
Victorious – Carrier: 36 aircraft. Speed: 30 Knots
 Sunk in the Bay of Biscay in December 1938
Illustrious – Carrier: 36 aircraft. Speed: 30 Knots

5th Battle Division

Vanguard – Class ship.
 8 Fifteen-inch guns. Speed: 30 Knots
 Sunk at the Battle of Suez in December 1938
Temeraire – *Vanguard*-class battleship

Ark Royal – Carrier: 54 aircraft. Speed: 30 Knots

Sunk at the Battle of Suez in December 1938

1ˢᵗ Battlecruiser Squadron

Marlborough – *Iron Duke*-class battlecruiser

Benbow – *Iron Duke*-class battlecruiser

Hood – Class ship.

8 Fifteen-inch guns. Speed: 32 Knots

Sunk at the Battle of Mogadishu in August 1938

Tiger – *Hood*-class battlecruiser

Renown – Class ship.

6 Fifteen-inch guns. Speed: 31 Knots

Indefatigable – Carrier: 80 aircraft. Speed: 32 Knots

JAPANESE NAVY

1ˢᵗ CARRIER STRIKING FORCE

1ˢᵗ Battlecruiser Squadron

Amagi – Class ship.

10 Sixteen-inch guns. Speed: 30 Knots

Akagi – *Amagi*-class battlecruiser

Atago – *Amagi*-class battlecruiser

Takao – *Amagi*-class battlecruiser

Sunk at the Battle of Suez in December 1938

Sōryū – Carrier: 63 aircraft. Speed: 34 Knots

Hiryū – Carrier: 64 aircraft. Speed: 34 Knots

Shōkaku – Carrier: 72 aircraft. Speed: 34 Knots

Zuikaku – Carrier: 72 aircraft. Speed: 34 Knots

Unryū – Carrier: 72 aircraft. Speed: 34 Knots

Kasagi – Carrier: 72 aircraft. Speed: 34 Knots

AIRPLANES

GERMANY

BF 109E – Fighter introduced in 1937.

    Speed: 575 KPH   2-20mm cannons and
                                    2-8mm machine guns

USGA

IK-3 – Fighter introduced in 1938.

    Speed: 575 KPH   20mm cannon and
                                    2-7.92mm machine guns

FRANCE

MS.406 – Fighter introduced in 1934.

    Speed: 486 KPH   20mm cannon and
                                    2-7.5mm machine guns

D.520 – Fighter introduced in 1936.

    Speed: 560 KPH   20mm cannon and
                                    4-7.5mm machine guns

MB.174 – Bomber introduced in 1936.

    Speed: 530 KPH   400 Kilograms of bombs

LeO.451M – Bomber introduced in 1937.

    Speed: 420 KPH   1400 Kilograms of bombs
                                        or 1 torpedo

MB.175 – Bomber introduced in 1938.

    Speed: 550 KPH   500 Kilograms of bombs

MB.152 – Fighter introduced in 1938.

    Speed: 509 KPH   2-20mm cannons and
                                    2-7.5mm machine guns

D.530 – Fighter introduced in 1939.

    Speed: 625 KPH   20mm cannon and
                                    4-7.5mm machine guns

ITALY

CR.32 – Biplane Fighter introduced in 1934.

Speed: 360 KPH.   2-7.7mm machine guns

CR.42 – Biplane Fighter introduced in 1937.

Speed: 441 KPH.   2-12.7mm machine guns

G.51 – Fighter introduced in 1938.

Speed: 570 KPH   20mm cannon and 2-12.7mm machine guns

SM.79 – Bomber introduced in 1936.

Speed: 467 KPH   1200 Kilograms of bombs or 1-2 torpedoes

Z.1007 – Bomber introduced in 1937.

Speed: 458 KPH   2200 Kilograms of bombs or 1-2 torpedoes

Br.20M – Bomber introduced in 1937.

Speed: 440 KPH   1600 Kilograms of bombs

SM.82 – Bomber/Transport introduced in 1938.

Speed: 347 KPH.   4000 Kilograms of bombs

SM.86 – Dive Bomber introduced in 1939.

Speed: 350 KPH   250 Kilograms of bombs

UNITED KINGDOM

Gauntlet – Biplane Fighter introduced in 1934.

Speed: 370 KPH.   2-.303 machine guns

Gladiator – Carrier-based Biplane Fighter introduced in 1936.

Speed: 400 KPH.   4-.303 machine guns

Fulmar – Carrier-based Fighter introduced in 1938.

Speed: 438 KPH.   8-.303 machine guns

Hurricane – Fighter introduced in 1936.

Speed: 500 KPH   8-.303 machine guns

Spitfire – Fighter introduced in 1937.

Speed: 570 KPH   8-.303 machine guns

Blenheim – Bomber introduced in 1937.

Speed: 420 KPH   540 Kilograms of bombs

Battle – Bomber introduced in 1937.

Speed: 410 KPH   680 Kilograms of bombs

Swordfish – Carrier-based Bomber introduced in 1936.
    Speed: 230 KPH   1 torpedo

JAPAN

D3A – Val – Carrier-based dive Bomber introduced in 1936.
    Speed: 430 KPH   370 Kilograms of bombs

B5N – Kate – Carrier-based Bomber introduced in 1937.
    Speed: 378 KPH   800 Kilograms of bombs or 1 torpedo

A6M – Hachi – Carrier-based Fighter introduced in 1938.
    Speed: 533 KPH   2-20mm cannons and 2-7.7mm machine guns

TANKS

GERMANY

Mark III – Light Tank introduced in 1936.
> 15mm of front armor. 37mm/L45 main gun.

Mark IV – Medium Tank introduced in 1936.
> 30mm of front armor. 75mm/L24 main gun.

Mark IIID – Light Tank introduced in 1938.
> 30mm of front armor. 50mm/L42 main gun.

Mark IVE – Medium Tank introduced in 1938.
> 60mm of front armor. 75mm/L43 main gun.

FRANCE

AMX35 – Light Tank introduced in 1935.
> 25mm of front armor. 47mm/L35 main gun.

S36 – Cavalry Tank introduced in 1936.
> 40mm of front armor. 75mm/L34 main gun.

G1 – Medium Tank introduced in 1936.
> 60mm of front armor. 75mm/L48 main gun.

B1 – Heavy Tank introduced in 1934.
> 60mm of front armor. 75mm/L34 main gun.

AMX38 – Light Tank introduced in 1938.
> 30mm of front armor. 47mm/L40 main gun.
> Magazine for main gun.

S39 – Cavalry Tank introduced in 1939.
> 50mm of front armor. 75mm/L48 main gun.
> Magazine for main gun.

G2 – Medium Tank introduced in 1939.
> 80mm of front armor. 90mm/L56 main gun.

B2 – Heavy Tank introduced in 1939.
> 100mm of front armor. 90mm/L56 main gun.

PD90 – Assault Gun introduced in 1939.
> 80mm of front armor. 90mm/L70 main gun.

ITALY

L3/35 – Light Tank introduced in 1935.

10mm of front armor. 20mm main gun.

L6/38 – Light Tank introduced in 1938.

25mm of front armor. 47mm/L35 main gun.

M13/38 – Medium Tank introduced in 1938.

30mm of front armor. 75mm/L34 main gun.

UNITED KINGDOM

Matilda I – Medium Tank introduced in 1936.

50mm of front armor. Machine Guns as main
gun.

Cruiser Mk I – Light Tank introduced in 1937.

10mm of front armor. 40mm/L52 main gun.

Matilda II – Medium Tank introduced in 1938.

70mm of front armor. 40mm/L52 main gun.

Cruiser Mk IV – Light Tank introduced in 1938.

20mm of front armor. 40mm/L52 main gun.

9 798889 330541